TORCHFIRE

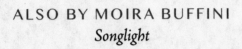

ALSO BY MOIRA BUFFINI
Songlight

MOIRA BUFFINI

TORCHFIRE

BOOK TWO OF
THE TORCH TRILOGY

STORYTIDE
An Imprint of HarperCollinsPublishers

To the boys, Joe and Jack

HarperCollins Children's Books, a division of HarperCollins Publishers,
195 Broadway, New York, NY 10007

HarperCollins Publishers, Macken House, 39/40 Mayor Street Upper,
Dublin 1, D01 C9W8, Ireland

Storytide is an imprint of HarperCollins Publishers.

Torchfire
Copyright © 2025 by Moira Buffini
All rights reserved. Manufactured in Harrisonburg, VA, United States of America. No part of this book may be used or reproduced in any manner whatsoever without written permission except in the case of brief quotations embodied in critical articles and reviews. Without limiting the exclusive rights of any author, contributor, or the publisher of this publication, any unauthorized use of this publication to train generative artificial intelligence (AI) technologies is expressly prohibited. HarperCollins also exercises their rights under Article 4(3) of the Digital Single Market Directive 2019/790 and expressly reserves this publication from the text and data mining exception.
harpercollins.com
Library of Congress Control Number: 2025930644
ISBN 978-0-06-335826-3
Typography by Molly Fehr
25 26 27 28 29 LBC 5 4 3 2 1
First Edition

PROLOGUE ✦ LARK

Lying with my mother in the bottom of a boat.

A half dream, half memory comes.

I am a tiny girl again, in my parents' bed. The four of us are curled in a heap: my brother, Piper, a year older, his long legs and boyish feet digging into me; my pa, his big seaworker's arm stretching over us both; and Ma, Curlew Crane. She gives me slow smile like a beam from her soul and Pa says my name.

"Elsa." I hear it in my core.

I am warm and safe in my dream memory and I fight against waking, but the cold creeps in. I feel the motion of the waves, hear the low whir of the boat's turbine. The battery hums underneath me, powering us south.

I remember.

We are on our way to Brightlinghelm, four of us, fleeing on the waves: Ma, Heron Mikane, Yan Zeru, whose true name is Kingfisher, and me. Piper is not here, nor Pa neither. Our family is split by war and death. Pa only lives in my dream world now. And Piper proved himself my enemy last night. It was on the tip of his tongue to tell the whole town I had songlight and denounce me as unhuman. I saw the look in his eyes as he stared at me and I can still feel the pain of it pulsing through my body.

My arm is wrapped around Ma. Her face is ghostly in the moonlight and she smells of congealing blood. My hands are sticky with it. There's a bullet lodged in her shoulder threatening her life. We left Northaven in a hail of gunfire and the sound of it is ringing in my ears.

My consciousness sharpens as I sit up on my elbows. Kingfisher is lying next to Ma, resting, warming her with his body heat. The moon casts enough light on his face for me to see the shape of his jaw, his fine brows, his long hair falling over his cheek, his muscular shoulders. I am instantly vexed at myself. For even in a situation as desperate as this, I'm still distracted by this boy's fine looks.

I wrench myself upright and see a large figure, hunched at the tiller in a silhouette, the moon over the sea behind him. Heron Mikane is steering the boat. His face is in shadow but I know his expression—broken fortitude. The past follows Heron like a rising wave, ever threatening to overwhelm him. He twists and looks behind us at the moon trail on the water, as if Death herself is running toward us.

Curl is bone cold. Her chest is barely moving when she breathes.

"Ma . . ."

"Don't wake her," whispers Kingfisher in his low Aylish lilt. "She's holding well. Sleep is what her body needs."

His hand brushes mine and in an instant, I feel like I'm back in the fire and turmoil that we fled from in Northaven. In my fear and anger then, a roar came out of me. I had sent my songlight far and high. *Nightingale!* I had cried.

There was anguish in her beam as she saw what was being done to us.

Lark! Her songlight had felt like it was burning through me, turning me into a thousand stars.

LARK!

Nightingale helped me, even though she's locked in Sister Swan's gilded cage.

I will find her. And free her.

The dawn will soon be here and our boat will be visible. The chase will close in on us. I lie once more next to Ma, trying to warm her with my body, trying to rest my racing mind.

I breathe, while the sea moves us up and down, holding us between the earth and moon.

PART 1

PETRA'S DIARY ✶ CELESTIS

DAY FOUR

Four days have dragged by since our voyage on *Celestis* began. Ten days since I last saw Fenan. I'm writing his name all over this page, as if I'm scoring it upon my heart. Fenan Lee. Fenan Lee. Fenan. Why should I bother writing anything else?

I feel a heaviness, despite being up so high. This airship drifts more slowly than the clouds, nothing but ocean underneath. The airship *Angelus* flies ahead of us. It's an impressive sight but I stare at it unmoved. *Angelus* will veer north first, up the west coast of the great continent. Shortly afterward we will follow, taking the east coast. *Solarus*, flying behind us, will continue on across another ocean, the longest journey of all. We will soon lose contact with Sealand, our home. In the days of antiquity before the Great Extinction, there was a network of satellites all around the globe and communication was as easy as my truevoice. On our journey, we'll be quite alone.

Things are still tense, even with my mild-mannered father. He is patient with me but something in him has withdrawn. I can feel his disappointment and it's worse than Mother's anger. There's an iron frost all over her. I caught her looking at me and it was like she was looking at a stranger.

DAY FIVE

How will I stand it, stuck in this cabin with my parents? Five months until we return home.

The only possibility of privacy is this little book. Fenan pushed it into my hand at our last meeting and said words I won't forget, beautiful mouth-words with his gentle voice.

"I can't change the way things are. Our lives will be on separate paths," he said. "But write your thoughts, Petra. That way, I can read them, even if we're far apart. Think freely."

"I will," I said. And I kissed him, lovingly, wholeheartedly.

Mother caught us. She sacked Fenan as my language teacher and in her screeching truevoice, she called the Division Enforcers—how I HATE HER; she didn't need to do that. I was screaming at her, pleading, but she wouldn't listen. She told me to SHUT UP, I was giving her a HEAD PAIN. Now she and Father have forced me to come on this STUPID VOYAGE.

MY HEART WILL BREAK. I want to be with FENAN, back in Sealand City.

I LOVE HIM.

WHAT HAVE THEY DONE TO HIM? HOW WILL HE BE PUNISHED?

DAY SIX

I'm avoiding the rest of the crew. I talk to them at mealtimes but spend most of my time in the cabin. When my parents come in, I hide this diary under my mattress. At night, Father fills the silence, talking about his work with the cartography team. He's kind to me but everything he says is unbelievably boring. I stare out the window at the clouds below.

I hardly see Mother, THANK GOODNESS. She's mostly on the viewing deck, looking at pictures of extinct ocean animals, drawing boring diagrams, making boring plans. Tonight she came back looking all self-satisfied.

"This is the first global assessment that we eximians have made in generations," she said, mistaking me for someone who cares.

I have earplugs at night because my parents snore.

DAY SEVEN

I have picked up my language work again but nothing pleases Mother. She has had another rant at me, telling me I am letting the family down with my morose behavior. I must be prompt and smiling at evening communion. I was late yesterday and almost ran into Air Admiral Xalvas, our commander, as he was entering to begin the thought-share. He said, "Good evening, Petra," but I could sense his affront. If I'm late again, Mother will slow-roast me. She said Xalvas is a man of first merit from one of Sealand's sovereign families. She went on and on and after a while, all I could hear was blah blah blah.

I concentrate on the ancient sapien languages that Fenan was teaching me. When Mother sees I'm working, she leaves me alone.

I'm not the only offspring on this voyage. Xalvas has brought his son, three years older than me. He's training him for leadership. Charlus. I instantly don't like him. He's too tall and looks a bit like a mantis. I'm the next oldest at seventeen—but not old enough to be treated like crew, as Charlus is. Perhaps that's why I feel I don't belong. Mother says I'll get treated like a child if I act like a child and I want to tell her to GO AND JUMP.

DAY EIGHT

Dear Fenan,

I want to pull your lips to mine and press my body close to yours. It felt as if both our spheres of being were pulled into that kiss and all our differences dissolved. What does it matter that you are not eximian? Fenan Lee, I want to kiss you and hold you, listening to your sapien heart. Because how different are we, really?

DAY NINE

This afternoon, I walked the whole length of *Celestis*, staring down at the blue, up at the blue, feeling so small in this cruel blue world. Sky and ocean. They have brought me on this trip to punish me. Or save me.

DAY TEN

In communion this evening, I spoke for the first time. Xalvas asked me to describe the ancient sapien audio I've been studying, voices coming down the veins of history—our ancestors. I am practicing their grammar and pronunciation, mouth-words, as Fenan taught me, in one of the old global languages. I told the crew that although millennia had passed since those tongues were spoken, some of the word roots and structures might endure. If we do find sapien civilizations of any kind, it will give us a starting point for communication. Air Admiral Xalvas remarked how interesting that was.

Beautiful view of the stars tonight. The Southern Cross is the brightest constellation. *Celestis* is a tiny ship, crossing a small planet, on an outer spiral of a commonplace galaxy. We are insubstantial small fry and our existence is a second in time.

DAY ELEVEN

We started passing over atolls and islands midafternoon. It was such a relief to see land down below. The airship *Angelus* has left us and turned north to explore the western coast. We will not see her again for many months. I watched until she disappeared and Garena came to join me. She's our archivist, only four years older than me, and I feel kindness emanating from her. I helped her to capture images of an ancient sapien town—a tumble of ruins, poking through the snow. No one has lived there since before the Great Extinction. *Celestis* has slowed to a snail's pace now, while Father's cartography team maps the coast.

LATER

I wonder if Garena might be the kind of person I could talk to about Fenan? I asked her if she's ever been up to the sapien quarters and she said no. She would need written permission from Commodore Bradus, our Division Enforcer. The sapiens do everything for us. But no one seems to think it's weird how separate we are.

DAY THIRTEEN

Father lost his patience. He told me how lucky I am to be on this mission. He said, "We're here making a new future." He says everyone is sick of my low spirits and I'm letting him and Mother down. He made me cry.

He said Garena needs an assistant in the archive and I am to work with her from now on. I arrived at Garena's desk, hardly able to communicate. But she was kind and after a couple of hours she was making me laugh. I wonder if she knows why I am here? Does Air Admiral Xalvas know?

Thinking back to that awful day when they discovered me with Fenan. My mother's truevoice was full of shock and pain.

"How could you think we'd let him be a match for you?" she had cried.

"Don't you understand?" cried Father. "We'd have to cut you off; we'd never see you again."

DAY SIXTEEN

Huge excitement today. We saw our first wild sapiens, down below. There was talk of sending a landing party, but Xalvas urged us northward. "This voyage is for reconnaissance," he said. "The next will be about contact."

Charlus asked if I wanted to see the scouting crafts. He took me down to the hangar and showed me how one worked. He acted like he could fly it, but I know that he's still training. He's only flown the simulator.

DAY TWENTY

Garena has seven brothers and three sisters. Her parents used sapien surrogates, like mine did. It's nice that our bodies will never be stretched and ruined by childbirth. We talked about how messy and awful it must have been. It's made me think about the sapien who carried me. That woman looked after me until I was three because my parents were away doing an off-planet tour of duty on our Martian colony, Terra Nova.

There's a hole in my memory about my surrogate. I suppose I must have called her mama and I remember the feeling of her tight hugs but I never knew her name. What did she think about me, growing in her womb? Did I hurt her? I wish I could remember more about her and I ache with trying.

DAY TWENTY-ONE

We're over a vast river basin. Garena showed me the signs of ancient habitation under the water. She said that thousands of years ago, there was a population of fifteen million down there. Fifteen million, loud with the filth and music of sapien life. Now it's silent but for lapping water. An underwater city, home to little fishes. I look in the archive for some record of its name. I find an audio recording where an ancient sapien woman calls it Benos Arees.

The biology team is ecstatic because they saw a flock of rare migratory birds. I haven't seen Mother's face look so bright since we left Sealand City.

DAY TWENTY-FIVE

Garena told me how, in a suicidal frenzy of destruction, the sapiens here cut their rainforest down. Why did they destroy the Earth when they had science and culture and knowledge? What madness gripped them? It's the greatest mystery of ancient times.

Learning of the Great Extinction has made me feel so sad. Perhaps we eximians have this sadness in our souls.

I could never be with Fenan. In my heart, I know this.

DAY TWENTY-SEVEN

We ate at the Air Admiral's table last night. An honor. Xalvas's family are survivors from our red planet colony, Terra Nova. Charlus spent his childhood far from Earth. That might account for his sallow look. The Terra Novans all have it, even though their genetic heritage is the finest and most advanced. They were reminiscing about the days when the space transports came and went from Sealand City all the time. All young Sealanders had to do a tour of duty on Terra Nova. Xalvas and his wife liked it there and stayed. How terrible it must have been when the gravity field began to fail. Charlus and his father left before the solar storm but his mother died there. We shared communal grief, remembering the lost.

DAY THIRTY

So much to do. Mother is off-ship again today. Her scouting craft is at ground level, taking samples of soil and flora, testing toxin levels. Charlus has been put in charge of replenishing our water and he went down with her to test a freshwater spring.

Yesterday we saw nomadic sapiens again; herders, a group of families on horseback, their livestock chewing at the patchy grass. They were staring up at us with children on their backs. I sent out my truevoice and the strange thing is, I could have sworn I felt a greeting in return, a curious question coming from one of the tiny figures down below. Garena laughed and told me I was fantasizing. Our ability to communicate has been honed with genetic intervention and generations of careful breeding. It's a romantic notion to imagine the same refinement in the sapiens below.

This evening, we passed a viable town, built from the ruins of an ancient city, but once again, Xalvas insisted that we pass on. First contact is not our role. Mother has brought plant cuttings up and she is testing them for pathogens and radiation. All I see of her now is the bright white suit, the visor over her face. Father works on his maps and snores.

DAY THIRTY-TWO

Charlus was telling me that he came back on one of the last ships from Terra Nova, when he was eight years old. Twelve years now since we lost all contact with the red planet. His mother's remains lie in the ruins of the colony. I didn't know what to say to him. We sat silent for a while and then he started talking about how different this airship is to space travel. He says it's impossible to imagine being without gravity, until you have experienced it. After the long journey home from Terra Nova, he'd lost so much muscle mass that he could hardly walk. His body had to learn how to do it all over again. But on the ship, he would air-dance. I asked him how it was done. He says it was the best feeling and nothing on Earth could come close. He liked everything about Terra Nova and he misses it terribly. He says that people who were born there have a special bond.

LATER

SO HAPPY! Garena has asked if I want to share her quarters! I moved my things in with her just now. Her bunk room is TINY but I love it already and it means I have privacy at last!! She is so much fun. And she KNOWS about life. She told me she was matched with a geologist called Marcus but she broke it off and applied for a different airship. She said some men's behavior left a lot to be desired. "Was he unfaithful to you?" I asked. She just laughed, as if the answer was "of course he was." I'm going to the ship's store to buy her chocolates.

At night, new constellations are appearing in the north.

DAY THIRTY-FOUR

Tonight at dinner, Xalvas asked me if I'd like to train with Charlus to be in one of the scouting craft crews. I said yes immediately and I could see that both my parents were glad. I felt a sense of relief at the thought that finally, they might be proud of me.

Charlus came up to me after supper. He was full of himself because he'd passed his scouting craft proficiency and he said that one day soon he'd take me for a ride.

I hope my parents don't want us as a match.

DAY THIRTY-FIVE

There are lots of sapiens in the scouting craft hangar and none of them will really meet my eye. They say "yes, miss," or "I don't have that information," no matter how open and friendly I am—and I know I have good mouth-word skills. I have accepted that they don't want to talk to me.

I crashed in one of my flight simulations because I was thinking of Fenan. Charlus could've been nice about it, but he laughed at me.

DAY THIRTY-EIGHT

A narrow escape. Mother's scouting craft was attacked!!! Sapiens came out of the forest armed with poisoned crossbows. Torens, her assistant, has been injured. The poison is strong and he's very sick. I am to take my part in his vigil of care tonight. Mother is all right—but shaken. When Torens fell, she took charge of the blaster and had to eliminate the sapiens. I think it has upset her. Father reminded her that the sapiens will die out anyway. "We will inevitably supersede them," I heard him whisper as he held her. "My darling, *this* is our Terra Nova now."

DAY THIRTY-NINE

Torens died. In a solemn ceremony, Xalvas addressed us all. After his eulogy to Torens, he said, "We eximians faced great peril and hardship in building our colony on Mars. We might have thought that peopling the Earth would be easy by comparison. Not so. This shows us all how hard it's going to be. We mustn't forget how strong the sapien is. In some places, we may make the sapien our ally, but where he is our enemy, we must be prepared to do what it takes." He praised my mother's courage and presence of mind in repelling the sapien attack.

I told her how brave I thought she was. I think she is forgiving me.

"We're doing this for you," she said. "We're risking ourselves to forge a new dominion, for you, for the young. Everything you see below you . . . one day that will be eximian land."

Her words have inspired me. I want to do my part for this great mission. I am proud to work hard for *Celestis*, for the future of all eximians.

DAY FORTY-FOUR

Too busy to write. We're way north of the equator now, floating above a crystal sea. My training continues: using the tech, weapons practice, first aid. My mother is an amazing scientist. It's no wonder that Xalvas relies on her more and more. We sit at the top table most evenings now.

DAY FORTY-SEVEN

The land below us is woefully bleak. No wild sapiens, hardly any large fauna. Wasteland and desert for hundreds of miles—the remains of one dead city after another. The ancient wars have left this place devoid of all but the most basic life. The ship has risen to avoid the radiation and we are high enough now to see the curve of the planet. We pass over the endless badlands, toxic and exposed. We're running low on fresh water but for five days no landing parties have been granted permission to leave. Xalvas has insisted we accelerate. He doesn't want us up here in the freezing stratosphere for long, so my father is working around the clock, mapping the badlands.

Busy all day—tired out at night. Far to our north, there are mountain peaks with snow. We hope this might mark the end of the badlands. *Celestis* begins to descend.

DAY FORTY-NINE

I was learning combat and my partner was Charlus. I got him on his back but he grabbed my ankle and pulled me down on top of him. Strictly speaking, it was cheating. He said sapiens won't fight with rules and I have to be prepared. I could feel his hip bones as I got off him.

Garena says he likes me. I should be happy about that. He is from a sovereign family. But all I could think of, when he was on top of me, was how inferior he was to Fenan.

DAY FIFTY

I was watching the sun go down when I heard it. A voice.

Ark . . .

It came again, as if beaming from a satellite of old. *Ark* . . .

It was cried with such feeling, coming from the farthest reaches of the north. An eximian. Garena came in. She strained to hear the voice but she couldn't pick it up.

"You must be hearing things."

"Listen," I cried. It came again. *Ark* . . .

Garena could hear nothing. "Everyone knows how strong your truevoice is, Petra. Perhaps you can hear the *Angelus*, right across the continent."

She's brushing me off. The cry lingered in my soul, full of pain and care. *Ark* . . .

A girl. I listened, straining my psyche until I heard it again. When it came, I could feel the pull of love and desperation in her cry. I realized that she was calling a name.

Lark.

1 ✳ LARK

In the cold light of dawn, I sit up, panicking—townspeople are calling me a dirty, unhuman, mind-twisting bitch. I wake and press my hands over my eyes.

"Sweet dreams?" asks a gruff voice. Heron Mikane, still steering our boat, has his one piercing eye fixed on me. I let my nightmare blow away. A month ago, I didn't know this man. Yesterday, he saved my life. He picked up my ma and carried her out of the fray. Today, I think I probably love him like my pa.

"Let me steer the boat while you rest," I tell him.

"Not tired," he says. "How's Curlew Crane?"

Ma must hear her name, for her eyes flicker open and she half smiles through her pain. "I'm fine," she says.

Heron looks relieved and I kiss Ma's cheek. In the first fingers of light, I look over the edge of the boat. I'm expecting to see a line of distant coast and nothing else but open sea. To my surprise, we're heading up an estuary.

"Where are we?" I ask.

"Heading to Borgas Market," says Heron.

"Why?" I ask. "Kingfisher has to get back to his people. Peace is hanging in the balance—we have to get to Brightlinghelm."

Heron addresses Ma, trying to keep the worry out of his voice. "I've seen enough gunshot wounds to know that bullet needs taking out—today. It needs stitching, proper, somewhere clean."

The moment Ma was injured suddenly fills my mind. She ran toward me—my brother was trying to hold her back—and she took the full force of the bullet that Emissary Wheeler meant for me. Piper and I met over her bleeding body—a chasm between us.

Wheeler's dead now. Heron sliced his throat. I sit and gulp the cold air, breathing down a wave of shock as my body remembers. When I look down at Ma again, I see that she's gazing at Heron. Neither of them speaks but there's a charge between them, as if they want to be alone with each other. It makes me feel embarrassed.

Heron is right, of course. Ma's life comes before everything.

"I reckon Borgas Market is the first place they'll look for us," I say.

"You got a better suggestion?" he asks.

"No."

The estuary is narrowing as we move upriver. "We should take down the sail," I say. "It makes us too visible."

I stand and get on with the job as the boat dances on the incoming tide. The choppiness doesn't bother me. Boats are my gravity. But as I haul the sail, I realize I'm impeded by the deep gash in the palm of my hand. I recall how it felt in the jail cell, the blade of Greening's knife cutting into my skin as I knocked it from his grasp. My hand sears with the effort and the sail flaps out of my control. Two strong arms come round me, helping me to grasp it. For the briefest moment, I think Rye Tern is here. I remember, in a flash of pain, how he would come to me in songlight, when I was on my boat.

But it is not Rye. It is Kingfisher, here in the flesh, and to my confusion, my body is reacting in a similar way. With longing.

"Did you manage to sleep?" he asks.

"An hour or two, maybe," I say. "You?"

"About the same."

I show him how to tie the sail and as I watch him I think of his grace as he fought in that jail cell, holding off two armed men with nothing but his skill.

"Teach me to fight like you do," I ask.

He smiles at my impatience. "This morning?" he asks. "You fight very well, Lark. You saved my life."

"That was chance," I tell him.

"It was courage. The rest is just footwork. I can teach you that."

I fear that color is creeping into my cheeks and I turn away, thanking him, in songlight, for everything he's done for Ma. Kingfisher doesn't reply and I remember that it goes against the grain for an Aylishman to use his songlight when there are people present who don't have the skill. It's a courtesy I admire.

The boat's battery finally dies and Kingfisher joins Heron on a bench, helping him to row. The two men put their backs into the work. Heron looks bleary with fatigue.

"You should rest," I tell him. "I can row."

"Can you now?" he asks skeptically, glancing at my injured palm. "Look after your ma."

I sit and draw Ma toward me, pulling Mrs. Sweeney's blankets tightly around her. Once again, I see Mrs. Sweeney fall into the sea, her back full of bullets. I offer a prayer to Gala for her soul, knowing that those bullets were really meant for me.

Ma resists my help as if it's against nature for her to be weaker than her child. But at last she sinks into my lap and I breathe with her, listening to the low, hypnotic rhythm of the oars hitting the water.

"Kizzy Dunne . . ." Curl's voice has no power in it and I lean in. "Her family had the grocer's store." Each breath is an effort. "We'd stay with them every year when we came out of the Greensward. We'd set up shop in their courtyard."

"In Borgas Market?"

"Kizzy was my friend." Ma half smiles. "She was there when I met your pa . . ."

"Do you think she might help us?"

Ma grew up in the dense forest that covers much of Brightland. The whole center of our island is a mountainous canopy of green. Ma's people—my grandparents—are Greensward nomads. Ma doesn't often speak of them but I know how much she misses them.

"If Kizzy's still living," says Ma, "she'll help."

18

It starts to rain and in my heart I curse the sky. I try to cover her as best I can and for a while, we just endure it.

"We can't take the boat into the harbor," says Heron, "in case Elsa's right and they're looking for us. We must hide it ashore and go into town on foot."

"Ma needs shelter, somewhere soon," I say. "She's not walking anywhere."

Kingfisher and Heron row with renewed effort. The tide is almost at its height, helping our course, drawing us inland. Once it turns, going will become impossibly hard. The estuary closes in, becoming the wide River Borgas. I perceive small farms and a scattering of black trees, blown by the sea gales into startling shapes.

My eyes meet Kingfisher's. In a heartbeat, I know what he's remembering. When I thought that we were going to die, I kissed him. The cold air is vaporizing as he breathes and I look at his lips, thinking of how they felt on mine. Yesterday, I thought I'd part from him forever. Today, something is different between us and I don't know how to name it. It's like a hunger that takes the edge off the cold.

We turn a bend in the river and through the gray gloom of the rain, we see the distant harbor lights of a large market town. The river is too wide for a bridge here and I see that it's connected to the moors and mountains of the north by means of a horse ferry, a large floating platform that's pulled back and forth across the water. I hope it slows the progress of anyone pursuing us from Northaven.

Among the trees on the nearside bank, I see a decrepit wooden boathouse. There is no light coming from it. The jetty outside is rotting into the mud.

"What about that place?" I suggest.

We're almost past it before Kingfisher and Heron can slow the boat. I leap out, the freezing water shocking me as it runs into my boots while I wade to the river's edge. I approach the low building, using all six senses to feel if it is safe. I peer in through a window, where the dry carcasses of moths and flies are turning to dust in a massive spiderweb. This place is long abandoned. It's ramshackle and falling down but it's shelter from the rain, which is falling in sheets. I wipe it from my eyes as I beckon in the boat. I help Kingfisher pull it onto the bank and we hide it as best we can, under some low-hanging trees.

"Let's take the sail," I tell him, thinking we can lay Ma down on it.

Heron lifts Curl out of the boat. "How are you?" he asks her.

"Never better," she replies. But she looks small and deep-down weary in his arms, not like my strong, vivid ma. There's a lump in my throat the size of a stone.

Kingfisher pushes in a half-rotting door and in the gloom, we see we're in a place that nature has invaded. The floor slopes down to the river. Rain splashes and patters through holes in the roof, and at the bottom of the slope, the high tide swirls in around an old, rotting boat. Some kind of animal is disturbed as we enter—a beaver maybe?—and it startles us, rushing into the water. Moss and ivy make a forest of the walls. Only the highest corner of the place looks dry. There's an old stove with a couple of chairs in front of it. Perhaps this place is still occasionally used by seaworkers or herders. We can't build a fire as the smoke will give us away, so as Heron lays Ma down on the sail, I pile all the blankets onto her, tucking them around her freezing feet.

Kingfisher is washing his hands in the river, scrubbing under his nails, preparing to help Ma. Maybe the salt in the tidal water will help him get clean enough.

"What do you need?" Heron asks him.

"Antiseptic, pain relief, more dressings, a sterile suture kit. The bullet needs removing and she needs stitching. The risk of infection is high." He's not making it sound good.

Heron nods and turns toward the door, as if he's going to stride into the town.

"You can't go," I tell him, shocked at his stupidity. "You're Heron Mikane.

20

You're on every mural from here to Brightlinghelm. What if they've heard about us on the radiobine?"

"Your ma needs stuff," insists Heron.

"I'll go," I tell him strongly. "No one will notice me. You'll attract attention, and so will Kingfisher."

"Who's Kingfisher?" questions Ma. I forget that she has only ever heard him called by his Aylish birth name, Yan Zeru.

"It's my true name," Yan tells her. "My songlight name."

"A songlight name?" Ma lies back, taking this in. "Do you have one?" she asks me.

"Lark," I say. "I'm Lark."

She turns it over in her mind, then looks at me with a kind of pride. "Lark . . . Go to Kizzy Dunne."

"How will I find her?"

Ma's memories come slowly through her pain. "There's a sign outside her store: a dancing hare."

"I'll be back before you know it," I assure her, and I turn away, trying to swallow the lump in my throat. Heron follows me to the door.

"I see you're our commander now," he says wryly.

"Yes," I tell him. "And you need to rest."

"You'll want this." He stuffs a pocketful of money into my hand. "And this." He reaches into his boot, giving me a switchblade knife. All Brightling soldiers have them hidden there. I stick it in my own boot, hoping that no one will look at me twice and that I never have to use the thing.

2 ✴ RYE

I've hugged the coast of Brightland for days, putting off the moment when I must heave out into the Southern Sea and make my crossing to Ayland. This stolen boat is not made for high seas. It's nothing but a farmer's boat with a tattered sail barely bigger than a tablecloth. I have no map, no talent for the water, and the likelihood of drowning looms large.

I've been hiding by day and sailing by night, working my way west. The first time I got into a headwind I was so inept with the sail that it swung around and almost knocked me overboard. But I've begun to get the hang of it. Yesterday, I made good progress. But I'm living on raw fish and I'm forever shaking with the bone-numbing cold. I don't think I would feel it so badly if I were strong, but my reserves are spent. The arrow wounds in my back and leg are not healing. There's a soreness round them that is growing worse. In short, I need proper food, fresh water, medicine, and a coat. I must be prepared for that crossing.

I curse myself for not learning to sail when I was in Northaven. I could have asked Elsa to teach me—but all I could ever concentrate on was her smile. And her eyes. And the beautiful curve of her waist and hips. I'd watch her leap from bow to stern, playing with the sea winds, making them work for her. I swear she could make her boat fly. I was transfixed by every inch of that girl and I realize now that I never much focused on what she actually did. There have been times when I have felt like giving up, with this lead band pressing painfully into my skull. And I have filled my mind with images of Elsa: Elsa in her boat, or on the beach, or glancing at me in the town, our secret glowing in her eyes. I feel the sensation of her in my arms, her lips on mine. I think of her songlight, like sun on water—dazzling. Elsa keeps me going.

Elsa—and vengeance.

Over the days my path has come clear. I'm going to make my way to

Reem, Ayland's capital, and tell them everything I know. I will enlist their help and at the head of an Aylish force, I'll sail into Northaven and rescue Elsa. Then, together, we'll lead an attack on Brightlinghelm. We'll slaughter every Brethren-loving, Torch-hating bastard that we find and when they're all dead, we'll burn down the Chrysalid House. We'll be heroes of the people and we'll rule Brightland together from our palace on the hill.

These fantasies keep me warm at night.

The sea feels heavy as daylight breaks. My arms are sore with rowing. I may be somewhere near Whitecliffe. I try to remember the map of Brightland that hung in our barracks, back in Northaven. How far is Whitecliffe from Ayland? If I push off into the open sea, will I miss the Aylish landmass altogether, and drift into the endless oceans of the south?

I've never much fancied the idea of drowning. Or of slowly starving to death at sea. But Ayland is my only hope.

There's a deserted cove coming into view. It looks a likely hiding place and I row toward it, pulling my boat up onto the sand. There's a bad smell and I notice a dead seal lying some feet away from me. Flies are eating what the seabirds have left. I hide my boat and beach lice jump all over me as I cover it in great armfuls of seaweed. This cove has a bad atmosphere, but it also has what I need—a freshwater spring running down from the cliffs. I drink deep and fill the water canister. I think of the boat's owner, the pig farmer, looming over me. I plunged my knife through his eye and killed him. The thought of it sickens me and I double over. I try not to retch all the water I've just drunk. It was him or me.

I hide the canister in the bottom of the boat. It'll give me enough for few days. Then I climb up a steep path, looking for signs of human habitation. Food, something warm to cover myself with—that's the bare minimum I need.

I walk through cow fields for a mile or so, watching it get properly bright. I avoid villages and clusters of farms. This part of the island is more populous than the north. Every corner of it is farmed and it's neat with hedges and little lanes. The landscape is more rolling here, woodland and pastureland. In one copse, I see a herd of deer and there are plenty of well-fed cattle, which fill me full of hope for food. In the distance, as the coast curves round, I see the wooden roofs and turbines of a military depot.

There's a lone house ahead of me, painted a dirty shade of pink, with a walled garden at the rear and a stable yard at the side. I see Third Wives' laundry, strung up on washing lines at the back. Food. I smell food. I cross an orchard, making my way from tree to tree, moving closer to that walled garden. There's row upon row of vegetables and I am going to steal some. I'll have some of that nice fresh laundry too.

I'm on the point of running forward and leaping the wall when a man rushes out of the side entrance. He's wearing a greatcoat, which he must have won in a card game or something because it's at least a couple of sizes too big. His cap is down low and he strides along in his military boots. He glances in my direction and I throw myself down on my belly. I need that coat—but something in me cannot bear the thought of ambushing him. I've had enough of violence. Two men are dead because of me: a guard on the prison barge and that fucking farmer. I don't want another angry soul hovering round my deathbed, waiting to harry me to Hel.

I watch the departing soldier climb a fence into a field. Keeping to the hedgerow, he sprints away from the main road. At the far end of the field, I see him leap the gate and he is gone from view. What's he running away from in that furtive, sneaky way?

Suddenly, a scream comes from the Pink House. I creep closer, curious. I can hear women's shrill voices, men shouting in fury—something's really kicking off. The back door opens. A girl with a pink band around her neck steps out into the garden and is promptly sick. Another girl comes out and comforts her.

"Blood," the first girl cries. "There was a lake of blood. . . ."

The second girl sloshes a bucket of water over the vomit and pulls her distressed friend back inside. No sooner are they gone than three soldiers come hollering out of the side entrance, shouting at the housefather, threatening him. The housefather, a burly brute of a man, gives as good as he gets, cursing them all to wild fuckery. I crawl forward to watch the drama. The soldiers grab their horses from the stable yard, one of them still doing up his breeches. They each set off in different directions, clearly after their comrade in the greatcoat—at breakneck speed. One heads toward the woodland, another down to the coast. The third gallops back to the depot—but none of them think to go over the fields.

I look into the back garden. The Third Wives have left the kitchen door open and the smell of fresh bread turns my stomach upside down. Can I? Dare I?

I jump over their wall and land in a flower bed, hidden by the lines of windblown laundry. I move closer to the house, stealing a clean shirt as I go. I put it on and find a neckerchief to go with it, tying it round the lead band on my head. I've seen some of our soldiers in murals wearing neckerchiefs round their heads like this and I don't want to look like a runaway unhuman. I hope my mud-caked trousers and boots look military enough.

In the Pink House, women are wailing, their voices fearful. I hear the housemother cursing the day someone was born. But when I peer in through the window, the only thing I see is a table laden with breakfast. I am prepared to die for a taste of that delicious bread.

I pull a pillowcase from the washing line to use as a sack and sneak in through the back door. Here I am, Rye Tern, reduced to stealing from a houseful of women. I stuff the pillowcase full of bread, cheese, a chunk of ham, and hard-boiled eggs. I'm virtually slavering with hunger. I'm about to run for the hills when I see a huge pie resting on a dresser by the stove. I drool at the thought of that fine pastry in my mouth and move toward it like a mangy, thieving fox. My hands are on it when I hear a girl's voice.

"What are you doing?"

I spin round, hoping the stove hides the bulging pillowcase from view. She's seventeen or eighteen, the most ordinary girl you could ever see. A pink leather band is sewn around her neck. I have no time to pity her. My only chance is to brazen it out.

"I'm fresh home from the front," I say. "I did call out when I came into the hall—but no one answered me."

"What do you want?"

"Same as any soldier in a Pink House," I say, for want of a better excuse. I see her look of weariness and it makes me feel ashamed. "I'm straight off the ship from Montsan Beach. Not even had time to bathe. Maybe your housemother can find me a companion?"

"Not now," says the girl. "You have to go."

I'm using my foot to hide the pillowcase down beside the stove.

"I didn't mean to startle you," I say. "But you don't get pies like this on the front lines." I give her what I hope is a friendly grin but I suspect it's more like a starveling leer because the girl takes a few steps backward.

"Our house is closed."

A screeching voice yells from upstairs. "Greta, bring that fucking mop!"

"You need to leave."

"Tell your housemother I'll be back tonight." I bow to her and pretend to go, walking confidently into the hall. Behind me, I hear the girl rapidly splashing water into a bucket. Good—she hasn't followed me. I just have time to hide myself in an understairs cupboard when the housefather comes in through the front door, his jacket pulled tight over the acres of his belly. I squeeze myself against a heap of coats and clutter.

"The Emissary's on his way," shouts the housefather as he thumps his way upstairs. "He says we're not to touch that soldier's body."

It must be a brawl of some kind. One soldier has killed another. The housemother's voice is shrill. "If I don't clean up this blood it'll stain my floor forever." She yells loudly: "Where's that mop, Greta?"

The girl from the kitchen hurries past me, sloshing water up the stairs. I hear someone start crying bitterly, pleading that she wants to go home. Another girl tells her not to be such a baby. "No one wants a little whore like you at home."

26

I take my time, fumbling in the dark, choosing myself a coat from the cupboard. As I open the door, I see that it's a sergeant's coat, moth-eaten, but it fits. I make sure no one is around and go back into the kitchen. I lower the pie into my pillowcase, taking a sharp kitchen knife so I can cut it—and within seconds I'm out the back door. As I go up the garden, I pull some carrots out of the soil and throw myself over the wall. Quickly, I run through the orchard and across the fields. I search for cover, as we soldiers have been trained. My stomach is growling, cramping with hunger, but I restrain myself.

I wait until I'm in the woods before I stuff my face with bread and ham. I eat until my jaw aches. I use my fine new knife to cut a big slice of pie, praising Gala for her bounty. I don't know what dreadful deed has been done at that Pink House but it feels like the gods are looking down on me.

This is an ancient wood. The trees are moss-covered and beautiful. After my feast, I walk back in the direction of the cove and I stop in a glade to eat some more bread. The sun has heat in it now and the food in my belly is making me feel sleepy. I mustn't overdo it. I've been on the edge of starvation for days and I know I must eat slowly. There's an old oak in front of me with thick, twisted branches and I climb it with my sack of food, hiding out in the warm morning sun. In the distance, I hear horses galloping up the coast and inland to the forest. They must be searching for that lad in the big greatcoat. I'll lie low, in case they find me in his stead. Whatever he did, I'd buy him a beer and slap him on the back. This food might just save my life.

I settle down in my warm sergeant's coat, my back against the trunk of the tree, my legs stretched out on a thick branch, and I look at the patterns the leaves make on the sky. Maybe Elsa Crane has been praying for me. Gala, thank you, everything is beautiful.

3 ✳ LARK

The rain is easing off. I walk through a wet wilderness of hawthorn, gorse, and brambles, climbing a hillock that leads to the road. It seems that every damn prickly thing on earth grows here, tugging at my dress and scratching my shins. A flock of sheep and a startled grouse are the only living things I meet. I do what I've been longing to do since I awoke: I send up my songlight to Nightingale. Once more, I recall her anguish as she cried my name last night. *Lark.*

I send my songlight in a high beam, just as Nightingale instructed me, thinking of her in the Brethren's Palace. Almost immediately, I feel the ever-strange sensation of being pulled toward her small, bright presence. Every second we're together, there's a danger of discovery, so we must keep our encounter brief.

I find her walking down a corridor, at the back of a crowd. My vision doesn't have full clarity in songlight, as Brightlinghelm is so far away. Images lose and gain distinctness; lights and sounds distort and dazzle me.

"Lark," she says.

"Nightingale," I reply, and in our names we exchange our deep care for one another. I never had a sister. But Nightingale feels like family to me.

She holds me steady in her light and I see the Brethren's Palace through her eyes. Ahead of us glide the pale figures of Sister Swan and her veiled ladies, following a hazy group of dark-clad men. Striding ahead is their new leader, Brother Kite.

"Haven't you slept?" I ask Nightingale in concern.

"Kite won't let anyone sleep," she tells me in low tones. "He's too busy securing his power. He gathered his allies in Peregrine's chamber, before the old man's body was even cold."

Our country is in a dark place. Brother Kite has taken power, Kite the warmonger, a cold machine of a man who chills me to my bones. He forced

Swan to poison Great Brother Peregrine, because Peregrine was contemplating peace with Ayland.

Nightingale points out Kite's new council members one by one.

"See that man who looks like a toad? That's Brother Drake." I focus on a squat man with short legs, falling over himself to keep up with Kite. "He would sell his own granny to advance himself. That uniformed man next to him is Commander Ouzel. He helped Kite develop firefuel and he wants to use it against Ayland as soon as he can. That tall man is Greylag, High Priest of Thal." As if on cue, the somber, frightening man that Nightingale is pointing out turns round and glares at Sister Swan. His skin is sallow, his expression grim. "He hates women and girls," says Nightingale. "I think he'd make us all chrysalids if he could." Last, she points out a bald man. "That's Ruppell, Surgeon in Chief. He's governor of the Chrysalid House."

My courage fails me then. Ruppell bounces along with a spring in his step, his head as shiny as an apple, jockeying for his position close to Kite. The Chrysalid House is a place where Torches like us are sent to die, and this vision of triumphant evil is too much to bear. I can't believe that Nightingale is anywhere near these men. How can I help her? What can I do?

"We're going to the Chapel of Thal," she says, "so that Kite can be sworn in as Great Brother."

As Kite leads his bootlickers across the great hall, every vassal and flunky salutes him. Kite slows his pace, taking ownership of the magnificent space.

"It's all his now . . . ," I whisper. It's hard not to be cowed with bleak dismay.

Kite pauses in front of the towering statue of Peregrine and suddenly, he bows his head with his fist against his heart, as if he's praying to Thal. Either his conscience is pricking him or he's putting on a shameless spectacle of grief. Peregrine's marble face is fixed on the man who killed him.

Nightingale is sensing my surroundings and she's full of concern. "You're not on the sea. Where are you?" she asks.

I explain my mission to get medicines for my ma.

"Be careful, Lark. Telegrams have been coming through the night from Northaven," Nightingale warns me. "They know you're fugitives, they know that one of you is injured. I don't know how far the news has spread but they'll soon be looking for you everywhere."

I thank her for the news. Kite and his entourage are moving on, climbing the great staircase.

"Is no one there standing up to him?" I ask in desperation.

"Brother Harrier is," says Nightingale, and I sense her warmth of feeling for him. "He has escaped the palace and they haven't tracked him down. Kite's blaming him for killing Peregrine but Harrier's clever. He'll fight back." I feel Nightingale's hope lift when she speaks his name.

"I hate to see you in this crowd of villains with no friend at your side."

"I have you," she says simply.

I surround her with my songlight, as if I am embracing her.

"I don't know what I'd do without you, Lark. You keep me strong—and I have Cassandra."

Nightingale moves her gaze to show me the woman standing at her side. I see gauze over what must have once been a striking and animated face. Cassandra has no expression now. Her eyes are blank, the empty eyes of a victim of the Chrysalid House. I stand with Nightingale, sharing her outrage, her sorrow at what has been done to her friend. Nothing can be said.

In my own reality, I see the town of Borgas Market down below and pause in apprehension. It's far bigger than Northaven and nothing like as pretty. The streets sprawl around a large market square, with turbine towers toiling all around the boundary fence. Nightingale looks down with me.

"Go carefully," she says.

We hold one another in a harmony of light. Then Nightingale goes, leaving me standing in the cold, wet field.

4 ✳ RYE

I must have dozed for a few minutes and I wake to find a tiny centipede crawling up my wrist. I put it on the bough, so it can live its life. Before I leave the tree, I eat more bread. It's delicious. I have a chunk of cheese with it and savor a mouthful of the gorgeous pie. My stomach, unused to food, feels like it's about to burst.

I climb down the tree and drink from a brook, then I retrace my steps toward the cove, keeping to the cover of trees and hedgerows. It's slow progress but at last, the steep sides of the cove come into view.

I have everything I need. The stolen food and the moth-eaten coat might keep me alive while I get across that sea. A flame of hope begins to burn that if I make it, some Aylish soul will help me get this tormenting lead band off my skull.

As I descend into the cove, the smell of dead seal pervades the air. I look for my boat and my stomach hits my boots. Gala in Hel—that soldier in the oversized greatcoat is stealing it. Suddenly I'm running. Cunning, thieving fucker.

"Hey," I yell with useless outrage. "That's my boat!" He looks up—and leaps in, grabbing the oars.

"Bastard," I yell, dropping the pillowcase on the sand.

I try to sprint but the deep shingle slows me down. I throw off my coat and hurl myself into the waves as the soldier starts rowing.

I'm a strong swimmer and this soldier is struggling to get the boat over the swell. I might just catch him. The guy's not big and it looks like he's never rowed a boat before. I come for him like I'm a shark, powering through the water. The salt is half blinding my eyes but in a few more strokes I should be able to grab the side. I'll heave myself up and throw that puny fucking villain in the sea.

But the gods are having their final laugh. The food I have eaten makes my stomach cramp. The cold water makes it convulse and suddenly I'm not swimming anymore. I try another stroke but the pain is sharp and I curl up involuntarily. Weighed down by the lead band, my mouth drops below the waves. Instead of heaving in oxygen, my lungs fill with water. Then I'm thrashing. I'm in too deep to feel the seabed and the cramping in my stomach makes me sink.

Gala, don't let this happen. It's too sudden, don't let it end this way—a thief chasing a low-down thief. Gala, please. Elsa, please. Elsa, the lead band is weighing me down.

Elsa, I tried. I am failing.

Elsa. Your smile.

I make one last effort to break the surface—and someone grabs my wrist.

It's him, the thief, the killer. Shall I pull him in and take him down to Hel with me?

The fucker puts a rope in my hand and I pull my head above the water.

I take in a breath, clinging to it as he rows us back to shore.

When I feel the shingle under my feet I know that I will live. I crawl out of the waves. I'm on my knees, coughing up seawater, heaving in the air. There are beach lice crawling over my hands and pathetically, I start to cry. I cry with sorrow for my short and measly life, with relief that I've been spared, with pain, humiliation, a thousand different things. I cry like a little fucking boy. I cough up brine again, and finally I feel like I can breathe.

I see a figure in a greatcoat standing before me. A baggy military shirt, crumpled trousers rolled up over boots—the short-arse murderer. Why has this bastard saved me? I look up at his face. And suddenly, it all makes sense. The heavy greatcoat is drooping off her shoulders and, just visible in the fading light, a pink leather band is sewn tight around her neck. Her eyes are hidden under her cap and she holds an army-issue knife.

"I killed one man with this, Unhuman. And if you touch me, you'll be next."

She's calling me unhuman. I put my hand up to my head. The neckerchief has floated away. She can see the lead band.

"Big fucking crybaby," she says.

"I saw you this morning," I say, "running from that Pink House." I see a flash of desperation in her face. "Why did you help me?" I ask. I genuinely want the answer.

She's shorter than Elsa. She has a cut lip and there's bruising round her neck. She's been through the wars all right, but underneath it all, she looks like a farm girl, bred on milk and butter.

"Turns out I couldn't watch you drown."

Her brows are furrowed and I can see she doesn't know what to do. Under her bravado she is scared of me. Her eyes steal up the beach to my pillowcase of food. Is that what she wants? I'm impressed. She's a cunning survivor like myself.

"My name's Rye Tern," I tell her. "I killed two men escaping from the Chrysalid House and I'm leaving Brightland in my boat."

"You're going nowhere, boy. You're a murdering thief."

I nod in agreement. "That makes two of us."

"Go get that bag of food," she orders me, "and throw it in my boat."

I stand. "Your boat?"

"That's right, soldier," she says, holding her ground. "It's no theft, stealing from a thief. I spared your life but now the boat is mine."

How do I play this? There's no way I'm giving up my boat to this stab-happy Third Wife. But I'm not going to fight her either. I don't doubt she could hold her own but something about it goes against the grain. She spared my life. And I respect her for it.

"So where are you sailing to on this fine day?" I ask.

"None of your business."

"I'm heading for Ayland myself," I tell her.

"That's nice. How're you going to get there?"

"In the boat I stole from the man that I killed. You're welcome to come with me."

That look of desperation again. "Can you sail?" she asks. I know from her terrible rowing that she hasn't got a clue.

"I'm learning. We stand a better chance of making that crossing if there's two of us. I'll share my food—unless the beach lice eat it first," I point out.

"Fuck!" cries the girl, and she runs to where I dumped the pillowcase. She grabs it, shaking the crawling lice out of it. I pick my coat up and do the same. The half-eaten dead seal is grinning away at us as we disturb his swarm of flies. He's a pungent reminder of how close we are to death.

"You know there's a whole pack of soldiers on your tail?" I warn her. "We should go."

I walk down to the water. One of the oars is floating away and I wade in, grabbing it. I ready the boat. To my surprise, I feel a blade at my throat. I'm aware that the wrong move could kill me.

"I thought we'd established a lovely sense of trust," I say.

Her voice is steely. "You lay one finger on me and I'll slice you from ear to ear."

I wish I could open my mind to hers and show her the myriad reasons why she needn't fear me. Instead I whisper, "That's understood."

Slowly, she lowers the knife. She climbs in, eyeing me suspiciously. I sit and row, facing her. I get us over the swell and out beyond the rocks.

"You should lie on the floor under the coats," I tell her. "In case they're watching for you from the coast."

The sun comes from behind a cloud and lights up her cut lip and the bruising on her neck.

"That's some beating you took," I say.

She puts her hand up to the bruises on her neck. "I left him looking worse," she tells me. And she shudders.

It takes a full two hours for her to relax enough to take her eyes off me and look at the receding coast. Even then, the knife is her hand.

"Where the fuck is Ayland anyway?" she asks.

And this is how I meet Wren Apaluk.

5 ✳ PIPER

I'm flying south, through heavy rain. I'm keeping below the clouds, following the coast. It might be better to ascend but I'm looking for a boat: four fugitives, my mother.

What would I do if I saw them?

I don't know.

Ahead, I can see the sandbanks of the Alma Straits where Brightland sits close to the enemy shore. On a good day I could probably see the peaks of Ayland. Today, everything is charcoal gray. They say that before the sea levels rose in the Age of Woe, Brightland and Ayland were all one landmass and the Alma Straits was where they joined. Sergeant Redshank told us we were once all one people. He said that's why we have a right to Aylish land.

Do we though?

I look down at the shifting sands below and nothing seems certain. Until yesterday, I was clinging to certainties I've believed in since I was a junior cadet. Now those certainties seem threadbare, blowing in tatters like a flag in a gale. There's no one to discuss this with, no one I can ask. Sergeant Redshank is dead—and for company I have only Wheeler's corpse, strapped into the gunner's seat in front of me. Wheeler has lost his certainty, that's for sure. His rigid faith is glassy-eyed and dead.

During the night, order in Northaven was restored. Gyles Syker put himself in charge. The junior cadets, armed with loaded weapons, helped the eldermen round up anyone who sided with the insurrectionists. I could hear Hoopoe Guinea crying, "This is a mistake! There must be some mistake!" as she was led away to the barracks. Gailee Roberts had to be pried away from John Jenkins's body. They put her in manacles.

Then Syker's First Wife, Tinamou Haines, was found, drowned in the harbor. No one knows how Tinamou fell into the water but Syker was yelling, convinced that the traitor Elsa Crane had pushed her in out of spite.

"That's not true," I told him. "Whatever my sister may be, you can't lay a murder at her door." A man pulled me away and I found myself looking at Mozen Tern, Rye's pa.

"Calm yourself, lad," he said under his breath. "There are winners and losers in life. And you'd better make sure you stay with the winners."

He offered me whiskey and I took it, feeling its fire in my belly. Mozen Tern helped me get Wheeler's stiffening body in my plane.

"You must tell the Brethren how he died—cut down in his prime by Heron Mikane."

I let Mozen talk, remembering one day long ago, when Rye stole a bottle of his best single malt. Rye shared it out in our dorm at the barracks and we thought he was a hero for defying his pa.

We managed to position Wheeler's corpse in the gunner's seat, trying to keep the head from lolling off the neck. Mozen Tern kept talking in my face, giving me his bad advice. His breath was so hot with liquor fumes that I could have put a match to it and watched his beard explode.

"You've no family of your own now, Piper," he rasped. "I'd welcome you as my son, in place of that miscreant I engendered."

How could he think I'd want him as a father?

"Rye was a good friend to me," I told him.

"Don't use his name," growled Mozen. "That name no longer exists."

As I prepared to fly, a posse on horseback approached, ready to pursue the fugitives down the coast. They had a spare horse with them, saddled for Mozen. Gyles Syker looked at me in mistrust.

"There's a list of the guilty here," he said, handing me a document. "Put it in the hands of Brother Kite."

I took this as a warning to tell the Brethren the right version of events—Syker's version.

"I'll see you in Brightlinghelm, Crane," he said, and he kicked his horse into a gallop.

There's something dangerous about Gyles Syker and I don't want him as an enemy.

I shut myself in the cockpit with my dead passenger as the horsemen raced off down the beach. For a while, I didn't move. I stared at the sea, thinking nothing. Perhaps I am concussed.

I circled over Northaven, wanting to see what happened one more time. The burned-out warehouse was sending up plumes of thick gray smoke and there was a bloodstain on the street where Ma was shot. I saw a huddle of defeated people corralled in the barracks, craning their necks at me, their hands cuffed behind their backs. I picked out Gailee, Hoopoe Guinea, Mr. Malting, and some of Heron's men. The losers.

Everything that's formed me seems as insubstantial as these clouds. My beliefs are seeping out of me and without them, how do I behave?

I ascend higher, trying to get beyond the dismal, driving rain, and at last, I rise through the clouds and light floods my cabin, warming my skin, making my eyes stream. It's like a different world up here, a world where only birds, gods, and the Light People have ever come before. I am a pioneer in a land where the earth is made of cloud. Blue sky and sunshine are all around—and what have I brought with me to this heavenly place?

A dead man and a pack of lies.

In my thick airman's jacket, I am not cold, yet I find myself shivering. There's something heavy on my chest and soon I'm shaking uncontrollably.

I almost sent my sister to her death.

I sit with that thought. I sit with my betrayal of Rye. I saw them put his body on a barge and take him upriver to the Chrysalid House. I think of what they will have done to him by now. Even if his body lives, the Rye I knew is dead, his face behind a gauze. I have done that. I have killed my friend.

I let go of the controls.

It's like I'm outside my body, watching myself as the plane begins to make a downward arc.

I have killed my friend. I loved him—and he's a chrysalid.

Elsa loved him and she hates me now.

Redshank is dead. Ma's the only person I have left. If Ma's dead, I can't go on.

The plane is falling rapidly now. I hit the soft cloud bank and plummet back into the sunless mist. I feel gravity in the pit of my stomach, pulling me down toward the earth. How many seconds before the death that I deserve? The plane is rattling, battered and hammered by the rain. I am hurtling at top speed toward the ground. I brace myself for the annihilating impact. Some farmer will find me crashed on the ground, a stupid, broken boy.

In an instant, I see Tombean Finch in front of me, turning round as if he's in the gunner's seat. He slaps my face, a memory so vivid I feel it sting my cheeks.

"Fly this plane, you fucker." His eyes are full of determination. "If you don't get us back alive, I'll fucking kill you."

I fall through the base of the clouds—the ground is racing toward me. It's too late for Rye. I killed him.

But I take the controls.

Pulling with all my might, I skim the top of a mighty oak. Startled sheep race beneath as I make it back into the sky.

This emptiness. I must fill it. If I cannot put things right, I must at least atone.

I can't ever bring Rye back. But I look at my hands as they grip the controls. I will use them in Rye's name.

I don't know exactly what that means. But I know it is my journey now.

6 ✸ LARK

I'm almost at the gates of Borgas Market. As I draw closer, I see the walls are topped with jagged spikes. It won't be easy to get in. There's a straggle of market traders on the road ahead, carts laden with goods and people stooped with loads of produce on their backs. In a way, this is fortuitous. If it's market day, I'll be less exposed as a stranger. But I see that the traders are forming a queue at the town gates, where two guards are checking permits to travel. Obviously I don't have one.

I quickly turn off the main road onto a farm lane. I let the barns and the outhouses hide me, running through vegetable patches and gardens, until I find myself in a timber yard by the walls, facing the dead end of a big locked warehouse.

Stay alive, help Ma.

I climb onto the top of a logging cart loaded with heavy timber and use a metal drainpipe to make my ascent—quite a feat with my injured hand. After an undignified scrabble over the guttering, I find myself crawling on my belly over the warehouse's mossy roof. If my thinking is right, this building forms part of the town walls. Visibility is poor in this driving rain and I can only pray that the guards that I see in the watchtower keep their gazes fixed on the river. I crawl on and at last I find myself peering down into a street. It feels like a triumph to have gotten this far until I realize there is no way off the roof. The only thing that I can do is drop. I imagine my bones snapping as I hit the ground and I brace myself. I must make myself soft like a cat and use my hands and feet like paws. I will fall with feline grace. I squash the little voice that tells me this idea is desperately bad.

I swing round my legs and grip the side of the roof, letting myself down as gently as I can. My hand wound opens up immediately and blood starts pouring down my wrist. I let go, dropping like a sack. Pain shoots up my ankles and I curl into a ball—but the damage isn't lasting. Thankfully, the alley is deserted and within a few moments, I am able to walk on. But a trail of blood drips behind me and my hand hurts like Hel.

Stay alive, help Ma.

The streets are like a maze and I move as quickly as I can, working my way toward what I hope is the town square. I have to stop by a trough and plunge in my hand. The cold water numbs the pain and washes some of the blood away. As I look at the wound, thoughts of Northaven crowd in. I try to fight away the fragmented images.

I left Northaven in fire and fury, neighbor fighting neighbor. With a pang, I realize I can never go back. I see Gailee Roberts crying over John Jenkins as he lay dying in the street. I see the look on Mrs. Sweeney's face as the bullets hit her spine. I try to force the violence from my mind—but my thoughts are mired in it. What's to become of those who helped us: Gailee, Soldier Wright, Mr. Malting? There's a wound in the town like the slash in my palm. It might scar over but it will never be the same again.

I tear some fabric from my petticoat and wrap it round my hand. The physical pain is making me feel like a pathetic little girl. I want Rye. I want him to tell me that everything will be all right. He was so good at making a joke out of adversity. But Rye is lost. A dark fire takes hold of me: grief, anger, loss, injustice. It presses down on me like a force. How can I fight it? I let out a cry at how hopeless it is.

No one sees me but a wet cat.

I walk on, my heartbeat telling me to stay alive and help Ma. My narrow alley comes to an end, feeding straight into the town square, and I stand at the edge of it, unnerved by the big, exposing space. Brightling flags hang heavy and damp outside a grand elders' hall. Shops and taverns line the sides, and in the center, a bronze statue of Great Brother Peregrine stands grandly in a fountain, with water splashing down his shoulders like a cloak. The square is busy with people setting up market stalls. There's a queue already forming outside a bakery and the smell of baking makes my stomach growl. I walk forward, looking for Kizzy Dunne's store—and come to a halt completely. At one end of the square stands a set of gallows. Four bodies are hanging: three men and a woman.

In Northaven, our gallows are up on the headland, a grisly but distant sight. Here in Borgas Market, it seems they are in everyone's face as they go about their business. I step closer, something drawing me toward the dead. Who were they? What were their crimes? I can't bring myself to look at what is left of their faces but their clothes look ordinary: farmer's clothes, shopkeeper's clothes. The woman was a widow, her gray veil now dripping with rain. What did these people do?

Nearby, a family is setting out their wares but their voices are hushed, shoulders bent, as if they know no good can come of commerce done in the shadow of death.

At last, I see a metal sign in the shape of a dancing hare—Kizzy Dunne's place. Keeping to the edge of the square like an ordinary shopper, I slowly approach and peer through the windows. I'm crestfallen to see empty shelves, right up to the ceilings. Perhaps the place has closed down; perhaps Kizzy is that woman hanging on the gallows. I try the door: locked. Hopelessness seizes me. I have no other plan.

Then I see a figure come in from a storeroom, moving behind the counter. A woman, neatly dressed, her hair tightly sculpted on top of her head. She must be about Ma's age. She sets a heavy block of cheese in front of her and starts to cut it with a wire. Maybe none of the stores have goods on the shelves anymore. This woman is portioning out rations for her customers.

I give the door a light knock. The woman startles as if her nerves are on edge. She looks at me and her expression changes, as if she's seen a ghost. Slowly, she comes to the door and as she opens it, a bell rings over our heads.

I should have spent my time preparing a story, instead of churning over the shocks that I have lived through. The woman is staring at me, her expression strange.

"Curl?" she says. I suppose I do look a little like my ma.

"I'm Elsa," I tell her. "Curl's daughter, Curl and Gwyn's girl. Are you Kizzy?"

She gives the slightest of nods, looking at me as if she knows I'm bringing trouble to her door.

"Ma sends her regards," I say, hoping my manner is friendly and not as scared as I feel. "She thought you might help." Kizzy says nothing so I carry on, filling the silence with improvised lies. "We're going to see my grandparents in the Greensward. I've never met them and Ma got permission to travel from our elderman but she fell from her horse, not far away. She's a bit shaken up, so I said I'd come. We need antiseptic, pain relief, a warm coat." Still nothing from Kizzy but a stare of dismay. "I have money . . . ," I say hopefully, showing her Heron's crumpled notes.

Kizzy glances across the square at the gallows. "You can't come here, child. Get back in your boat and go, as quickly as you can."

At that moment, I realize she knows. News must have reached Borgas Market from Northaven. Either she's heard about our escape on the radiobine or there's a search party here already.

"I'm sorry to have troubled you." I say. "My mother remembers you fondly." I'm about to turn on my heel when Kizzy grabs my hand.

"You need to hide," she says under her breath. As she pulls me into the store, the bell rings again, loudly, over our heads. "Get down," she says, and she pushes me toward a barrel of grain. As I hide behind it, my stomach flips. Coming into the square I see two Emissaries and a uniformed Inquisitor. A chain around the Inquisitor's waist binds his Siren to him, like a dog upon a leash. I shrink from the sight of her—a young woman, not much older than me, her hair shaven, wearing a shapeless dress in the nastiest shade of yellow I have ever seen. There's a cruel red welt around her skull. Her lead band is off, held by her Inquisitor, and her head is tilted upward like she's listening. She is seeking songlight. They're already hunting for us here.

"Stay put," whispers Kizzy. "My husband is coming."

42

As I crouch out of sight, a man comes out of the storeroom, pulling on a rich, dark coat. His self-importance leads the way and I notice that his fingers are covered in fine gold rings as if he's the wealthiest man in town. Kizzy is plain by comparison.

"Who was at the door?" he asks.

"No one."

"I heard the bell."

Kizzy stands in front of me, keeping me out of his eyeline. "I was sweeping the step and I saw the searchers coming," she tells him in a singsong voice, pointing out the approaching officials. "I was going to offer them a cup of tea."

"Tea, are you daft? Didn't you hear the radiobine? There are riders coming from Northaven. We're going down to the harbor to meet them."

"What will you do?" asks Kizzy nervously.

"If those unhuman traitors have snuck their way in here, we'll soon unearth them in a house-to-house search. If we don't find them, we'll get a posse together to search down the coast."

Kizzy goes to the merchant and dusts the dandruff off his fancy coat. She'll give me away. Any second now, she'll tell him who I am. What's she waiting for?

"It sickens me to think that someone in this town might be hiding them," says Kizzy.

"They're scum," says her husband. "Heron Mikane—what a betrayer. Who'd have thought he'd side with the Aylish?"

"It just goes to show," says Kizzy, "treachery is everywhere."

I'm heartened to realize that she's lying for me. I close my eyes in the vain hope it will make me more invisible.

"One of them is injured, by all accounts," says the merchant. "A woman. It'll make them desperate and we'll soon pick them up."

The merchant opens the door and strides out. I notice that his riding boots are made of softest suede. I see him shaking hands with the Inquisitor and

43

the eldermen. He ignores the crop-haired Siren, as if she's too distasteful to contemplate, even though her awful yellow dress makes her the most vivid thing in the square—a canary among crows. The Siren's gaze is on the ground but I know she's listening, searching for any tiny hint of songlight. Did she hear Nightingale and me outside the town? Can she sense Kingfisher, using his songlight to help Ma? I am desperate to warn him but the Siren makes this quite impossible. I have to get back to him—now.

I look up at Kizzy. Kizzy looks down at me.

"What's happened to Curl?" she asks.

"She's been shot." There's no point lying. I tell her the story as quickly as I can: how the Aylish were coming to make peace, how Heron Mikane welcomed them, how Great Brother Peregrine cordially agreed to talks in Brightlinghelm, how the Aylish were given safe passage. And how Wheeler, the Emissary, tried to murder Kingfisher, and Heron Mikane wouldn't stand for it.

"How do you know all this, child?"

"I'm Heron's Second Wife," I say, trying to keep the tale as simple as I can. "The town was divided. There was a fight. Emissary Wheeler shot my mother—and Heron cut his throat."

"How bad is Curl?"

I feel my face distorting into hot distress that I then struggle to control. "She's bled a lot. The bullet's in her shoulder. Our neighbors helped us to escape. But our eldermen were killing them. I don't know how many are dead."

Kizzy takes in all I've said. "That pressure, that feeling of neighbor against neighbor. It's the same in Borgas Market," she says. "Since the hangings last week, it's been like a powder keg just waiting for a match. It could all—"

"Mama?" comes a voice from the stockroom. I step behind some shelves.

"Hello, my pet." Kizzy turns and I see a junior choirmaiden aged around twelve. She's as bonny as a June meadow, wearing a nightdress covered in hand-embroidered flowers. She reminds me strongly of Chaffinch Greening.

"Who are you talking to?" asks the girl, looking around in puzzlement.

"Your pa." Kizzy approaches her. "The Inquisitor's here. There's trouble—and we must step up and help."

"What kind of trouble?" asks the girl in excitement. Gala, how easily she could betray me.

"I need you to stay upstairs," Kizzy instructs her. "There are bad people about."

"What bad people?"

"Traitors."

The girl lingers, troubled. "Will there be more hangings?" she asks fearfully.

"No," Kizzy assures her. "I pray not."

The girl pauses, her eyes searching the store, knowing that she heard my voice.

"I told you, my pet, go upstairs. Put on the radiobine and get yourself dressed."

"Can I listen to *Music Hour?*" asks the girl.

"Yes," says Kizzy, and her daughter leaves. I feel Kizzy's torn emotions.

"Thank you," I whisper.

She looks out the window. I sense her deep anger at me for putting her in danger. She has lied to her husband and her daughter and I hardly know what to say.

"I'm sorry to have brought you my trouble. I want you to know that we're not bad people."

I realize that Kizzy's eyes are fixed on the gallows.

"Neither were they," she says.

We look at the hanging figures in silence. Then Kizzy turns to me.

"My husband is the law here, you understand? Nothing stands in his way, not me, not anyone."

I nod. *Yes, I understand. You're scared of him.*

"Come," she instructs, leading the way behind the counter and into her storeroom. "Your ma needs a doctor. I can't help you with that."

45

"She'll be all right if we can get the bullet out and stitch her shoulder," I say with more confidence than I feel.

"You might kill her," says Kizzy.

I think on my feet. "Heron has some knowledge in that line. Battle-field medicine." I fear that if I tell her that one of us is an Aylishman, an unhuman Torch with healing skills, it will break the spell that is currently binding us together. Kizzy opens a wooden box full of bandages and dressings. She hands me one.

"You'll need that for your hand." I look down and see that blood is dripping once again.

"I'm sorry," I tell her.

I wrap my hand as Kizzy takes a big cloth bag from under the counter. She starts throwing things in. I see her grab a pot of pills. "These are for pain," she says. She gives me a bottle of antiseptic. "There might be infection." She goes to the kitchen and I see a sewing box by an armchair. Kizzy gives me scissors, needles, tweezers, and her finest silken thread. "Clean it all before you use it with the antiseptic," she says.

I thank her again, following her like I'm under her enchantment.

"My husband is a righteous man," she tells me as she picks up more supplies, dropping a loaf and a hunk of cheese into the shoulder bag. "He accused some of our neighbors of aiding insurgents from the Greensward. They're hanging on the gallows now."

The risk she's taking is enormous and I honestly don't know what I can say.

"You must have loved my ma, to be helping me like this."

Kizzy looks away so I can't see her emotion. "I was a different person then."

Kizzy opens her back door, peering out to make sure we're alone. "Into that barn, quick as you can," she says, pointing across her wide yard, and I sprint, disappearing through a pair of high wooden doors. I hope her daughter doesn't see me from a window.

I gasp with shock. Before me are two of the biggest horses I have ever

46

seen. Their legs are like young trees. I've heard of the existence of these beasts but no one has them in Northaven. They are great-horses. Our forebears bred them during the Traveling Time when they lived as nomads, to carry heavy loads. I stand looking up in awe at the great-horse nearest to me. She lowers her head, which is almost the size of my torso, and snuffs at me with her big velvet muzzle.

I put my hand up to her.

"That's Yura," says Kizzy as she closes the barn doors behind us. "And that's Uki, her son."

I look up at a young stallion. He has the same brown coloring as his mother and he's almost twice as tall as me. He's eating from a huge bale of dried grass that's hanging from a wall. I'm drawn to these horses like a magnet and I feel a longing to use my songlight to show them who I am.

"Yura," I say aloud, "I'm pleased to meet you."

"You've no time," says Kizzy. "Your path lies this way." She clears the straw and muck from a worm-eaten trapdoor in the barn floor. She heaves it open. A rank smell comes up and I see a filthy set of steps leading down into a black hole. Suddenly I realize her game. She intends to make me a prisoner and wants to be credited with the catch.

"No," I say, stepping back.

"Your path is down there," says Kizzy.

"I'll go back the way I came."

Kizzy stands between me and the barn doors. One more breath and I'll push her aside and run. She must see my horror.

"It takes you into a storm drain," she assures me. "There's a narrow footpath running beside it. It'll bring you out downriver, just past the harbor and the town walls. My father used it for smuggling." Kizzy fetches a hurricane lamp and lights it. "You'll never get back out through the square. They're watching for you now."

Reluctantly, I see her logic.

"My advice is head inland as soon as you can get Curl on her feet. And child . . . ," she says, handing me the lamp, "don't come back."

47

She fetches a warm riding coat and a thick shawl from a peg. "For your ma," she says. Kizzy helps me into the coat and shawl and suddenly I am clinging to her.

"Thank you" is all I can say.

"When we were about your age," she tells me, "Curl and I would go down this tunnel, keeping out of our parents' way. We'd wander down by the riverside, looking for clams. The currents down there are fierce and one day, I fell into deep water. Curl leaped in to save me."

"My ma saved your life?"

"No," says Kizzy with a wry smile. "She couldn't swim."

I feel such a pang of love for my mother that tears spring to my eyes.

"That's why I'm helping you. Curl leaped in that river and she couldn't swim."

"What happened to you both?" I ask. "How did you survive?"

"You don't know the story?" she asks in surprise.

"No," I admit.

"Ask your mother."

Taking the lamp and the heavy bag, I make my way down the slippery steps. Kizzy holds the trapdoor, ready to close it over me.

"I never saw you, Elsa Crane," she says. "Now Gala go with you."

At that moment, the barn doors open and I see a small figure walking in: Kizzy's daughter.

"Ma," she says. "There's blood—" The girl's eyes meet mine, and she looks like a startled deer. Kizzy slams the trapdoor down, leaving me in the suffocating dark.

She saw me. The girl saw me.

I lift the lamp, my heart pounding. A dank tunnel with walls covered in slugs and snails runs narrowly in front of me. Slipping on the rocks, carrying my load, I hurry away as fast as I can.

7 ✷ NIGHTINGALE

I'm standing with Swan and her veiled ladies in the small chapel of Thal, which adjoins the council chamber. It has gray-black drapes from ceiling to floor and the altar is rust-red marble. Upon it, Thal himself, made in muscular bronze, dwarfs us all, holding the lightning bolt of war and invention.

We are watching as Starling Beech fits Peregrine's heavy robes of state onto Kite's shoulders. Kite is preparing for the ceremony that will make him our Great Brother. He has finally schemed and maneuvered himself into the position that he's always craved. Brightland is his. And he got it by murder. One little yellow almond was all that it took, laced with the poison he forced into Swan's hand.

Kite is shorter than Peregrine and the thick fabric trails on the ground, threatening to trip him. The robes, which were probably august and statesmanlike on Peregrine, look like a dressing-up costume on Kite.

How did I get here, watching this abhorrent man grab power? I feel hollow with defeat, as if the gloomy bleakness of the chapel is acting like lead, taking my songlight, taking my courage. What can I do to keep myself alive, under the eyes of these terrible men?

I look to Swan, my vivid mistress who lights the room with her presence. She is the beginning and the end of my survival. Radiant, she steps up to Kite. She too will be looking for a way to stay alive, to make herself needed, to ingratiate herself.

"You don't need Peregrine's robes," she says adoringly. "This is a time of new beginnings. You need a look that plays to your stature and your strength."

She takes the robes off Kite and holds them, as if Peregrine himself is swooning in her arms.

"Look at yourself now," she says.

Kite looks down at his impeccable suit. He has hardly acknowledged Swan since their murder was done. Now he turns his gaze on her, inspired.

"Yes," he says. "I am the modernizer, the radical, the purifying force. I will be myself." He looks to Starling. "Let them in."

Swan lays Peregrine's robes on the altar. Starling opens the doors and Greylag, the High Priest of Thal, leads in Kite's new councillors to witness the inauguration ceremony. Kite surveys his eleven men. Swan stands with them, making twelve.

The veiled ladies and I are ignored by all. We might as well be moths, clinging to the drapes.

Greylag begins a prayer for Peregrine but Kite soon cuts him off.

"We cannot pause for mourning," he says. "Brightland must have steady government. From here, we will proceed directly to the council chamber and we will not rest until we have restored order, crushed the rebellion, and captured Peregrine's murderer. We know his name—Raoul Harrier. We know where he will hide—in the base streets of Brightlinghelm. We will root him out and bring him before us, to answer for his crime."

I instantly resolve to help Harrier in any way I can. He had no more to do with Peregrine's death than these voiceless sisters of mine. But Kite hates Harrier for being a decent man and I fear he won't rest until Harrier is dead.

Greylag takes the rod of state and in Thal's sacred name, he swears Kite in as our nation's leader.

"As our Great Brother, you must solemnly swear to devote yourself to Brightland."

Kite cuts him off again. "I will not be known as Great Brother," he announces. "That title was Peregrine's and his alone. Brightland must look to its future. Our nation is being reborn. We are rediscovering firefuel technology," he continues, "and to honor this renaissance of the Light People's power, I will from henceforth be known by one of their titles: Lord Kite. And you will be my Ministers."

Kite talks on, about how brilliant everything is going to be now that he's able to do exactly what he likes. He will be Thal's own son, the master of war and invention. As I look at the councillors, all I can see are their teeth and glinting eyes. Kite names them, giving each his new position. Ouzel is Minister of War; Ruppell is Minister of Purity, a title that chills me to the core; and Drake is Minister of Home Affairs. The councillors exchange glances as they all invisibly transform into Ministers. Last in the line is Swan. I see her anticipation, waiting for what's due to her. She's sick of being the Flower of Brightland. She's the Queen of Propaganda, an expert at turning Kite's lies into glowing truths. But Kite passes her by without a word.

I sense Swan's affront. Humiliation rises off her like hot vapor.

"Hail Lord Kite," cries Ruppell with fervor. The other men follow suit and Swan adds her voice to theirs. "All hail Lord Kite!"

There are not enough people to make much noise and the ladies and I cannot join in, as we have lost our will to speak. There is no cheering, no trumpet fanfare. These men celebrate their new regime like robbers in the night.

Lord Kite gets straight to business, his efficiency as impressive as ever. "Great Brother Peregrine's remains will lie in state in the temple of Thal," he informs us, "so that our citizens can pay respects. We won't hide the effects of the poison on his face. We'll let all of Brightland see what the traitor Harrier did to him."

This is barefaced by any standard. And it will be effective. Harrier will be made a villain.

"What are my orders for the Aylish diplomatic ship?" asks Ouzel. "It's due to arrive in Brightlinghelm tomorrow."

Kite considers. "We will honor Peregrine's commitment to talk peace," he says, "but our real intention is attack." This sends a thrill of excitement through the room.

"I knew it, my lord, I knew it," cries Ruppell. "I knew we could rely on you. Peace would be unthinkable. The first thing the Aylish would insist upon is the closure of the Chrysalid House."

"We must make sure that the Aylish get the welcome they deserve," says

51

Kite. He looks to Ouzel. "We'll plan his funeral, timing it as their ship arrives. They will see as soon as they step ashore that their hopes for an easy peace are about to be burned on a funeral pyre and floated down the Isis."

I know why I am here now. I'm a spy.

I'm here for Lark, for Kingfisher, for Heron Mikane, for Harrier. I'll do whatever I can to forward their cause.

Kite's Ministers proceed out of the chapel of Thal toward the adjoining council chamber, congratulating each other. Brightland is their playground now and Kite is the man of the hour. These Ministers will back him to the hilt in return for their own advancements. They smile at Swan as they pass, muttering salutations: "dear lady," "sweet flower." I'm sure her jaw aches with smiling. Each one is like a hungry snake, carefully guarding his territory, on the lookout for a better position, all vying for a moment to strike. Kite has them tamed for now. But keeping their loyalty will be his daily task.

For the first time Swan turns round and glances at me. I instantly fill my eyes with outrage on her behalf, and she looks grateful.

"I'd like to know what my new position is, my lord," she asks.

Kite remains with Swan and us moths. He kicks the door shut. Being lord of the snakes must be the greatest aphrodisiac—as he suddenly grabs Swan and pins her up against the altar.

"This is your new position," he says. His kiss is ugly and his hands invade her. I scrunch up my eyes, closing out the sight. I hate it here so much. I pray to Gala to make this stop. If he takes her on that red marble altar, I will scream.

Swan is stopping him.

"My lord," she says. "I'm happy to devote my life to you, as you devote yourself to Thal. But first, you must give me my new title. I wish to be Lady Swan and I will accept a position of Minister for Public Enlightenment. I am the conduit between you and your people. And you owe me no less." She raises her eyes to his.

"I owe you nothing. You have murder on your hands," whispers Kite.

"And your role is going to be different from now on. Mistress of the Bed. All our business from here forward will be conducted in your rooms."

It's as if he has just punched her.

Kite moves away, opening the council chamber doors. I see his Ministers rising to their feet, grinning like a cabinet of death masks. He closes us out, leaving us in Thal's dark chapel.

I move toward Swan. Her shock is so great, Kite's ingratitude so galling, that for a moment she doesn't speak.

"Sister, you have to fight back," I whisper. "Do nothing for him until he's given you everything you want."

I'm not sure that Swan hears me. There's a ringing sound in my ears, as if her songlight is burning to escape from the confines of her Siren's lead band. It must be so painful to have it constrained in that way. I try to hold her, calm her with my light, but she moves away from me.

"Let's go," she says.

We leave the chapel. The ladies follow behind as we walk down the great staircase.

"I have tarnished my soul with murder for that man," says Swan, "and he will not reward me. He will hold it against me, using my body and mind until he's ready to discard me."

I can't argue with any of this. My songlight tries to reach through her band. I feel for her desperately. Kite has a core of viciousness and spite, and I hate what Swan is forced to endure. The whine of her trapped songlight doesn't relent.

The great hall is busy with small groups of men. I expect they're discussing Peregrine's murder and Kite's assumption of power, trying to gauge if others are for or against him, making guesses as to where to put their loyalty. Anyone truly opposed to Kite would be wise to leave at the first opportunity.

Swan doesn't seem to see them. She stops to look up at Peregrine's statue.

"I'm remembering his last words to me," she says quietly. "He said,

'Zara, the persecution is going to stop.' He said he was going to demolish the Chrysalid House."

I stand with Swan, looking up at the stone man.

"He was going to destroy it," she continues. "But I'm the only person who knows he said this. And it will go with him into the grave."

"It can't," I whisper urgently. "Sister, you have to act."

Swan's eyes are locked on Peregrine's face and the ringing sound of her trapped songlight grows louder and louder until something in her is about to shatter.

"Forgive me," she murmurs aloud. And she collapses.

I put my arms around her, holding her up. The other ladies assist us. Swan has gone pale. I grip her as she emits an ugly sob. This isn't picturesque sorrow. This is a raw guilt that knows no bounds. Peregrine stares down at her, the cold, wily, marble raptor.

"I loved him," cries Swan. She emits another dreadful sob and I hold her as tightly as I can. "I killed him," she says in the quietest whisper, into the folds of my dress.

What do I do? Silence has fallen in the great hall and I can say nothing in case I give myself away. At last, Swan wipes her face with her hands and begins to recover herself.

All the activity in the great hall has stopped. Every man has taken off his hat as a sign of respect: servicemen and merchants, Emissaries, aides, Inquisitors, and the lowliest of guards are all looking at Swan in concern. They mistake her guilt for grief.

Swan is as slim a reed but she feels as heavy as an ox as the ladies and I support her out.

This woman will keep on taking all the strength I have.

Back in the white rooms, we lay Swan down.

"Those men all felt your sorrow," I say in my most gentle voice. "Everyone loves you."

"That's not true," she says. "I'm a monster. I chose the wrong side and Peregrine is dead."

My body is faint with the effort of holding her. It takes me a moment to get my words in order.

"If you think you are a monster, then you must atone for what you did."

Swan looks at me uncomprehending, like a child. I stand upright and the room starts spinning. My head feels light. I cling to the bedpost, steadying myself.

"My poor dolly," cries Swan, noticing how drained I am. She barks at one of her ladies. "Get us food—drink—do it now!"

As the lady turns, I see it is Cassandra. It's the last straw. My energy fails me.

Swan fusses around me, propping cushions, finding me a coverlet. I wonder, in my dizziness, if she has ever done anything this kind before. She never thinks about anyone else. She certainly doesn't think about the state of her ladies, whether they need food or drink or rest. There's a little door behind Swan's bed, where the women come and go. Presumably they eat and sleep in there. I have not been in. It feels like a hidden place for chrysalids, where the fully living should not go.

"Kaira, you're precious and you need special care," says Swan tenderly. "I must learn to look after you better. I should have sent you back here to rest hours ago."

"I'm glad I was with you," I say with feeling.

I eat the bread Cassandra brings and drink the cool, refreshing water. The dizziness leaves me and my thoughts begin to clarify. An idea forms.

"You can't let Kite push you out," I tell her. "I know you feel grief about Peregrine, but you must act, strongly, as Peregrine would have wished."

"I have to survive, Kaira."

"Then show Kite you won't be used and bullied anymore. You have an opportunity to act," I urge. "People respect you; they love you and they know you loved Peregrine."

Swan eats and drinks too, letting the cold water revive her. "If I do anything against Kite, he'll send me to the Chrysalid House."

"He wants you to think you're powerless," I press. "But his position isn't safe. He's murdered Peregrine and everything's in turmoil. He might have the loyalty of the palace but things are different in the city. Ordinary people like me, we don't know Kite and we don't trust him. We hear you speaking every day and we believe in you. Speak for yourself, Sister. Show Kite you have power in your own right."

Swan takes in what I have said. "How can you see this so clearly, Kaira?"

"Because I'm not from the palace," I say. "The real world is out there in the city. That's the world that's important. Without the people, a leader has nothing. Kite bullies and uses you, but Sister, you have influence."

Swan looks as if she's piecing something together. "Harrier once told me the same thing. He said that I should use my influence for good." She sighs, her eyes downcast. "But there's no such thing as good. Only failure or success."

"That isn't true," I argue. "I can feel your goodness." I voice my idea. "Kite hasn't yet spoken to the people. They don't know that Peregrine is dead."

Swan looks at me and I see a plan of action forming.

We ready ourselves, eating a little, drinking more water. And together, we walk to the recording room. Swan treasures her radiobine engineers and they all seem to adore her. Seeing her grief, they greet her with reverence. She tells them that this morning her address needs some heart-rending music, befitting the death of a great man. She sits down in front of the big, insectile microphone, where she has sat so many times before. The engineers respectfully prepare Swan, adjusting the microphone, fitting her headphones. A calmness comes over her as she begins to speak. I listen in amazement. Her speech exceeds all my expectations.

"Today," she says, "I am speaking from my heart . . ."

It's as if Peregrine's hand is on Swan's shoulder, telling her what she must say.

8 ✳ PIPER

Flying over the lush south, the rain clouds peter out. I'm over a verdant landscape of rolling hills, farmsteads, and sleepy little towns. I trace the fields and the hedgerows, following the rivers and streams as they run like veins upon the living earth.

"Brightland is beautiful," I muse aloud.

Wheeler, his head still balanced on his gory neck, makes no reply.

I'm thinking of Tombean Finch, my gunner, my friend. I did him wrong. I rejected him, ran from him in fear. Finch was offering me love, an interdicted love that goes against the *Anthems of Purity*, a love that does not conform to Great Brother Peregrine's *Definition of a Human Male*. I lost him his job as my gunner. It's a small wrong compared to what I did to Rye, but it's a wrong that I must try to right.

I drink from my canister and realize that no food has passed my lips in more than a day. I open the pocket where our emergency supplies are kept. I cram a few dry biscuits into my mouth and wash them down with water. The shaking in my body has finally eased off and by the time I see the distant turbine towers of Brightlinghelm, I'm pretty sure that if I'm spoken to, I will be able to reply.

I'm flying on my fuel reserves when I come in to land. I remember the euphoria I felt when Finch and I brought our plane down on the River Isis. Today, I'm more sedate. I climb out of the cockpit and stand on the wing as the ground crew run to meet me. I scan their faces, looking for Finch. He's there, keeping his eyes turned from mine, doing his job with professional indifference.

"Fuel check," he shouts, and he climbs the other wing to look at my controls.

"Fuck," he exclaims when he sees Wheeler's corpse. "What happened?" He's looking right at me.

"I need . . ." My voice is hoarse. "I need to talk to Wing Commander Axby."

Finch runs to get Axby. I evade the barrage of questions from the rest of the ground crew and leave them struggling to get Wheeler's rigid body out of the cockpit. I've spent enough time with that fucking corpse. Grateful for the fresh breeze, I walk down the airstrip toward the main hangar. Axby has his office there.

There's something comforting about the thought of Axby. He's nothing like Redshank in appearance—he's an educated, cultured man from one of Brightlinghelm's rich families—but he has the same kind of gruff care for us that Redshank did.

I must give him Syker's document and get my thoughts in order. How much can I tell him? Dare I unpack my confusion? Is Axby someone who might help me find the truth?

Ahead of me, I see Finch interrupting Axby, who is listening to a radiobine address. His expression is serious. Finch begins to speak but Axby raises his hand, causing Finch to fall silent. Axby turns a dial, flicks a switch, and the radiobine transmission is suddenly heard at full volume throughout the hangar. The space fills with the velvet voice of Sister Swan.

". . . This must come as a great shock to you all," she says gravely. "Peregrine was in good health. He was a man in the very prime of his life and it pains me to tell you that his death has not been natural. He was discovered in the early hours, poisoned. . . ."

Silence falls in the hangar. All work stops. We are all listening in disbelief.

"We do not yet know the perpetrator of this crime," continues Sister Swan, "but Lord Kite will not rest until justice is done. My task is simply to bring you the news, to tell you the facts as far as we know them, that we may stand together and share in our grief. . . ."

Lord Kite? . . . What is this? Kite is our leader?

I struggle to take in what Swan's saying and I'm not the only one. The shock among us all feels palpable. Our Great Brother is dead. And now Kite is in his place. How can he suddenly be leader of Brightland? Every certainty is gone.

Sister Swan is telling us that Peregrine will lie in state. "He would want you to see him, to pay your respects. His funeral pyre will be lit tomorrow at sundown on the Isis." Swan pauses. What she says next is electrifying. ". . . Last night, I sat with our Great Brother along with the rest of his council. I heard him speak about the vision he had for our future. He wanted his legacy to be peace. Before he died, he invited a diplomatic ship from Ayland to Brightlinghelm for talks."

Finch inhales, as if this can't be true. "Peace?"

"She's right," I say, loud enough for my comrades to hear. "I was in Northaven, where the Aylish ship landed."

My brothers in arms turn their eyes on me. Perhaps I shouldn't have spoken. But they need to know what Peregrine wanted.

Swan's voice has a fire of urgency in it now. "More importantly, Peregrine spoke about songlight. He said there had been a time when we needed to cull the unhumans. In his youth, the People of Song had become a corrupt elite and Peregrine, in his anger, wanted them eliminated from our race. Last night, he told me this was a fatal error of his judgment. He said the persecution of songlight was weakening our nation. He said it had to stop. His next edict would be to demolish the Chrysalid House."

This comes like a bolt from the blue. Finch is staring at the radiobine as if Swan is inside it, speaking just to him. I look at Axby and see that he is flushed with strong feeling—but I can't tell what that feeling is.

Sister Swan rushes through her next sentence. "I'm sure Peregrine's able successor, Lord Kite, will honor this last wish. You are all witness to it now."

Suddenly, there's nothing but static. Swan has been cut off. I see a troubled look cross Axby's face. The static lasts for a few seconds and then a man's voice is heard:

"There will now be a three-minute silence to honor the passing of Great Brother Peregrine."

All around the hangar, men straighten their backs, lowering their eyes. The silence is slow and heavy. I wonder if the shock on Finch's face is mirrored on my own. I feel a kind of fever as understanding dawns on me.

The Chrysalid House is going to close. The cruelty of this pierces me. Another week and Rye would have been spared.

Sister Swan hasn't told us enough. Who killed Peregrine? Who made Kite our leader?

I remember the last time I saw Brother Kite. It was here, in this hangar, only a day ago. I would have walked on hot coals if Kite had asked me to. I was mesmerized by him. I saw only honor and valor in his face and truly I thought that loving him would save me.

Then the memory that's nagging at me comes into focus.

I overheard something that Kite said. The recollection of it makes me step forward involuntarily.

I heard Kite say, *Leave Peregrine to me.*

9 ✳ LARK

Halfway down the storm drain, I trip and drop my lamp. It smashes and sputters out, leaving me in total darkness. I try to control my horrible panic, terrified of slipping down some hole or falling into the torrent that is racing along beside me. The noise of rushing rainwater is deafening. I hoist my precious bag of supplies over my shoulder and put my hands on the slimy wall, displacing slugs as I grope my way along. I feel like a child caught in a nightmare, imagining attack at any second from some eyeless monster. The darkness is appalling. I want to scream—but instead, I cry out, "Stay alive, save Ma, stay alive, save Ma." I hope the roaring of the water drowns out my frightened voice.

At last, I see a spot of light. It grows bigger as I hurry toward it and the rushing river takes on shades of gray. Daylight is ahead. Another storm drain joins the water with a great force and the walkway I am on narrows until it's no wider than a brick. I have to edge along, keeping out of the torrent. There's a big broken grill at the end of the drain and I pause, breathing in fresh outdoor air, watching the torrent cascade out, roaring over the rocks and down into the river.

There's a hole in the grill big enough to climb through and a narrow ledge on the other side, with a drop of about five feet. I can see a way to land that will avoid the rocks. Dare I make my leap? Or will I find myself surrounded by townspeople on a traitor hunt? I look downstream—all clear—nothing but boggy fields and willow trees. I look upstream—and I step back into the drain, clinging to the grill, praying to Gala that no one has perceived me.

The great horse ferry is being pulled across the River Borgas from the north. On it are six horsemen, collars high and hats down low against the rain. I pick out Gyles Syker, Elder Haines, and Rye's pa, Mozen Tern. The horses twitch impatiently as the ferry travels over the swirling water.

Waiting for them on the town's quayside is a small group of men. I see the weighty figure of Kizzy's husband in his fine riding coat, and in front of them all, dripping wet, at the end of her Inquisitor's leash, stands the Siren.

I think of Kizzy and my throat tightens. Has she managed to explain to her daughter who I am? And what will her daughter do—go straight to her father? I imagine the wrangle between them, Kizzy pleading, her daughter crying, Kizzy denying, her husband accusing, Kizzy confessing, and her marriage ending on the gallows. It will be my fault.

My head spins. John Jenkins, Mrs. Sweeney—people perish when they help me. The apprehension makes me dizzy and I have to shut it out.

The horsemen reach the other side of the river. They greet the group on the quayside and I can almost hear Gyles Syker cursing the weather. The Siren stands, bent on her task, listening for songlight. The Inquisitor tugs her leash and they all move out of sight.

I jump, miss my footing, and slither down the wet rocks. I scramble back up as quickly as I can and waste no time climbing over the top of the drain and down the other side. My progress is slow; the mud is thick under the trees at the edge of the field and my feet keep disappearing, ankle deep. I am appalled to see the trail of footprints that I'm leaving behind me. I make my way down to the riverside. The tide has turned while I've been in the town and it is ebbing out again. There's a narrow shingle bank that I make my way along, over tree roots and under great fallen boughs. I am sweating with exertion when at last, I see the broken-down boat shed. My bag is weighted with water now. The straps are digging into my shoulder blades and I hope the medicines and dressings that I'm carrying aren't ruined. I fear the bread will be a soggy mess.

Kingfisher must have been keeping watch because he comes out to meet me, taking the bag. I see relief all over his face.

"You were gone too long," he begins. "I feared the worst, I couldn't sense you—"

62

I cut him off. "Did you use your songlight?"

"Not in any direct way."

"They have a Siren in the town, searching for us. Horsemen from Northaven have arrived."

Kingfisher's face falls. "We must go, as soon as we can."

"How's my mother?"

"Resting. Come out of the rain."

Kingfisher virtually lifts me into the boathouse and I don't stop him. For a moment, fatigue has gotten the best of me. Heron is at the window, keeping watch, close to Curl. She wakes as she sees me. I take Kizzy's warm coat off and, shaking it dry, I give it to Ma.

"This is for you, from Kizzy Dunne. She helped us."

"Kizzy's solid gold," says my ma, trying to sit up.

"She guessed who I was as soon as she saw me," I tell her. "She hid me from her husband, a powerful man in the town."

I hear Kingfisher telling Heron about the horsemen. Heron turns, alert to this, and looks at me in concern.

"They have an Inquisitor and a Siren. They were already hunting for us. As I was leaving, I saw horsemen from Northaven come across the river."

"How many?" asks Heron, readying his gun.

"Six, led by Gyles Syker and Elder Haines. They're doing a house-to-house search but it won't take them long to start looking farther."

"We must go," says Curl.

Kingfisher has been going through the bag of supplies. "We can't go anywhere until that bullet is out of your shoulder, Mrs. Crane."

Ma sighs. "If you're going to dig about in my body, you had better call me Curl," she says.

Kingfisher acknowledges this with a smile. He opens one of Kizzy's pots and takes out a pink pill. "This is for your pain, Curl."

"I always think a woman should know how much pain she's in," says Ma, refusing it.

63

"Take it," says Kingfisher. "You don't want to be awake through this."

"I'm not taking anything that'll knock me out," says Curl. "I won't be a dead weight when those horsemen come along."

"Take the pill, Ma," I urge her. "It'll hurt like Hel."

"I birthed two big babies with no pain pills. This can't be any worse." Ma is adamant.

I look at Kingfisher, knowing Ma means business. He prepares himself to work, with the rain hammering on the roof.

"Those riders must have set out at first light," muses Heron. "They'll be just as tired as we are and wet to the bone. They'll have to pause at some point to eat and feed their horses. We should eat too. Yan—put some food in your belly before you start on that wound."

"After," says Kingfisher, and he looks across to me. "Clean your hands," he says, and I realize that he wants me to assist. I don't like blood at the best of times, especially not Ma's blood—but I brace myself, washing my hands in the river, cleaning my wound with the stinging antiseptic and wrapping it tightly in a sterile bandage. Kingfisher comes to join me.

"I wish I could use my songlight, but if there is a Siren close by I must tell you this in words," he says quietly, out of Ma's earshot. "The bullet is lodged over one of her arteries. When I remove it, we may find that the artery is ruptured and her blood will spout, like Wheeler's did when his throat was cut."

My stomach turns upside down.

"If it happens, I will say 'clamp' and you must pass me these without delay." He has Kizzy's tweezers in his hand. "I will put them in place and then you must take hold of them and hold that artery closed as best you can, while I stitch."

I see how hopeless it is. Sewing scissors, tweezers, a silly silver thimble in the hands of a young Ship's Torch and a girl who doesn't like the sight of blood.

"If I can't get it stitched, your mother will slowly bleed to death."

Kingfisher isn't sparing me. I nod, and I expect that I am turning pale.

"I have to prepare you, Lark, I'm sorry. When I say 'swab,' you must use those dressings to soak away the blood. You understand?"

His eyes are boring into mine. I nod.

"Have you any questions?" he asks gently.

My mind is a blank. "I'll do everything you say."

We go back to Ma and kneel at her side. Curl looks up at me.

"Get me something to bite down on, so's I don't make a noise," she whispers.

"I wish you'd take that pill," I say.

"Just get it done, my love," says Ma.

Heron's eye is on the rain at the window.

"Give Ma your belt," I say. I see the apprehension on his face as he hands it over. Ma takes it, looking at him. There's some kind of moment going on between them.

"I'll walk up the hill," says Heron. "I'll get the view of the town from there."

I know why he's going. He can't fucking bear it and I don't blame him.

"Heron," I warn him. "The road is busy. Keep your face out of sight."

The door closes behind him.

Kingfisher is on his knees, bent over the wound, with a sterilized needle, ready to begin. "We should be grateful for this fine silk thread," he says to Curl. "If all goes well, your body will heal and eventually absorb it."

"Kizzy Dunne was a terrible seamstress," says Ma fondly. "Her embroidery was a dog's breakfast. I'm amazed she's got silk thread. I bet someone gave it to her as a bribe. . . ."

"That store of hers is some place," I say, trying to keep Ma's mind occupied.

"Tell me, who did she marry?"

I don't want to tell Ma that Kizzy has married a man she is scared of—not now.

"I didn't catch his name. But they have a lovely daughter."

Ma smiles at me. "So do I," she says. She puts the leather in her mouth, readying herself.

"Keep your breathing slow and steady," Kingfisher tells her. And without further pause, he delves down into her wound with the tweezers and Ma's face contorts with pain, biting down on the belt. She breathes through it, in, out, in, out. My eyes flash to Kingfisher.

"Almost there," he says, peering at the bullet.

"It'll soon be over," I say, trying to reassure Ma. "Kingfisher knows what he's doing. He's been to Torch School in Ayland and they've taught him how to heal. Can you imagine?" I chat on, saying everything that comes into my head, but another long, drawn-out groan comes out of Ma and she grinds the leather with her teeth.

"You're doing great," I say uselessly. "You're doing really well."

Kingfisher has the bullet on the end of the tweezers. He pulls—then everything happens at once. He drops the bullet into my hand as a spurt of blood fills the wound.

"Swab!" he cries. He delves down again as I put one of the dressings over the blood. In seconds, it is soaked. I use another. Ma is desperately trying not to yell.

"Clamp!" cries Kingfisher. He has got the tweezers on the artery and he is showing me where to hold them. I pray to Gala as a low, guttural moan escapes Ma.

"We got the bullet, Ma," I cry.

"Swab!"

I soak away the blood as Kingfisher picks up the needle. He starts to stitch. And I can see that this is where we'll fail. He's slow and clumsy and his hand is shaking with nerves. He's been taught this out of books. I bet the first time he did it out of a classroom was when he sewed up the orca bite on my leg. Even at the time, I thought it was a jagged mess.

I learned enough from being a choirmaiden to know what good stitching looks like.

"Hold the clamp," I tell him. "Give me the needle."

"I've got it," says Kingfisher, resisting.

I raise my voice. "Do it now," I order. "I can sew."

He sees the sense in this. He takes the tiny clamp and I move around him. Quickly, he hands me the thread.

Gala, it is strange seeing the inside of a body, especially your own ma's.

"I don't want lazy mending, Elsa Crane," whispers Curl. Her face is a bad color like she's going to faint.

"This'll win Hoopoe Guinea's prize," I tell her. I peer down through what must be muscle and I see the edge of a white bone. The artery is small and purplish and I focus on the puncture wound where it has rent.

I imagine I'm at marriage training, creating yet another tablecloth and matching napkin set. I pull the thread through the tissue—oh, the weirdest feeling. I can't think about what I'm doing, I must just make one stitch after another, so neat that even Chaffinch Greening would give me praise. I can't look at Ma's face. I can't let myself be distracted by the agony she's in. She sweats and breathes, low moans escaping her, and at last, the wound is closed. Kingfisher looks at me. Slowly, he releases the clamp. The blood begins to pump through the artery again. And the stitches hold. I look at Ma. Her eyes are fiercely closed.

"You'd be proud," I whisper to her. "It's the best work I've ever done."

Ma nods and grimaces. Her ordeal is not yet over. Kingfisher shows me where to stitch next and I draw the muscle closed. Finally, I stitch the skin. Ma's skin is usually darker than mine but now it has a greenish hue. On and on, one stitch after another, until my eyes are aching with the strain.

"Ma," I say, sitting back, cutting the thread. "It's over."

Curl opens her eyes. Her breath is heaving as Kingfisher cleans and dresses the wound. She's almost bitten through Heron's belt.

I give Ma the bullet and she looks at it.

"How are you?" Kingfisher asks her, somewhat bashfully.

Ma looks at us both, taking in our anxious faces.

"I should have taken that damned pill," she says.

We go down to the ebbing water and wash the blood off our hands, off our clothes. Kingfisher stills and I realize he is gazing at me. I gaze back.

"There's blood," I tell him, "on your face."

"Yours too."

We wash again, the freezing water invigorating us. My hands are really shaking now and my cursed cut is throbbing with pain. We dry ourselves as best we can.

"Thank you," I say, heartfelt.

"You should thank yourself," he replies. "Not many people could've done what you just did. It was very brave."

His lips.

"I've seen your dreadful stitching on my leg," I say, breaking his gaze. "I didn't want that for my ma."

He smiles. "Oh, you're cruel."

"True, though."

"I don't think I've been more terrified in my life," he admits. "I learned anatomy and I'm good with surface wounds but I'm no surgeon. You are."

"Any choirmaiden could have done that."

"Bullshit," says my Aylish friend. He's smiling, but that strange awkwardness is still between us. I've always sensed a reserve in Kingfisher, underneath his open charm. It's like he's holding something back, like his heart belongs to him alone and is never to be shared.

Except—when I kissed him in the jailhouse. It was like he let something go. I felt something in his core, that wanted me as much as I want him. Not just because we were about to die. This boy is an enigma, that's for sure. I want to pry him open with a kiss.

He stands to leave. Any second he'll be gone.

I'm grabbing his hand. I feel his arms coming around me and my breath suspends.

"She'll be all right," he says.

I exhale, realizing that this is a comforting hug, a brotherly hug. Not the kind of hug I want. My hands run down his back. I want to let go of everything except his lean body. I want to pull him toward me, press myself against him. I want to kiss him full and hard.

"Kingfisher." I say his name—and I realize in dismay that I haven't used my voice.

He releases me immediately and the moment breaks. I have let a wisp of songlight escape.

In my dark periphery, I sense a shaven-headed girl, who stays alive by finding moments just like this.

"Stay with your mother," says Kingfisher quietly. "I'll find Heron. We must leave."

The silence stretches between us. He holds himself apart. Then he turns away and is gone.

10 ✴ SWAN

With every word I say, I feel my stature grow. My dolly is right, Kite must be resisted. I tell the nation Peregrine's last words, hoping they might make a difference to my fate. But as soon as they're out of my mouth, Starling Beech runs into the radiobine recording room, beside himself with anxiety. He grabs the microphone and pulls out the plug.

"You can't say that," he screeches. "You can't just make things up!"

"I haven't made it up," I retort. "I'm telling the nation our Great Brother's dying wishes. He wanted the Chrysalid House to close."

"But—but—Lord Kite hasn't authorized it," says Starling in a panic. "I'm supposed to watch over you. He'll sack me for this. He'll throw me from the palace; I'll never see you again!"

I stare at him, quite astonished by this outburst. Starling, hot with embarrassment, plugs the microphone back in. "There will now be a three-minute silence," he says, "to honor the passing of Great Brother Peregrine."

I stand in silence with Kaira. My radiobine engineers join us, moved, I can tell, by what I have said. But Starling is pale with fear and his reaction is shaking my composure. As the three minutes come to an end, the door opens and two grim-faced Emissaries enter.

"Lord Kite wants you in the war room, immediately."

This is it. The punishment begins.

Kaira walks by my side, her eyes straight ahead, her white gauze covering her face. Her voice is low.

"You were brilliant. You have honored Peregrine."

"And angered Kite," I whisper.

"Let him see your strength," she says with fire in her eyes.

The game Kite plays with me is more contorted than Kaira could ever understand. When I defy him, he either punishes me or, after an eternity of dread, he rewards me for standing up to him. If he rewards me one day, he'll punish me the next. A treat or a punch—which will it be? Whatever I do, it's a losing game. Kite's skill is to make me believe that I might win.

Everyone we pass is talking about my radiobine address and people fall silent as I approach: guards, flunkies, civil servants, military personnel. Some make smalls nods of respect but others look at me, aghast at the news I have delivered. I hear whispers of outrage about the closure of the Chrysalid House. My breath starts to rise in panic as we climb toward the military wing. Kite will make me suffer.

"Everything in your speech was true," whispers Kaira. "It was magnificently brave and I love you for it." This is said with such passionate integrity that it takes my breath away. Kaira truly cares for me—and it's so precious and poignant it's reducing me to tears. I come to a halt, turning to her. We have reached our destination.

"Take this little dolly to my rooms," I say to Starling. "I don't need her here."

Kaira questions this furiously with her eyes. She wants to be with me. But the scene is likely to be ugly and I want to spare her. I can't bear her witnessing the things I have to do with Kite. I don't want her to see my physical servitude to him. When he grabbed me in Thal's chapel, I saw how much she suffered.

Kite once said that love is a burrowing insect, a parasite that lays its eggs in the sufferer's chest. *No sane man should entertain it.* I understand his meaning now. My feelings for this girl are causing me pain.

We part. Starling walks away with her and I notice her small frame, her spectacles, her ill-fitting dress. My heart melts some more. Then I follow the Emissaries into the war room.

I'm on the mezzanine floor. Down below me, a sea of servicemen wearing headphones sit at rows of intricate machines. I have no idea what they are for. I pass the vast map with all its flags and markers. It's pockmarked with pinholes, like craters on the landscape, telling a history of war: advance, retreat, advance, retreat. The south of Ayland is pitted with them. The sea is full of holes where our ships have been lost. Our dotted coastline tells the story of their raids.

Lord Kite is in front of me, standing at the balcony, addressing his military. His status has grown with his new role and he holds himself like a toy Thal, even with his back to me. I realize that he's halfway through a speech.

"The Aylish ship will arrive here tomorrow," he declares. "We'll welcome their diplomats and show them hospitality. We will talk peace, as Peregrine desired. It's right that our citizens should see this and I asked Lady Swan to tell them so in her address."

He's already taking ownership of everything I said. How sly of him. He's called me Lady Swan too. What's his gameplay? I walk forward, as if nothing in the world is wrong between us.

"Ah, here she is." Kite gleams with a smile, welcoming me to the balcony. "The peerless Flower of Brightland."

I smile graciously, hating that title, as the servicemen applaud me. I stand tall, giving them my full radiance, looking, I hope, like a statue of victory.

"We'll begin peace talks," continues Kite, "but as Peregrine's most trusted heir, let me tell you this." He pauses, as if he's looking every serviceman right in the eye. "Our Great Brother's real aim remained unchanged, right up until the moment of his death. Perhaps he was murdered because of it. The faction led by Raoul Harrier was determined to have peace at any cost. Such a peace would be a shameless betrayal of everyone who has died. Peregrine knew this. I believe that the traitor Harrier discovered Peregrine's real aim—and killed him for it. His intention was to lure the Aylish here and use the talks to prepare for an attack. Those who genuinely loved our Great Brother knew that his true aim was and always has been victory!"

"Victory! Victory!" A host of voices chant from the depths of the war room, as if inspired by the sight of us. "Death to the Aylish, death to the Aylish!"

I raise my arm in a victory salute and Kite basks in his power, with my beauty and my glamour adding to his standing. Underneath his relaxed stance I sense his ice-hot rage at me.

A punch. It will be a punch.

We go into a side room. More maps. A boardroom table.

"My lord," I begin.

Kite ignores me while he greets a wing commander and one of his airmen. This boyish airman is invited to speak and Kite listens, without interruption. The young airman describes what he saw. He is a witness to the violence in Northaven and he tells us how an argument erupted over the imprisonment of the Aylish Torch. Events turned violent and Heron Mikane killed Emissary Wheeler. Shaking with emotion, he takes a document from his inside pocket and hands it to Lord Kite.

"These are the names of all those who sided with Mikane," he says. "Northaven's eldermen are seeking your guidance on what should be done with them."

Kite peruses it. "Curlew Crane," he says with interest. "Is that your mother?"

"Yes, my lord."

"She was with the mutineers?"

"Yes, my lord."

"Where is she now?"

"She was shot. I fear she may be dead." The boy swallows and I can tell that Kite is impressed by his sincerity.

"Songlight is hard to resist," he says. "I'm sure your mother's mind was twisted. Sadly, it cost her her life. But you are stronger. You were not swayed."

"No, Lord Kite, I was not."

"Tell me, if your mother survived and tried to reach you, would you let me know?"

"Yes. I want her to be saved."

"I'd like to trust you, Airman Crane, but there are liars in your family. Your sister is a traitor."

"I no longer have a sister," he says. "That unhuman no longer has a name."

His sincerity is impressive. Kite walks toward him.

"Our Great Brother's funeral is arranged for tomorrow. I want a fly-past of my planes. You will lead it, Airman Crane."

The airman's eyes grow wider. "You honor me too much. Great Brother Peregrine was—"

"Dismissed."

The airman holds his ground. There's something else he wants to say. "I have upon my arm an ink drawing of Thal. He has your face, my lord."

Kite regards him in surprise. This is a declaration of loyalty, bordering on love. Kite commends the wing commander on his young airman and he sends them both away.

"My lord," I begin again, but an Emissary offers him a telegram. Kite takes it, ignoring me. He reads it and screws it up in his hand.

"Tell them to proceed. I want the Aylish Torch alive."

I have only twice seen an Aylish Torch. One was the warrior who slit my father's throat. The other was the youth I dueled with, here in these very war rooms. He beat me that day. He made me look weak in front of Kite and the thought of it brings up a host of powerful emotions. I try to quash them. The wrestling match between us was so intense that I swore one day I'd put my foot upon his Aylish neck and force him to surrender. He stole my dignity and I stole his true name. Kingfisher.

Kite is sprawling in a chair, his legs spread, giving his final orders to his men.

My punishment is coming. I perch nonchalantly on the corner of the table.

Brazen it out. Take the punch.

When his men leave, I say: "It's been a good day for you, my lord. And I have helped."

Kite considers me. "How was that radiobine address helpful?"

"Without the people, you're vulnerable," I tell him. "I have the population on my side and it is my gift to make them love you. You should realize that."

"The rabble?" he sneers.

"The people loved Peregrine, they love Raoul Harrier—but they don't love you," I point out. "That could cost you dearly." I'm aware I'm using Kaira's words.

Kite eyes me, listening, preparing to strike. I try to keep the dread out of my voice.

"The people are sick of war and privation," I say. "There's rebellion in the air, we've seen it in Northaven. You need your population to believe in you or they won't support you. You may have power in the palace but without the people, you're susceptible to every threat. I have the population in my hand. Without me, Lord Kite, you're by yourself."

I dare myself to meet his eyes. I see him weighing me up, his Siren, his antagonist.

He comes close. I wait for the punch.

He raises his hand—I flinch—and with one finger, he caresses my face.

"Minister for Public Enlightenment," he says.

It's the title I wanted.

A treat.

11 ✳   LARK

I watch Kingfisher run up the hill to fetch Heron, then I pack our things. As Ma sleeps, I pick up all the blood-soaked dressings and drop them into the river. I feel torn up by my carelessness. I let that Siren see me, and my moment of weakness has betrayed us all. I let desire get the better of me. And desire for what? An Aylishman who doesn't want me? This is my punishment for forgetting Rye. My stupid, fickle heart has given us away.

I have to get Ma ready to leave and I wake her as gently as I can. She smiles up at me.

"I was dreaming about Kizzy," she murmurs. "We were girls again. . . ."

I remember Kizzy's story. "She said you once leaped in the river after her, when the current carried her away. She said you couldn't swim. That was brave, Ma."

"We were a pair of fools." Curl smiles. "I went in after her without a thought. Then there were two of us, swirling downriver, paddling like dogs."

"How did you survive? Kizzy said you'd tell me."

The memory fills Ma, bringing back some of the glow to her skin.

"A seaworker was coming upriver to market, from Northaven. He pulled Kizzy up into his boat, then he threw out his nets and he caught me like a flounder. His name was Gwyn Crane."

"Pa," I realize in delight. "You met Pa." I cherish this story. But I can see it's tiring Ma to talk.

"I need to get the coat on you," I tell her.

"I'm ready," says Ma. But she is not ready and we both know it. I'm as gentle as I can possibly be, but putting the coat on causes her great pain.

"Do you think you can get to your feet?" I ask.

"In a minute," she says—but to my dismay, she immediately drifts off into a deep slumber.

She's not fit to travel, not at all. And where will we go? How will we get there? They'll be watching the river by now and if we flee by road, they'll pick us up before the hour is out. Ma can hardly walk, never mind run.

I peer out of the dirty window and see Heron and Kingfisher running down the hill. This dull day is almost over. The gray light will soon be thickening into night and the darkness will help us. There is that, at least. I turn back to Ma, waking her, urging her to stand, and Heron and Kingfisher burst in.

"The horsemen are riding out through the town gates," says Heron.

Kingfisher starts putting sticks and kindling into the stove. He chucks in a match and blows a fire alight. Heron goes straight to the window. He smashes a cracked pane of glass and pokes the gun out through it.

"What are you doing?" I ask them.

"Making it look like we're still here," says Heron in his commander's voice. "Gather our supplies." And I jump to it.

Heron balances the gun on the back of a chair, tying it in place.

"Are you leaving that here?" I ask.

"It might buy us some time."

"What if we need it?"

"My plan is we won't get seen."

It's not much of a plan—but Heron doesn't need me to say so. Kingfisher blows the fire aflame as I help Ma to her feet.

"You must use your songlight just before you leave," says Heron. "Make that Siren believe you're still here."

"Are we going in the boat?" I ask, desperate.

"We can't," says Kingfisher. "But we'll make it look as if that's what we're doing."

"Where will we go?" I ask.

Ma speaks up, pretending a strength that she doesn't have. "My people came overland from the Greensward," she says. "I've been retracing the route in my mind."

"Then lead us," says Heron, and he scoops her up in his arms, carrying her to the door.

"Mind her stitches!" I cry.

"I'm not made of glass," says Ma, reassuring me. Heron strides out with her and I see her hand reaching up to cling on to his neck.

Kingfisher picks up the sail, no longer needed as a groundsheet.

"Help me with this," he asks, and together we take it outside. As Heron climbs up the hill carrying Ma, Kingfisher and I arrange the sail in the boat, covering the seats, as if it could be hiding people. The awkwardness between us pulls like a violka note.

Then Kingfisher strides right up to me and kisses me.

My senses are flooded with it. My lips melt into his.

Then I pull myself away. "What are you doing?"

"What I should have done before."

"Don't mess with me, Kingfisher," I tell him, my anger rising.

He looks sheepish then, boyish, like his perfect self-control has let him down. There's no time to ask him what he's playing at. We push the boat into the river, putting our weight into the task. We heave the boat into the water and it slowly floats out.

"Let's get out of here," I say, and I turn away from him. I sense his songlight then, reaching for his ship. He's drawing the Siren.

I do the same, sending my songlight to Nightingale. She's walking through the palace with an aide. She looks so weary—but she brightens at my presence.

"They're coming for us with a Siren," I say. "It's my fault. I gave us away."

I show Nightingale a fast blur of images: Kizzy, her daughter, the storm drain, the way Kingfisher and I took the bullet out of Ma. I show her how I reached for him—and how I let my songlight go.

"Oh, Lark," says Nightingale, "sometimes love escapes us and we can't hold it back. You mustn't blame yourself."

"But I don't love him," I cry. "I love Rye. He's just messing with me. All I can do is avoid him—which is pretty hard when there are only four of us."

I sense the Siren's creeping songlight, trying to break into our harmony. It makes me shudder. Nightingale says she will stay close. "I'll help you, however I can."

We part. Quickly, Kingfisher and I follow Heron, jumping from rock to rock, so as not to leave footprints, watching in fear for the horsemen.

"Did you reach Alize and your ship?" I ask him.

"No" is all he says.

Ahead, we see Heron disappearing under one of the great willow trees at the top of the hill and we race to follow him under its leafy boughs. As he lays Ma down against the trunk of the tree, we hear hoofbeats. We hide ourselves as best we can and I thank Kizzy Dunne for choosing a green coat, as Ma is near invisible.

"Can you ride a horse?" Heron asks me.

"It can't be that hard," I say.

"Tell me straight."

I shrug. "As if a Northaven girl would ever get to ride a horse. . . ."

Heron looks to Kingfisher. "Elsa's with you."

Kingfisher nods. So much for my plan of avoiding him.

"We're going to steal their horses?" I ask.

Heron puts his finger to his lips. Coming over the brow of the hill are the six horsemen from Northaven plus five more from Borgas Market. I gasp to see that Kizzy's great-horses are leading the others. They are all laden for a trek.

"My fear was they'd bring a pack of hounds," whispers Kingfisher. "They've spared us that, at least."

The great-horses are truly magnificent. I look at their long stride, how

79

they walk as the other horses trot. If they were to gallop, no other horse could catch them. These are the horses that we need. But the merchant sits on one of them and on the other is the Inquisitor with his Siren. Her nasty yellow dress stands out in the gloaming.

"We must take those," I whisper to Kingfisher. "The mare is called Yura and the stallion is her son, Uki. Talk to them," I tell him, "like you talked to that orca."

"The Siren would sense me in a moment," he whispers.

Gyles Syker raises a hand, bringing the horsemen to a halt. They survey the view of the boathouse. The fire has made a tiny glow in the window and smoke is rising. Syker sees the gun, poking through the broken window, and the horsemen fall back, wanting to keep out of its range. They begin to dismount. I see that the great-horses have rope ladders that uncurl from the saddles, letting down the riders. The saddles are like raised seats, strapped tightly on the horses' massive backs. The Siren stands on the wet grass, her eyes fixed on the boathouse.

"The burst of songlight came from down there," she says.

Something stirs in me. A memory of Nightingale's anguish as she cried my name in Northaven. *Lark* . . . My head filled with a painful flare of light. It was overpowering. I wonder if her strong songlight could help us now?

The horsemen make their way down the field, readying their rifles. Gyles Syker positions himself behind a tumbledown stone wall. Our tree is only a hundred yards higher up the hill.

"We know you're in there, Mikane," yells Syker, his attention on the gun pointing out of the window. "Turn yourself in and we'll spare your life."

The men ready themselves, rifles raised. The Inquisitor tugs the Siren closer. He pushes her down, keeping her shaven head out of the firing line. He quietly instructs her and I sense the Siren's discordant songlight. I refuse to let it in—but it grates on my very being. She tells us we're caught, we're surrounded, resisting is pointless. This girl is wretched, truly, and I

80

can see that Kingfisher is pained by her too. She wants to rest. She wants food and sleep. She wants this to be over. She tells us there's no hope. It's better to give up.

Personally, I'd rather die.

The men have surrounded the boathouse now, leaving their horses grazing. One man remains behind, watching over them, his gun in his hand. It's that old bastard Mozen Tern. How such a man could have produced a son like Rye, I will never know. Mozen's gaze is fully concentrated on the boathouse, a scarf wrapped high around his neck against the cold. Heron looks at us. He doesn't need songlight to tell us what he's going to do. He leaves the cover of the willow tree, heading round behind us in a large circle, using gorse and hedgerow to hide himself. He will disempower Mozen—and I don't care how. Night is falling in earnest now and the only light is the tiny fire-glow, coming from the boathouse window.

"Lark," says Ma, using my new-discovered songlight name. I turn to her, propped up against the tree. "If it comes to it and we can only get one horse, you must go with Kingfisher. Get him to Brightlinghelm, back to his people."

"It won't come to it, Ma."

But it disturbs me, what she's said. I tell her to be ready to get to her feet and I return to Kingfisher. His eyes are fixed on the great-horses. They are not so far from us, the rope ladders hanging down their sides. "Let's take them," I whisper. "They're our best chance."

I'm expecting him to disagree with me, to have some better plan, but he says, "You take the mare, I'll take the stallion."

"Just as soon as Heron deals with Mozen Tern," I say.

Syker keeps up his yelling from behind the wall. "Your last warning. Give yourselves up or we'll fire!"

As soon as those men realize the boathouse is empty, they'll be back on their horses. It's now or never. I risk everything.

81

"Help us, Nightingale," I cry in songlight. "Take on that Siren!"

Immediately the Siren turns toward our tree.

"Wait," cries the Inquisitor. "Hold fire—she senses something!"

The Siren gets to her feet, her eyes searching the line of willow trees. Then suddenly, she turns to face south, her face raised. Her whole body is taut. Her breathing heightens. I can sense Nightingale's forceful songlight. Kingfisher grips my hand. He can sense it too.

"What is it?" yells the Inquisitor. "Where are they?"

The Siren suddenly cries out in pain, as Nightingale's songlight fills her senses. The Inquisitor tries to pull her back down behind the wall, out of range of the boathouse gun. She must be a valuable asset for him. She lands on her knees in the boggy grass.

"No, no," she cries out loud—as if replying to Nightingale. "I can't!"

"Where are they?" interrogates her Inquisitor. "Tell me what you see, or I will take my whip to you!"

A cry of woe escapes the Siren, as if she's torn and cannot act. At the same moment we see Heron step into the gloaming behind Mozen Tern. He grabs him, putting his huge hand over Mozen's mouth. Mozen struggles, his arms and legs flailing like a beetle's.

"Now," says Kingfisher.

I turn to Ma. "Be ready," I say.

The men's eyes are all on the Siren. "No," she wails. "You're hurting me!"

Kingfisher and I leave the cover of the willow tree. The Siren's despairing is at a dreadful pitch.

"It is no good," she cries. "He'll kill me!"

"They're mind-twisting her," realizes her Inquisitor, grabbing hold of her dress and using it to pull her to her feet. "Do your job, girl, or you'll pay for it!"

We run like shadows as Syker opens fire on the boathouse. Others join him and the volley of gunfire unsettles the horses.

The Siren's mind is completely dazzled by Nightingale's bright light as I reach the giant mare. The Inquisitor threatens her with his night-stick.

"Yura," I say, trying to make my songlight as calm and gentle as a meadow. "We're Kizzy's friends. My mother needs your help. . . ."

The great-horse seems willing to come and I lead her toward the willow, reassuring her in songlight all the way.

The Inquisitor slaps his Siren around the face, as if it's common practice. It's horrible to witness.

"I see a boat," cries Kizzy's husband. "They're getting away!"

Syker holds fire on the boathouse. He and the rest of the horsemen run helter-skelter toward the river's edge and the Inquisitor drags the Siren after them. I look over and see Kingfisher, his forehead pressed against the stallion's great muzzle.

"This will be a race, Uki," he says in songlight, "with freedom at the end of it."

The great-horses follow us up to the willow and Heron meets us there. None of our pursuers have their eyes on us—thanks to Nightingale. I look around and see Mozen, splayed on the ground.

"I only knocked the old gizzard out," says Heron.

He's already helping Curl as high up the rope ladder as he can. She manages to get herself into the saddle. Gala, that must have hurt.

There's more gunfire down by the river now, startling the rest of the horses. One of them turns, whinnying, and canters back toward the town; the others are skittish, about to follow. Mozen, unconscious in the mud, does nothing about it. Kingfisher is already up on Uki's back and quickly, I scramble up the ladder. I feel horribly unsafe, so high up off the ground.

"Tie yourself on," he says. I see that the saddle has straps on each side. I tie them but I still don't feel secure. We hear shouts coming from the river-side and I sense Nightingale's songlight fading away from the Siren, leaving her in wretchedness to face the wrath of her Inquisitor.

Heron has his arms round Ma, holding her in place. She is leading us to

83

her childhood home, the Greensward. I see her whisper to Heron and he steers Yura toward the east. Uki follows, as a good son should. The movement takes me by surprise and I grasp Kingfisher's back.

"Hold on tight," he tells me.

The great-horses leap into a gallop and we head into the dark, leaving Borgas Market far behind.

PART 2

12 ✳ PETRA

CELESTIS—DAY FIFTY

I am trying to concentrate on my scouting craft proficiency test. I am learning the manual by heart. But I can't stop thinking about that voice.

Lark . . .

I listened long into the night, straining my mind in case it came again.

I've always known my truevoice is keener than most. I played it down when I was a girl, not wanting to be special in any way. But I found learning how to use it easy, when all my friends were struggling. Instead of teaching me how to hone my voice and make it stronger, my instructors had to tell me how to quiet and protect it. I hardly ever use my full voice. The last time I did was in Sealand City, when the Division Enforcers came for Fenan—and Mother immediately sedated me. *You're hurting my mind!* she cried.

I can't imagine what Charlus would make of my full truevoice. Maybe he'd think that I'm a freak, like the kids at college did. Perhaps one of the things I liked so much about Fenan was that he came from a world apart—the sapien world—and he couldn't hear me. Whispering on a low note has become second nature to me now. Yet sometimes, I wish I could throw off my constraints and see what my truevoice is really made of.

I went to the labs, looking for Mother. I wanted to tell her about the strange voice and see what she made of it. What if there are some kind of natural eximians down on the ground? We've passed over many sapien habitations now and sometimes I've sensed questions curling into the air, far-off wisps of truevoice, as people crane their necks to see *Celestis* pass.

On the way to Mother's lab, I saw Charlus. He was some distance ahead of me and I was about to call his name but I realized he was talking to the gatekeeper, one of Bradus's Division Enforcers. The man let him through and Charlus went up to the sapien floor! As far as I was aware, none of us are allowed up there without Xalvas's permission. Maybe Charlus has special privileges as his son.

When I found Mother, I asked her if this is the case. She said I should really mind my own business. She didn't lift her eye from her microscope and her tone was curt, as if she was busy. So I didn't tell her about that mysterious voice.

On the way back to my cabin, I decided to wait for Charlus to come down again, but after a whole hour, there was no sign of him. Then I thought, what if I was to go up?

I tried!! But the Division Enforcer on the door said he couldn't let me through. "Come now, miss," he said. "You'll get me in trouble." He was being playful but underneath I could see his iron authority.

DAY FIFTY-ONE

We're coming out of the dead zone now. Although the land is still hostile, radiation levels are no longer an immediate threat to human life. Roaming herds of ruminants have appeared and in the evening we see a gigantic murmuration of starlings, bigger than this ship. We are heartened. There may be viable lands ahead.

I am putting all my energy into my training, so that I get chosen for the next landing party. Commodore Bradus is impressed with how quickly I have learned. I work twice as hard as Charlus and I have my mouth-word language skills as an advantage. Bradus knows they might be useful on the ground. The sapien engineers are becoming less unfriendly. One of them taught me how the water-pumping mechanism worked. He had a kind face so I asked him his name and he said Caleb Ableson, which has a nice sound to it.

LATER

Caleb Ableson left some tools lying on a gangplank and Charlus tripped and fell. He lost his temper, shouting with clumsy mouth-words at Caleb

Ableson, and he was really stunningly rude. I saw the look on Caleb Ableson's face, such bitterness it almost scared me. Later, when we were practicing evacuation procedures, Charlus said, "In my humble opinion, the writing's on the wall for sapiens." I asked him what he meant. He said eventually they'd be wiped out, like the bipedal hominids of old.

"I can't see any difference between us," I said, looking him full in the face.

Charlus was impatient at that. "The difference is there in our genome, in our ability to communicate. There isn't one sapien I've ever met who can communicate as we do."

It's strange that Charlus should pick up on this. Because I don't like his truevoice.

LATER

As we were leaving the scouting craft hangar, Charlus said something that I couldn't hear in mouth-words to Caleb Ableson. Caleb Ableson caught hold of Charlus, turned him round, and gave him a massive punch—BAM. I heard the cartilage squelch in Charlus's nose and blood was plastered across his face. He was knocked out cold. Commodore Bradus sounded an alarm and Caleb Ableson was contained.

The whole airship speaks of nothing else. The offense is grave. But what did Charlus say? Why did Caleb hit him? Xalvas will pass sentence tonight, at communion. The eximians have all turned on Caleb Ableson. Father says it's a danger to have a violent sapien like that on the ship. I try to tell him of Caleb's kindness to me but Father says it's about time I learned my lesson with sapiens. They cannot be trusted. That's why we live separately.

I am full of dread at what Xalvas will decide. It's a foundational crime for a sapien to harm an eximian. But after the punch, Caleb Ableson looked at Charlus like he was glad, like Charlus deserved it.

DAY FIFTY-TWO

Horrendous. Horrendous. I am so upset I will never come out of this room again. Garena says I must come to dinner but I won't go. She has left without me.

They executed Caleb Ableson by sky burial.

We all had to watch it from the viewing chamber.

The sapien crew were brought downstairs and they stood in ranks. Many of them I have never seen. One of them was a heavily pregnant girl and she was crying. My eyes were drawn to her because we never see pregnancy. Xalvas spoke in mouth-words so the sapiens would understand. He said Caleb Ableson had shown violence to an eximian and he would be sentenced, according to the law. It was an act of mutiny, and mercy was not possible. He ran a tight ship. Hierarchy and discipline had to be maintained.

He gave the signal to Commodore Bradus. A trapdoor opened in the underbelly of the airship and Caleb Ableson fell through it with his arms tied behind his back. His body twisted as it hurtled down through the cloudscape. We watched until he was a dot far below.

I hope that he was dead before he hit the ground.

The pregnant girl had to be led away. She was distraught.

Can't write more.

We have committed murder.

13 ✳   RYE

The open ocean is nothing like the sea around the coast and Wren Apaluk doesn't like it. She makes her feelings clear by spewing over the side. She sits looking green, hunched and shrunken in her coat. The roll and fall of the swell is huge out here and we go up and down, up and down, surrounded by an unstable world of ever-changing gray and blue. I've realized that the best thing to do is to try to meet the waves face on. When they hit us from the side, the boat feels likely to capsize.

We messed up badly yesterday. We lost the water canister. I hadn't tied it down and as we careered down a wave, it rolled into the sea. I leaned over the side, desperately trying to pull it back, but it sank like a rock. Wren Apaluk cursed me loudly for that. She learned good swearing in that Pink House, I will say that for the girl. We tied everything to the boat then, including our good selves.

I've got one eye on the sail now and I'm pulling at ropes, using my weight to get the wind flowing in the right place. There have been times when all we can do is lower the sail, grip the sides, and pray, then hours where the water seems to flatten out, the sail fills, and we shoot forward like a comet. We're intruders in a world of wind and wave and I wish for the thousandth time that Elsa Crane were here because somehow, that girl can speak the language of the sea.

I try not to think about how vulnerable we are. This boat feels no stronger than an acorn cup. I mustn't dwell upon the slow fall to the murky seabed or on what might lurk down there, waiting to suck clean our bones. But on the positive side, each hour carries us farther from Brightland. As night falls, I set the sail so we're heading toward the sunset, west toward Ayland, please, Gala.

As the moon climbs, the temperature plummets. Wren sits as far from me as possible and I never lose sight of the knife in her hand. I find myself looking up at the night sky. The Silver River arches over us, its waters made of millions of stars, and the moon sends a line of diamonds reflecting on the water. If only it were a path to follow, leading us to safety. I think of Elsa, always Elsa. I bet she knows how to navigate with stars. I wish I could send my songlight up to ask her where to point this boat.

I don't know how long passes when I hear Wren's voice coming out of the dark.

"He didn't even bother to take off his boots," she says. Somehow, I know she's talking about the man who she escaped from. I look at her, so she knows she isn't talking to the wind. After a while, she speaks again.

"I said, 'Can you get your boots off my sheets, please?' He said, 'Shut up, bitch.'" There's another pause, as if the memory is vicious and hard to relate. "Anyway, he strangled me."

The bruises on her neck are proof enough of that.

"He kept a knife in one of his boots. I felt the end of it as I was struggling. I didn't even think." She makes a stabbing motion with the knife.

She falls silent. I see that her hands are shaking.

"The fucker should have taken his boots off," I say.

Wren sighs a long sigh, running her hands through her hair. "Some girls can do it; they can be Third Wives. They're good at it. They're nice to the men, the men like them and they keep coming back. I could never pretend. The girls would say you've got to imagine you're far away but I could never do that. I was always stuck there. A man gets insulted when you freeze up. But that's the way I'm made. I don't want their hands on me and I can't lie about it."

I don't know what to say to any of this. She has no reason to trust me and I expect she's only talking because she thinks she's going to die.

"I've never been in a Pink House," I tell her.

She looks surprised. "Why not?"

"First one I was in was yesterday, when I robbed your kitchen."

"What's wrong with you?"

"They found out I was a Torch before I left my hometown."

"So you've never . . . ?"

I'm immediately with Elsa on Bailey's Strand, feeling a kind of ecstasy I didn't know humans could feel.

"There was a girl, back at home, a girl I cared about," I tell her, leaving all the rest unsaid. Wren puts down her knife and ties her hair back out of the wind. Her pink band looks gray and her bruises are lurid in the moonlight.

"What did she do when they caught you as unhuman?"

I close my eyes, remembering Elsa's face as she saw them force the lead band on me. I was screaming at her in songlight: *save yourself*. I kept up the cry until they silenced me. At the shaming post, I begged her with my eyes not to give herself away. She picked up a handful of soil and threw it in my face. *Unhuman*, she said. It still stings me now.

"She saved herself," I say.

I think Wren can tell I don't want to talk about it.

"Where's home, then?" she asks. "You've got the same dumb accent as this new girl in our house."

"I'm from Northaven."

"That's it," she says. "Northaven. This girl arrived a day or so ago; right pain in the arse. Name of Una or Uta or something, do you know her?"

"Uta Malting?" I ask in surprise. She was one of Northaven's princesses, the baker's daughter.

"The housemother told me to show her the ropes. This girl Uta was full of shock, like all the new Thirds. Kept saying she shouldn't be there. She went on and on. She said she would've got Second Wife—but some girl stole her man. 'We're all rejects here,' I told her. 'You have to make the best of it.' But she moaned and wept about how she could have been a commander's wife, only some girl Elsa made a play for him."

I am incredulous. "What did you say?"

"Apparently this Elsa climbed a tree and flashed her fuzzy at Heron

Mikane." Wren is amused and I see her white teeth flashing as she smiles. "Fair fucks to her, I say."

"That isn't true," I say. "That can't be true." I realize that my voice is raised.

"Listen, I don't give a shit," says Wren, seeing my dismay. "I'm just telling you what this girl Uta said. She was from Northaven too. I'm just filling up the silence here."

I turn away. The moon path dances across my eyes and I close them. I'm going to be sick.

"What's the matter, unhuman?"

Elsa is married to Heron Mikane. Gala.

I let the boat take me up and down, up and down.

"You know her, don't you?" asks Wren gently. "The girl who climbed the tree."

I nod.

"She your girl?"

I don't reply.

"I expect this Uta was exaggerating. She was peeved and bitching, that's for sure."

Silence falls between us again. Silence for a long time. I knew Elsa would have to marry. I knew this. And I should be glad. It means she's still alive, uncaught—they haven't tied her to the shaming post. But Heron Mikane . . . I am struck dumb.

I try to put myself in Elsa's boots. As a survival strategy, I can see the sense in it. There's a mural of him on every fucking street. Plus, Elsa thinks I'm dead. She thinks that I'm a chrysalid. What's she supposed to do? I want her to be safe. I want her to be happy. But Wren might as well have stuck that knife right through my heart. Mikane, with his flowing black locks and his battle-chiseled face. . . . How long will it take Elsa to fall in love with him?

Wren leans a little closer.

"I'm sorry, soldier," she says. "I only told that story to stop me thinking about that man with his boots."

"Best to know," I say with a shrug. And then, when I can speak without a croaking voice, I say, "It means she's still alive."

Rise and fall, up and down, plowing through the swell. The moon goes in behind a cloud. The night is getting colder.

"Rye," she says, using my name for the first time. "Do something for me." To my amazement, she hands me her blade, putting her neck within my reach. "Don't fucking slip," she says.

By the light of the moon, I kneel beside her, cutting the thick pink leather band, stitch by stitch. At last it comes off in my hand.

"There," I say. Wren takes it. She stands and hurls it far into the sea.

"I wish I could do the same for you," she says.

I nod my thanks and tap the lead band. "This is a bit harder to remove."

Wren curls up like a fox in the bottom of the boat. I can see her eyes, glistening in the dark.

I don't know how I pass that night. The hours crawl and my chest feels as heavy as the sea. All I know is that at some point exhaustion carries me away because I wake and it is morning.

I sit, thirsting for some water, looking for the coast.

There is nothing but the vast, moving surface of the blue and gray. I look toward the sunrise. And slowly I begin to fill with dread. The east should be behind us but it's at our side. We're heading south, not west.

How long have we been going off course?

How far are we from land, in this floating acorn cup?

Then I remember Elsa. Elsa is married to Heron Mikane. She's his wife and she'll forget me.

I know that I should shift myself and turn this sail. But at this moment, I can't bring myself to care.

14 ✳ LARK

The trouble with great-horses is the unmistakable hoofprints that they leave. We may be moving fast but we'll be easy to follow. Uki takes us under trees and we have to crouch low to keep the black branches from knocking us off. He follows Yura up colossal rocks and makes his way across gullies that we cannot see in the dark. We try to wade through water whenever we can to hide our progress—but we're trackable, even without that Siren beaming her gaze on us. We lurch forward as Uki makes another leap and I am gripping fiercely to the saddle.

I think of the pain that Ma must be in and hope my stitching holds. For a whole hour, we go at full pelt. When the horses tire we slow our pace, hoping we've put some distance between us and our pursuers. We daren't use a light and I thank Gala for the horses' good eyes and for my ma's instinct for direction.

I reckon the Greensward must be calling her.

I sense Nightingale on the edge of my consciousness. She wants to talk but I daren't join with her, knowing how close that Siren is. Nightingale is insistent, though, as if, with the very last of her energy, she needs to unburden herself.

"I hurt her, Lark," she confesses. "My beam was too bright and I hurt her. I think she's in a deep faint. She won't be using her songlight for a while." Nightingale is sitting on a white cot in her white gown, alone in Swan's white rooms. She's hovering above a deep exhaustion, using the last of her stamina.

"Let Kingfisher join us," she says. "I want you both to hear this."

I invite Kingfisher and his songlight opens into ours. The first thing he does is to thank Nightingale.

"That Siren is wretched," she tells us. "Her Inquisitor is cruel."

"Yes," says Kingfisher, immediately agreeing. "Her songlight was piteous. It was terrible to hear."

"We have to help her."

This is the last thing I'm expecting Nightingale to say. And it's the worst idea she's ever had.

"I pity that Siren too," I say. "But she's pulled you into her suffering. She *wants* you to pity her. She's trying to entrap you because that's what Sirens do."

"Lark, there must be a way that you could get her free."

My heart sinks at Nightingale's compassion. "Of all people," I tell her, "you should know how Sirens work. You're an Inquisitor's daughter. You know that girl will betray us to her master."

"Her name's Bel Plover," Nightingale insists, "and she's no different from you and me."

My songlight is firm with disagreement. "She *is* different. Would you ever choose that role, to stay alive by betraying others? How many Torches like you and me are in the Chrysalid House because of her?"

Nightingale is silent at this.

"You see the good in everyone," I tell her, "but that Siren will send us all to Hel."

"Bel Plover isn't evil, she's abused."

This gets under my skin. "So what do we do, turn around and fight that Inquisitor and all those men?"

Nightingale doesn't give up. "I told her things were going to change," she argues. "I told her you carried hope for every Torch in Brightland. I told her peace was coming. I said the Chrysalid House would close—I told her you were good people. It made her cry, Lark. I said you and Kingfisher would help her to escape."

"You told her *what?*"

"She wants to die. She hates herself." Nightingale is passionately upset. "We have to give her hope. If we can't help Bel Plover, what are we even striving for?"

"I thought we were striving for peace," I say.

Kingfisher is listening intently, aware perhaps that this is not his country, nor his culture.

"But there are things that peace won't fix." Nightingale speaks from the heart. "I know you see it, Lark. You've rebelled against it all. Peace won't fix the way we are treated. It won't fix forced marriage or Sirens or Third Wives. Surely we're striving for more than peace?"

I take this in.

"We'll do what we can for Bel Plover," says Kingfisher quietly. And I realize he means it.

I'm kind of furious—but I don't contradict him. I don't want Nightingale to be overwrought. She's grateful to us both and I want her to be comforted.

Kingfisher leaves the harmony but Nightingale and I linger in each other's company. I sense that there's something else weighing on her mind that she hasn't expressed. She doesn't want to share her troubles but I press her, wanting her to talk.

"I'm afraid of what's happening to Swan," she says. "I'm afraid of what Kite might do to her. But more than that . . ."

I wait for her to share her thought and finally, she voices it.

"I'm afraid of myself."

"Why?" I ask, sensing her disquiet.

"How did my songlight make Bel Plover collapse?" she asks, desperate for an answer. "I hurt people, Lark. I hurt you and Kingfisher, I hurt Swan. Why am I like this?"

"You were saving all our lives," I tell her. "Nightingale, there's nothing wrong with you. You're strong, that's all."

"I'm dangerous." Her worries come tumbling out. "What if I go too far? What if I hurt someone and they don't recover? What if I hurt myself?"

It's as if she's on the great-horse with us, her arms around me as we hurry on. I try to think how we can help her.

"When you're free, we must get to Ayland," I say. "Kingfisher says they have schools there, where Torches learn to use their powers. Commander Alize will take us—I know she will. We just have to get to the Aylish ship. I'll get you out of the palace and we'll hide with them on the *Aileron Blue*."

We both know that this is wishful thinking, but it comforts Nightingale. "I bet there are others like you," I assure her. "I bet you're not the only one."

At last I feel her beginning to calm. She takes in my surroundings.

"I can't believe I've troubled you with this, when—"

I cut her off. "You're not alone. You're never alone."

I feel the emotion in her songlight. "Nor you neither," she says.

Before she leaves me, Nightingale regards Kingfisher.

"He must know you're still in love with Rye," she says. "Perhaps he's only trying to protect his heart."

She rises away, leaving me to consider this.

Kingfisher's eyes are on the path ahead and he is silent, concentrating as Uki follows his mother through a long valley filled with scree. That reserve sits between us once again, despite our physical proximity. I am literally holding him, my arms clinging round his Aylish uniform.

Is Nightingale right?

He smells of the fire in Northaven, the salt of the sea, the sweat of our escape. I think of everything we've been through together in the brief time we have known each other. I feel a strong desire to lay my head on his back, to see if I can fathom his beating heart.

"Lark," he says. "I sense her."

I hear it—a plaintive wail of songlight, so forlorn and lonely that it makes me want to weep. The Siren is on the prowl again. We hear another distant cry, so full of suffering that every instinct I have wants to reach out in comfort.

"Don't fall for it," I say. "I bet she's reeled a hundred poor souls onto the end of that Inquisitor's whip, using that selfsame cry."

I try to block it out. But Kingfisher keeps listening and it pains him to the core.

"It's a classic system of divide and rule," he says.

"A what?"

"The Brethren fear the power of Torches, so they have set you against each other. They have divided you, so you can't unite against them."

"She's a machine, Kingfisher, that's all I'm saying. She's trained to hunt and she'll use any means."

"You've dehumanized her," he says. "That's exactly what the Brethren want. That's how their system works."

"Are you trying to explain my own society to me on a horse's back in the middle of the night?"

Silence falls again as Uki climbs up the side of the valley. The land gets so steep that in spite of the straps holding us in place, I feel as if I'm sliding. I hold on to Kingfisher with all my might and we sense another high, woeful wail of songlight.

"I'd love to help her," I tell him, "truly I would. But we'd risk your mission and most likely end up dead."

Kingfisher acknowledges this—but I can't help feeling his disappointment.

The land straightens out again and I think we must be on some kind of high plateau because Uki's pace picks up and we are galloping. I wish we could see this strange terrain. Apart from my shipwreck and my brief trip to Ayland, I have never been outside Northaven. When the moon comes out from behind a cloud, I see the outline of mountains against the sky. It's a magnificent vista. We ride alongside Heron and Ma blows me a kiss, wrapped in her warm green coat. I see that she's conscious and comfortable and I am reassured.

There is such tiredness in my bones that finally, I let my head rest against Kingfisher. It feels so very, very nice that I drift into a kind of half sleep. When Uki suddenly lurches down a steep ravine, I jerk awake. I slide forward and I think we'll both go over on our heads. I hold on to Yan Zeru as fiercely as I can.

I can hear a river down the valley, and at last, after a horrible descent, Uki follows his mother to the water. Heron pulls Yura alongside us.

"Daylight's coming soon. We need to rest," he says. "Your mother knows a place."

"We're looking for a rock, like a wolf's head," says Ma, her tired eyes fixed on the view ahead. "It's up this river somewhere."

The great-horses walk in the wide shallows over fine shingle and I am thankful that the water will cover our tracks. Uki drinks deep as we watch the gray dawn begin to saturate the sky. The horsemen will soon see the muddy lines of hoofprints we have left behind and I long for the Greensward to hide in. The interior of Brightland is so impenetrable that the Brethren have still not created a road through the middle. In the north, all the towns are along the coast. Trade and human traffic comes and goes by ship and the vast mountain forest is left to its own devices.

"How far are we now from the Greensward, Ma?"

"We have to cross Garbarus Moor," she tells us.

"Shouldn't we plow on," asks Kingfisher, "while we have the advantage?"

"It's open country," says Heron. "No cover. Soon as dawn comes we'll be seen for miles. We'll hide for the day, let Curlew rest, and set off again as soon as it's dark."

The horses walk on, the water splashing round their sturdy legs. The sky is turning pink when I see a group of rocks jutting out of the escarpment. I point them out to Ma. They look like a creature with its jaws wide open.

"That's it," she says. "We can rest at Wolf's Head."

There's a wide shingle beach in front of the escarpment. It seems too open and exposed to offer us much safety. Heron dismounts, using the rope ladder to get off Yura's back. He holds it steady for Ma and she manages to slide her way down.

In the growing light, I notice the great panniers that each of the great-horses carries on their sides. I open them. One is full of oats and hay. The other has the Inquisitor's supplies. There's some food, a pistol, neatly folded linen. I unhook the panniers and hand them down to Kingfisher. Then I climb off Uki's back.

I'm happy to see that Ma is stable on her feet, looking steadier than yesterday. On Heron's arm, she leads us up to the top of the beach. There's a narrow cave entrance in front of us, barely visible under ivy and creepers.

"Here," she says. "The great-horses won't like it but we must persuade them in."

Yura resists. She won't go near it. Kingfisher is about to use a whisper of songlight to coax her but I stop him.

"That girl will be hot on our heels by now. You'll give us away." I hope he notices that I've called her "girl" and not "Siren."

Heron, who has a way with horses, persuades Yura in with a big bag of oats, and Uki reluctantly follows. The narrow entrance opens out into a large cave. Heron lights a match on the wall. It stretches back a long way. Stalactites and strange mineral growths make it seem like the entrance to the underworld. I gasp as bats flit around our heads, angry at being disturbed.

We give the great-horses oats in huge nosebags and they eat in sight of the entrance. I go to help Ma but I see that Heron is already making her comfortable, laying blankets on the rocky ground.

I watch them, remembering the vivid dream I had, lying on the floor of the boat as we escaped. A tumble of limbs in our family bed: Ma, Pa, Piper, and me. That golden time is lost and gone. I felt Pa's presence then and I'm feeling it now. What would he think about Ma and Heron? It makes me want to cry for him. It's not that I begrudge Ma. She's lived in loneliness for far too long. And it's not that I don't love Heron—I just miss my pa.

I turn, heartsore, and help Kingfisher ransack all the panniers. We find food enough for two days, generously packed by Kizzy for her husband. This gives me hope that he didn't discover how she helped me. Her daughter didn't give her away.

The merchant carries a rifle, ammunition, a map, a battery turbine lamp, dry clothes, blankets, a groundsheet, and a bottle of strong-smelling whiskey. The Inquisitor carries whiskey too. And along with his food and clothes, we find a lethal-looking crossbow, sharp, metal arrows, a curled whip, manacles, and three lead bands—all the splendid tools of his trade.

At the bottom of the pannier is a little yellow bag. I open it. Bel Plover's pathetic things fall out. Another vile yellow dress, a carving of a rabbit, and a pair of knitted baby's shoes.

Somehow the tiny shoes turn my heart upside down.

I pick them up. The wool is grubby and frayed, as if the shoes have been held and handled, over and over. Damn it.

The Siren becomes human. The shoes are made of love.

15 ✷   PIPER

He can't keep this act up forever.

I saw him last night, drinking with some of the ground crew, and I went up to his table.

"Finch," I said, "could I have a word?"

"Sure, mate," he said casually. "Sit yourself down, join us."

His words were friendly but not his tone. His tone was saying, "Fuck off, Crane."

"I'd be grateful for a word in private," I said.

"How's your pal Lord Kite?" asked Finch. One of the crewmen snickered at that.

I stood my ground. "I just want to talk."

"No secrets between friends." He grinned. "Sit yourself down. Talk all you like."

There was no room at his table.

As I walked away, I heard him mutter an insult under his breath. I turned to look at him and saw a fierce resentment on his face.

Finch loved being a gunner; he was made to be a gunner. He saved both our lives when I was panicking in the sky. And now he's in the ground crew because of me. Because I told Wing Commander Axby he was unreliable.

I knock on Axby's door before our morning training flights. How do I begin to say I want Finch back? How do I tell Axby that I lied? I will say that I was mistaken, that Finch is the best and most solid lad that I have ever met and the finest gunner too.

Do I tell him the truth? *Finch kissed me, sir. We were about to make love and I panicked. I'm an aberration, sir. And I've turned on Lord Kite.*

Axby calls me in. "Sir," I say as I enter. And I don't know how to go on. There are already three men in the room, three gunners, and one of them is mine, Finch's replacement, the quiet and dependable Lenny Habib.

"A timely arrival, Crane," says Axby. "Kite wants more men trained as pilots and these men have all scored highly in their tests. They're off to Camp Meadeville later today. You're going to lose Habib as your gunner, I'm afraid."

"Congratulations," I say to Habib, pleased that one of my burdens has been so swiftly lifted. "You'll make a fine pilot, Lenny. No one deserves it more." I mean every word and I shake his hand.

Habib thanks me, wishing me luck. "I'll be flying alongside you soon, taking down the Aylish," he says.

I'm not sure what I reply. I hope it's sufficiently warlike and daring. Axby dismisses the gunners and they leave.

"Training flights have been suspended until after Peregrine's funeral," he informs me. "Are you ready to lead the fly-past?"

"Yes, sir."

"You're to take off when the Aylish ship is just about to dock. Kite wants a show of respect to Great Brother Peregrine but also, rather usefully, a show of our new airpower."

"Sir."

"He's taken a shine to you, Airman Crane."

"Sir."

"Play your cards right and you'll soon be flight lieutenant."

I say nothing. My shoulders are so tight I feel a pain crawl up my neck. Where do I begin?

Kite may have done something unthinkable, sir. I want the truth. I intend to get as close to him as I can.

"What else can I help you with, Crane?"

There's a small painting of a boy on the wall above Axby's desk. My eyes keep going to it. The boy is ten or eleven, just too young to be a junior cadet. Axby's son? Himself as a child?

"I'll need a new gunner, sir."

"Yes, I was thinking Keever."

"Finch, sir, Tombean Finch."

"You told me Finch was volatile, unstable in the air."

My eyes hit the floor and I force out the truth.

"No, sir. I was the volatile one in the plane. Finch kept his head. He got us down."

"Then why did you say otherwise?"

"We argued about another matter, a personal matter, and in my anger, I..."

"You had him demoted?" Axby's look is hard with disapproval.

"I came to confess it, sir. I'll take any punishment. It's no less than I deserve."

My throat is wobbling and my eyes are stinging so I fix them on the painting. But the child's face is not comforting. It makes my eyes sting even more. The silence goes on as Axby regards me.

"That's my son, Roland," he says. "He died of wasting fever when he was twelve."

"I'm sorry for your loss, sir," I manage to say. I don't know how to speak to this man's grief. If I blink, tears will fall. It will look worse if I wipe them so I stand in front of Roland Axby and pretend that I'm not crying.

The wing commander is silent. Now my fucking lip is shaking.

"I'm sure that trip to Northaven took its toll on you, Crane. You lost your sister and your mother. If they're caught alive, they will face justice."

"Yes, sir."

"Lord Kite's justice will be harsh."

Ma. I swallow down a desire to sob. Swallow. It. Down.

"Is there any news of them, sir, the fugitives?" I ask. "My mother, is she...?"

Dead. Is she dead?

Axby says, "They were last seen fleeing Borgas Market. No further news as yet."

"Thank you, sir."

106

"As for your punishment, send Finch to me. He will decide it."

"Yes, sir."

"You realize he may not wish to be your gunner?"

I nod. "I was no friend to him. But I must try to put things right."

Axby holds me in his gaze. It seems that something is passing between us and I don't know what it is.

"My son would have been your age," he tells me. "I'm conscious of that every day, as I send you and your comrades up into the air. I'm aware of the risks you take. My son taught me that life is very precious. It must not be wasted."

"No, sir, no."

All my concentration is forced into keeping my composure. I think he's telling me not to waste my life.

"We're all grieving this morning, Crane."

I salute him.

"Dismissed," he says.

And I go.

I find Finch straightaway. He's at the side of the airstrip under a leaking engine, wrench in his hand, overalls covered in grease. I am transfixed.

"Axby wants to see you," I say.

Finch stares up from his position on the ground. "Why, you having me sacked?"

Gala, he's so angry.

"Finch . . ." I try to force out what must be said.

"What?"

It's like you understood me without words. You offered me love without judgment and I fled. I was scared. I was a fool. You're in my mind, all the time.

I don't say any of this. I say, "What I did to you was wrong." My throat tightens. "I'm sorry."

I say it to Finch, knowing it's too late to say it to Rye Tern.

When he doesn't reply, I walk away, alone.

16 ✳ NIGHTINGALE

Sunlight is already streaming in. I don't want to open my eyes to these dazzling white sheets. I don't want to think. The sun is warm and lovely on my face and I want to rest for as long as I can. I collapsed on this cot last night after leaving Lark and I realize I'm still in yesterday's dress. I want to hover here on the edge of a dream, where I can imagine I live a different life. Maybe my mother would still be alive. Maybe I wouldn't have songlight.

I try to imagine what it must be like to have a mind that's at peace, a mind that can't hear anything but its own thoughts. Always on the edge of my consciousness there's the hum of voices. It's become second nature to block them out but when someone is hurting, their distress draws me in like a moth to a flame. That Siren—her wretchedness made me sore in spirit.

I think if Lark had not held me, I would have cried all night.

I imagine I'm on Bailey's Strand, feeling the freedom of the warm sun, listening to the falling of the waves. I stretch my legs and imagine I'm a strong boy who never had wasting fever.

Today I might die.

Today, I have to live.

Then I remember that I have a task. I sit upright, wakefulness surging through me. I reach for my spectacles and put them on and the world comes into focus.

The first thing I see is a woman with white gauze over her face standing by the window, pouring me a basin of water to wash myself in. It's not Cassandra. This woman has long dark hair cascading down her back and Sister Swan calls her Lady Scorpio. I wonder what her real name is. I get out of my cot in my crumpled dress. The floor is cold under my bare feet.

"Is that water for me?" I ask the woman.

She stands aside.

"Thank you," I say.

Another gauzed woman, Lady Orion, enters with a clean dress, ready to help me put it on.

"How kind of you," I say to her. "Thank you very much."

Through her gauze, her eyes acknowledge nothing.

"What a fine sunny morning after all the rain," I say. "It's really the loveliest time of year." I feel as if I'm being stupid and ingratiating but I have to try to talk to them because they're human and my sisters. I wash and dress as quickly as I can, telling them how lovely it is to have hot water brought for me. I tell them about my stepmother, Ishbella. I describe our cramped apartment—and then I stop because I have a sharp and unexpected pang of homesickness.

"I miss my papa," I tell them. "He's in jail for helping me escape." I think of the journey he went on that day when he decided to help me. He stopped being an Inquisitor and truly became my pa. I feel a powerful wave of love as I think of him, incarcerated.

One of the women gestures to a tray laid out with breakfast. She is quite expressionless.

"I'll eat it in a little while," I tell her. "Thank you for your pains."

The door to Swan's bedchamber is open but her bed has not been slept in. Did she spend the night with Kite? Or has her radiobine address already led to her arrest?

I will find out soon enough.

I can't bear to think about Swan: capricious, unstable, magnificent, volatile. Gala, how she scrambles me. I put out a tendril of songlight but I get no sense of her. Either she's asleep, or Kite has locked the lead band round her skull.

I move across the chamber until I get to the door the songless women use. I push it open and see a dormitory with a row of narrow beds, evenly spaced, and hard chairs with high backs. Three women sit motionless, gauze over their faces, eyes wide open. What are they seeing? What are they thinking? They are at rest.

109

She's there, Cassandra.

I approach her. In the quietest whisper, I say, "Cassandra, it's me, Kaira."

Nothing registers on her face. I put my hands on the sides of her chair and kneel down in front of her, peering through the gauze and into her eyes. Cassandra is staring right through me.

"It's me," I repeat. "Kaira. You used to call me Little Bird. . . ." My voice trails into silence as my memories catch me.

I once dreamed I was embracing Cassandra, kissing her lips. I woke up in utter confusion. I'm sure I only dreamed such a thing because Cassandra was the one person in the whole world who really knew me and she was offering me hope of freedom and escape. But these confusing feelings come to the surface now and they start to plague me. What if I kissed her now, like princes do in folktales?

Would she awaken?

The thought is so sad and so ridiculous that I catch a tear running down my cheek and angrily wipe it away. There is no hope of such a thing.

"You are Cassandra Stork," I say. "You worked as a nurse. You helped me. You saved my life. Cassandra, it's me, Kaira Kasey. . . ."

One slow blink. The dull focus of her eyes doesn't change.

It's just as well I know another way to speak.

I remember how I slipped inside Peregrine's mind. It seemed so easy and so natural. I try with Cassandra, asking her forgiveness for the intrusion. Instead of finding myself in a world of her memories and perception, her daydreams and musings, I find what I can only describe as a landscape of impenetrable fog. There is simply nothing there.

I'm not trying hard enough. I know there'll be a way through. Some of her senses are still intact. She can hear, she can see, she can understand instructions. Somewhere, her selfhood must still exist. I don't believe the surgeons can take her soul away. I walk into Cassandra's mind and make myself appear as Cassandra knew me. I want her to see the girl she saved and taught and cared for.

110

Soon I become aware of something in the eerie emptiness—a wall. I look up and see it disappearing into the fog. Somewhere, there must be a chink in the edifice, a way through. I walk and I walk and at last, I see a tiny opening. I crawl inside and all is dark and red, as if I am standing in her living flesh. I see a long staircase spiraling up. It looks as if it's made of sinew. I put my foot on the lowest step and it sinks, as if I'm walking upon tissue.

"Cassandra," I say, "I want to help you, like you once helped me. You kept me alive."

I begin to climb. The staircase turns and turns, getting narrower until I feel I'm squeezing my way through her flesh. I hear Cassandra's breathing, the workings of her heart. I make my own breath blend with hers. My heart begins to beat in time. I repeat her name, over and over.

"Cassandra, you taught me how to use my song."

The walls change from red flesh to painted bricks but the steps continue to feel soft.

"You made me believe in myself. You're the first true friend I had." I tell her that I love her. I say it with my songlight, where it sounds so much better.

At the top of the flesh staircase, I turn the tightest corner. I have to squeeze through a narrow gap, being careful of the cleaning supplies I see all around me.

I don't understand. I seem to be in some kind of cupboard.

I sense that Cassandra was hiding here and that she was afraid. Suddenly I feel as if I *am* Cassandra. I sit hunched behind some shelves. The door opens, and two men dressed in green come in, searching. Dread is pounding in my heart. They see me—they see Cassandra—and they pull me out. I'm struggling against them and they drag me along a corridor, lit with low-grade turbine tubes. One of these lights is broken, flickering. Is this a hospital? I see rooms with wheeled beds inside.

"Cassandra, I'm here with you. It's Kaira."

The cells have bars on the doors. In one, I see a pool of blood upon the floor. In another, a man lies wrapped in bandages.

111

Oh, Gala, I know where I am. I know what I see.

This is Cassandra's memory. The men pull her—pull me—into an operating theater.

Ruppell, bald and grinning—he is there.

I struggle. I'm fighting as the men lift me, screaming in protest as Ruppell pushes me down. I feel a jabbing pain in my arm. A cold liquid seeps into me. I try to fight it but it knocks me out and everything is dark.

In a flash, I'm back in the cupboard, hiding behind the shelves. The men in green come in again. The memory replays. I can't bear to go through it again.

Is this all that's left of her, this agonizing fragment, before they took her mind?

I refuse to believe it. Somewhere, she's here. I close my eyes and I'm back on the soft, visceral staircase again. With my songlight hand, I touch the flesh. Scar tissue. Nothing can flow here. I listen to her heartbeat, thinking that maybe my strong songlight can do some good. I concentrate on controlling it. I beam my love and light on one of the hardened thorns of flesh. Is there a way that I could try to make a flow?

"Cassandra," I say. "Perhaps there is a different—"

Suddenly I feel a cold hand on the back of my neck.

"What are you doing?"

I feel a shuddering jolt as I pull myself away. For a moment I can't find myself. I see my own body, kneeling in front of Cassandra. And I see Sister Swan, standing over me, suspicion on her face. My heart is pounding as I rejoin my own body.

"Why did you come in here?" she asks coldly.

I search for what to say. "To look at the veiled ladies."

"Why?"

"To remind myself what you saved me from."

This irritates her. "You were trying to commune with her—why?"

"To find her."

"And there's nothing there, is there?" cries Swan. "Do you think I haven't tried the same thing? I gave up years ago. They're dummies, they're ruined and there's nothing you can do. Stop wasting your songlight when I need you."

She turns away. Cassandra's expression is the same unbearable blankness as before.

"Wash me!" demands Swan, and the women prepare to do her bidding, running a hot bath. Swan restlessly pulls me into her bedchamber.

"I am your new Minister for Public Enlightenment," she says, smiling. "And I have a title, Lady Swan." She's behaving as if this is something to take pride in.

"That's good," I say. "That's very good."

"Did you listen to my morning address?" she asks.

"No," I confess. "I'm so sorry."

"It was an anthem of praise for Kite," she tells me. "I prepared the population for Peregrine's funeral and the arrival of the Aylish—but Kite was at the head and heart of everything I said."

So Kite has given her some power. I hate to think of what she's had to do for it. No wonder her mood is brittle and weird. I want to ask her if she's all right but her energy is manic.

"Go and eat something, Kaira. It's my first cabinet meeting and I need you." She pushes me into her reception room and prepares for her bath. "Today," she tells her ladies, "we're in mourning. Get me a bouquet of lilies and my plaited wig."

I look at the food and force a sweet pastry into my mouth. It explodes with flavor. Swan's breakfasts are like nothing we ever had at home, but my anxiety about what the day might bring is making it hard for me to swallow the food. Which Swan am I going to get? Sometimes she is her real self—thoughtful, reflective, courageous—and sometimes she's this hard and brittle creature, who'd do anything for power, as if Kite's poison has seeped into her skin. There's something in her mood this morning that makes me feel afraid. This is ruthless Swan. I eat as much as I can, knowing that the food will give me strength.

"Have you been in touch with the fugitives, Kaira?"

I turn, my heart thumping. The ladies have put a long wig on Swan, styled into a simple plait. She's in a plain but elegant dress, perfect for a funeral. She looks very young—but something in her eyes is very old.

"No," I tell her. "I haven't heard a word since Lark was in Northaven."

Swan takes me in. "I think you're lying," she says. "And you know how I feel about people who lie."

"I'm—I'm not the kind of person who courts trouble," I say. "I daresay the fugitives know that using songlight would endanger them. So they haven't contacted me."

Swan studies me in silence. She walks toward me.

"I love you very dearly, Kaira," she says.

"I love you too," I tell her.

Swan takes my face in one of her cold hands and she gazes right into my eyes. "You must always obey me. That's just the way it is."

I nod.

"So tell me about Lark."

She'll get it out of me, I know she will.

"There's nothing to tell."

Swan doesn't let me go.

"If you betray me, it would break my heart," she says. "And if I broke my heart, I might do something bad."

Every muscle in my body has tightened in fear. "I'd never betray you," I assure her. "I think about you from morning to night. I owe you everything. I owe you my life."

"If Lark contacts you, I want to hear about it straightaway."

Swan's cold hand ever so gently squeezes my face. I can hardly get my jaw to move.

"Yes, sister."

"Promise, on your father's life."

"I promise," I whisper.

"There. We are friends."

Swan doesn't know what friendship means. She turns, taking a bunch of drooping calla lilies from Lady Scorpio.

"Come," she instructs us, and we stand in our ghoulish formation of white. "Today, we bid farewell to our Great Brother."

Swan is a hero and a monster. She is capable of love and murder. As we make our way out of her cold, white rooms I reflect on everything she's taught me. I've seen her courage and incredible tenacity. She's taught me how to twist a mind and steal another person's heart. But her best lesson has been on how to lie.

I will never give her Lark.

17 ✳ LARK

A stale gust of air blows over me, a musty reek coming from deep down in the black throat of the cave—and I wake. Perhaps we're disturbing ageless creatures of the underworld.

Let's hope so.

I'm wrapped with Ma in a pile of blankets. Strong afternoon light pours in through the cave entrance. Heron is keeping watch, crouched on a rock, a rifle resting on his knees. Kingfisher is near the horses, sleeping with the Inquisitor's crossbow primed and ready by his side. I wonder how many nights he has spent in his life armed to the hilt and ready for violence?

"So," Ma says to me, in a low voice. "Kingfisher."

I see that she's following my gaze and there's a curious question in her look.

"What about him?" I ask.

She raises her eyebrows. She's a wily cat, my ma. She might be in ten shades of agony but not a thing gets by her.

All my confusion comes to the surface.

"I can see he likes you," she says. "What's holding you back?"

I shake my head.

"Are you thinking of Rye?"

As soon as she mentions his name, the image of Rye at the shaming post fills my consciousness, the desperation in his eyes as I called him unhuman. I close my eyes at the pain of it.

Ma strokes my hair. "Two things have come clear to me on this journey," she says. "The first is that the heart has a tremendous capacity to love. You won't love and honor Rye any less by living. He's gone from us, my darling. Rye's gone and I've watched your heartache over him. You must live for the future, not the past."

"So," I say, when my emotions are back under control. "Heron Mikane."

Ma smiles slowly and her face glows with color. "The second thing I've learned," she says, "is that when life offers you a gift, you should take it. I don't love your pa any less."

Songlight or not, Curlew Crane could always read my mind.

"It's none of my business anyway," I say. "It's old people stuff."

Ma laughs at my cheek and the sound of it gladdens me. She's so much better. I go to get her some food and water but when I return with it, I see that she's drifted into a slumber again. I leave it by her side, not wanting to wake her.

I join Heron. He's looking down into the valley, alert to every sound.

"Don't you ever sleep?" I ask him.

"Not much use for it," he says.

"People go mad when they don't get any sleep."

"I've been crazy for a long time, then."

"I'll take the watch. Go get yourself some rest."

He looks at me as if I'm not qualified for the job.

"I've got two good eyes," I tell him, "which is one more than you."

This amuses Heron and he stands.

"Hadn't you better leave me the rifle?" I ask.

"Do you know how to use it?" he asks.

"I'm guessing that I aim it at some bastard and pull the trigger," I say, being clever.

Heron's smile fades. "Don't make light of it, Elsa. It's not easy, killing a man. You carry it with you. Don't wish it on yourself."

I'm beginning to think that Heron Mikane has to drop the burden of dead people that he carries on his shoulders. He has to start living for the future too.

"Teach me to shoot," I say. "I need to be useful."

But Heron takes his rifle and goes into the cave. He looks back at me.

"You are useful," he says.

His approval warms me. I take his knife out of my boot and sharpen

117

it, making the blade gleam as I look up and down the valley. There's a big jagged rock that splits the shingle beach in two and for a while, I watch an osprey who's sitting on it tearing apart the trout she has caught. I play with the knife, liking the way it cuts through the air. The blade folds away in the bone handle and snaps back out at the touch of a button. It's a neat weapon.

The sky is clear today, no more than a few scudding clouds, after all the rain. The river is heavy with water and we're lucky that the great-horses are such a size. They made the crossing effortless, holding themselves against the flow, keeping our supplies dry. I hope the horsemen are having all sorts of trouble. Their small beasts will have to swim through every watercourse they come to.

The osprey finishes her meal and takes off, sweeping up with an easy grace. I sit for a long time, watching the light change in the breeze-blown trees until the sun is nearing the hill line. It will soon sink down below.

I drink from Kizzy's husband's water flask. It's almost empty and I wonder about going down to the river to refill it. That would be useful, one task less for everyone to do. I find the Inquisitor's flask and pick up our own. I look upriver and down beyond the jagged rock, as far as I can see. This is a perfect wilderness, not a human soul in sight. Two minutes, I'll be two minutes. I think of waking Kingfisher and setting him to watch but I'll only be gone a matter of moments and we'll be glad of that fresh water as we cross the moors tonight.

I make my way down the shingle, careful not to dislodge any stones. I fill the flasks and take a moment to splash some water on my face. It's freezing and I gasp, almost laughing at how cold it is. I am—

I see a black hat.

Fuck.

Fuck.

They're down the valley. They're crossing the river. The first man is over. They are coming.

No time to get back up to the cave. I grab the flasks and dive over the rocks.

"Kingfisher," I hiss, hiding behind a fallen tree. But I know he will not hear me. I can't use my songlight because of that Siren and if I scramble back up that shingle I'll alert those fuckers straightaway. Two of them over now, holding a rope for the rest. I feel for Heron's knife.

Fuck.

I curse myself for being such a fool, for thinking for one second I was safe. I'm supposed to be watching—and I have left them all vulnerable. The group of men slowly get across the water. The Inquisitor is last, Bel Plover behind him, her shaven head raised. I'm aware of her songlight, searching. She's looking for her baby boots. She wants them back. The cave entrance is small and high and covered in hanging creepers. I'm comforted by the fact that you'd hardly see it if you didn't know it was there.

But what if one of them does know?

The sun is low in the sky as they begin to approach. I'm about to make a dash into the wilderness when Syker, who is riding at the front, gets off his horse on the other side of the big jagged rock.

"What about this place?" I hear him yell.

The men join him and dismount. This gets worse and worse. They're going to make a fucking camp. They want to dry out and eat. In one way this is good. It means that they have lost our trail. I see Mozen Tern and Elder Haines picking up bits of driftwood. Soon a fire is blazing and their horses are drinking at the river's edge. Most of the men are hidden from me by the jagged rock but I see the Inquisitor throw Bel a biscuit, then a carrot, then a piece of cheese. He makes her run to catch them and the men find this amusing. When Bel has her paltry share of food, she sits down to eat.

I see a figure coming to the cave entrance. Ma.

Get back, I want to cry. I suppress my songlight, which wants to wrap itself around her, urging her back into the dark where she is safe. Ma is standing almost straight, far more steady than last night. She's looking for me—she sees the horsemen—her eyes meet mine—and she vanishes.

I pray to Gala to bring down the darkness fast, to make me invisible. I can work my way back up to the cave when nightfall comes and maybe the horsemen will never spot the fissure in the edifice, maybe they will ride on by.

I see Gyles Syker having a piss. In an act of pure meanness, he aims his piss at Bel.

She cries out with disgust, glaring at him, wiping his urine off her dress. I hear Syker's laugh ringing out and some of the other men laugh along with him. But the Inquisitor hasn't taken kindly to his Siren being pissed on. As far as I can tell from their body language, he's having a proper rant at Syker. I suppose he's got to ride with Bel and she won't smell too good. The Siren pleads with him. She wants to wash. The Inquisitor impatiently pulls her up the river.

They're close. They come round the jagged rock and they're near the spot where I filled the water. I can hear their voices now.

"Let me off my leash so I can wash myself," pleads Bel as they trudge over the shingle.

"And watch you swim away? Do I look like an idiot? Get that stinking dress clean. I'm sick of the smell of you." He vents his temper as Bel walks to the water's edge. "When I get you back to Borgas Market I will flay you raw. You let them get away."

"I told you, I was blinded."

"You let them mind-twist you."

"There was a force, an overwhelming force."

"Coming from the Brethren's Palace?" sneers the Inquisitor. "Do you expect me to believe that?"

"I'm not lying. It was the strongest songlight I have ever felt."

"You're full of lies and bullshit, girl. I want those fugitives tonight."

"They know we're following. They won't use their songlight. I'm doing my best."

120

"You're a useless, stinking little wretch. I don't know why I keep you alive." The Inquisitor holds out some soap. "Wash," he orders her.

Bel walks into the river, waist-deep, fully clothed. She doesn't even take her boots off. She washes her dress with the soap. She washes under her arms and between her legs. She turns her back to the Inquisitor, making no fuss about the cold. She washes her cropped hair and floats as she rinses it off. She makes it look as if the water is lovely and inviting. How is she not freezing to death? She walks out, dripping, and dumps the soap in the Inquisitor's hand.

"You don't smell so good yourself," she says.

The Inquisitor pulls Bel toward him, using the leash.

"You're the worst Siren I ever had," he tells her. "You're spoiling my career. Get me those unhumans tonight or I will finish you. Do you understand?"

The Inquisitor pushes her and she trips, sprawling on the rocks. The Inquisitor takes his boots off. He takes his socks off and neatly folds them up. He puts his toes into the river.

"Thal's teeth," he says, "it's cold." He bends down and starts to wash his feet.

This is what Bel Plover does.

She reaches down and picks up a stone, a stone so big she needs both her hands. It's heavy and one edge is sharp. She lifts it. She's going to bring it down on him. Bel Plover's had enough.

I watch in dull fascination. At the last second, the Inquisitor senses Bel. As she brings the rock down with all her force, he turns. It hits him on the nape, instead of on the skull. I am watching open-mouthed, unable to move, as if I'm frozen in a block of ice. The other men are huddled round the fire on the other side of the jagged rock, eating their food, their banter covering the thud.

Bel's missed; she's missed her chance.

She tries to get away, scrambling on her knees, but the Inquisitor pulls her back toward him.

"I'm going to snap your fucking neck," he says.

I see him put his arms around her, forcing all the air out of her lungs. He lifts her like a wet rag and puts his arm around her neck. Bel chokes. She sounds like a dying animal, her legs kicking hard against him.

Suddenly the enchantment that I've been in breaks and I'm running toward them. The Inquisitor's back is to me and without pausing for a second, I plunge Heron's knife into him. But his coat is thick and the blade hits something. His belt, the thick belt he wears around his waist. Why didn't I aim higher? The Inquisitor releases Bel and turns toward me, jolted with surprise and pain.

In the fading light, his grimace makes him look like a skull. He comes for me straightaway, careless of the knife in my hand.

"Unhuman bitch!"

I try to hold him off, swishing the blade—but he grabs my knife hand by the wrist. I thump him. I hit the bastard, hard as I can. I'm in real danger now. He's prying the knife out of my hand and within seconds he will finish me.

My songlight leaps out. "Bel, help!" I cry.

Bel grabs the metal leash in both her hands and pulls it hard round the Inquisitor's neck. He jerks backward. This man is strong and he's fighting for his life but he's in between us and we're both determined to be free. Bel pulls with all her might. He hurls me backward, away from him, using his hands to get the leash off his windpipe. I stand, grasping my knife as hard as I can. His belly is revealed. I run at him—but something flies past me with a near-silent swoosh and hits the Inquisitor in the heart. It has missed me by an inch. An arrow, one of his own metal arrows.

I look up. Kingfisher is at the entrance to the cave, holding the crossbow.

The Inquisitor jerks and thrashes, trying to get the thing out of his heart. Bel puts her hands over his mouth, preventing him from crying out—and that's how he dies. In agony.

Bel is staring at me.

"Let's go," I say in songlight.

But the leash is padlocked round her waist. I squat down by the Inquisitor, trying to unfasten his thick leather belt, but I can't get it loose and I am wasting precious seconds. Those men will notice us, now, now. Bel comes to my side and together, we pull the belt off. I give it to Bel and she is free.

"Quick," I say in songlight.

Kingfisher is pointing to the far end of the escarpment and I lead Bel upstream. I'm hoping we can climb around and drop down on the cave mouth from above. Bel is still dripping wet and she's left a trail of water that any fool could follow.

As the cave mouth nears, I see Elder Haines getting up and going around the big jagged rock. I expect the nasty old grunter wants a shit. He sees the Inquisitor and stops in his tracks.

"Hey!" he yells. "Hey!"

We're nearing the cave mouth, coming at it from above. But the last few feet are bald of trees and we'll be dangerously exposed. I see Kingfisher below us, standing with Heron. Their weapons are raised.

"Up here," I cry in songlight. "Help us!"

Haines runs across the shingle, calling out the Inquisitor's name. The other men are alerted and begin to follow him round the jagged rock.

I lower Bel into Kingfisher's arms but as soon as she sees him up close, she begins to struggle.

"Aylish." I feel fear and loathing pour out of her in songlight. "Aylish!"

"That's Kingfisher," I say to Bel in forceful songlight. "He's one of us."

"You're free," Kingfisher says, taking her into the cave. "We'll help you. Come."

I jump down and Heron catches me, pulling me quickly out of sight. He turns me to face him, his eye glaring with an anger I have never seen.

"I set you to keep watch," he upbraids me, keeping his voice low in the echoey cave. "Not to get in a fight and kill an Inquisitor."

"It needed doing!" I tell him, with a bravado I don't feel.

"We saw it," says Ma in a low voice. "We saw."

I look over at Kingfisher and see a strange expression on his face. "You could have died," he accuses.

"I would've killed him," I say. "You didn't have to interfere."

"You're welcome," says Kingfisher.

Down below, I hear the men yelling. Bel's wet prints will soon lead them here.

"Get on the horses," says Heron. I'm glad to see that the great-horses are packed and ready to go.

"And go where?" I ask. "We've got the advantage up here. We can pick those men off with the guns and the crossbow."

"That's not what we're doing," says Heron firmly.

"We're taking another way," says Ma.

Bel has found the Inquisitor's keys. She's using them to unlock the girdle that has bound her to him. She pulls it off and throws it to the ground, a hated thing.

"I hope you can ride, child," says Ma in a gentle tone.

Bel nods, still looking suspiciously at Kingfisher. "Aylish," she says again.

"Ride with me or stay behind," says Kingfisher, climbing up onto Uki's back. He reaches down a hand for Bel. She quickly climbs the rope ladder, ignoring Kingfisher's hand, as if she doesn't like to touch him. All this has happened so fast. I remember my own confusion as Kingfisher pulled me off my wrecked boat and up onto the Aylish ship. It took me so much time to accept him, to take a wider view of things.

I see something on the cave floor left behind so carelessly—a little patch of dirty white.

"Here," I say. I reach up and drop the tiny boots into Bel's hand. She puts them to her heart and bends her head. I feel a great confusion of emotions coming from her. I don't think Bel can find any words, not even in songlight.

"Elsa," says Ma. "We should have a Torch on each horse, in case we get separated in the dark. You ride with me."

I love the way Ma has called me a Torch, like it's a normal, ordinary thing. I am climbing up on Yura's wide back when a gunshot hits the mouth of the cave. Heron runs with the rifle and fires twice. I hear a man screaming outside, shouts of anger from the others. As Heron leaps up on Yura, hordes of bats, disturbed by the noise, suddenly descend from the cave roof. They flit around us, inches away from our hair, our faces, making a high-pitched communal screech that pierces our songlight and gets under our skin. They swarm out of the entrance and into the night—thousands of them. I hope they'll slow our pursuers.

It takes all our songlight to calm the horses. We go to the back of the cave, far from the entrance. Ma lights our stolen turbine lamp. A narrow passageway can be seen, leading downward and away. An old mining tunnel of some kind.

"This is it," she says. "My people used to walk this way."

Is that where she is taking us, down into the underworld? I feel Yura's reluctance, and behind us, Uki stalls, panicking. Kingfisher and I pour our songlight into calming them once more.

"The meadows lie this way. Have no fear. You'll soon graze on fields of freedom."

Bel's songlight is incoherent, overwhelmed with shock and confusion. I worry that she'll undo our efforts and unnerve the horses.

"He's dead," she cries, "he's dead." Her songlight reminds me of John Jenkins. Truthfully, I am shaken too and if I had the time, I'd huddle in a wreck and cry. Heron is right. It isn't easy to kill a man.

"He can't hurt you anymore," I say. I tell her that Kingfisher won't let her fall. We are all on the same side and nothing divides us but a spiderweb of systems. I tell her she can look to the future, that things will get better—but it's like we're going through the very gates of Hel and my voice soon falls silent as we plunge into the dark.

18 ✳ SWAN

Our first appointment in the hours before the funeral is a ministerial meeting. Lord Kite makes a point of introducing me as his Minister for Public Enlightenment. He said the radiobine is to be my sphere.

The other Ministers don't like this. Ruppell's usual grin slips right off his face.

"With respect to Lady Swan, is she qualified for such a role? Her improvisation around Peregrine's last words has caused total consternation in the Chrysalid House," he accuses. "Our loyal staff have done years of sterling service and now they're worried for their jobs. One of my interrogators came to me this morning and the man was virtually in tears."

I find the thought of one of Ruppell's torturers being upset about his job darkly ridiculous.

"I reported Great Brother Peregrine's last words most faithfully," I tell him.

Greylag, who smells of boiled carrots and surgical wipes, suggests that I should submit all my speeches to him for approval before I am allowed on air.

"You fail to understand my rapport with the people," I reason patiently. "It's based on honesty. My addresses to the people are never scripted. I speak from the heart and that's why they trust me. And through me, they'll trust our lord."

I turn to Kite then—and I take in the new throne he has organized for himself. Strange that he doesn't want to sit in Peregrine's.

"Lady Swan will be given a script to deliver and she will deliver it in her own way," Kite tells Greylag. "Only if she goes off script will we review the situation."

Kite gives me a thin smile and I can almost hear his threat: behave, or you are out. The other Ministers most certainly see me as an interloper, a malign influence, here only because of my womanly wiles. I will have to work day and night to prove my value.

My second appointment is to represent Kite at Peregrine's lying in state. Unsurprisingly, Kite can't find the time to attend. My ladies and I make our way into the great Temple of Thal and stand by the catafalque, holding our lilies in a tableau of mourning. My dolly is at my side, loyal and steadfast. All day long, we stand and watch citizens file past our Great Brother's corpse. I wish I could say that he looks serene in death but he looks shocking, his tongue and lips black with poison. In the afternoon, I have the guards bring a stool for Kaira, conscious of her fatigue. I am resolved to look after my little dolly better.

I stand, watching people with keen interest. Some kneel before the corpse, wanting to know who killed him; others swear him silent vows of vengeance. Mothers bring babies; the elderly force strength and dignity into their limbs. Our Great Brother has been part of our lives for so long. He's on our murals and our money, we know his books and sayings by rote. He has seeped into every facet of our lives and these people are grieving as if they've lost a father, a brother. I can also sense their disquiet now that their all-controlling anchor has gone. There is a vacuum that Kite needs to fill—but he is nowhere in sight. Instead, I represent the state. Many of the people meet my eyes, nodding as they pass. I sense they're glad that I am there and feel strangely comforted to be among them. We are sharing our loss together.

"Sister," an old woman says, tears flowing down her face. "It can't be Harrier. Tell us it wasn't Harrier who killed him."

"Lord Kite believes it was," I say.

"Lord Kite?" The old lady looks as if she wants to spit. She squeezes my hand and goes. Her sincerity is powerful.

A one-legged veteran comes forward on crutches. As he looks at Peregrine, I see his face is wet with tears. This man is clearly a derelict but I take his hand. I do this because I think it will look gracious but a strange sensation comes over me as I share his pain. For long moments afterward, I feel it in my heart, even though I badly want to wipe my hand. I look round at Kaira and she comes to stand at my side. As more people file past, my emotions feel more and more raw. I am sharing eye contact, grasping hands, sharing grief, and again and again, people show me something I am quite unused to: kindness.

Harrier once said, "I wish you'd come into the city with me, Swan." He spoke in that easy way of his, with the half smile I found so dangerously attractive. "I'd like to see you walk in freedom through the markets and the streets. You should meet the people, talk to them." Harrier was trying to tell me something then and I didn't know how to listen. Perhaps Kaira has tried to tell me the same thing. When I'm with the people, I will find myself.

Kite doesn't appear until the last moment. He is wearing a newly tailored suit, Light People style. As I look at him it galls me that he's blaming this murder on Raoul Harrier. I decide then and there that I won't have any part in it. I will fudge every attempt to find Harrier and it makes me glad that he's still free.

The flow of citizens is halted by guards and Kite approaches the catafalque. I greet him with a ministerial bow. Kite looks right through Peregrine, as if he's made of glass, and I feel him recoil at the poison on his lips. The drummers play a funereal beat and after yet more prayers to Thal, Greylag takes his place behind Kite. Peregrine's bier is not lifted by a guard of honor, it is lifted by Kite's Ministers, and I realize that our Great Brother's body is being used to give his approval to the new regime. Ruppell, Drake, Ouzel, and the rest of the black-clad collective of hypocrites and nothings lift their dead leader onto their self-serving shoulders. Clever.

My ladies and I take our place behind, our heads bowed.

Kite leads the cortege down to the esplanade. The palace grounds are full of citizens and soldiers. It's the first time Kite has been among his people as their leader and I can see he doesn't know how to conduct himself. He nods, greeting them with a tight smile, which seems completely at odds with the gravity of the situation.

Peregrine is taken to the wide esplanade, where a floating pyre has been made ready. In a tradition that dates from the Age of Woe, when the dead were too numerous to bury, pyres have been set alight on the river. Peregrine's remains will drift down to the sea. Kite offers me a place at his side but I keep my distance as much as is polite.

The funeral is a military spectacle. Every marching band in Brightlinghelm is present and our troops are out in force. We take our positions at the exact moment when the Aylish ship comes into sight. I am close by the pyre, my loyal dolly at my side.

As the ship comes in, there's a dramatic fly-past of our Firefly planes and I must say they look inspiring, filling the sky with whorls of smoke in Peregrine's red and white colors. The firefuel engines roar and Kite has made no attempt to conceal them. His flouting of the First Law is there for all to see. He's showing the Aylish that he scorns the ancient covenant that says mankind must burn no firefuel.

It's a confident move.

There's total silence as the Aylish disembark. And memories of my childhood in Fort Abundance come flooding in. The town was a Brightling trading colony on the southern shore of Ayland. I think of the last day I was there, the day my father locked me in the water tank. I remember the sensation of the dark water up to my chin and the dreadful anguish that I felt. Father had discovered my songlight, thrown me in the tank, and abandoned me to die. Later that day, the Aylish rode in. There was a frenzied battle that resulted in a massacre and in their attack, they slit my father's throat.

The image of that Aylish warrior, his knife gleaming in the sun as my father's blood arced into the sky and spattered on the ground, plays in my mind over and over as the Aylish ship docks. I think of my mother and my sisters, who tried to escape the town in a small boat as their neighbors lay dying, and I feel the pain and terror of their drowning.

I hate these Aylish. I hate them.

The gangplank is lowered. I'm sure these foreign dogs are expecting to be met by a smiling Peregrine, and I take pleasure from witnessing their discomfort. Not one Brightling Minister steps forward to greet them. The Aylish, in their plain blue uniforms and soft sea boots, walk toward us at the funeral pyre. As they make their formation, they must see that Brightlinghelm is now cold and implacable against them.

One of them walks forward, trying to look undaunted as she stands before Lord Kite. Can this really be their leader, this plain, one-handed woman with an unstyled crop of hair? I see Kite take the insult. The Aylish haven't even sent a man to negotiate with us. But this woman a very clever operator, I can see that straightaway.

"My name is Drew Alize," she says. "I'm a commander of Ayland and my title there is Eminence." She gives us her condolences. She says that Peregrine, although an enemy to Ayland, was acknowledged by her people as a visionary statesman.

Kite tersely welcomes her to Brightlinghelm, declaring that he is now Lord of Brightland. "I will honor Peregrine's desire to hear what Ayland has to say."

"How did he die?" asks Alize, with disarming candor. "His telegram to Northaven gave no hint that he was ill or indisposed."

"Not everyone in Brightlinghelm loved Peregrine as I did," says Kite smoothly. "He was poisoned by one of his councillors, Raoul Harrier."

"Why?" I see deep concern on the Aylishwoman's face.

Kite ignores her question and informs her that he will be leading the peace talks now. "They will begin when our period of mourning is over, in three days' time."

Alize replies, quiet and respectful. I don't hear what she says. Then to my surprise, she walks up to me.

"Sister Swan, you have every reason to hate us," she says quietly. "The massacre at Fort Abundance is a stain upon our history. There is never an excuse for the murder of civilians. I can only imagine what you must have suffered. No apology can ever be enough."

How dare she. How dare she bring up my family's death. Not a word comes to my lips.

She holds out a scroll. "This is from our Great Circle House in Reem, agreed by our vast network of parliaments. We acknowledge that a war crime was committed and we take responsibility, as a nation, for every civilian death. We apologize wholeheartedly, to you and to the others who survived that day."

How dare these people insult me with a scroll, a scrawled and meaningless apology, done for political effect. I despise it.

The eyes of the city are upon us. My hand goes out. The Aylishwoman places the scroll in it. I give it straight to my dolly, unsmiling. Alize suddenly looks quite riven with dismay. I don't know whether it's my refusal to engage that upsets her, or the sight of my gossamer chrysalids.

"May we pay our last respects to Brightland's Great Brother?" she asks, and before Kite can reply, she turns to the pyre and kneels before Peregrine. Her crew follows suit, saluting him with a discipline that doesn't belong with their casual blue uniforms.

Clever of her. Respecting our dead leader in front of the whole city.

The Aylish stand aside and the funeral ceremony begins, led by Greylag. A somber drumbeat, growing in intensity, and some soaring violkas underpin a speech from Kite about the strength of Brightland. He promises to bring Peregrine's murderer to justice. It's time for my eulogy but my stomach is still churning from the delivery of that unspeakable scroll.

I climb to the podium and talk about the day I first met Great Brother Peregrine. I remember his kindness as he asked me to describe what I had seen in Fort Abundance. I remind the whole of Brightlinghelm what the Aylish did. My voice distorts through speakers as I describe my father's murder. Kite stares at me while I am speaking and I can see that he approves of every word. But my dolly seems to be in some discomfort. I feel her fidget next to me and her big eyes burn me, if she's longing for me to say something else. I'm sure she wishes that my words were those of an appeaser. I spare no detail. "I arrived in Brightlinghelm an orphan," I say. "And Great Brother Peregrine became my second father."

Afterward, people tell me that my words were most affecting.

Kite gives the signal and the pyre is set alight. Not once do his eyes land upon the corpse. Perhaps he's afraid that Peregrine will sit up as the flames lick, and accuse Kite of his murder. Troops push the pyre out into the river. The great drums pound a slow beat as Brightlinghelm watches Peregrine burn. I have to close my eyes against the embers blown on us from the river. The breeze comes with the smell of burning human flesh.

Peregrine. Forgive me.

Kite withdraws as soon as the drumbeat ends. He parts from the Aylish commander. "As you understand," he tells her, "this is a time of great change for my people. I will see you in three days' time. In the meantime, Lady Swan will entertain you."

This takes me by surprise and I grip my dolly's arm.

I feel Alize stiffen. She's taken this as a slight. Which is exactly what it is. Kite has dumped her with me, a woman who has no real power, for three long days. I too am livid.

"Our Torch, Yan Zeru, was kept behind in Northaven," says the commander. "May we communicate with him on your radiobine?"

"Not during our period of mourning," says Kite. "No state business is being done." He's made this up on the spot and the Aylish hag looks thwarted.

"May I have your assurance that he is all right?"

"He's being shown the best of Brightling hospitality." Kite smiles his thinnest smile.

I think of the Aylish Torch I dueled with. Kingfisher. I feel the

132

humiliation of being beaten. That sharp-eyed, long-haired bastard knows I am a Torch. Who did he tell? Does this bitch know? Do all the Aylish know?

I am in danger from these people.

"I'll leave you women to make your arrangements," says our lord, and without so much as a bow, he walks back to the palace.

"Sister Swan," says the Aylishwoman. "You're welcome on board the *Aileron Blue*."

I'd rather walk on broken glass than step aboard her ship. I indicate Starling Beech. "My man will be in touch with you," I say, dismissing her.

I remain with my dolly long after the Aylish retreat to their ship, my face turned to the river. I watch the flames until the pyre is out of sight.

Farewell.

19 ✸ PIPER

We wait on the airstrip for what seems like hours. The whole city has assembled for the funeral and from up here we have an excellent view. We watch the last phalanx of troops march into place on the esplanade and I see the tiny dots of Lord Kite and his councillors. Sister Swan and her chrysalids are the only specks of white. The Aylish ship comes into view, sailing up the Isis flying the flag of peace, surrounded by our military vessels. I'm struck by its fine engineering: the shape of the sails, the way the turbines are clustered, the bow, rising gracefully out of the water. It's as aerodynamic as my Firefly plane. I immediately want to draw it and model it. Features could be scaled down and reused to make our fishing boats more efficient. Then I catch myself. Is it traitorous to admire Aylish engineering?

Axby gives the signal and we prepare to fly. My spirits fall as I watch my comrades climb into their cockpits with their gunners. I am the only one who flies alone. I suppose Finch has made his decision and will have nothing to do with me. Then, at the last minute, I see a small, sturdy figure walk out of the hangar. Without so much as a glance at me, Tombean Finch jumps up on my wing and drops himself into the gunner's empty seat. He doesn't speak or acknowledge me.

"Ready, gunner?" I ask, pretending that I'm confident.

He nods. I taxi to the head of the runway. We carry canisters of red and white smoke under our planes, Peregrine's colors, Brightland's colors. I take off and circle high above the palace, noticing how well the golden sunset glances off our wings. We veer southeast, over the docks, and we make our formation. I am a nose ahead of my comrades, forming the tip of an arrow of Fireflies that spreads out on each side behind me. We start our fly-past over the river.

"Release the smoke," I say to Finch, and he follows my orders without question. We fly low and I notice the citizens staring at us from Peregrine Park on the hill. There is awe in their faces. We are surely the pride of Brightlinghelm. A few days ago, I would have reveled in such status, but I feel strangely light and empty now, as if the only thing that's holding me to Earth is this flimsy fuselage. The Aylish are standing on their deck, a host of men in their uniforms of blue. Finch puts his thumbs over his guns and pretends to fire at them. I expect that every other gunner does the same.

"Fuck," he says, peering down. "There are women in the crew. Fucking savages, bringing their women to fight a war."

"Their leader is a woman," I say. "She's called Drew Alize. I saw her in Northaven."

"Bastards," says Finch. "Peace, my arse. We should mow the fuckers down."

I'm glad that he's speaking to me but I'm taken aback by the violence in his words.

When we reach the city limits, I veer round and fly past again, my comrades keeping a wonderful symmetry. I see Great Brother Peregrine's open coffin on its bier, ready to be set alight and consigned to the river. As the Aylish ship pulls into the quayside in front of the palace, we swoop low, leaving trails of red and white smoke behind us. We've proudly shown the Aylish what we've got.

I try to fathom how I feel about the peace talks now, in my new world of mistrust. A few days ago I'd have been gunning at the Aylish with Tombean Finch. But now?

I recall that vivid Aylish Torch in Northaven, who crawled through the flames toward Ma.

"I can treat the wound," he said. It looked bad to me, a deep, red hole in her. Has he saved her?

"My children," she said, "we must have peace."

Gala, whether she's alive or dead, I'll strive for what Ma wanted. I will strive for peace.

I search for a handkerchief, trying to keep my grief at bay before Finch sees the state of me. But I blow my nose and my throat catches. Finch turns round and stares at me.

"What's the matter?" he asks glibly. "You crying for that corpse you brought back home?"

"No."

"You crying because you're an uptight prick?"

"My ma. She was shot."

He pauses then. "Fuck, man, I'm sorry." His tone is not cruel.

I wipe my eyes so that I can see my plane's controls and I prepare to land. If Tombean tells Axby of the state I'm in, I'm done.

When we're back in the hangar, I don't want to get out. I don't want this to be over. Finch is here with me again. I look at the short hairs on the side of his neck, the way his sinews move beneath his skin. As I come to a stop, he stares at me. We sit in silence for a while.

"Axby's letting me choose your punishment," he says.

"What's it to be?" I ask.

I notice that he's looking at my lips. "I'll think of it, in time," he says. "For now, you can clean my kit." He opens the cockpit and pulls himself out.

I join him on the wing. "Where do I find you?"

"After the funeral. In the laundry room, fuckwit." He turns his back on me and walks away.

There's a funeral supper, speeches, we must drink a toast. It goes on for an age. At last we are dismissed. I sneak away from my comrades and make my way to the laundry room. It's a good place, warm, underground, windowless. Finch enters and stands with his greasy ground-crew kit. He dumps it at my feet.

He takes off his shirt and throws it with the rest. I leave off my dress uniform and roll up my shirtsleeves. I throw his things in a tub, with a handful of detergent.

"I'll let it soak," I say.

136

Neither of us moves. Not an inch. We're maybe two feet away from one another. I know what we're both doing. We're scanning every door and corner to make sure we can't be seen. The moment holds so long I feel it's going to shatter.

"What are you looking at?" he asks.

There's no point answering. He knows.

Finch moves. I grab his arm. And it begins.

I pull him toward me and his lips are suddenly on mine, hungry, beautiful.

Transforming everything.

20 ✳ NIGHTINGALE

It pained me, watching the way Swan disdained the Aylish. I hold their scroll of apology, half running to keep up with her as she strides angrily back to her rooms.

"Can't you see?" I whisper as we approach. "You have an opportunity to decide Brightland's future. Why are you behaving as if Commander Alize is beneath you?"

"You have the reason in your hands," Swan declares. "That disgusting apology, that vile insult. Don't ask me to be cordial to that witch. She killed my father."

I know the story of Swan's father. She let me into her mind to share her memories.

"The same father who disowned you and put you in a water tank to drown?"

Swan reaches her rooms. "You have no right to speak of him."

The other ladies file in and the door shuts on our closed white world.

Why has that scroll upset her so much? I know she hates the Aylish but they made a massive concession in signing it. Admitting responsibly for an atrocity seems like a genuine step toward reconciliation. Why does Swan find it so objectionable? She is still agitated to an extreme. I take the horrible gauze off my face, so I can breathe easier.

"Haven't you ever wondered what provoked the Aylish to attack Fort Abundance?" I ask. "What triggered their assault? You shared your memory with me, Sister, and I'm only thinking that you must have been in great distress when your father locked you up. Is it not possible that your songlight was wild with anguish, and the Aylish—"

Without warning, Swan slaps me hard around the face.

"Don't you dare use my memories against me," she says.

She has knocked my spectacles off my face and I replace them, blinking at her. Silence falls. My cheek is stinging. No one has ever hit me before.

I have nothing to say to her. Nothing.

"Now what?" she asks. "Are you going to tell me I'm a monster?"

I turn my back and walk away. Something in me is recoiling. I don't care what happens to this woman. I sit on my cot, facing the wall.

"Kaira," I hear her say, "you've been crass and insensitive. You have to understand that my father's death was—" She can't find the words. "It's formed me. And you cannot speak about it. But you wouldn't know how sensitive I am. So I forgive you."

She forgives me? Truly, that is funny.

Swan walks into my line of vision. I curl up, lying on the cot, closing my eyes until I hear her walk away. Why have I wasted my care on her? She's no different from Kite. They're both disgusting murderers. No matter what I do for her, Swan will turn on me one day. She would betray me on the toss of a coin and send me to the Chrysalid House.

I hear her approach again.

"Kaira," she says, and her voice sounds more contrite. "That Aylish devil woman upset me. Stop sulking now."

I say nothing, staring at the cold white wall.

"Share these chocolates with me," urges Swan. "We must comfort one another. Funerals are always very hard."

I feel her sit on the cot and she puts some chocolates down right by my face. I don't touch them. She starts stroking my hair. I push my hand through it, forcing her to stop. I lie there, feeling as lonely as I have ever felt.

"Kaira, I care about you very much," she says, laying a blanket on me.

I'm not thinking about Swan and I don't care how she feels. I am thinking of my papa, lying lonely in a jail cell, my papa who lost everything because he chose to love me. He abandoned every value that he thought was true and he tried to save me. My tears are for him.

"I want my papa," I say, and it comes out loud and angry.

I hear Swan pacing, as if the silence between us is becoming a screech.

"Get out, all of you, get out!" she yells at my silent sisters. Obediently, they leave. Swan continues to pace in her opulent white cage. Then a stillness descends on her. She comes to sit on the bed and after a long time, she speaks. Her voice has lost its sharp and brittle tone. She's speaking from her heart.

"My father," she says. "His last words to me were, 'It's better if you die.' He dropped me in that water tank and locked the door. I was screaming, pleading—no, Papa, please—I was so afraid."

I sit up. I don't interrupt her, aware that these words are the real undertruth. Swan is pulling it out of the black pool that is her wretched heart.

"I've always feared that my actions brought the Aylish to our town that day," she confides. "I expect my songlight was pouring out my anguish. I was pleading to Gala for somebody to save me. What if they heard? What if those Aylish rode in to save me, a child, a fellow Torch? They fought so fiercely. And one of them, the warrior, was yelling at my father, just before he cut his throat: 'Where is she?'" Swan can say no more. She is shaking with emotion. "In my life, I have destroyed everyone who's loved me. So beware of me, Kaira. You are right to turn away."

I can't bear how broken she is. I put my arms round her.

The clock ticks and everything is hushed in the airless room.

We are still holding one another when Starling Beech comes in. He tells Swan that Lord Kite desires her company.

"The city's full of unrest," he says, his voice tight and panicky. "There have been windows smashed. People don't believe that Harrier killed Peregrine. Graffiti is appearing. People think it's Kite."

Swan's arms are still tight around me.

"I don't care," she says.

Starling waits, thrown. He looks at me with a flash of envy, as if he would like to be held so lovingly by Swan.

"Lady," he says, "I'll tell Lord Kite you're indisposed."

Swan wipes her eyes.

"No," she says. "The beast must be fed."

140

I see Starling puzzle over this remark. As he understands it, his compassion is aroused. He watches Swan in hungry devotion as her ladies fix her face. The makeup forms a perfect mask. She chooses a shade of vermilion for her lips, knowing what her task will be. Kite's bed awaits.

When she is ready, Swan accepts Starling's proffered arm.

"Thank you," she whispers, and Starling's feet float off the ground.

I lie, staring at the whiteness, while Swan, the consummate survivor, goes toward her conqueror.

21 ✳ LARK

Heron holds Yura's reins in one hand as we ride through the tunnel, gripping Ma in front of him as I cling on behind, holding the turbine light. Kingfisher follows us, supporting Bel.

Far behind us in the cave, I hear the distorted yells of men, exhorting us to reveal ourselves and our lives will be spared. We hear a volley of gunshots and I hope they're wasting lots of ammunition.

It won't take them long to realize where we've gone.

I'm glad that Bel Plover's songlight can't travel far underground. She is so overwrought that if there was any other Torch within ten miles, they'd hear her.

"Bel," I tell her in firm songlight. "You're worrying the horses. Calm yourself."

She tries. But she's tied on a horse with a fearsome Aylishman and the shock of the Inquisitor's death runs deep. We descend for a long time. In a couple of places the passage is so narrow that I have to jump down off the saddle ladder and coax Yura through using the reins. The ceiling lowers and I worry we'll be trapped here but at last, the tunnel widens out.

The texture of the walls changes from natural rock formations into something gouged and hewn by powerful machines. These tunnels have been made by the Light People. Slowly, dripping minerals have made weird shapes from the ceiling to the floor. Some of them look ghostly in the weak turbine light, as if they could be human figures, frozen in time, calcified by the gods of Hel.

I wonder what this place once was. Occasionally other man-made tunnels open out on either side like black, gaping mouths. Heron slows Yura as Ma considers our direction. I hear her whispering to him: "left here," or "take the right-hand fork." I don't know how she is finding her way. And then I realize she is doing it by pictures. Every so often we come to small, bright markings drawn on the cave wall, swirls and symbols, animals and handprints. The pictures are a language that my ma can read, a Greensward language.

Curlew Crane is so much more than just my ma. She's a wonderful enigma, that's for sure.

At one point, the tunnel opens out into a cavern, bigger than our Elders' Hall. We see the bones of a horse, a rotting saddle, and a machine so rusted that its purpose is impossible to fathom. Farther on, the walls are decorated with ancient paintings. In the flickering turbine light we hurry past images of houses and landscapes. We see a huge painting of men and women with their children. The Light People stare at us as we pass. These paintings must be ancient, thousands of years old. Perhaps the Light People made these caves for shelter in the Age of Woe. Perhaps they were some kind of mining system and people moved down here as war raged and flames burned above. Maybe they were sheltering from disease. Whatever they were doing, they have painted their landscapes and architecture on the walls, images of their lost world, perfectly preserved. For a moment, we slow the horses, looking round in eerie fascination.

"This is the cave of the ancients," says Ma.

I sense Kingfisher's hunger for knowledge. He wants to get off his great-horse and sketch the vivid artworks, preserving them in his memory. There are more of the calcified humanlike rocks, formed by drips of minerals. Perhaps Gala turned the Light People to stone, to punish them for their crimes against creation.

Bel doesn't like the place one bit. "We're in Hel," she mutters. "This is Hel."

"No," I say. "We rescued you from Hel."

"Our people have a long history in these caves," says Ma, reading more of the strange markings. "When winters were bad, we'd shelter from the snows here and travel back to the Greensward in the spring."

"I wish you'd told me more about them," I tell her.

143

"I missed them so much," she explains. "And I didn't want to make you yearn for a place you'd likely never see. I could sense your restless spirit and I didn't want you entertaining thoughts of being a runaway."

"Rye and I were going to run anyway," I confess. "We had to."

Ma's voice has strength in it now. "It feels good to be out of Northaven," she says.

Heron listens to all of this with interest and neither of us minds having him there. He's not intruding in any way. Strangely, it feels like he belongs. He surveys the dark tunnels off to each side, looking for enemies in each.

"I hope we'll find news of our family in the Greensward," she says. "When Peregrine came to power, he tried to destroy our way of life. The Traveling Tribes cared nothing for nations or politics and they refused to show him any allegiance. So he brought in the travel permits to force them to stop moving and trading. But my parents could never keep still. You'd never catch them living in a house."

"Where did they go?"

"I don't know. But I hope for news." I feel the pull in Ma's heart and I wonder how much she must have missed the traveling life when she chose to marry Pa. "They'd be proud of you, Elsa. And of your brother too."

I feel a catch of pain between us as she mentions Piper. Wrongheaded, purehearted Piper, caught up in the Brethren's dream of power. We both fall silent, drawn into the hole he's left between us.

"Go left ahead," I hear her say, and Heron leads Yura down a narrow tunnel. It's flooded with water and we have to turn around and find a different way. Another tunnel that we try has fallen in and once more we retrace our steps, but as the hours go by, we're making progress. We're rising now, and the air doesn't smell so dank. Far behind, voices echo. I hope those men are getting lost in the labyrinth. I hope they disturb the sleeping ghosts.

Bel falls into an exhausted sleep, her head against Kingfisher. He draws her into his arms to make her safer and I feel a weird pang as I look round

144

at them. Kingfisher holds my gaze and I can't tear my eyes away. The moment is intense and lasting—but no words pass between us and neither of us smiles. The light in his eyes draws me closer and closer until I feel I could fall right into them.

The crunch comes when our turbine lamp runs out. The horses come to a halt, nervous in the thick dark. Bel wakes up and her songlight turns electric with fear. Kingfisher and I try to keep the horses calm. Her lack of control is worrying to me and again I'm reminded of John Jenkins.

"Here," says Heron, giving me a box of matches, and I start lighting them, one after another, letting them burn down to my fingers.

"We're almost there," I say to Yura in my calmest songlight. "You can taste the breeze. Follow the breeze."

"This way," says Ma. "Keep going."

We move forward, upward. We can see a square of light ahead. Yura and Uki pick up their pace. The tunnel is clear. Moonlight shines in.

"Slow the horses," cries Ma. "Slow them or we'll fall!"

Heron reins in Yura. At the exit, there is a sheer drop. The tunnel comes out halfway up the side of an ancient quarry. One side of a hill has been blasted clean away. It's dizzying.

When we get our bearings, we see that a narrow path meanders down. Yura takes it, breathing in the fresh night, glad to be out of the oppressive caves. We come to a place where the path falls away and Yura leaps over the gap as if it's nothing. The great-horses seem to have no fear of heights but there are times when I must close my eyes in dread. The path is impossibly narrow. At times, it's just a mess of scree. But the horses' heavy feet find a purchase on it and we make our way across. After half an hour or so, we come to level ground and I start to breathe more easily.

Ahead, the moon pours through a gap in the clouds, showing us a vast expanse of bogland and heather.

"This is Garbarus Moor, the last open space before the Greensward," says Ma.

Sure enough, in the far distance under the stars, I see a different, denser kind of dark—a tree line perhaps. I'm thinking maybe we can stop for a rest, maybe I can breathe freely just for a minute—when a shot booms out behind us and a flare slowly falls, lighting us up in a garish silver beam.

"Mikane," yells Syker. "You can't outrun us. Give yourself up."

Our pursuers are up high, at the end of the tunnel, their turbine lamps glowing against the quarry's side.

"You've been mind-twisted by your whoring Second Wife," cries Syker. "She's unhuman, Heron. Hand her and the Aylishman over and we'll show you mercy."

Heron ignores him. "So," he says, looking at Kingfisher. "It's going to be a race."

Kingfisher holds Bel firmly, gripping Uki's reins. "Let's go," he says.

Bel, Ma, and I hold on for our lives as Heron and Kingfisher kick the great-horses into a gallop. Another flare lights up the sky and I turn and look over my shoulder as we sprint away. I see the snipers taking aim. Judging by Syker's words, I'm the number-one mind-twisting whore of Northaven and those rifles will be looking for my back. Gunfire ricochets through the night and I fully expect the agony of dying. But their shots fall short. We are too far away.

Their flare dies out and we gallop onward, into the dark. The remaining horsemen will have to wind their way down the treacherous quarry path. They can't catch us here.

My relief is short-lived. The track is waterlogged and terrible. Our going will be slow. There are places where it's pure bog and we have to avoid great tracts of swallowing mud and standing pools of evil-smelling water. Crumbling ancient brickwork and corrupted metal tell us this was once a sizable town. The moon comes and goes. It lights our way but it reveals us to our foes. At one point, I dare to turn around and I wish I hadn't. Six horsemen still follow and they're gaining on us. Perhaps they're not hindered by the mud, the way our heavy great-horses are. In truth, Yura and Uki are exhausted, they're hungry and thirsty, they want to go home to their comfortable barn.

The dark line of the Greensward is closer now. But before us, at the bottom of the fell, is a long silver ribbon. A flood-swollen river separates us from our destination.

"If we can get under those trees, we'll lose them in five minutes," says Ma. "They'll never find us in the Greensward."

"We're almost there, Yura," I tell the wonderful beast as she carries us forward.

I look ahead to the roaring silver river. The water is fast, full of the rainwater pouring off the moors. None of us have any idea of its depth. Suddenly, the path stops dead in front of us. The bridge has been swept clean away.

Heron takes out his gun. Kingfisher lifts the crossbow. My hand grips the knife—although Gala only knows what I will do with it.

"They'll hang me," wails Bel in songlight. "They'll send me to the Chrysalid House."

"In my country," says Kingfisher, "a Torch will never let another Torch be taken. We'll live or die together, Bel."

Bel is silent, struck by what he's said. She looks at him, mistrustful.

"Find cover," Heron tells Kingfisher. "This is not what I wanted. We must shoot our way to freedom."

But there is no cover. Only windblown gorse and the small stone foundations of the bridge.

"This can't be how it ends," I say. "I don't like this moor and I don't want to die here."

"That river will sweep us away," he says. He grabs his rifle and swings his leg round to climb off Yura.

"Heron, wait," I urge. "The odds are bad on a fight. They've got more bullets—and I'll bet these great-horses can swim."

The ground is vibrating under us with the hoofbeats of the horsemen, growing closer with each second. Heron urges Yura into the river. A gunshot is heard behind us and a bullet whistles past me.

"Go! Go!" yells Kingfisher to Uki, and he follows us.

I've gone beyond being scared. I only pray these beasts can swim.

Bullets hit the water around us and then—thankfully—the moon goes behind a bank of cloud, confounding the aim of our pursuers.

The water is freezing. It comes up past our waists. We cling on to the horses as tightly as we can. I grab the saddle with one hand and Heron with the other. The sheer force of the water takes us quickly downstream, but our horses have the strength to keep their heads above the flow. Slowly, they are swimming through the current, crossing in a great diagonal.

"Freedom lies on the other side," I promise Yura. "We're almost there."

One of the horsemen fires another flare, high into the sky, illuminating us. Foolishly, two horsemen ride in after us. The floodwaters consume them almost straightaway. The river is narrowing, the current's getting faster. The banks are high on either side and I see that we're approaching a deep muddy gorge. The rush of water is phenomenal. We have to make it to the far bank now or truly, we'll be swept away. Yura puts in a last effort. And suddenly, there's solid ground beneath our feet.

We rise up out of the water—and I hear gunfire. Bel Plover screams on Uki's back as Yura gallops up the bank with Heron, Ma, and me. A bullet whistles past me as the flare dies out. I see Uki behind us. We're safe, we've made it.

But Bel is shrieking "Aylish! Aylish!" not in hatred but concern. When I look round, my heart is in my mouth.

Kingfisher is gone.

22   LARK

I slip off Yura's back and jump onto the ground.

"The water took him!" cries Bel as I run back to the riverbank.

"Yan," I cry in songlight, "Yan!"

A bullet flies past me and I hit the ground, pouring out his name.

"Kingfisher! Where are you?"

There is no reply. My songlight thunders out.

"KINGFISHER!"

On the edge of my consciousness, I hear Heron and Ma calling me, telling me not to be a fool. "Their bullets will get you." But I get to my feet and run on by the river's edge. If I see him, I'll jump in. I have to rescue him, I must.

I think of my ma, jumping in after Kizzy Dunne.

"KINGFISHER!"

Rifle fire sends me to the ground again. They're tracking me from the other bank. They can see me in this bastard moon. The river roars beside me, murderous. The plateau we are on is descending down rapids. Why can't I hear his songlight?

I can't endure another loss.

Please don't take him, please don't take him.

I run on, keeping low to the ground. Ma is distant, crying my name, terrified I'm drowning in the flood. I can't reassure her or I'll give myself away.

"YAN!" I cry in songlight. "YAN!"

And suddenly a small figure is next to me. Nightingale.

"I hear you," she cries. I tell her what has happened in a rush of pain.

"Help me," I beg her. "Save him. Don't let him die."

Together we search. I let Nightingale hold me in her songlight and take me into the water.

Sometimes in Northaven, we'd go with our songlight into the blue sea, searching for shoals, finding Light People ruins down on the seabed. But this river is nothing like the sea. It's black with peat and mud, angry and churning, an irresistible force. There are great rocks down in the depths; I sense their massive shapes. Kingfisher could have cracked his skull. I think of the pain of drowning and grief terrorizes me.

"We'll find him," Nightingale assures me.

Meanwhile my body runs on, staying low to the ground in the long grass, heedless of Syker and his gun.

In the river's depth, we sense a human shape, a boot caught in the rocks, his arms outstretched. A dead man. A wail builds in my core—

"It's not Kingfisher," says Nightingale with certainty.

It's the merchant, Kizzy's husband. There's nothing we can do for him. His lungs are full of water, his spirit extinguished.

In our harmony, we concentrate with all our force.

"KINGFISHER!"

That cross-legged figure sitting on my upturned boat.

Blowing kisses to girls as his ship drew into Caraquet.

His lips meeting mine in a prison cell.

Kingfisher.

I think of all the things I want us to do.

Perhaps I am a curse. Perhaps every fine and handsome boy who gets close to me will end up dead.

Perhaps Heron's demon has caught up with us. This time, Death has done herself proud. This time, she's taken the cream of the crop.

"Don't despair," says Nightingale. "He might be unconscious, not dead."

On my hands and knees, I have reached the top of a waterfall. I listen to it plunge. I feel the force of water vibrating through my being. Could anyone survive it? Nightingale and I search the pool beneath. Water crushes everything.

As I begin my descent of the rocky escarpment, I look for the horsemen, but their silhouettes are gone. Perhaps they think I'm dead. Perhaps they've headed downstream to find a place to cross. All my songlight is with Nightingale, searching for Kingfisher, and I'm not looking at my steps. Suddenly, my foot lands on nothing. I grab at some creepers as I fall—but most of them rip away from the rock walls. Only one or two strands of them hold me and I'm left dangling, way above the ground. That bastard wound in my hand opens up again and I scream with pain. The creepers start to break, dropping me down. I can't hold my connection with Nightingale and I beg her to keep searching for Kingfisher. She vanishes. The final strands of creeper snap and I fall. The jolt of landing is so intense that it takes a few seconds before my body feels it.

It's a while before I can pick myself up. Then I carry on, shaken. I can walk, I can run. Any other injuries can wait.

At the side of the waterfall's pool, something takes my breath away. Nightingale, in songlight, is with Bel Plover. Bel is waist-deep in the water, dragging out a body.

Has Bel been with us all along? Has Bel been sharing my distress? I help her pull Kingfisher onto the rocks and we don't stop until we've dragged him out of sight.

I know what to do with drowning men. Seaworkers have these skills in their blood. I turn Kingfisher on his side, forcing the water out of his airways. I see a wound on the side of his head. A bullet. A wave of sorrow blinds me with tears. I keep pumping hard, but Kingfisher doesn't breathe.

"He's dead . . . ," whispers Bel.

"I don't think so," says Nightingale in songlight. "Touch his skull. See if the wound is deep."

I do this, telling Bel to keep pumping the water out of him.

"It's grazed the surface," I say.

"The coldness of the water might have been his friend," says Nightingale. "It's kept the oxygen in him. Can't you feel the light in his core?"

I try to focus my songlight. I sense Nightingale's strong force, concentrated on the core of Kingfisher's being. But all seems dark and lifeless to me.

"He's there," says Nightingale. "But I can't reach him."

Bel suddenly speaks with a quiet clarity that totally surprises me.

"We must join our songlight," she says. "We become one. That's what they train us to do as Sirens. It makes us stronger. That's how we hunt. And if we can hunt, maybe we can heal."

Right now, I'll try anything.

"We'll give you our light, Lark," says Nightingale. "We'll become one force and you must lead us. You know him best."

We join our minds together in a harmony and I feel like I am full of lightning.

"He needs air," says the Nightingale part of me. I share my air, blowing it into Kingfisher's mouth.

"His heart has to beat," I say to the Bel part of me. And Bel starts pumping his chest.

All is cold and dark in Kingfisher. We look for the tiniest light.

I let go of everything, falling.

And I find myself suspended above a black night sea.

I scan the horizon. There are no stars, no constellations. This is a place where the living don't belong.

A ship. I sense it. He's on the prow of his ship, far away. The ocean he's sailing on is midnight black and if we fall too far, Death will welcome us too.

I think of our light: the truth in my heart, Nightingale's courage, Bel's determination to be free. We become a comet, lighting this airless sky, and we come closer to the ship. Kingfisher is on the deck, colorless, fading. Death is walking toward him over the water, beckoning him.

"Breathe," we tell him. "Breathe." We burn like a bright meteor, filling the darkness with our songlight.

Death is standing with Kingfisher on the deck. She holds out a bony hand and Kingfisher is in her trance. She's coming to take him in her skeletal embrace. I use every last bit of our joined energy and take form. I am a spirit made of us, all three. I place myself in front of Death.

Kingfisher sees me.

"Breathe," I tell him.

Death sees our trinity. Then she runs at me—I feel her fury—an icy cold right though me—and I open my eyes by the river, in my body, feeling an icy chill. Kingfisher's ribs move almost imperceptibly. He's trying to take in air.

"Bel," I say. "Help him."

Bel forces her hands down on Kingfisher's ribs, shocking his heart into action. I give him lungfuls of my breath. Those lips, his lips.

Death will not have them. They are the living, they are for me.

"Breathe," I yell.

His lungs open. His heart beats. Water-vomit comes up from his guts. He heaves out the muddy water that so nearly killed him. Nightingale's songlight envelops us all.

He breathes.

Bel and I make Kingfisher sit up. He is still ice cold but his breath is steady.

"Say something," I demand. "Talk to me. Tell me you're all right."

His eyes meet mine. And everything falls still. It feels like the air is suspended in my lungs.

I don't know what Kingfisher saw or what he remembers from that spirit place. Maybe it was all a dream to him, gone upon his waking.

"So you do care," he whispers.

And I see the faintest hint of a smile. *That* smile.

The tension breaks. I feel my body fill with life. And I burst into sobs. I lie with him, crying in terror and relief. Bel comforts me.

That's how Ma and Heron find us.

"The stupid fool got shot in the head," I say. "He got washed down a waterfall. Bel Plover pulled him out."

"That's good work, Bel," says Ma, and Bel flushes, unused to hearing kindness or praise.

153

"Get your body moving, lad," says Heron. "We must reach the safety of those trees."

He pulls Kingfisher to his feet, as if he's light as goose down. We support him away. Over the river, we hear a loud gunshot and see another flare, lighting up the sky.

"You're a fucking traitor, Mikane!" yells Syker. But his voice is far away, beyond the roar of the waterfall. He hasn't found a crossing place. "You're a wanted man. We know where you're going and we'll be there ahead of you."

"Two of them drowned in the river," I tell the others.

"Maybe they're cutting their losses," says Heron. He leads us on toward the forest edge, looking over his shoulder, his gun at the ready.

Nightingale remains with us in songlight until we reach the tree line. Kingfisher thanks her. His beam is still faint, like a whisper. "Have my people arrived in Brightlinghelm?" he asks.

Nightingale shows us Alize arriving and the cold reception that she gets. "Peace talks will begin in two days' time," she says.

Kingfisher takes this in. "One of my crewmates, Renza, she's a sensitive," he says. "She can sense songlight but only at close quarters. Her full name is Carenza Perch. If you find yourself near to her, please can you find a way to tell her what happened in Northaven? Tell her I'm alive and that we're coming?"

"I'll try my very best," says Nightingale.

"How are you?" I ask, sensing the strain on her. She says she's well, she's safe and things are fine. I immediately know that the opposite is true.

"Come to me tomorrow," I tell her. "When we're safe under the trees, come to me and we'll talk."

"Stay out of trouble, Lark," she says, giving me a final smile.

"You too," I say. And Nightingale fades. I miss her as soon as she has gone.

At the tree line, we take the saddles off the great-horses and let them go.

"Beautiful creatures," says Ma. "But they'll only hinder us in the Greensward."

It feels good to leave them in these lush meadows. The panniers are soaked from crossing the river but we rescue what we can and quickly, we pack it on our backs. I put my hand on Yura, bidding her farewell. She glances at me, tugging at the fresh, wet grass.

I see Kingfisher standing with Uki, his face pressed against the horse's muzzle as if something is passing between them. I think of Kizzy Dunne. I took her food, her medicine. Now her great-horses are gone and her husband too. I hope she and her daughter will be all right. To my mind, she will make a powerful widow.

Together, the five of us face the forest. Under the trees, all is black as pitch. Even Heron looks daunted. The darkness is thicker and more eerie than the caves. This darkness is alive.

Ma is handing out long strips of cloth. "We must tie these round our wrists," she says. "The only way to travel, pathless through the dark, is if we're bound together. My childhood was full of tales where ten people would start out through the forest and by morning, there'd be only one."

This doesn't reassure us. Yura and Uki stay grazing as we walk under the mighty trees, leaving the moon and the starry sky behind.

23 ✳ LARK

Before we've gone ten feet into the undergrowth, the outside world has disappeared. The air is thick and dense, the ground soft and crawling with unnamed things. Every inch of our way must be felt. We are wet, cold, and exhausted, and the effort of forward motion is intense.

"No one could find us in this," I say.

"They might, when daybreak comes," says Ma. "We must get in as far as we can before we rest."

We creep onward, aware of our own noise, the swishing of branches and the snapping of twigs. Kingfisher's close presence fills my senses. I'm glad I am bound to Bel because it forces me to resist the urge to throw my arms round him.

I almost lost him. He almost died.

Weird night creatures quiet as we approach and all around us, a teeming silence hangs. We are aliens in this place. After a while, Ma lets us pause. We all rest together on a mossy bank with nothing but wet blankets to keep the insects off. I don't sense any reserve from Kingfisher. He seems newborn and glad to be alive. I lie with my head on his chest, warming him, listening to his heart to make sure it doesn't stop again. We drift, each of us processing what we have just come through. I must eventually doze because when I wake up, Kingfisher is warm and his heart is steady. Ma's already on her feet, getting ready to move on. I hope that she has rested well.

"The forest knows we're here," she says. "It has its own wisdom. Each tree is entwined in the whole and it has a kind of perception that we can't understand, no matter how we try. If the forest thinks we mean it harm, it might treat us like infection. So we must tell the forest we're just passing through." I think she's saying this for the benefit of Bel, who is struggling the most with her terror of the dark. Ma is giving her a job to do.

"Greet the forest, Bel. Be polite. And you too, Heron Mikane." Ma's voice sounds soft among the trees but there's a quiet strength to it. "The worst thing that can hurt you is your fear," she says, "so greet the beetles that run over your hands, the leaves, the thorns, the twisted roots, greet the moss beneath your feet and say you are just passing."

I endeavor to do this but my thoughts are soon pinned on Kingfisher again. I feel his hand clasp mine and it has lost its deathly chill. He helps me to my feet and his presence is all the more vivid because I cannot see him with my eyes. He's not protecting himself with that reserve. Since we saved his life, since I lay on him sobbing with relief, something has changed. Maybe Nightingale is right and he has been protecting his heart.

I don't want to let him go. I want kiss his chest, his neck, his lips, and whisper that I'm glad he is alive. I want him to love me, to lose himself in passion. I want to lose myself. The force of desire renders me speechless and quickens my breath. I'm worried that a wisp of songlight will give me away and I try to bury it. But as we move on, I listen to his breathing, sensing his presence, body and soul. When I stumble, he grips my waist. When he loses his footing, I steady him.

"Stay close," I whisper.

And I can almost feel his smile in the dark. "I'm not going anywhere."

We come to a place where the ground is soft, too soft. In front of me, Bel whimpers as the mud pulls and sucks and she almost loses her ill-fitting boots. We find our way around the swamp but I sense how easily the forest bed could swallow one of us. We pull ourselves on, avoiding insect nests and huge gnarled roots, but the undergrowth is an ever-changing obstacle. At every step, tiny crawling creatures fall into my hair, run up my sleeves, and occasionally I wipe them from my eyes. The smell is heady, thick in our nostrils: trees, fungi, leaf mold, decay.

We walk on, bound to one another. Heron leads, a phosphorescent compass needle guiding us southeast. Ma follows—then comes Bel, strung between us like a little piece of laundry on a line. I feel a whine of her songlight and she starts pulling at the rag that ties her to my wrist. The whine grows as fear overwhelms her. She is spinning into a panic, trying to get herself loose. I feel her pulling at Ma, trying to wrench herself, and I worry for Ma's shoulder wound. Bel's songlight is rising in distress. I join with her, trying to calm her. She is seeing a vision in the darkness and snatches of it flash before me. Maybe Kingfisher sees it too.

In her mind, Bel is bound to her Inquisitor again, but he's a phantom in front of her, leading her to Hel, where all the people she has sent to the Chrysalid House await. I force myself into this horrible vision, bringing my songlight.

"He used you, Bel," I say. "That Inquisitor can't get you now. He can't harm you anymore."

But Bel's songlight begins an awful wail. I worry that she'll break free of us and flee into this perilous dark.

"He's waiting for me down in Hel."

"It's the binds, Ma," I say urgently. "They're making her think she's a prisoner again."

"Oh, Bel," says Curl, immediately drawing Bel into an embrace. "I am so thoughtless. You are bound to no one here."

Ma holds her, shushing her like a lost child. Bel stills, taken aback by Ma's affection. Kingfisher helps me free Bel's wrists.

"Come and walk with me, my lovely," says Ma. Bel's distress begins to fade.

"We should find a proper resting place," says Heron. "We'll carry on at dawn. We're far enough now from the forest edge."

"Light a match," Ma instructs him. "Let's see where we are."

Heron flicks a match ablaze and I see my four companions, eyes like owls. As the flame begins to flicker out, I see a gap some way ahead in the gnarled trees, long grasses growing up.

"I think there's a glade," I say, pointing.

Heron and Ma move on, taking Bel between them. Ma is telling Bel how her people used to sing the forest paths into their memories. Each tree, each brook would get a verse and that way, a route could be remembered. Ma sings an example in a low voice and after a while, Bel finds a harmony. Their voices quell the impenetrable dark and Bel's anguish ebbs away.

I am about to follow them, still bound to Kingfisher. My free hand feels ahead, my fingers stretched into the pregnant air like antennae. But Kingfisher pulls me back.

I turn—and my outstretched hand lands on Kingfisher's chest.

"What is it?" I whisper.

I feel his body, taut beneath the fabric of his clothes. And I know what he wants.

"Lark" is all he says. But the sound of my name on his tongue turns me molten. I let my hand run down his lean body to his waist. And I feel his breathing change. I know what I'm doing lacks all propriety but Gala, I find his lips and pull them onto mine.

It feels like lightning, shooting through my core.

We are defying Death, showing her how life triumphs.

We're clinging to each other, feeling every inch of our bodies as they press together. His hand creeps up to my breast and my breath turns into rags. We kiss with a silent fury. Kingfisher pushes me against a tree and I lean into him. I want this darkness to close around us. I want this moment to last and last. One hand of mine is still bound to his. The other grasps his back. No words pass between us, no songlight illuminates us from within. Another language is at work.

A moan of pleasure escapes me—and he breaks away.

We breathe in unison, our foreheads pressed against each other.

"We should make a covenant," I whisper. "To live life to the full."

"Life," he says in agreement, his body pressing against mine. "To the full."

We seal this pact with another long, exquisite kiss. And if the forest spirits hear, I don't care what they think.

"Elsa?" cries my ma. "Elsa!" I can hear the panic in her voice.

"We're here," I shout. "We're fine. Yan fell." And then I whisper to him, "He's fallen hard . . ."

Yan laughs a low laugh, as if he's telling me he won't fall so easily. He puts his hand up to my face.

"I heard you," he whispers in songlight. "I heard you, calling me."

He's speaking of the spirit place.

"There was a woman, drawing me toward her," he says, reliving what he saw. "I wanted to go with her—but I saw a light. You." A chill runs through Kingfisher. "She spoke to me," he says.

"What did she say?"

He pauses. The darkness all around us leans in, listening.

"She said she would come back."

Fear pounds through me then. I hold him. And I know that it's me who is falling hard.

"This might be all the time we have," he says.

We kiss again, freeing our bodies to do what they will. I want to chase that bony demon away, proving to her that we are living flesh—and vulnerable as we are, we will love, however short our day. We are lost in each other when Ma calls for us again. Kingfisher pulls back and I know that we've gone far enough.

"Tomorrow," I say. "There is tomorrow."

He holds me, recovering himself, his arms around me, his face buried in my hair.

"Lark," he says again.

I'm glad the darkness hides us.

As we head toward Ma's voice, I know that we are bound together now, by far more than a piece of ragged cloth.

PART 3

24 ✴ RYE

Another night without fresh water. We're beyond crazed with thirst. Wren and I have been quiet for a long time, lying top to tail in the cradle of the boat, looking at the starlit heavens. We've drifted into warmer, calmer seas and as the stars cross the sky, I feel like I'm floating up to join the great Silver River.

"Do you believe in Gala?" asks Wren.

The question brings me down. People always think of gods when they're about to die. I want to say, "No, I don't, and if I did, I'd ask her why she's given us such short and shitty lives." But Wren deserves a more considered answer.

"I don't believe in Gala as a being," I tell her. "Gala's just a word for creation."

"We're part of creation, though, aren't we."

"Yes."

"So, we're part of Gala. We are Gala." Wren falls quiet again, philosophizing. The next thing she says is, "She made us. And our flesh will go back into creation."

I wish she hadn't voiced it. Somehow, voicing it makes it true. We're about to become fish food, gull food, foam on the ocean. There must be a way out of this.

"Maybe it'll rain tonight. We could catch some water in the sail and—"

"The sky's clear. The food's gone, we're losing strength. There's nobody to save us." Wren says it like a fact.

"Hard to hear it, Wren. I would rather keep denying, if it's all the same to you."

She agrees. And we fall silent.

"I've been trying to comfort myself," I tell her. "Saying at least we'll die free. But it's no fucking consolation."

"Actually, it is."

The cradle rocks us on the gentle waves. The sea is being kind to us tonight.

"I'm glad I'm not alone," I say.

Wren turns around, lying on her side so she can look at me.

"I feel like we should tell each other stuff," she says. "Anything that's weighing on us, we should say."

"All right," I say, although I'm not sure I want to prod the mess inside me into actual words.

"My family's from Harmony Mills, down below Lake Lunen," says Wren. "We're herding people. When I was a kid," she goes on, "I always saw myself with my own herd, my own family. That was going to be my life."

She's saying this like it's a secret that she wants off her chest. I'm puzzled.

"That's a good life," I say.

"But I wasn't ever a wife in my thinkings."

"How do you mean?"

"When I was a kid, I always thought, 'When I grow up, I'll be a man'—as if I'd have a choice. I'd imagine leading my family up to the high ground in the summer. I'd have thirty golden cattle and a hundred sheep and my sons and daughters would mind them all. I'd have a wife, not a husband. I thought that I could just choose to be a man." She pauses. "Gala put me in this body, Rye. But I am not a girl."

My first instinct is to contradict her. "But you are."

"I look like a girl." She breaks our gaze, lying on her back, sighing. "I know I can't make you understand. I just want to say it aloud, one time, and have someone to hear me. I tell you, in my heart and soul I am a boy."

I see the gravity in her expression. This is her deepest secret, her truest self.

I lie beside her, trying really hard to understand. I think about what it must be like.

"You're a boy in your soul?"

164

"I am a boy."

I let it sink in for a few more breaths.

"So in that Pink House . . . ," I begin.

"That Pink House was Hel," she snaps at me. "It's gone. I don't want to think about it."

But she is thinking about it because the next thing she says is, "When things got bad there, I'd imagine I was in the high meadows back at home. We'd wander up by Lake Lunen and pitch our tents for summer. It's heavenly up there. . . ."

I'm still trying to understand what she has told me. "So, in your mind, you are a boy?"

She gets up on one arm and looks down at me, trying one last time to explain. "Rye, I am a boy. But Gala gave me this body."

I ponder on her words, his words.

"You get what you're given, don't you?" I say. "Elsa and me, we didn't choose to have songlight. It is who we are."

Wren nods in agreement. "It's who we are."

I sit up. The mention of Elsa's name has sent another wave of loss and longing through me. Wren seems to sense it.

"I bet your girl is grieving for you, Rye. She won't forget you. Trust me, you're a good man and there's a scant supply."

This makes me smile. The smile cracks my salt-dry lips. "We had this dream, Elsa and me," I tell her. "Of a place where we were safe, where we could be who we were."

"I wish you could have got that," says Wren.

"I wish you could've got your dream too."

Wren sits and I begin to see the boy in her eyes—his eyes.

"I used to swim in Lake Lunen, near the veterans' hospital," she says—he says. "I would imagine going into the water a girl and then by some miracle, Gala would hear me and I would come out a boy. I knew when I was twelve years old that it was never going to happen. The eldermen sent my brothers off to be cadets and they put me in a dress. I had to go to marriage training then. But we all knew, every person in my family knew, that I did not belong there."

I see it now—his foxlike face, his boyish smile.

"You were becoming yourself, though, Wren," I tell him. "You escaped from that Pink House. You took that soldier's clothes. When I saw you at my boat, I fully thought you were a man."

This pleases him.

"Gala," vows Wren, "if this is my last night on earth, I will live it as a boy."

"We're not done yet, soldier," I say. "As far as I'm concerned, no one's dying here." It sounds as confident as I can make it. But the endless canopy of stars is making me feel my insignificance.

"They made us grow our hair long in the Pink House," says Wren. I see the knife glint in front of my face. "Cut it off, soldier." Wren is determined. This is an order.

I do my best job, throwing long tresses into the ocean depths. I cut it close to Wren's scalp at the back and sides and leave it a little longer on the top, the kind of haircut I would like myself. I take my time with it. It feels important.

"That's my best work," I say when it is done. Wren turns to face me, more foxlike than ever. "You brush up well as a boy," I add.

She—he—runs his hands through his soldier's cut and looks at his moon-shadow on the water, liking his new shape.

I look at this new-sprung boy, thinking of Piper Crane.

Piper has been on this journey with me, every step of the way. I think back at all the anger and rage I have felt, the betrayal, the sorrow and the desperation. If this is my last night on Earth, I must try to forgive him. Perhaps I should share it with Wren. Of all people, Wren would understand. But it's just too hard to start the long and bitter story. And I can't spare the fluid for the tears. I say it to the stars instead.

Piper, my friend, I hope you will find peace.

Wren is peering at me. "I wish that there was something I could do for you," he says. He puts his hands up to my lead band.

"I've tried every which fucking way," I tell him. "This thing's not coming off."

His hands are tender on my raised and angry skin. The pain is constant around that band and it feels good to let Wren touch the dreadful ugliness.

"What's it like having songlight?" His question dances on the water.

"Hard to describe," I say. Then it comes to me. "It's kind of like this." I gesture up to the night sky, to the calm sea, to Wren and me. "Sometimes you don't need songlight to have songlight. You feel that sense of connection without it. You, me, everything. Songlight's our connection. People of Song can access it more easily, perhaps. That's all."

Wren appreciates this. "Whether you believe in Gala or not," he says, "we're part of creation. We came from air and earth and water. And that's what we'll go back to."

We lie once more in the bottom of the boat. This time, our heads are together. Wren takes my hand. I really see him then, his whole soul in his eyes. And I believe that he sees me.

"Dream well, soldier," I tell him. And we fall into our last and final sleep.

25 ✳ RYE

The crunch of land beneath us jolts us both awake.

It's dawn.

For a long time, I don't believe it's real.

This is the far shore of the underworld, a misty, crepuscular world of ghosts.

The waves are lapping at a long beach. Flat land stretches out before us. There is flotsam all along this coast, strange sculptures of sea-decaying wood and weird relics from the Light People time. It feels like a dead zone. We have drifted in with the tide and some big current has dumped us here.

Wren is clearly thinking the same as me. "Have we died?" he asks uncertainly.

"Let's find out."

We get out of the boat. The water is cold and real around our legs. The strength we exert feels palpable as we pull the boat onto the beach. After so many days being rocked by the sea, my legs are land-dizzy. I collapse onto the pebbles. Wren remains standing, holding on to the boat, looking down the beach.

"Do you think this is Ayland?"

"I fucking hope so, with all my heart," I say.

We're too near thirst exhaustion for any jubilation. All we can see in the eerie mist is the beach.

"We will find a stream soon," I say. "A stream or a river. Think of that, Wren, a drink."

"Which way do we walk?" he asks.

"You choose."

We trudge down the beach—and never has a beach seemed so horribly unending. The salt waves tumble in, mile after mile. The land is dry, drinking moisture from the mist, nothing but strange water-grabbing plants and dry seagrass. We force ourselves on. Somewhere, we will find fresh water.

After an exhausting hour or so, the pebbles give way to sea-slimed rubble. The mist momentarily clears. My heart leaps as we find ourselves staring at the towers of a distant city. Hope surges and I swear aloud.

"Fuck . . ."

We pick up our pace. Cities mean people, they mean water, they mean life. But the nearer we get, the more our brief ray of optimism fades. The windows of this city are all black and empty, and around them, lifeless rubble stretches for miles.

"I don't think this is Ayland," says Wren. "I think we're in the badlands."

My heart is in my boots as I agree with him. We've all heard tales about the southern badlands. Nothing thrives. Most of the travelers who venture down here never come back and those who do have their children born unhealthy. Wren's shoulders sink, dwarfed by the oppressive towers. In the swirling fog, it's obvious the buildings are just skeletons.

"This is a city of the dead," he says.

Some of the precipitous towers have half collapsed, leaving twisted, rusting innards reaching for the sky. I start to worry that this is a land of toxins like our own Tenmoth Zone. On Sergeant Redshank's map, it's an area marked with brown crosses, and he told us no one ever goes there. What brought about its destruction? What caused the deathly atmosphere that lingers there?

Wren puts my fears into words. "Are we shortening our lives just by walking on this beach?" he asks.

"If we don't find water," I say, "our lives will be short enough anyway."

The fog closes in again, hiding the tops of the buildings.

"Where there's a city, there must be fresh water," says Wren, trying to stay positive, and we walk on. But the place presses on our spirits. Nothing moves and the fog-muffled sea is the only thing we hear.

169

Then, as we near the great towers, I sense something in my periphery. I spin around, knife raised, and Wren immediately crouches, alert, ready to attack. We watch, waiting. It's eerie as hell.

Something weaves its way out of the seagrass.

It's a fucking cat.

"Bastard," says Wren.

The cat comes a little closer, staring at us with ancient, almost reptilian eyes.

"If there's a cat, there's water," says Wren desperately. "Come on, puss, where do you drink?"

The cat doesn't look like the domestic kind. It's huge and it's dirty; an old fighter, scars in its fur, jumping with fleas. It keeps its eyes on us as we walk and I reckon this cat must have feline songlight because soon another joins us, a black-and-white hunter with one ear torn clean off. More cats are approaching. A flea-bitten gray with yellow eyes comes right up to Wren's feet.

"All right, cat?" he says, trying to be friendly. The cat turns its head and walks on, disdainful. I am unnerved.

"I'm not being funny," says Wren, "but are we gonna be cat food?"

"Cats don't hunt in packs," I tell him. "They're lone predators."

"But these are badlands cats. They might be different. They might have evolved."

"They're just checking us out." I curb my desire to boot these cats into the sea.

This city is a graveyard, for sure. Rolling waves break into the old towers, booming through the empty halls. What did the damage here? Was it war? Was it abandoned to disease? Did the Light People simply flee the flooding seas?

We walk inland and after a while, we reach a higher place where a pattern of streets is still visible. The cats are assembling. More and more of them stroll toward us.

"They're stalking us," says Wren, "getting ready to pounce."

"I'm not so sure," I counter. "They're not starvelings, they look well fed."

The buildings here are lower-rise and many still stand. They're not so stark and dangerous as the great towers. I turn and stare back at them again, the broken tops smothered by the fog. How did humans ever live in them? What did they grow to eat; where did their children play? They must have had pulleys or flying machines to get them to the top.

The sea is distant now but the eerie quiet is just as unsettling as the boom and roll of the waves. We see a broken shop sign hanging in the dust, bits of glass in some of the windows. But the city is sinking into the ground as nature does its job. Trees have forced their way up through the paving and the ground is soft with moss and mold.

"There must be water under our feet, water to sustain those trees," I say.

"We've landed on the coast of Hel," says Wren.

If I had my songlight, I could get more of a sense of these fucking cats, but they are an inscrutable mystery. Something tells me that disaster will befall us if we stop but Wren is seriously flagging. He sits on a concrete block and I can tell his stamina is near its end. My friend needs water or he will die and I am wracked with a sore pain at the thought of it. Wren is a precious and unusual soul and I want to know him better.

"We'll find water soon," I reassure him. "Then we can get out of here." But my own mind is fighting a dreadful weakness of privation. I feel that any decision I make is going to be the wrong one. The lead band is so heavy and this relentless thirst is scrambling me. I look up into the yellow eyes of a large, brindled cat, not three feet away.

"Water, fuckface," I say to it. "We need water."

This cat couldn't give a shit. It turns and walks away, like it's checked us out and found us of no interest.

"Come on," I say. I help Wren to his feet and we follow the imperious brindled cat. It turns a corner, away from the main street.

There's a straggle of birch trees growing here, like a desert oasis. We wind our way under their long branches, following the cat into a large, rectangular courtyard. There are buildings on three sides, six or seven stories high, still fairly intact. It looks like an awful lot of families once lived here. Now the windows and the walls are covered with some kind of brown fungus—no, it's too shiny and lacquered for a fungus—some kind of weird plant? Perhaps the thirst is making me hallucinate because the walls all seem to be vibrating.

"Listen," says Wren, clutching my arm. "Water."

I hear it, water, flowing under our feet.

At the other end of the long courtyard, some of the timeworn paving slabs are lying in a heap. Perhaps other travelers have passed here and uncovered an ancient underground stream.

Wren lets me go and starts hurrying toward it but as he moves, the brown lacquer starts swirling over the paving slabs. We have disturbed the new residents of this square. The ground and walls are swarming with polished brown cockroaches.

"Get back," I cry to Wren, and he stops.

We slowly back away. Gala, these fuckers are the size of mice.

"What do we do?" asks Wren. "We have to drink."

Then my eyes alight on something strange. It's a tripod, with a small machine on it.

"What's that?" I ask.

We approach it. It's a small black device with a thick glass lens on it.

"Some kind of Light People thing?" wonders Wren.

"But how can it be?" I ask. "It looks brand-new."

I take a few steps toward it. And suddenly the ground rocks with an explosion.

BOOM.

A bomb blast.

"Run!" yells Wren. "Run!"

The cockroaches, disturbed by the explosion, are swarming. Before we

172

move five paces, I feel them all over me and we both start screaming. I see Wren writhing, trying to get them off. I feel them running up my sleeves; they're over my face, my eyes. All I can hear is our double screaming.

Curse the gods of Hel for bringing us here, for tempting us with water. This is the worst death, the worst. These monstrous things will run into our mouths and choke us.

Suddenly, I hear another BOOM. Some kind of weapon has been fired.

Within a second, the creatures make a dash for the shadows. They flee from our bodies, finding no sanctuary there, disappearing down into the watercourse and up into the broken buildings. With unnatural speed, they scale the walls, disappearing into the darkness inside.

Standing at the end of the square is a figure, wearing a white suit made of a strange and brilliant fabric. I think it's a woman but it's hard to tell. Not one inch of her is visible. A glasslike visor covers her face.

She's pointing a weapon at us. Two more people appear at the other entrance to the square, both wearing the same bright white suits with visors over their faces. Their weapons are trained on us. The first woman speaks. There must be some kind of machinery built into her suit, because her voice sounds mechanical, like the radiobine in our Elders' Hall.

"Sapiens, raise your hands!" Her accent is strange, like nothing I have ever heard.

We raise our hands.

"Help us," I plead. "We need water."

26 ✳ PETRA

We're a crew of five. Mother, Charlus, two sapien engineers, and me. I am the first of the eximians to arrive in the hangar, over-keen of course, as it's my maiden expedition. *Celestis* has been descending to a lower altitude, to enable us to take on water. The scouting craft will take a long hose to the ground and our mission is to find an acceptable water source. If we are successful, *Celestis* will pump it up to our refinery, so we can fill our tanks.

"Good morning," I say to our sapien engineers. I try to engage in conversation, using mouth-words to ask about wind speed and surface temperature. The man is called Jem Kahinu and the woman is Tayla Cross. We've worked together throughout my training but today, the conversation flounders. They answer my questions politely but I feel as if a chasm lies between us. The atmosphere on *Celestis* has changed completely since the execution of Caleb Ableson.

I see his death again, as I do many times a day, his body falling through the clouds with his hands tied behind his back. I wish I could say something to these engineers, some words of solidarity or consolation, but I feel so guilty. As if it's my murder.

It's the meanness of tying his hands that upsets me most.

I've been avoiding Charlus since it happened. It was easy at first because he was in the medical wing, getting his broken nose fixed. But yesterday, he was back at training, sporting bruises and a gray ring round his eye. He came straight up to me. I was preparing for my final tech theory test and I didn't want to be disturbed.

"Hello," he said. He wanted me to say, "How are you?"

"How are you?" I asked.

"I thought you might have checked in on me." He leaned against a pillar, nonchalant. "It would have been nice to have had a visit."

"I've been prepping for my tests."

He turned, showing off the profile of his new nose. "How do I look?"

Like a mantis.

"They've done a really nice job."

"I asked them to make it more aquiline."

"Yes. It suits you."

He smiled then, having squeezed this compliment out of me. "Glad you approve."

I turned back to my work.

I'm so proud to be on this scouting craft team but I profoundly wish I wasn't stuck with Charlus. I don't like him and I don't trust him. I can't make an enemy of him but one thing is for sure: I don't want him as a friend. I saw Charlus go up to the sapien quarters. Something happened up there that no one's talking about. The next day, he fought with Caleb Ableson. And Caleb was executed as a result. Charlus is dangerous.

My mother arrives in the hangar with a list of orders and instructions. The engineers are to assist her with any observations. She will require them to document her findings. She's clear and businesslike and they nod their understanding. She treats me like an ordinary crew member and I'm glad she's not making a fuss—but a "Good luck, Petra" would have been nice. Affection is just not my mother's style.

Charlus is late and when he finally appears, the atmosphere turns really sour. The engineers prepare for flight, turning their backs on him. Charlus makes light conversation with Mother as we ready ourselves. He barely throws the engineers a single mouth-word. They go through the safety checks and Charlus eases the craft out of the hangar.

Can't he feel how much these sapiens despise him?

I sit by the window, marveling at the speed of our descent, feeling my stomach turn over and my ears pop. There is no view. A thick mist surrounds us—but after so long in the air, I'm itching with anticipation. I will have my feet back on the earth.

Our craft has been given a search sector near a ruined city. As we approach, I get a sense of its cracked and forbidding towers, hauntingly dramatic in the fog. Charlus detects an underground stream with his divining device and sets the craft down as near to it as possible on the outer edge of the ruins. The sapien engineers must keep guard of the craft, while we eximians explore. Our task is to find a water source, bring the craft to it, set up the hose and pump water to the ship.

It feels momentous as I step on the ground. I make sure I keep my true-voice under control in case I start singing my inner thrill. I, Petra, am exploring new lands; I am here for future generations, to make a new world for our people, a better, eximian world.

I concentrate on getting used to my suit. There are speaker devices so we can communicate in mouth-words with our sapien crew. My breath sounds loud and strange and I can't see what's in my periphery, so I keep imagining that something's creeping up on me, out of the fog.

We quickly discover that the water source is useless. There's a perfectly horrible ecosystem here. Cats, rodents, cockroaches. The cockroaches live on the toxic ground mold and the stream is crawling with them. They would clog up our pumping hose within minutes. But Mother is fascinated.

"It's possible that the cockroaches are actually breaking down contaminants with their digestive processes," she says. "Rather than being a blight, they're an example of how an ecosystem might eventually begin to recover."

Charlus wants to leave immediately and search inland, but Mother asks if she can make some observations first.

I do what I can to assist her, as it keeps me from talking to Charlus. I set up her camera where the underground stream is open to the sky and a vast swarm of cockroaches has congregated. Mother picks one of them up with a small pair of pincers. She turns it on its back and inserts a scalpel, starting to dissect it while its legs flail. My disgust must show on my face.

"Don't be sentimental," says Mother. "I want to test the enzymes present in its gastric cecum." She slits the creature in half. "This is the mid-gut, which is responsible for nutrient absorption. That yellow tissue is fat." She sees my expression and it irritates her. "This is what the voyage of *Celestis* is all about," she informs me, as if my lack of enthusiasm is a personal slight. "We're increasing our store of knowledge, observing the ecosystems that we find, discovering ways that these benighted places may one day be livable again."

"Yes," I say as she squeezes cockroach juice onto a slide. "It's wonderful."

"Livia," says Charlus, approaching. "May I borrow Petra?"

My heart sinks.

"Of course," says Mother, giving him a winning smile. "I'm not detecting much appetite for my roachoid anatomy lesson."

The last thing I want is to be alone with Charlus. But what can I do? He's our craft captain.

"We'll walk this way," he says. "We can open that watercourse up to the sky with our blasters and get the hose in where it's clean."

"Sure," I say. He uses his divining device to follow the route of the underground stream. Fog hangs over everything and the fearless cats watch our every move. I see one crunch a cockroach and swallow it down.

"So," remarks Charlus. "How are you enjoying your first trip?"

I look around at the dismal ruins, as the giant insects scoot over my feet.

"It's great," I tell him. "But we shouldn't leave my mother for long. We should be alert for sapien marauders."

"Sapiens avoid these ruined places. That's what we've observed so far."

"I suppose there's nothing for them here."

We walk on.

"You're a curious person," he says. "For the first month on the ship you were as dull as soup. You barely said a word, but recently, you've proved yourself to be a total dazzler." He pauses. "You know I'm crazy about you, don't you?" I look at him, tongue-tied. "And I'm guessing that you're pretty keen on me."

His new nose waits expectantly behind his visor. He wants a response. I have to stand up to him and tell him straight. I have to nip this in the bud.

"It's nice to have you as a friend, but I'm not—" He doesn't let me finish.

"You know our parents want us for a match. So what's stopping us?"

"It's very gratifying, Charlus, but—"

"You don't have to be shy."

He's come right into my personal space, we're virtually visor to visor. I want to yell "Get away from me!" but I remain polite.

"I like you as a friend. But I'm not looking for a match." I hope this is clear and final. But Charlus is still smiling.

"Come on, you've been following me for weeks."

"I've been working with you."

He needs me for something, I can sense it. Maybe Xalvas is angry with him. Maybe he knows his reputation on the ship has been shaken by the death of Caleb Ableson. Whatever it is, I'm a pawn in his game.

"We could have a lot of fun, you know."

"Thank you, Charlus. I'm overwhelmed by the offer. But I can't accept."

"What do you mean?" he asks me, irked.

Don't insult him.

"I'm not ready for a match," I say, searching for something to tell him. "I'm in love with someone else."

Charlus stares down at me, trying to ascertain if this is the truth. His grin turns into a disappointed smile. He turns and walks a little farther up the stream, looking down at his device, dealing with the setback I have given him.

"I know all about that sapien tutor in Sealand City," he says. "Your parents shared everything with Father and me."

I imagine my parents sitting there discussing me as if I'm one of Mother's specimens. I feel like Charlus has me held in a little pair of pincers.

He goes on. "A lot of us have dalliances with sapiens. It happens. I won't hold it against you."

"It wasn't a dalliance." I look into his eyes so he can feel the truth of this but Charlus brushes it off.

178

"We've both made mistakes," he says. "We've got that in common. You've got some passion and frankly, it makes me want you even more."

He grabs hold of me, pulling me toward him by the waist, and I feel the same dizzy revulsion that I did for the flailing cockroach. Charlus's truevoice is surrounding me like a miasma, pressing itself up against my white protective suit. I hold my ground.

"I'm honored," I say. "But I'm not ready and I don't want a match."

For the longest time, he doesn't move, his truevoice pressing in on me. "Your coyness is very fetching," he replies. "I'll wait."

He releases me, leaving me breathing my reluctance.

"Let's get to work," he says. He marks a cross on the ground with his foot. "Full power. Let's make some noise, Petra."

We shelter behind a wall and set our blasters to full. We aim them at the cross on the ground until the earth is cracking with the heat. When the pressure grows too great, it explodes.

BOOM.

Debris falls all around us and the air is full of dust. As the ringing in my ears subsides, I realize I can hear tumbling water. The river at the bottom of the crater is racing under us and the water looks clear. As Charlus contacts the scouting craft, I hear screaming coming from the square. Mother.

I immediately leave, running away from Charlus as fast as I can.

I hear blaster fire—and when I enter the square, I see that the cockroaches are streaming away out of sight.

Mother is aiming her weapon at two primitive sapiens. They are filthy and ragged—young males, wearing long coats and heavy boots. The smaller reaches for the taller, grabbing his arm. I notice that the taller wears some kind of metal crown. I aim my blaster right at them and when Charlus appears at my side, he does the same.

"Sapiens, raise your hands!" orders Mother, in rudimentary mouth-words.

"There might be more of them," says Charlus, panic in his truevoice. "This might be an ambush."

The last time she met sapiens, Mother blasted them to pieces—but these two look starving and pathetic. Charlus is about to fire.

"Don't shoot," I tell him in my firmest truevoice. "Don't hurt them."

The sapiens have raised their hands.

"Help us," begs the taller one in mouth-words. "We need water."

"Don't kill us," says the other. "We mean no harm."

I recognize word roots from one of the old global languages. Fenan has taught me to understand them.

"How many of you are there?" I ask. "Where's the rest of your tribe?"

"There's just us," says the one with the crown. "We came by boat. Please help us, we're dying of thirst."

"They need water," I say.

"What if there's more of them?" says Charlus, and I can see he's scared. "They'll overrun us."

"They're alone," I assure him. "We can let them drink at the new blast-hole that we've made."

Mother decides the matter. "I want to study them," she says.

I lower my blaster but Charlus keeps his aimed at their heads. I walk forward, keenly curious about these wild sapiens, using my best mouth-word skills. I feel like a pioneer, a true explorer.

"Felicitations," I say, hoping that this is the right greeting word. "My name is Petra. We're a reconnaissance team from the airship *Celestis*. We can offer you water."

The primitives are staring at me in shock and bewilderment.

"Thank you," says the one with the crown, in quiet disbelief. "Thank you."

"You must put down your weapons," I say.

The taller sapien slowly puts down a pathetic knife. As my mother walks toward them, the younger, smaller boy slowly backs away. Mother picks up the knife and puts it in a specimen bag. Charlus trains his blaster on the one who wears the metal crown. Perhaps he is some kind of tribal prince.

180

"Petra," he says, "my name's Rye Tern, and this is Wren Apaluk. We thank you."

He's so polite! And what interesting names. I return his courtesy.

"This is Livia, our chief biologist, and Charlus, our scouting craft captain. We're from the airship *Celestis*." The sapiens look totally puzzled. The smaller one looks younger than me.

"Please, come this way." I lead them out of the long courtyard. My mother takes her camera off the tripod, filming the encounter. Charlus walks beside us with his blaster raised.

"Their clothes," says Mother, "the fabric looks like it's been made with some kind of rudimentary machine technology. Ask them about it."

They're wearing vaguely militaristic coats, like something from a history book.

"Livia would like to know about your clothes," I say to them in mouth-words. It instantly feels like a stupid thing to ask.

"What's wrong with our clothes?" the one called Wren asks defensively.

"Do you know if the fabric is machine woven?" I can't believe I'm asking this. These people are near-death with dehydration.

"They're just our uniforms," says the one called Rye Tern.

"Are you engaged in some kind of tribal warfare?" I ask. He looks puzzled. My questions are hopeless.

"We're refugees, from Brightland," he says. He points back toward the sea in a northerly direction.

"Charlus, lower your weapon," says Mother, who outranks him. "I don't believe they're any threat."

Charlus finally lowers his blaster and the smaller sapien grabs the taller, his chest heaving in relief. I hear something in low mouth-words that sounds like "thank fuck."

As we hear the scouting craft approaching, the sapiens look up into the fog, perturbed at the roaring noise. When the craft appears, they gaze at

181

it in wonder. As it lands beside the blast-hole, they start talking to each other, their voices raised in excitement.

"They're like the Light People," says the one called Wren Apaluk.

"There's civilization, here in the badlands," says the crowned one. "This is an incredible discovery, Wren."

"I expect they think we're gods," posits Charlus.

"I've seen this kind of thing before," muses Mother. "These primitives don't have high-level communication and our technology is too much for them to comprehend. They can't understand how we're communicating. I fear it won't take them long to interpret us as hostile."

"Just watch," Charlus warns me. "I bet we'll soon have trouble."

"Not if we communicate in a way they understand," I urge. I pity these sapiens heartily, scratching a living in this wretched place.

"Where are the rest of their people?" asks Mother.

"They could be surrounding us," says Charlus. "We must be prepared for an attack."

"They say they came by boat and they're alone," I say firmly.

Then the one called Rye Tern takes my breath away. He says, "There's a lad I know who's a pilot. He'd give his back teeth for a plane like yours."

His confidence throws me. And I think I must have misunderstood.

"A pilot?"

"He flies a Firefly," says the sapien. "But it's a piece of tin compared to this. Piper Crane would fall over backward to see the blueprints for your plane."

Do these primitives have air technology?

"This is just our scouting craft," I tell him. "Our airship is above. What's a Firefly?"

"It's a two-man plane."

I think this is incredibly exciting and Mother asks me to translate. When I tell her what Rye Tern has said, she's skeptical. "Show me their two-man plane," she says, "and then I will believe you."

Jem Kahinu and Tayla Cross disembark in their protective suits and I explain how we found the wild sapiens. Our engineers have no hesitation in helping the sapiens down to the water hole and giving them ship's flasks to drink from. The ragged pair are relieved almost to tears as they quench their thirst.

"Drink it slowly, soldier," says Rye Tern to the smaller one. "Too fast and you'll throw it up." The one called Wren Apaluk nods. They're both in terrible condition: skin blistered by the salt and sun, lips cracked, and the one with the crown has various wounds that look like they're infected. They need medical help as well as food and I can see that our engineers are also moved by their woeful plight. They greet them in low mouth-words and the primitives thank them over and over. The one called Rye Tern pours water over his head and face, washing away some of the dust and dirt. The younger one follows suit, almost laughing in relief.

"Thank Gala," he keeps saying. "Praise Gala."

"We can't abandon them here," I say to Mother.

"That's exactly what we're going to do," says Charlus.

"This mission is about reconnaissance, not contact," says Mother, agreeing with him. "We've already stepped over the mark. We can leave them some food and medical supplies, but you can't be sentimental, Petra."

The sapien Rye Tern stands, looking at me. He walks toward me and I notice that his striking eyes are full of some kind of revelation.

"You have songlight," he says.

I am puzzled. "Songlight?"

"I couldn't think how you were all communicating with each other. I thought you must have some kind of radiobine in those suits. But it's songlight. Are you Aylish?" he asks. Hope is shining in his eyes.

"What is songlight?"

"Your thoughts connect, without the need for words," he explains.

I am amazed. "He knows we have truevoice," I tell my mother.

"Petra, I am like you," says Rye Tern. "I have it too."

"But you don't," I say in mouth-words. "If you had a voice like ours, I'd hear it."

He is full of emotion. "In Brightland, songlight is forbidden. It's persecuted, that's why I fled. My people put this lead band around my head and it has stifled me. Please," he says, his voice shaking. "Can you help me get this band off?"

"He's suffering," says Wren Apaluk, coming to his comrade's side. "Please, help him to be free."

I translate what they have said as best I can, deeply affected by what he has said.

"That's not possible," says Charlus. "He must be some kind of trickster. They've had their water. We should leave as soon as we can."

Our engineers have set up the hose. It disappears into the fog. Water is now being pumped to *Celestis*.

"Let me see," says my mother, the scientist. She walks toward the ragged sapien, giving me the camera.

"Livia wants to look at your crown," I say. "She doesn't mean you any harm. She's my mother."

Rye Tern lets Mother examine his thin metal crown.

"It's lead," says Mother. "It's been crudely welded to his skull," she continues. "It must be causing him great pain."

We look at one another. Every eximian knows that proximity to lead affects our ability to communicate. It's a substance that we never use. There's none of it aboard our ship.

"We have to help him," I plead.

"A laser should remove it," says Mother, before Charlus can interrupt.

She gives the engineers a clear order. The engineer called Tayla Cross goes into the craft and returns with a laser. The smaller wild sapien is supporting Rye Tern and it touches me deeply to see their affection. I wonder if they might be brothers.

Tayla Cross instructs Rye Tern to lie down. I explain what the laser is and what it will do in the simplest terms. Rye Tern nods his understanding.

"Thank you," he says. "Thank you."

He lies in the dust and the younger boy takes his hand. Carefully, Tayla Cross applies the laser and the sharp beam soon cuts through the metal. It must be hard for the wild sapien to bear the heat. His scalp must be burning but he endures it. I pour water over the lead crown, trying to keep it from searing his skin.

At last, the job is done and the lead band is sliced in two. Rye Tern sits up. Tayla Cross helps him take the band off and he thanks her over and over.

We all hear it. Low at first, but growing in intensity. His voice, his beautiful, deep truevoice.

His first utterance is a cry of love.

"Elsa! Elsa. Wherever you are, I am free." I feel an ache of loss—and then Rye Tern is crying with relief and gratitude. The boy Wren Apaluk hugs him tight. I think that I am crying too.

My mother looks pale with shock and wonder.

"This changes everything," she says.

Rye Tern is an eximian.

27 ✳ RYE

We sit in the back of their aircraft, making the seats dirty with our coats. I hear a roaring sound and the whole thing rises straight up from the ground. Fuck, it's incredible. I'm losing my guts with fear, but I'm not telling Wren that.

"Are you sure we're not dead, Rye, are you sure?" Wren asks, laughing in delighted terror.

"My guts are telling me that we're alive," I tell him. "I've just left them on the ground."

The one named Petra turns round and smiles at us, reassuring.

"It's my maiden flight too," she says. "I've only used the simulator up to now."

We smile back. Neither of us knows what she's talking about. Wren begins to relax his shoulders and I sense his deep joy and relief. I look at the white-suited people strapped into the seats in front of me. This unbelievable piece of the future must be everyday business for them. A scouting craft, they call it. They look as relaxed as I'd be on a cart.

What must they think of us? We might look like filthy, cockroach-bitten cavemen, but I want them to know that we're more than that. I thank them again in songlight but the tall, skinny lad looks round at me.

"Keep it calm for a while, okay?" he says. "I need to concentrate."

I apologize. My songlight must be a spark shower of uncontrollable emotion.

The one whose name is Petra speaks in support of me. "He can't help how he feels," she says. "He's been cruelly silenced. Can you imagine such a thing? It's barbaric." She turns and looks at me. Her eyes, through her visor, are full of outrage and compassion.

"Who did that to you?" she asks.

"Save your story for the airship, young man," says the woman named Livia.

It's strange that Wren can't hear any of our songlight conversation. He's talking with the other crew members, the non-Torches, asking them how far away their airship is.

"You'll see it ahead, when we get through the fog," says the woman who took my band off. I will love this woman forever for what she did for me. I ask her for her name.

"Tayla Cross," she tells me. "This is Jem Kahinu."

"Thank you, brother," I say to Jem, and I warmly shake his hand. He seems surprised and pleased—but afterward, I notice him cleaning his hand with gelatinous stuff.

We're rising fast, almost vertical—the strangest sensation. Petra turns round again, speaking aloud, beaming a smile at both of us. "I was so nervous this morning," she says, her voice sounding tinny through the visor. "But can you imagine? We've made contact with intelligent primitives and found a natural eximian. This is an incredible day." There's a sweetness to her enthusiasm that's so disarming that it takes me a moment to realize that she's called us primitives. And what was that she described me as? A natural what?

"I'm sure we're not looking our best," asserts Wren, "but we're not primitives."

Petra seems mortified at this. "No, of course not. I used the wrong mouth-word, forgive me."

Fog clings to the craft's windows. It's disorienting, like we're flying blindly in a thick gray soup. But then, all of a sudden, we rise through it into bright, dazzling sunshine. We're above the cloud bank. A rolling sea of soft white stretches out as far as the eye can see. Above us, the blue heavens trail with wisps of cirrus cloud. We're in a world where people don't belong.

Piper leaps into my mind. This is what he dreamed of when we were boys. This is what he was yearning for, this magical, unfathomable sky.

Piper Crane . . . if you could see me now.

The scouting craft turns in a wide circle. And there it is. Their ship.

"Gala in heaven," says Wren under his breath.

It's as big as a battleship, made of a burnished alloy that glows in the sun like coppery steel. It looks as if it's kept afloat by—I want to say immense eggs, filled with some kind of light gas. In truth, it's indescribable; everything about it looks impossible. There's no sign of an engine, yet it hums with power.

"She's called *Celestis*," says Petra with pride, as if she's seeing it through our eyes and noticing its beauty.

"*Celestis*," says Wren, trying the sound of it in his mouth.

"Incredible," I say. I start asking what I hope are intelligent questions and I don't use songlight. "Where have you come from?"

"Sealand," says Petra, which leaves us no wiser.

"Where are you going?" asks Wren.

He's trying to draw Tayla Cross and Jem Kahinu into the conversation too but they defer to Petra, letting her do all the talking. Petra tells us Sealand is in the Southern Hemisphere and that *Celestis* is on a voyage of scientific discovery.

"How is it powered?" I ask.

"You'd have to have a good grasp of physics to understand," says the tall lad who's flying us.

"It's like a town," says Wren in wonder, "a floating town."

As we get closer, I see two stories of high windows and a deck at the bottom, made almost entirely of glass. Inside, there are people working. Some of them look up from their tasks, watching us approach. Their plane—scouting craft—heads toward the stern of the mighty ship, where great metal doors are opening to the sky.

The skinny pilot brings in the scouting craft. My stomach turns upside down with fear as he knocks against the metal doors and we fall back and plummet. I feel a sharp spike of terror and Wren inhales in fear. The skinny lad steadies the craft and has to make his approach again. I notice the man called Jem Kahinu rolling his eyes in grim frustration, flashing a look at Tayla Cross. I imagine how easy would it be to lose control of this thing and spin to the ground like a sycamore key. Wren leans over and grips my hand. We're both shit-scared.

This time, the skinny lad doesn't fuck it up and we enter a large hangar in one piece. The great doors close behind us, cutting us off from the dazzling sun and the dangerous blue-cloud paradise outside.

I sense a growing hum in the air and at first I think it's some kind of turbine noise, but as we exit the craft, I realize it is songlight.

"The ship is full of Torches," I say to Wren in wonder. "I can hear them all. I can hear them." Wren grips my arm, aware of how moved I am.

"You can be yourself here, Rye. You can truly be yourself."

I nod, choked with emotion. Using my songlight is so beautiful, so incredibly freeing. I realize that in Northaven, I never really fully let it go. Even with Elsa, there was always something in me that was constrained. The constant fear of capture was never far away. I think Elsa had more freedom on the sea and so her songlight grew more dynamic than mine. Mine was always reined in like a wild and dangerous animal. To have this kind of freedom after my long incarceration under that lead band . . . I don't know what to do with myself. I could curl up and weep.

"Get a grip of yourself, soldier," says Wren. "They think we're primitives. Let's show them who we are."

I pull myself together and we walk out of the craft with as much dignity as we can muster. The hangar is bigger than our Elders' Hall. The walls are made of the same burnished alloy as the outside of the craft and the floor is rubbery jet black. Uniformed engineers secure the scouting craft in place and I notice that some of them are women. Everyone is gazing at us with a kind of friendly curiosity.

"See how the women are all working with the men," says Wren. "It's like they respect each other." I can feel how this pleases him. "This must be a place with no Third Wives."

There's a small group of people descending a staircase in smart suits made of a fabric I have never seen before. They're communicating in songlight so quickly that I cannot keep up. It seems that they're not keen on our arrival but I can't decipher why. It's too long since I used my songlight. It feels clumsy and inept.

One of the approaching Torches is a thickset man with shoulders like an ox. He's clearly some kind of leader, as everyone defers to him. He is angry with the woman called Livia—and gradually, I pick up on what he's saying.

"This is not the purpose of our mission. We were specifically instructed not to make first contact."

"Bradus, you must understand. This is an exceptional—"

Livia tries to interject but the man carries on.

"Not only have you gone against a direct order—you've brought wild sapiens onto *Celestis*, endangering us with their pathogens."

Livia points at me. "That one speaks with truevoice. I don't know how—so I have acted in the name of science."

She describes to the thickset man how she found us and I can hear her songlight going further, as if she's choosing to open the story up to every Torch on the ship.

Wren turns to me, puzzled. "What are they saying?" he asks.

"Their songlight is too fast," I tell him. "I can't follow it. They keep calling me eximian. I think that's their word for Torch. That man there is called Bradus. He thinks we'll give them pathogens. He called us wild sapiens."

"What does that mean?"

"I don't know but it's something inferior, that's for sure."

Wren looks down at his salt-stained coat. "Well, look at the state of us," he says. "Can hardly blame them. I wish they'd speak with their mouths, though, so we can all understand."

I'm not surprised Wren is feeling excluded. I look at the other people on the deck, the ones without songlight. They're waiting patiently, neither interjecting nor asking the Torches to translate. Why not? It must be a sore aggravation.

190

"Rye Tern," says Livia to me in strong songlight, "tell us where you're from."

"Brightland," I say. "We're refugees."

"Don't use your mouth-words," instructs Petra. "Mother would like you to use your truevoice. Commodore Bradus needs to hear it."

"They want to hear my songlight," I say to Wren, filling him in, so he understands my silence. Then I address the austere man as clearly as I can, using my songlight to describe in images how Wren and I survived the seas and came to be in the cockroach city. "We were trying to get to Ayland," I tell him. "We thought the Aylish might help us—but we found you." I make a polite bow.

"We thank you for your hospitality," says Wren, and he bows too.

All their songlight has fallen silent. It's as if the whole ship is listening. The man Bradus looks shocked to the core.

"This is a discovery that profoundly alters our knowledge of the Earth," says Livia as if she's pressing home her point. "It's exactly what this mission is about."

Bradus is quiet for a moment. "Why did you bring the sapien?" he asks. I think he must be referring to Wren.

"They're inseparable," says Livia.

"We won't be parted," I say firmly in songlight.

There's an awkward silence among our hosts. Then another man enters the hangar. I know immediately that he is their leader. He walks with a kind of easy authority that only the very powerful have and his uniform is unmistakably that of a commander. He has a neatly trimmed beard, just beginning to turn silver, but the most compelling thing about him are his eyes. He beams them on me, and I feel his keen curiosity.

"I am Air Admiral Xalvas," he says to me in vivid, charismatic songlight. "Tell me your name." I've never felt a keener desire to impress a man.

"Rye Tern, from Brightland," I tell him. "This is my brother, Wren Apaluk."

"Rytern," says the Air Admiral, running my names together as if they are all one word. "Is Brightland your name for the wilderness below?"

"No," I tell him. "We stole a boat to escape and sailed a long way to be free. We're refugees."

"You stole a boat?" he asks, smiling. "So we have thieves here?"

"You have two very grateful people, sir. We would have died down there, without your crew."

"Why did you leave your Brightland?" he asks.

I find myself stuck for the right way to begin. It's so fucking painful. How do I explain a merciless system like ours to these principled explorers? And how do I tell Wren's story? I can't stand here talking about him in songlight, while he looks puzzled and excluded by my side.

"It's a long story," I say, in mouth-words.

The girl called Petra comes forward. "Admiral, they're starving. They were dying of thirst when we found them. Please may they eat something?"

"We must put them in quarantine," says Livia.

The Air Admiral nods slowly. "Rytern," he says in songlight, regarding me. "When you have quarantined, I'd like you to join me for communion."

I don't know what this is but my songlight gushes incoherently, telling him that I'd be honored.

The Air Admiral nods at Wren. "Welcome, young man," he says.

"Thank you, sir," replies Wren, who looks as dazzled as I am.

Livia fires some instructions at her daughter, too quickly for me to pick up. Petra walks forward, explaining to us both in what she calls mouth-words.

"We want to treat your injuries," she says, "and we must isolate you both to check for any illnesses you might be carrying. Our immunities will be different so we need to run some tests. We can inoculate you, which will keep you safe. It shouldn't be longer than a day or so. Then you can mix with us."

"Bring him to medical," says Livia to Petra, preparing to leave us.

"What about Wren?" I ask.

"Tayla Cross will take your companion to the sapien wing. He'll be well looked after there."

"I told you we won't be parted," I say.

Commodore Bradus is impatient. "If there's a problem, we can take you back to the ground."

I desperately don't want to get off on the wrong footing with these people and I sense that Wren feels the same.

"We should do as they ask," he says. "They could help us in so many ways. And look at them," he continues. "There are no chrysalids here and no Third Wives. We're safe."

I'm reassured by this and we prepare to part.

"As long as you're not scared without me, soldier?" Wren smiles.

"I'll try to be brave," I reply.

"This way," says Petra, gesturing for me to accompany her. And that's when I notice her perfect figure and the light in her eyes.

"Behave yourself, soldier," Wren says in farewell. I hug him.

"I'll see you soon, brother," I say as Tayla Cross escorts him away.

I don't know why I'm feeling so concerned. These are kind and civilized people.

And Wren Apaluk can look after himself.

28 ✳ NIGHTINGALE

I'm on Bailey's Strand. A figure is dancing on the sand, a girl in a choir-maiden's dress, carefree, joyful. I run toward her.

"Lark," I cry.

The girl turns and I stop. It's Swan.

Her hair is natural. She wears no Siren's band. There is no damage, no darkness on her soul.

She says, "You're the first to truly love me," and she pulls me toward her.

My body feels beautiful in her hands. We are kissing passionately—and I force myself awake.

What was that?

I sit up, staring at the windows, scrambled.

Morning light is streaming in. I get out of bed and plunge my face in water, trying to wash the dream out of my head. But the confusion will not leave me.

What did it mean?

Songlight can't penetrate dreams, so Swan isn't manipulating me, the way she has mind-twisted Starling Beech. The dream has come from me alone. Why?

Desperate for a friend, I go to find Cassandra Stork. She is blankly preparing breakfast.

"What's wrong with me?" I ask her, knowing that she can't reply. "Why did I dream something I don't feel?" It leads me to a bigger, more painful question. "I used to dream like that about you. I dreamed you loved me, Cassandra—why?"

Cassandra blankly offers me a seat at the breakfast table. I don't take it. I pace the room, trying to keep my energy from exploding through the walls. My life has always been so confined. I was cloistered by illness in our little apartment and now I'm caught in the snare of Swan's rooms. I have hardly met anyone my own age, certainly not any boys. No wonder I dream about girls—they are all I know. The only men I ever saw were my father's friends from the Inquisitor Station and I was scared of them all. Cassandra came into my life like a bright, exotic bird and I adored her with all my heart. I thought of her all the time and I longed for her to love me. When Lark was grieving over Rye, I recognized exactly how she felt. She was bereft of love.

Did I dream of Swan because my life is loveless? Cassandra pours me out a cup of tea. I can't stand it and I stop her.

"I'm sorry to enter your mind without permission," I say, "but I think I'm going mad here in these rooms and I need you."

I work my way into the tissue of her cortex. I'm going to fix this girl because I need her to talk to me. Soon I'm in the landscape of mist and I'm caught up in the harrowing fragment of memory that plays over and over in her damaged psyche—the Chrysalid House. I'm hiding in the cupboard. I am Cassandra, being dragged out by orderlies and pulled into an operating room. Ruppell looms over me—then I'm back in the cupboard and the trauma repeats.

There must be a way to access other memories, to make a link between this fragment and who Cassandra used to be. I concentrate my light but still, the same dreadful moment plays.

Cassandra grows restless. Perhaps she can sense my intrusion.

Even this would be a step forward.

I release her. "You have to help me," I say. "I don't know what else to do."

She blandly adds milk to the cup of tea.

"One day," I tell her fiercely, "you'll know yourself again. You'll realize what they did to you. And you will throw that tea against the wall."

Cassandra holds out the cup and saucer. I pause before I take it, lonely and defeated.

"Thank you very much," I say.

Cassandra blinks. She gathers up my laundry and exits to the little room behind Swan's bed.

I know why I had that dream.

Zara Swan has made herself the morning and the evening of my life. She fills my consciousness, even now, when she's not here. I have no illusions about her character. She's a self-serving bully and she's dangerous to me. But something in the dream was true. I love her, for all that she has suffered. That's the messy and confusing truth. Swan uses me, she kidnapped me, *she hit me*. But she fascinates me and the damage in her breaks my heart.

This love is bad for me in every way.

I put on the radiobine, hoping its noise will provide me with distraction— but Swan is giving her address. There's no respite—she's *everywhere*. Her gorgeous voice pervades the room.

"Lord Kite told me this morning that the first principle of diplomacy is to listen," she says. "I will go and meet with the Aylish today, not to talk peace—that is a job for our wise Lord Kite—but in this spirit of listening."

I put my hand up to my cheek and feel the risen skin where she struck me.

"I won't forget what the Aylish have done to us," Swan continues. "When I walk in to meet them, I will take with me the ghosts of my parents and my sisters, the ghosts of all the loved ones you have lost. There can be no peace without atonement, without reparation for their deaths." She ends on this strong warning.

I'm sure that Eminence Alize is listening too.

I'm about to turn the machine off when a news bulletin begins.

A masculine voice tells us that Heron Mikane and his unhuman Second Wife are still on the run with the Aylish fugitive. Men are urged to join the hunt for them. They're known to be in the Greensward. A very large reward is offered for their capture.

I'm about to reach out to warn Lark—but there's a hard moment of static and another voice cuts in on the radiobine.

"This is councillor Raoul Harrier." It's a voice that thrills me. "Peregrine was poisoned because he wanted peace." Harrier wastes no time as he takes

196

over the airways. "The war with Ayland could end tomorrow and we could all live free from persecution. But Kite has a fatal dream of triumph and his dream will cost us dear." Harrier leaves a momentary pause—and I feel his words taking hold of the whole city. "I am accused of our Great Brother's murder. I am innocent. Ask yourselves who's gained most from Peregrine's death. Look there, and you will find his kil—"

Harrier's voice cuts out. There's static, then a marching band.

I pace the room, unable to keep still. Harrier has accused Kite of murder, in all but name. His vision is alive—a peaceful Brightland, free from persecution. How did he take over the radiobine? He must be working with others. My mind whirs—the Brightlinghelm resistance. The thought is incredibly exciting to me. I wonder how many people are also pacing in their homes now, aware that a sea change has just happened?

There is an alternative to Kite.

I long to contact Harrier and tell him I am on his side, his friend in the palace.

I send my songlight up, honing my mind on the great throng of the city. Usually, my mental energy is taken up with blocking people's thoughts out. Now I open myself to the whole cacophony.

Harrier, where are you?

I remember how I crept into his mind the night that Peregrine died. Can I make the same connection again? And if I'm able to reach him, what shall I say?

A great stillness comes over me as I search.

Attic. I see an attic room, a radiobine transmitter, a man bent over a table, laughing at his success. There are others present; I see them as shimmers. But Harrier is clear. I recognize his laugh. I become aware of his breathing, of his inner life: his determination, his hatred for Kite, his fears for his family. And he senses me.

"Mind-twister," he says. "What do you want?"

Harrier doesn't have songlight but he is sensitive to mine.

"I'm your friend," I whisper. "I would help you in any way I could."

"It's a Siren," says another voice in the room. "Protect yourself, Raoul, cast it out."

Suddenly I become aware of strong songlight. Harrier is with a Torch and this Torch will fight for him. I withdraw immediately.

I take in my breath and let it out, processing what I've just done.

My body might be trapped here but my mind can be useful.

I send my songlight soaring high, searching for Lark. I have to share what's happened.

I find her on a rope bridge, high over a deep ravine.

"Lark," I say excitedly. "Harrier took over the radiobine. He's working with insurgents in Brightlinghelm. They're planning something, I'm sure of it."

This fills Lark with hope—but the rush of my songlight unbalances her. She clings to the flimsy bridge and glances down into the ravine. I feel a wave of gut-churning dizziness go through us both. It's a horrible drop and the bridge is in a dreadful state. She inches her way forward.

"I'm so sorry," I say. "I shouldn't have come. But I had to tell you."

She regains her balance and moves on, step by careful step. "This is good news," she says. "When we get to Brightlinghelm, Harrier might help us." At the far side of the bridge, I see Kingfisher anxiously waiting for her, his arms outstretched. I fall silent as she negotiates the last few feet. He grabs her, pulling her to safety. I sense the emotion between them. She's fallen for him in spite of herself, in spite of the pain she carries for Rye. She loves them both. Her heart has just expanded.

"There's one more thing I must tell you," I say. "Kite has put a price on your heads."

Lark takes this in. "I hope it's a lot," she says.

"People know you're in the Greensward—they might come hunting."

Lark walks ahead, leaving Kingfisher to help the others. Bel begins to cross the bridge.

"Tell me how you are," she demands. "Something's wrong, what is it?"

198

"Nothing." My loneliness bubbles up—but how can I burden Lark when she is in such real and present danger?

"I had a troubling dream about Swan, that's all," I say.

Lark pauses. "That woman spends all day churning you up. No wonder she's stalking though your dreams."

"I wish I were like you." I sigh.

"How?"

"Your heart is so clear."

"Clear?" laughs my friend. "Nightingale, I've never been more confused in my life."

Suddenly I feel Swan's songlight, like the wind tinkling through a crystal chandelier. "I must go," I cry, and I immediately retreat.

My anxiety rises. Swan will regard everything I've done since I awoke as one betrayal after another. Cassandra, Harrier, Lark, I've used my songlight in their service. Now I must devote myself solely to her.

I sense her, walking through the palace. She's in her brittle, ebullient mood. I check my appearance at the mirror, tying my hair into a chignon, trying to look more adult, more her equal, preparing for her entrance to the room.

Starling Beech escorts her in and she asks him to wait outside. Then she smiles at me wickedly, flexing her songlight, reveling in her liberty.

"Kite's freed me. He's charged me with finding Harrier," she says.

"Don't do it, Sister, please."

"Did you hear him on the radiobine? Harrier accused our lord of murder. He wants us to capitulate to Ayland."

I can feel Kite's influence in everything Swan says. "Kite hasn't freed you at all," I remark. "He's just let you off your leash."

Swan goes quiet. I can't bear to think of the night she has just spent with him. I don't know how she can endure it.

"Wash me," she says to her ladies. "Get me clean." They go to prepare her bath and Swan looks at me.

"It's hard to spend time with him and not be infected," she says. "Sometimes I find myself thinking like Kite does—because that's how I survive." I sense that the better side of her is fighting for ascendance.

"Harrier would free you," I remind her. "He'd close the Chrysalid House."

The brittle whine fades from Swan's songlight. "I won't do Kite's bidding," she says. "He can find Harrier himself." But it frightens me how changeable and mercurial she is.

I catch her looking at the welt on my cheek. "I want us to forget about last night," she tells me guiltily. "It's in the past and we've moved on."

I'm not sure I can let her brush it away so easily.

"I can't control what you do, Zara," I say. "But if you hit me again, I'll withdraw from you forever." I state this as a simple fact. "I'd rather give myself up to Kite than be hit by somebody I love."

Swan swallows hard and turns away. I can feel shame pumping through her and I'm glad.

"So you love me, then," she says quietly.

My lips stay silent. And my heart feels sore. Swan follows her ladies into her bedchamber, leaving me standing in confusion.

I have to grow up and get out of this place.

I will find out who I am. And I will find a better love.

29 ✳ RYE

People keep their distance as Petra leads me through the airship. They peer at me from doorways and I hear songlight in hushed whispers. Occasionally, someone retreats with an embarrassed smile, as if I might be toxic with disease.

One corridor is lined with huge dramatic artworks. They must have been made by a very great artist and are so vivid they seem to burst out of the walls. I stop and stare. They tell the story of a planet with two tiny, odd-shaped moons. People are arriving in crafts, sailing through a starscape that looks fully three-dimensional. A settlement is built and lines appear from one moon to the other, encircling the planet and protecting it. The next drawing shows a settlement with domed buildings and crops growing all around it. Then farther down the corridor, there's a shattering event as one of the moons explodes and some kind of storm engulfs the whole planet. I'm not sure what I'm looking at. Perhaps it's a creation myth—or a destruction myth. I can feel the artist's emotion as he conveys the loss. There's a sea of faces looking at the exploding sky. As if everyone knows they are going to die.

"That's Terra Nova," says Petra in songlight, making the subject of the art no clearer. "An asteroid hit one of the moons and the gravitational field we had created failed. The atmosphere was compromised and almost all our people died in solar storms. It happened when I was a child. Air Admiral Xalvas and his son Charlus are survivors. They were in one of the last ships that made it back to Sealand. There's nothing but ruins on Terra Nova now. It's a dead planet once again."

So these incredible people have been into space and have come back, carrying an unfathomable loss?

"Where were you when this happened?" I ask Petra.

"At home, in Sealand City," she says. "I never got to go to Terra Nova but my parents did a long tour of duty there." She shows me the final etched picture: a city on a large ocean island, a place with domed towers. "For many thousands of years Sealand was just our base camp on Earth. Now it's our capital. It's all we have left." These elegant artworks make our murals in Northaven look like a child's daubings. I try to take in what Petra has told me. None of it seems possible.

"Have you ever heard of Lark?" she asks, out of the blue.

"Lark?" I turn to her, puzzled.

"A few days ago I heard the faintest songlight coming from the north," she tells me. "I didn't think it was possible but the cry was so poignant. Is Lark one of your gods, like Gala?"

"It's a bird's name," I say, puzzled. "A lot of people have bird's names in my country. My family's named for a seabird, a tern. They say it harks back to the Age of Woe. We thought that all birds would die out and when they began to return, it was a sign of recovery, so we value them."

"Lark could be a person, then?"

"Yes."

Petra mulls this. "My friend Garena would love to talk to you," she says. "She's our archivist. She's writing the chronicle of our voyage and you're a major piece of news, Rye. No one can believe you're here."

She smiles again and I am dazzled. I stop looking at the art.

We turn down a corridor, then another narrower one into a clinical wing where everyone is quickly putting on body-covering white suits with glass visors. I'm an object of much curiosity. The medical staff are friendly and welcoming but they're treating me a bit like a dirty, untamed bear cub. I'm almost expecting to be shown to a straw-lined pen but Petra leads me to a cabin with a glass door. There's a clean white bed and a finely crafted chair.

"I hope you'll be comfortable," she says.

"It looks like heaven," I tell her. I take off my filthy soldier's coat and dump it on the bed. I'm dismayed when a dead cockroach falls out of the sleeve.

Gala, there's a mirror behind her and I see my face for the first time since I left Northaven. I look like a bog-man, risen from the dead. I turn away from her, ashamed. What must these sleek people think of me? No wonder that man Xalvas had compassion in his eyes. I am a pitiable wretch.

"You've been injured," says Petra. And I realize that she's looking at the unhealed arrow wound on my shoulder. It's been a minor pain compared with the ceaseless torment of the lead band but in recent days it's been hurting like a criminal and seeping pus. I feel even more ashamed.

"I got shot with an arrow."

"How?"

"I was escaping."

"From what?"

"A place called the Chrysalid House."

"I'd like to hear."

Those eyes of hers. So intense. I want to tell her. I want to pour it out for her, my whole story. She holds her songlight ready, waiting.

"You're dismissed, Petra," says Livia as she enters the cabin. It seems like a strange way for a mother to talk to her daughter. Livia walks up to me and Petra backs away toward the door, allowing a man to enter the tiny space—some kind of doctor, I presume.

"Now," says Livia. "Where do we start?" She looks to the doctor who has come in with her. "I think a full brain scan." Livia reels off a list of instructions in songlight so fast that I cannot follow them. The doctor nods, agreeing. Livia is clearly in charge.

"How long will it take you to get his genome?" she asks the doctor.

"Are you going to dissect him," Petra interrupts, "like you did that cockroach?"

"I didn't dissect the cockroach," says her mother. "I eviscerated it. I only wanted its digestive juice. I want this sapien's genome."

"He's not a sapien," says Petra.

"We can't prove that until we've examined his genetics."

I don't know where my genetics are, but I won't let this woman anywhere near them.

"What's a sapien?" I ask suspiciously. "What's a genome?"

"Why don't you give him something to eat and make him welcome, before blinding him with science?" asks Petra, raising her voice.

"You don't overfeed starving people," says Livia impatiently, giving me a bar of something wrapped in foil. "They need small amounts, not a banquet. Too much food will make him sick." As I devour it, Livia shines a small bright light into my ears. "Good gracious," she says. "We need to scrub you clean before we can do anything."

"Stop treating him like a specimen," cries Petra angrily.

"I'd like to wash," I say. "I'm longing to be clean."

"Good," says Livia. "Get yourself in that shower."

I look around. I don't know what she means. What shower? Petra realizes my confusion. She leads me into the tiny bathroom and touches a silver button on the wall. Hot water immediately pours out in a rain-like spray.

"Take those filthy things off," says Livia, squeezing in. "Then we can ascertain what state you're in."

Is she expecting me to strip in front of her?

"I'd like some privacy," I say firmly.

Livia turns to her daughter. "Make yourself useful," she says. "Take his clothes to be disinfected and give them to Garena. We should keep them for the archive. Find him a clean suit."

I close the bathroom door on them both and I strip. My body is a mess of cuts and sores and insect bites. On my ribs, there's still a yellowing trace of the battering that Wheeler gave me back in Northaven. How long ago was that? The day I lost Elsa and my world fell apart. . . . It feels like a lifetime.

I step into the shower. What a sensation. The hot water feels so good. I think of our washing facilities at the barracks—a line of rusty taps spraying us with cold jets. This is so luxurious. Everything in this bathroom is

204

beautifully made and the lights, tucked into the ceiling, refract a comforting rainbow of colors. The soap smells of a night garden.

Gala, there is so much pain I have to wash away.

Maybe Wren is right and Gala does exist. I've never been comfortable with prayer—I used to laugh at all of Wheeler's prayers to Thal—but as the water pours down on me I thank Gala for her bounty. Maybe she has led us to these people for a reason. What if they can help not just Wren and me but all Torches and Third Wives?

When I am clean, I stand at the sink and examine the broken skin on my skull, where the lead band has done its damage. I see a comb and I gingerly pull it through my hair. I shave off the beard that has grown since I left Northaven, then I soothe my skin with some delicate oil that seems to be there for the purpose. I stare at myself, wondering who I am now.

Some extraordinary twist of fate has spared my life and put me on this ship with these remarkable, sophisticated people. My purpose becomes clear.

I'll tell them what happens to Torches in Brightland. I'll tell them the whole sorry tale, from the shaming post to the Chrysalid House. I'll tell them what the Brethren do. I'll get their help. They will bring their airship to Brightlinghelm.

And these eximians will wipe the Brethren out.

30 ✴ NIGHTINGALE

"This is going to be a very special treat," says Swan. "Wait till you find out where I'm taking you."

Starling Beech leads us on a route that I have never walked before, toward the north end of the palace. There is a tram waiting at the entrance. Starling has commandeered it for Swan's personal use and he looks deeply uncomfortable.

"What am I to tell Kite?" he asks her.

"Don't tell him anything," replies Swan.

"But he'll find out," says Starling anxiously.

"You're always so clever with things like that," says Swan, brushing him off. "Tell him what you like."

The tram takes us up the hill.

"I don't have a father, Kaira," says Swan in songlight. "But you do. Last night you said that you missed your papa. I thought you might like to see him."

I want to throw my arms around her. "Oh, Sister," I say in warmest songlight. "Thank you—you're so good!"

Swan is just astonishing. I never thought she would do something like this.

"I don't know what to say," I tell her. "Thank you, thank you." It's all I can do not to cry.

"There," she says. "I like to make you happy."

This is her apology for hitting me. It's real and it's meaningful and I am very moved.

"I love my sweet little dolly," she says aloud, holding me.

I think this remark is for Starling's benefit. I notice him glaring at us. He must feel totally excluded from our silent conversation and I see a cold look on his face. Is he jealous? Does he resent Swan's dolly? I hide this disturbing thought away as the tram climbs up to a forbidding building.

Swan kisses my cheek. She's all kindness and goodness—but I'm already fearing her next change of mood.

The prison is not a recent architectural innovation like the low, underground horror of the Chrysalid House. It's an old fortress, with tiny, barred windows facing the sunless north, away from the palace complex. A high wall runs around it and the tram stops near the heavy entrance gates.

The guards are stupefied to see Sister Swan. She's clearly never been near the place before. They fall over themselves to obey Starling's orders, opening the great doors.

The smell of a thousand unwashed men hits us.

Starling is anxious. "Kite will want to know why I brought you here," he insists as we wait. "I have to tell him something."

"Darling Starling," says Swan, soothing him. "I'm here looking for information about Brother Harrier. Tell him that."

I walk through the gates with bated breath.

My papa, my papa. I last saw Papa crying out my name, down on the esplanade, fighting his own men as they came to arrest him. He was helping me escape.

"You won't be able to speak to him, of course," says Swan in songlight. "Your father must believe you're a chrysalid, along with everybody else. But you may look at him for a short while."

"Our meeting won't be private?" I ask, crestfallen.

"Of course not. How would I arrange that? Starling's right, it's risky enough as it is."

I'm instantly full of misgivings. "But he can't see me like this," I say. "It would break him. I have to be able to speak to him, to—"

"Your songlight is hurting me," says Swan. "Will you please learn to control it?"

Before I can say more, the prison governor and his chief officers rush out to greet us, groveling their thanks to Swan for her courtesy in visiting. She says a few gracious words, praising them, on behalf of Lord Kite, for all the excellent work that they do.

207

"Lady Swan, how may I serve you?" asks the governor, with his hands in prayer, as if Swan is the great goddess Gala.

"I'd like to see the Inquisitor who was arrested recently," she tells them.

"I have a thousand criminals, dissidents, and madmen here," he fawns. "Do you have his name?"

"Sol Kasey," I tell her in songlight.

"Sol Kasey," repeats Swan.

"It's best we take you to the exercise yard," the governor tells her, ushering us closer to the overpowering smell. "The interrogation rooms are, well, they're not fit for any lady, never mind the most radiant Flower of Brightland."

"I have to reveal myself to him," I say to Swan in songlight. "Papa has to know that I'm all right."

"He can't know about you, Kaira. He'd be a danger to us both."

"But he'll think I'm a chrysalid."

"I'm doing my best," she says, and her songlight flashes with irritation. "If your father has any intelligence at all, he'll realize why I've brought you."

Swan really hasn't thought this through—but it's too late to say anything else. The governor is already leading us into a dismal exercise yard. He's so happy she's come, he says. The prison desperately needs more space, more rations. The plumbing is broken, men are starving, overcrowding is so bad that things have reached a breaking point. He fears riot, he fears disease. He's sorry to trouble her serene presence with . . . Swan nods but I can tell she's not listening. In truth, I'm barely listening either. My heart is thumping in anticipation.

Papa. My papa.

The thing to do is to hide behind Swan. That way, he won't see that I'm a chrysalid. A door opens and two guards bring a man into the exercise yard. At first I think this can't be Papa, he's so thin and his face is hidden under an unkempt beard. But he still wears what's left of his Inquisitor's uniform and when he looks up at us, I see my papa's eyes. At first he's blinking, dazzled in the light. He stares at Sister Swan in awe, wondering why on earth he has been brought before her. He makes a bewildered bow.

Gala, he looks so ill and crushed. Where is my proud, confident papa? He's like a shadow. Remorse hits me—I am responsible for his terrible decline. Having an unhuman daughter has brought him here. Papa looks fearfully at his guards, as if they might be about to stand him before the firing wall.

"Sol Kasey," improvises Swan. "Tell me what you know about Raoul Harrier."

Papa looks at her, wiping his watering eyes. "I know nothing, Sister."

"Lord Kite wants him for murder. Think harder."

"My Inquisitor station was bombed by a cell of insurgents," begins Papa haltingly. "We caught one of the men and under torture he said that he was part of the Greensward militia. We broke that informer and drained him dry. He never mentioned Harrier."

I don't want to know that my papa has tortured a man. It's too dreadful. I take an involuntary step forward and Swan immediately grabs me. Papa's gaze alights on me. I see him studying my figure, the gauze over my face, my spectacles.

"No," he says in shock. "No." He falls to his knees. A moan of distress escapes him. "Kaira!"

I try to tell him in songlight that I'm here, I'm not a chrysalid. But he cannot sense me.

"This is my punishment," he cries. "My girl, my child!"

I pour my songlight out. "Papa, I'm here, don't despair!"

Swan grips me harder, flinching in pain.

"You're hurting me!" she hisses in songlight. She turns to the governor. "The man's lost his mind. He's useless, take him away!"

"Kaira!" screams Papa. "Kaira!" Papa is dragged back to the barred door, his eyes on mine, his face a mask of agony. "Gala have mercy! Gala forgive me! Kaira!"

209

My name reverberates in the air as they lock the door behind Papa. I am stunned. I cannot move. This visit has been a senseless act of cruelty.

"May I bring you someone else?" asks the governor. "We have many suspects here who—"

"No," says Swan sharply. "I've seen enough. This place is giving me a headache!" She turns to leave.

My distress is so acute that I can hardly see where I am putting my feet. I know nothing of how we leave the dreadful prison. When we're back in the tram, I find that I am shaking with the effort not to cry.

"You hurt me," says Swan in songlight. "I did that to make you happy and you hurt my mind with your Torchfire, that dreadful, sickening power you have to cause people pain. I tried to do a kind thing. I let you see your father."

She wants my gratitude and I must hide this wrecking grief.

"I'm only sad because I couldn't tell Papa how wonderful you've been," I say, trying to calm my distressed songlight. "I couldn't tell him how you've helped me to survive. But I wonder if there might be a way to send him a message, letting him know that I'm still—"

"Do you want to get us both killed?" Swan's songlight is hot with vexation. "You're the most dangerous secret in the whole Brethren's Palace. No one can ever know about you. I don't want to hear another word about your papa or about that stenching prison."

I pull myself together as the tram makes its way through the palace complex.

There's a word for my uncontrollable songlight: Torchfire. If there's a word for what I can do, it means that somewhere, there must be others like me. This thought excites me.

We're going down to the esplanade, toward the Aylish ship, and Swan firmly changes the subject.

"This is going to be a day of treats for you, Kaira," she says. "I'm taking you to visit the Aylish. And I will be polite."

"Sister," I say. "You're wonderful." And half of me means it. I decide that

210

if I can't help my papa, at least I can help Kingfisher and the cause for peace.

When the tram comes to a halt, Swan walks briskly down the esplanade, pulling me after her, and our frilly white dresses blow in the stiff river breeze. Starling looks on and I can feel his keen resentment. He should be accompanying Swan, not her dolly, her silly flapping moth.

As we approach the *Aileron Blue*, I am struck by its beauty. The white flag of peace looks so vulnerable as it flickers in the wind. Commander Alize is watching us from the deck with her crew. A young woman is at her side and they both come down the gangplank to meet us. Alize greets Swan warmly and thanks her for coming.

"This is Carenza Perch, our chief turbine engineer," she says.

She's the sensitive, the girl Kingfisher spoke of who is open to songlight. I have to find a way to communicate with her—but how, when Swan's possessive songlight is at liberty? I think of Kingfisher, how close he came to death. I must tell Renza that he lives, that he's coming.

Swan politely greets Alize and they exchange formalities.

"Who's your companion?" asks Alize, looking right at me. She does a good job at hiding her horror.

"Oh, she doesn't have a name," says Swan dismissively. "She's from the Chrysalid House, like all my ladies."

"How do you do?" says Alize, speaking to me as if I'm human.

"She won't understand you. She only follows orders. But I like to keep her with me. She's my dolly."

This is a crass and stupid thing to say and I can see that Alize is shocked. But Swan is not stupid. She just wants Alize to think she is.

That's clever.

"Come aboard," Alize says to me, "you're very welcome." She clasps my hand with her one good one. Alize has no songlight but a bolt of charge runs though me at her touch. It's so sincere. Having been ignored and despised by those in the palace for so long, I find it astonishing that someone should treat me with respect.

211

The Aylish crew has lined up in formation to meet Swan. She nods regally as she passes. They too stare at me with pity and horror, as if my existence as a chrysalid is an obscenity. I want the ground to swallow me up. Or rather, I want to turn to Alize and beg her to save me.

But my task is becoming clear.

As Alize and Renza show us their ship, it occurs to me that the Aylish could help Harrier. Maybe Harrier could help the Aylish.

Somehow, they have to be put in touch—Harrier and Alize. The idea is so frightening that I feel a sudden nausea. How? When?

"What's the matter?" asks Swan in songlight. "I can hear you all aflutter—what is it?"

I mustn't forget that her songlight is loose. I tell Swan it's nothing, a bad stomachache.

As Carenza Perch demonstrates how their new turbine technology works, I calm my racing heart. I will find my moment. I will speak to her.

At the end of the tour, Alize shows us to a low table laden with Aylish food and invites us to sit on cushions. I take my usual place, standing behind Swan.

"This boat is a tiny piece of Ayland," says Alize, "and it's our custom that everyone shares food." She speaks with quiet authority. "There's no hierarchy at our tables, that's why they're all circular. Zara, your young friend must sit with us."

"Sit," says Swan.

I sit awkwardly on a cushion. Swan lifts my gauze.

"Eat," she says.

I obediently pick up a shellfish and put it in my mouth. It's spicy and delicious. I notice how subtly Alize has started using Swan's name. She has become Zara, not Sister.

"We're most impressed with your radiobine technology," says Alize. "We have less need for it in Ayland as we have a network of Torches to communicate, but it has been entertaining us since we arrived. *Berney Grebe's Music Hour* is a delight."

212

"Yes," agrees Swan politely.

"I've been listening to your addresses too. You're a most compelling speaker."

"Thank you."

"What happened this morning?" she asks calmly. "Who's Harrier?"

Swan pretends she is not thrown. "He's a notorious ex-councillor, wanted by Lord Kite for the murder of Great Brother Peregrine."

"Did he do it?"

"He will be found and brought to trial. Justice will decide."

Alize remains silent, waiting to see if Swan says more. Swan meets her gaze.

"I'm curious about Lord Kite," says Alize.

Swan gives her nothing. She isn't going to make this encounter easy.

"I hope this question doesn't diminish you in your own right. You are clearly a very able politician—but is Lord Kite your romantic partner?"

Swan laughs, as if this is hilarious.

"This woman has some nerve," she tells me in piqued songlight. She turns to Alize. "What of your romantic life, Commander?"

"It's defined by monogamy, terribly dull," she says with a smile. "My husband and I have been together forever. Sometimes I think we're like a pair of compasses. I travel and he is my fixed point. We are apart but somehow, always joined."

"Why isn't he here, making peace?" asks Swan, who is clearly rattled by Alize's frank and open answer.

"He's with our youngest child, who's still at school."

"Why aren't you with your youngest child?"

"I wish I was," says Alize. "And when our nations are at peace, that's exactly where I'll be. But my partner is a teacher and I am a soldier. We each have our roles to play."

Swan doesn't know what to make of this. Perhaps the idea of a happy relationship is completely alien to her.

"Where did you grow up?" she asks.

"In Reem," says Alize. "My parents had a bookshop."

213

"Books," says Swan, almost wistfully. "I had books in Fort Abundance. I liked to read."

"Did you?"

"Yes, but of course my books were all removed when our Great Brother, in his wisdom, decided that girls and women didn't need to read. Our minds are better suited to practical tasks. You must have found that yourself? Your life as a commander has been very practical, I'm sure."

"What were your books as a child?" asks Alize, drawing the conversation back to Swan. "I wonder if we read any of the same things?" They talk on, sharing picture books and rhymes, myths and fairy tales. Swan is beginning to relax. There's nothing fake or politic about Alize and I can see Swan slowly unfurling little fronds of trust.

"Tell her what's close to your heart," I urge Swan in a whisper of songlight. "You may not get another chance."

Swan glances at me. She leaves a pause. "Peregrine was going to make you an offer," she says. "He wanted the Chrysalid House to close."

I'm so happy to hear Swan say this. She's thinking beyond her hatred of the Aylish and I beam her my support.

"The man Harrier said the same thing on the radiobine," replies Alize. "Perhaps Peregrine knew it would be our precondition for peace."

Swan turns steely. "You're not in a position to demand conditions," she says.

"No," replies Alize. "But I'm glad to know how Peregrine felt. And this is the first big thing that you and I agree upon. The Chrysalid House must close."

It makes Swan feel uncomfortable to agree with the Aylish on anything.

"Did you ever read *Arla, Queen of the Badlands?*" asks Alize.

"Oh yes," says Swan, in a glow of remembering. "It was one of my favorites. I kept that book when I lost all my others. I had it hidden under my bed."

"What's the name of the prince," asks Alize, "the one from Arkanzia, who Arla seduces?"

They talk on, steering the conversation away from the thorny subject of peace.

Carenza Perch keeps smiling at me with a painful look.

"Please, help yourself to more," she says.

How I hate being this silent, staring dolly. I hate this gauze and this white dress. I want to be Kaira Kasey.

I stand. All three of them stare at me.

I look straight ahead, my eyes wide and blank. "I need to go to the bathroom," I say to Swan in songlight, and I clasp my hands together over my abdomen. "I'm sick."

"My dolly is indisposed," says Swan, rising to attend to me. I'm taken aback by her genuine concern.

"Could Renza take care of her?" asks Alize. "Then you and I could keep talking. It may be the only chance we get."

Swan glances at Alize, seeing the truth of this. The turbine engineer springs to her feet. "I can help you, miss," she says. "Please come with me."

Swan's persistent songlight follows me. "What has made you unwell?" she demands.

I let her see that I'm in a cold sweat. "I'm so sorry. It's my papa. I'm upset."

Swan looks guilty. "Don't be gone for long. I need you by my side." As I exit the room, I'm glad to see her turn to Alize and say, "Sorze Separelli, your chief Torch. Tell me about him."

The cold sweat isn't about my guts. It's terror at what I'm about to do.

The chief turbine engineer leads me down a corridor to a small bathroom. She couldn't be more amazed when I pull her in with me and say in a hushed whisper: "My name is Kaira Kasey. I have a message from your comrade, Yan Zeru."

Renza Perch takes in her breath. She listens. And I tell her absolutely everything.

31 ✦ LARK

Our progress through the forest is torturously slow. We have been winding our way along a narrow mountain path between two huge, thickly forested peaks, each topped with snow. Curl uses her instincts and her memories to find our way and Heron religiously follows the needle on his compass.

"We need to get on to the Temple Line," says Ma. "We should be able to see it when we come out of this pass. From there, we can make faster progress down to Sherlham, a glade where two forest rivers join. Then we're only half a day's walk from Lake Lunen. That's where we must beg or steal a boat to take us down the Isis into Brightlinghelm."

"What is the Temple Line?" I ask.

"You'll know it when you see it," says Ma.

As we walk on, I look over at Kingfisher. After last night, I thought there would be some sort of sea change between us, some new, deeper connection. But all day, he has walked apart from me.

Why? What's in his mind?

We kissed in the darkness and I slept in his arms but when I awoke, he was not with me. He was seeing to Ma's shoulder, then helping Bel prepare us some food, then he walked ahead with Heron. Apart from lifting me off the rope bridge, he hasn't touched me all day and his conversation has been practical, polite. Now he walks along, talking to Heron and Ma about his boyhood in the prison camp. It's an intense conversation and all of them are fully absorbed.

He doesn't acknowledge me.

Maybe I'm imagining things. Maybe I'm unused to this kind of all-consuming passion and I'm being needy, seeking reassurance, wanting clarity about the way he feels. Everything between us has happened too fast. A worry starts to gnaw at me as I remember the Kingfisher I first met, the risk-taking Torch, the adored local hero, with his carefree smile and his pocket full of hearts.

Is he messing with me?

I try to push him from my mind but it's hard when he's so close.

Bel asks if we can rest. Her boots are bad, ill-fitting and full of holes, deviously chosen by her Inquisitor to impede her if she ever ran away. She's limping with effort.

"We mustn't rest for long," says Ma. "On the other side of that peak is the Tenmoth Zone," she says, pointing east. "We should pass it by as quickly as we can."

Bel doesn't argue with this. Nothing lives long in Brightland's zone of irradiance. I remember Nightingale telling me of it, back in Northaven. She said it looked like the rest of the forest, only it was a canker land. The plant life and insect life could survive but everything else got sick and slowly died.

I help Bel take her boots off and we wrap rags around her feet to protect them better. She catches sight of the cut on my hand. It's red raw today and as painful as a burn.

"That's going bad," says Bel. "It's full of forest dirt. You should get it seen to."

"It'll heal eventually," I assure her.

"It'll go rank," she tells me in a low voice. "It'll puff up and you'll lose your whole hand. It wants cleaning and stitching, or your sinews will rot."

This resolves me. "All right," I say. "Later."

We wind along the mountain path, mile after mile, as the sun moves across the sky. Bel is making every effort to be part of our team, hacking at the undergrowth where it blocks our path, offering a hand to Ma and carrying more than her share of our supplies. Kingfisher cuts her a sturdy stick, to help take the burden off her feet. He seems to be studiously avoiding my gaze. As the morning turns to afternoon, he walks with Bel, asking her about her training as a Siren. Bel is reluctant to talk about it at first but Kingfisher draws her into a long conversation.

Why won't he damn well look at me?

Ma and Heron are up ahead. I hesitate to join them, thinking that perhaps they only want each other's company, but they are talking about Harrier and I catch them up.

"I met him way back, when we were lads," Heron is saying. "Harrier was in the navy and I was assigned to his ship for a while. I liked him. But our paths never crossed again. I heard he got half his leg blown off at Fort Peregrine and then much later, I heard he'd joined the council. I never understood how he could stomach it."

"Stomach what?" I ask him, curious.

"Politics," says Heron. "It's a scoundrel's game."

"Nightingale believes in Harrier," I tell him. "He's fighting back against Kite—and that's good enough for me."

Ma turns and asks me about Nightingale. I tell them both our whole story, how Nightingale heard the anguish in my songlight when I was grieving for Rye and how she became my friend. Bel and Kingfisher come closer, listening as I describe how Nightingale was betrayed by a Siren and kidnapped by Swan.

"Swan has been using Nightingale's songlight for her own ends ever since."

"That poor girl," says Ma. "She's in a perilous position."

It occurs to me that since we left Northaven we have not had a moment, as a group, to properly assess our situation or discuss our course of action.

"When we get into the city, we have to help her," I say.

Heron looks thoughtful. "What does Nightingale know about Harrier? How many men does he have in this Brightlinghelm resistance?"

I tell him I don't know.

"If Harrier's to do anything lasting," he muses, "he'll need the armed forces on his side."

"Is that where you come in?" I ask him.

Heron shakes his head. "I made a vow after Montsan Beach that I'd lead no more soldiers to their deaths."

I take this in. "You're going to have to change your mind about that," I tell him.

"A vow is a vow," says Heron.

We're walking through the biggest trees that I have ever seen. Their trunks are taller and wider than our giant turbine towers in Northaven. We crane our necks to see their tops and the atmosphere around them is quite magical. But progress is slow. I can feel how desperately Kingfisher wants to be with his people. It must be dreadful to know that Alize has sailed into Kite's trap—and not be able to do anything about it.

"Nightingale will contact us again when she can," I tell him. "I know she'll find a way to help."

"She shouldn't risk herself," says Kingfisher, and he is almost curt.

I'm sure that what he felt for me last night was sincere and genuine. The best actor in the world could not have pretended that. Why has he withdrawn from me like this?

There's something he's not telling me.

We make our way down the steep mountain pass and every time I use my hand to steady myself, pain shoots through me. Damn this wound. This poxy cut will make it hard for me to hold a crossbow or shoot a rifle—all the things I may need to do when we get to Brightlinghelm.

Midway through the afternoon, the pass widens out into a long, densely forested valley. We are high enough up to see a straight line cutting through it—a vast road made of rocky, ancient concrete. It rears up out of the ground, straight and smooth, a huge construction of the Light People.

"The Temple Line," says Ma. "We should go faster now."

We climb up one of the ancient concrete legs. Someone has hammered steps into it, but it's precarious at best. My injured hand is screaming as I grip. I look down and see that the long cut is now full of rust. I join the others, who are all standing in awe, looking at the view.

It's beautiful. The Temple Line appears and disappears, rearing in and out of the ground from northwest to southeast for many miles. It's become a long, wide meadow, providing some relief from the rampant vegetation of the forest. Far away, deer are grazing, and all around our feet, flowers and grasses are rippling in the breeze. We walk and a sense of freedom begins to affect us. We're visible here and that is certainly a danger, but after the dense forest, we're relishing the open sky.

I purposefully walk next to Kingfisher, determined to cut through his weird reticence.

"It's some view, isn't it?" I say.

"Yes," he replies. And that's all I get. I want to ask him what's happened but I can't find the words and I know there's no point contacting him in songlight because there are others present who blah blah blah.

It's beginning to piss me off.

I walk on through the vast landscape at Ma's side, singing old Greensward songs with her, trying to forget about the Aylishman.

When the sun is low in the sky, the Temple Line takes a dip back down into the forest bed. There's a stream nearby where Ma lets us drink. We eat the remainder of our small store of food, sharing the last few bites between us.

"That's the end of our supplies," says Ma. "We'll have to find tonight's meal. Don't eat anything unless you show me first, not a single berry, understand? And only drink running water. If it's standing, don't touch it, not even to wash."

We bow to Ma's wisdom.

Bel looks as if she could sleep on her feet.

"I think we need to rest," I say. "Why don't we make camp here? Night will fall soon enough."

We decide to rest before hunting for food. Ma climbs a mighty tree with Bel. They curl up together on a bough.

Heron sits beneath them, keeping watch as usual. I suddenly feel like I can't walk another step and I let my legs go, sitting hunched next to him.

"Will you rest?" asks Kingfisher, staring at me pointedly. And I get the feeling that at last, he wants to talk to me.

"I'm not tired," I say, looking at him defiantly.

Two can play the cold-shoulder game. Let him see how he likes it.

Kingfisher nods slowly. He walks away and climbs a different tree.

Good.

Heron is peeling a birch rod.

"Why don't you sleep?" I ask him. "I'll keep watch."

"The last time I slept, I seem to remember you killed an Inquisitor and set a crowd of horsemen on our tail."

I ignore this. "If we get to Brightlinghelm," I say, "you have to find a way to get the armed forces on Harrier's side. You're a hero, Heron. The military will listen to you."

Heron looks at me long and hard. "Listen," he says. "Let's be real about what we can achieve. We're taking that Aylishman back to his people. And if there are insurgents in the city, we can try and join them. But there's only five of us, Elsa—"

"You're Heron Mikane," I say desperately. "You can make a difference. There has to be peace, there has to be an end to the Chrysalid House and to Peregrine's system of wives. You don't know what it's like to be a girl—or to be a Torch."

"So you want full-scale revolution?"

"Yes—everything has to change."

Heron pauses, taking in my strong opinions. "If we take on Kite, we're facing death, you understand?" he argues. "I don't want that fate for you, or for your mother. And I won't lead you there. I made an oath."

"There'll come a time when you have to throw that oath of yours to the wind," I tell him. "So you'd better be ready."

Heron looks at me as if to say, "We'll see about that." Then he turns back to his thin piece of birch, peeling the bark off layer by layer. My eyes fall on Kingfisher. He's lying stretched out like a mythical big cat on a branch opposite, listening.

"I'm strolling down to that stream," I say to Heron. And I walk away.

221

I sit on a rock and bathe my feet in a deep pool. I wash the filth out of the wound in my hand. The water's so delicious that I walk into it and wash myself clean.

Things were so different with Rye, where time had made us strong and deep. We had interwoven roots. Our world was Northaven and we held each other upright, like these trees. We grew together. So whenever we met in the flesh, it felt right and true, like it was meant to be.

The passion that I'm feeling for Kingfisher doesn't have those deep foundations. If I were to meet him in an ordinary way, would this still be happening? Or is it just the drama of fleeing from Northaven? I don't know what it is—but I feel as if a fever's running through me and even this cold water won't cool it down.

I decide that I'm going to confront him.

I turn—and I see he's come to find me.

"Elsa," he says. "How's the water?"

I stand in my petticoat, the water up to my waist. "Don't give me small talk," I tell him. "What is this? You kiss me every time you think you're going to die and then when the moment passes, you think you can ignore me?"

"No," he says. "What I feel for you . . ." I wait for more. "It's not what I intended."

I laugh at his impertinence. "Am I an inconvenience?"

Kingfisher wades into the water. He takes hold of my arms and, breaking his own rule, he uses his songlight. An intimacy suddenly opens up between us and it takes my breath away. In songlight, his feelings are strong and clear.

"I've been trying not to fall for you, not to give in to it. But there's no denying it."

"No denying what?"

I feel his deep and powerful emotion but he won't name it. "Last night, I let myself go. And I shouldn't have."

"Why not?" I ask. "We made a pact to live life to the full. Can't we just do that, for as long as we've got left?"

Kingfisher tells me there's another part to his mission.

In songlight, he shows me a vivid memory. He's on the deck of his ship, fighting with Swan, Torch against Torch, in a duel of power. I instantly recoil at the sight of her. Their struggle is unbelievably intense. He has her caught in his grip and I feel her attacking him, invading his mind. He counterattacks and they move from his ship to the Brethren's Palace in a locked embrace, from his space into hers. Kingfisher sees Swan's inner loneliness, her desperation, the fight of light and darkness at her core. He shows me her shaven head, her Siren's band, held in Kite's hand. He hears Kite insult and upbraid her and he sees the mastery that Kite has.

It moves him. Swan is so fucking beautiful, even in defeat. She tears into his mind and steals his name.

"Afterward," he confesses, "I couldn't stop thinking about her. I thought about nothing but Swan for days. I dreamed about her. I kept trying to reach her. Then . . ." He pauses. "Then I found this Brightling girl, washed up on a sinking boat, an orca swimming round her."

I wait for the end of this story. I don't think I'm going to like it.

"When we got back to Caraquet, I told Janella Andric about Swan. She said I must tell Sorze Separelli. So we contacted Reem."

I see what is coming.

"Separelli said that it was probable that Swan had also been profoundly affected. I described her wretched subjugation to Kite, and Separelli thought that Swan could be turned against him. Janella said I was the man to do it. Now that Peregrine's dead, it becomes even more vital that I try."

I take this in. "Your mission is to steal Swan's heart?"

Kingfisher leaves a silence. And in his silence is his answer.

A shocked laugh comes out of me. "That woman doesn't have a heart," I say.

"She does," he counters. "I felt it beating."

I'm about to leave the pool but he holds me back. "I overheard you talking to Heron and he's right, Lark. When we get to Brightlinghelm, the odds are stacked against us. I can try with Swan. It might even help Nightingale."

223

I hate to admit it but this last bit affects me.

"So where does it leave us?" I say, already knowing the answer. He can't risk Swan rifling through his consciousness and finding me.

For long moments, Kingfisher says nothing. Then he pulls me toward him.

I push him away and leave him in the pool.

"Don't mess with me," I tell him.

I grab my dress and walk into the woods.

Yan Zeru told me from the off that his mission came first. His heart is not free.

He's holding it back, as a gift for Zara Swan.

32 ✳ SWAN

My dolly seems much recovered when she returns to the ship's table and resumes her seat. I send out a concerned beam of songlight.

"Thank you," she beams back, "it was momentary. It has passed."

I made a promise to myself as I lay in Kite's bed last night. I will learn to love Kaira properly. I will become a better person. I have been acting upon this all day and it pains me that the visit to her papa was a failure.

In truth, I'm glad I don't have to take my ailing dolly back to the palace. In spite of all my preconceptions, I am enjoying my meeting with Alize. It's diplomatic but also personal. I've never known a politician like her. When I ask her a question, she gives an honest answer. I notice how relaxed she is as she sits cross-legged on the low cushioned seats. Gradually, I crumple up my dress and sit the same way. I don't feel the same need to perform as I do when I'm among men. And our conversation is different as a result—deeper. I have always been the only woman of note. But Alize is my equal.

"The apology you gave me when your ship arrived," I tell her, "the scroll signed by your highest parliament, I didn't receive it very graciously."

"We sprang it on you," says Alize, with feeling. "It was clumsily done. I felt terrible afterward." I like the way she uses the stump of her arm to emphasize what she is saying, as if she still has her hand. "But we didn't know what else to do. How does one atone for an atrocity of war?"

"One must first admit to it," I observe. "And you did. The gesture of that scroll carried a meaning I didn't perceive at the time."

"In my view," says Alize, "peace can only be lasting if it comes with a recognition of the human cost of the conflict. Both sides crave truth, justice, atonement. How can we achieve it?"

Again I am taken aback. When was the last time anyone asked me for my ideas?

"I'm not sure peace is possible," I begin. "There is too much hate."

Alize knows I am speaking of myself. My hatred is a part of me: it's the fire at my core.

"Then that is the question," she says. "What do we do with our hate? When my daughter was killed, I wanted Heron Mikane and his men to die the most horrible death. Hate was eating me alive. Moving beyond it is the hardest thing I ever did. But it has made me feel alive again."

"For those of us who have been bereaved," I say, "the war will go on, long after the fighting stops."

Alize nods slowly. "You're right," she says. "The bereaved must be front and center in our negotiations for a settlement."

I take this in. Alize has listened to me as if I am a powerful player. I bow my head, ashamed to admit that in all likelihood, I won't even be at the negotiating table. I sense my dolly giving me her support, telling me she has loved and appreciated everything I've said.

"Would you like to see our great hall, Commander?" The question comes out of my mouth before I really think it through.

"I would love to," says Alize, taken aback by my offer.

Kite has sent me here because he thinks this woman is beneath his notice. I can turn that situation to my advantage. I am determined to be at these negotiations now and there's something about taking this Aylish-woman into the palace that feels both statesmanlike and audacious. *I want to be seen with her.* I know Kite won't like it—and the thought of this minor rebellion pleases me.

I walk with my dolly, asking how she fares as we cross the lawns leading up to the palace. She puts her arm through mine and tells me in hushed songlight that she feels as if she's witnessed something very special. She says Alize and I could change the world. I laugh at her naivete but her sweetness warms my heart.

No one has ever believed in me like this.

Alize walks behind us with her engineer. They seem very close and the engineer chats with her the whole way to the palace.

When we enter the great hall, the sun is low in the sky, hitting the stained glass, filling the magnificent dome with a rainbow of color. The usual passing flunkies, military personnel, and government officials stare at the Aylishwomen, as if they're defiling our hall by their very presence. I show them the statue of Peregrine and the masterly artworks, pretending I'm oblivious to the sensation we are causing.

"This must have been your Circle House," says Alize, "in the days before the Brethren."

"Yes," I say. "But history changes things."

"It's an ever-moving force," agrees Alize. "But we can affect how it changes, that's our daily task."

"As women, our daily task is to heal the earth, according to our prayer to Gala," I say. "As a child I found that prayer very moving—but one soon realizes that some things can't be healed. We're never in control of change."

"I don't believe that," Alize counters. "Even in a culture like yours, that separates the sexes into—if you'll forgive me—an unnatural hierarchy, women are the potent undercurrent. They can affect the whole flow. Let me give you the example of a young Brightling woman I met recently. Her name is Elsa Crane, a choirmaiden, married against her will to a man she didn't know. That young girl has been inspirational in bringing change to her land. She is the reason I am here."

I stop. I can feel my dolly's heart beating. Alize has mentioned her precious Lark, her special, clever, inspirational Lark.

I begin to wonder if I am being played.

I know Alize has no songlight but I suddenly wonder if she has been subtly twisting my mind. It is a fallacy to imagine, even for a moment, that we might be on the same side. I watch her as she stares up at the statue of Peregrine. "He was a mighty man," she says, loudly enough for the Brightlings to hear. "But there are mighty women in Brightland too." She smiles at me.

She has her own agenda here. Lark, Mikane, these Aylish, they are all dangerous to me, I mustn't forget that. They want Kite to fall from power—but if Kite falls, surely I'll fall with him.

"I've heard tell that Peregrine was a great collector of Light People artifacts," says Alize. "I'd be most curious to see?"

Can I take this woman at face value? Kaira squeezes my arm, urging me to trust.

"Let me show you our Great Brother's rooms," I suggest. "I think you'd appreciate his love of history."

I lead the Aylishwomen toward Peregrine's library, offering commentary on some of the art and artifacts that we pass. I make a point of introducing Alize to everyone of note, causing as much consternation among Kite's bootlickers as I can. No one knows how to react to her. She is charming and polite, repeating how wonderful it is to be here in the palace, to be embarking on a historic meeting with the leaders of Brightland. I watch her: open, friendly, honest, and sincere. Perhaps Kaira sees the mistrustful look in my eyes and I hear her songlight:

"Alize isn't like the politicians here. She means what she says."

"Does she?" I ask her. "I've lived among vipers too long. Trust is something I have never had. So Kaira, you must tell me when someone's speaking true, and you must warn me when they tell a lie."

"I will," says Kaira earnestly. "I won't let you down."

I take the Aylishwomen into Peregrine's laboratory. Starling tags along behind us, clearly there as Kite's ears, but I leave him by the door, where he can't overhear.

"Our Great Brother was fascinated by the Light People," I tell Alize as I show her Peregrine's extraordinary floor-to-ceiling collection of Light People objects. Alize gasps at the well-preserved household implements and the time-obscured technology. "Lord Kite shares his fascination," I tell her. "He sees this era as a renaissance of their times."

Alize touches the ancient relics on Peregrine's worktable. She isn't interested in Kite.

"The war is entering a new phase, Zara," she says, a heaviness in her voice. "Airpower will change everything. As soon as the Light People learned to drop bombs on one another, it was only a matter of time before they began to destroy cities. You have your very impressive firefuel planes and I'm sure you're improving them. Soon, they'll fly to Reem with a cargo of bombs. We've known about your planes for quite some time."

I remember my duel with the Aylishman on the deck of his ship. He saw our war room; he saw one of our planes land. Kingfisher. Did he take what he saw back to Sorze Separelli?

Of course he did. Vile bastard.

"We have missiles," says Alize. "Our missiles are self-propelling bombs. The Light People called them rockets. They will do as much damage as your planes, if not more." Alize approaches me. "The Light People don't offer us a way forward. They are the way backward, nothing more. We must evolve into something better. You and I have an opportunity to—"

"Alize," I say, stopping her, pained by her hopefulness. "Thank you for your candor. There's nothing you and I can do to change the situation here."

Alize waits for me to explain.

"You know that I have no real power," I say. "You asked me about my relationship with Kite. I think you know the answer. You know my true condition here."

"But you are powerful, Zara. You have great public influence. And you're a Torch."

Alize has said this with such throwaway certainty that I know it's pointless to deny it. I feel Kaira gripping my arm in support.

"Who told you so?" I ask.

"A young man named Yan Zeru. He's currently a fugitive from Northaven."

Him. Kingfisher.

"He dueled with you on the deck of his ship. He told us of your power and he spoke with great respect." She walks toward me. "I live with Torches, Zara. My husband is a Torch; my daughter had songlight too. I don't have it myself but I know it when I see it. I've been aware of your songlight since we met."

"Who else knows?" I ask, feeling horribly exposed.

"Separelli and our Prime Minister, Odo Swift—only our innermost circle. We know what Kite has done to you. We know he makes you wear a Siren's band." I am still too shocked to speak.

"I can see that you don't trust me," says Alize. "But I don't want to hide anything from you. You have songlight. So read me. There's so much that we can do to change the prospects of our people."

I feel the commander open herself like a book. She's making me an offer, letting me in.

I enter her psyche. Usually, I am the subtle interloper, picking through secrets, planting suggestions and watching them grow. But Alize has invited me. She shows me her husband and her son in Reem. She shows me an image of her daughter, who died in the fire at Montsan. I see the deep scar of grief on Alize's spirit. Alize invites me to see a group of people she is part of, her inner circle, inspecting a line of missiles. These deadly things are being mass-produced. Next, I see her in a Brightling harbor town, joining hands with a wreck of a man, who I realize is Heron Mikane. I have not set eyes on Mikane for many years and it shocks me to see his battle-scarred face and his terrible decline. I feel the emotion of their exchange.

Then Alize speaks directly to me. Her inner voice is halting but I realize she has learned to do it from her long years interacting with Torches. She can make herself understood. I see a bright golden chain, linked over a map of both our countries.

"You and I can be a channel, where truth is spoken between our nations," she says.

"You're asking me to spy on Kite, to go around him, against him?"

"What are the true interests of your people, Zara: a real lasting peace, or a fantasy of victory ending in destruction? Consider—that is all I ask."

I consider. I look at what she is showing me and I feel her whole mind, open and honest in my hands.

What isn't she revealing? *Where is her vice?*

There's something else, something much closer, something she's not telling me. I chase it.

She suddenly presents me with a whirl of images—her parents' bookshop, titles of books that I loved as a child. She is blinding me with nostalgia. I cut through all this and grab what she is trying to conceal.

Carenza Perch. The engineer. I see her whispering to Alize as they cross the palace lawns. Before Alize can block me out, I hear the engineer say:

"The chrysalid is a Torch. She saw Kingfisher this morning with her friend Lark. He's coming. She says Raoul Harrier will help us. Kaira says she can find him—"

Alize throws me out of her mind—a difficult trick for one without songlight.

I stand, breathless.

The betrayal is complete.

On this day, when I tried so hard to love her, Kaira has spoken with these Aylish behind my back.

She's lied to me about contacting Lark.

She has communed with *him*, the hated Aylishman.

And she has found Harrier.

Alize looks utterly invaded. "You trespassed where I did not invite you," she says. Clearly in Ayland, this is some kind of crime.

"Are you accusing me of a breach of trust?" I ask sarcastically, trying to keep the devastation out of my voice.

"Everything I've said is true," says Alize. "We could change history. Please let's put aside our hate."

"I *am* my hate," I tell her with quiet certainty. "It's the only thing that's never let me down. What is left of me without my hate?"

I turn to Kaira. Her big eyes are full of concern, those eyes that I let in to my soul.

"*Traitor*," I say in songlight. And she quails.

"Poor little dolly," I say, keeping my voice as calm as I can. "She's been terribly unwell. She's really very weak. I must take her to my rooms."

But before I can move a step, there is an ear-shattering BOOM—like a crack of thunder coming from outside. Starling rushes, panicking, to the window.

"A bomb," he cries. "In the city!"

There's another ground-shaking BOOM.

I join Starling at the window and with the Aylish, we watch the flames. On the waterfront, on the other side of the river, a warehouse is burning. Farther up in the city, smoke billows into the evening sky, from the side of our military museum. A whole wall of it has been blown away.

BOOM—a third explosion happens as we watch, blowing a hole in a temple to Thal.

"So this is Raoul Harrier?" asks Alize. I can see the excitement in her eyes.

In front of these Aylish, Brightlinghelm has just revealed its deep divisions. I want these women out of here.

"I must go to Kite," I say. "My man Starling will escort you to your ship."

"Until tomorrow, then," says Alize.

"There will be no tomorrow. I am otherwise engaged," I inform her.

Alize looks disappointed. She glances at Kaira, then she thanks me for my hospitality.

Starling leads the Aylishwomen out.

I stare at the fires over the city. And I feel like I am burning.

Kaira Kasey has abused my trust.

She has made a fool of me.

And she is going to pay.

33 ✳ LARK

I'm walking away from Kingfisher because it hurts to be near him.

How has this happened? How have I let myself fall?

I was right to hold him at arm's length, to mistrust him.

Why did he make that pact with me: *Let's live life to the full?* Why did he let himself go like that, if he knew he wasn't free? I'm furious and I think the boy's an idiot.

Sister Swan? She'll chew him up and spit him out.

All my pain and frustration seem to have landed in my hand. It's hurting to sweet fuckery and I can almost feel the infection rise. It has been bleeding, congealing, and splitting open again for days, and only the intensity of the chase and the riot of my feelings has been keeping the growing pain at bay. It's constant now and my mind is one long cuss.

Ma has left Bel sleeping and when I return, I see her in an embrace with Heron. I hate to disturb them but she's already seen me. They separate but her warm glow doesn't fade. I want to be happy for her but I feel full of bitterness. Heron turns back to his work, attaching the wire from the Inquisitor's belt to each end of the birch rod. I realize he's making a longbow.

"How are you?" asks Ma, her expression changing to concern.

I'm unable to turn my boiling emotions into anything coherent so I just hold up my wounded hand.

Ma is horrified. "Elsa," she says. She takes hold of my wrist and I wince with pain. "We're going nowhere till this is seen to," she says.

Ma says she'll need some light to clean my wound. Heron builds a firepit and calls Bel and Kingfisher to gather some firewood. Ma makes me drink some of the Inquisitor's whiskey. I feel the heat of it in my throat and it makes me want to roar.

Kingfisher comes back with an armful of dead wood. I can't even bear to glance at him. Bel follows and together they build and light a fire, then

Kingfisher takes Heron's newly finished longbow and goes to catch us something to eat. It's like he can't bear to look at me either. Heron sits watching the tree line for danger, crafting hardwood arrows, while Bel gathers herbs and roots, checking with Ma which things are safe to eat.

"Right," says Ma, "this is going to hurt."

Ma helps women though childbirth and she has done a lot of stitching in some very private places. I trust her completely but a symphony of pain is running through my body and silent tears start running down my face.

"Anything you want to tell me?" asks Ma.

"No," I say. And she seems to know not to press me.

Moths and bugs are dancing in the flames as she begins to stitch. No point going into how much it hurts. Before Ma is done, I think I kind of faint because the pain stops for a while and when my vision comes back into focus, night has fully fallen. My hand is throbbing like a drum and is wrapped in a neat bandage. My eyes are drawn to the firelight and I can see some skinned ratlike things roasting on a spit. Heron is curled on a blanket next to Ma and to my amazement, I see that he's asleep, his head on her knee. Kingfisher is sitting cross-legged on the other side of the fire, keeping watch, making hardwood arrows. He glances at me and I see his concern but he quickly turns back to his task.

Bel Plover is showing Ma her little knitted boots. Ma handles the frayed and grubby things as if they're precious jewels.

"They're Lila's," says Bel.

"Your daughter?" asks Ma.

Bel nods. And I realize she is halfway through a story.

"I was lucky," she says. "I got chosen as a Second Wife. And my friend Mara was the First. The husband we got was a midshipman."

"Was he good to you?" asks Ma.

"He was fine, I suppose. He was polite. We had it better than a lot of other girls."

I suddenly think of Gailee Roberts and I miss her with an ache. I think

234

of how tight she clasped my hand on our wedding day. I think of Uta Malting and all the girls who were taken as Third Wives. Where are they now?

Bel did indeed have it lucky if her husband was polite. I had it lucky too.

"After his wedding leave, he went back to his ship," Bel continues, "and Mara and I found out we were both pregnant. We got heaps of praise from our choirmother. Our families were laying bets to see if we would both have sons. But I knew I had songlight . . ." Bel pauses like she's coming to the hard part of the story.

I sit up so she knows I am awake. It doesn't feel fair to eavesdrop. Bel holds my eyes for a moment—and she carries on.

"I'd known I was a Torch for years and I'd hidden it away," she says. "I pretended so hard that I was the same as everyone else that I began to believe it. When life was steady, I didn't think about my songlight much. I'd find myself outside my body from time to time but I kept it tightly under control."

"What gave you away?" asks Ma.

"Childbirth," says Bel simply. "My songlight went wild. I wasn't even aware of it."

"Oh, Bel," says Ma.

"I had a hard labor—but my girl was born healthy." A warmth glows in Bel at the recollection. "She was perfect. They laid her on my chest and I loved her straightaway. Her hand curled around my finger and I thought, 'This will be all right. I'm a mother now and I will find the strength. I'll hide my songlight for my girl. She'll need me to be strong.'" Bel takes in a breath. She looks into the flames. "But Inquisitors came. A Siren had heard the songlight in my pains. They pulled my girl out of my arms and they gave her to Mara. Mara was crying, I was screaming, begging for my girl, but they carried me to—" She pauses.

"They put you at the shaming post?" Ma exhales her shock.

Bel nods. "I was still bleeding," she says. "My milk had just come in. They were throwing dirt at me and . . ." She can't tell this part. The pain is too great and she moves on. "In the Chrysalid House I was leaking milk. I had so much milk and I thought, I will do anything, anything they say to get back to my baby. When they sent me to ensnare another Torch, I did what they told me." Bel pushes her fists into her eyes, forcing back her tears. "I sent nine people to the Chrysalid House. Nine souls I have destroyed. That's on me. That's waiting for me down in Hel. Everyone knows a Siren is unclean," she says. "I don't know why you rescued me. I don't know why your friend Nightingale told me there was hope." Bel turns away, hiding her emotion, hunched over her knees in her awful yellow dress.

"They used you, Bel," I say. "They terrified and tortured you. It's your Inquisitor who'll suffer down in Hel, not you."

Ma tries to draw Bel into her arms but Bel won't be held. She sits, unmoving. "Lila would be two now," says Bel. "I count the days. Two years, three months, fifteen days."

"Bel," I say. "We can take you home to—"

"My people don't want me," she says, cutting me off. "They never want me back, I brought shame on them. They all threw dirt at me, even Mara."

I edge toward her.

"I threw dirt at my friend Rye," I tell her. "It doesn't mean I didn't love him. I do love him. I will always love him"—at my periphery I see a flash of Kingfisher's eyes—"but I was scared for my life. I threw dirt at him and called him an unhuman. I've felt the shame of what I did every single day. I bet Mara has too."

Bel hears this. After a while she wipes her eyes on her sleeve and turns the rat things on the fire.

"What's this feast you're cooking up?" I ask her.

"Possums, with roast hazelnuts," she says, swallowing her grief. "It's going to be good."

It is good. As we eat, I stare into the fire.

There has to be a reckoning for this. Somebody must pay for what was done to Bel, for what's been done to all the Gailees and the Utas and Cassandras. There must be a reckoning for the system that marries us to strangers and makes us Third Wives, for the system that ties us to the shaming post and leaves us childless or womb-less or mindless. Somebody must pay. And his name is Kite.

I get to my feet, facing the others. "We need to talk about what we're going to do when we get to Brightlinghelm," I say. "Because it's going to be a fight. It's not enough to return Kingfisher to his ship and hope for peace. Peace will never come, as long as Kite's in charge. We need to plan how we can put that bastard in his grave."

"Sounds like you're talking treason," says a voice out of the darkness.

That's when I see them, men walking toward us, rifles out. Kingfisher's longbow is instantly in his hand. Heron reaches for his rifle but a warning shot is fired.

"Put your hands up," cries the voice. "There's a bounty on your heads, and we will have it."

Heron raises his hands and suddenly, there is a knife at my neck. My attacker's in the shadows.

"Drop your weapon, Aylish, or she dies," says the man behind me. Kingfisher puts down the bow and raises his hands. The men, all armed, walk into our clearing. I can't get a good look at them, the campfire has burned down too low. But from the smell of them, I know they're scum.

"How many?" I ask Kingfisher in songlight.

"Four," he says. "All armed."

Bel's songlight flies out in distress. "They'll torture me for what I did to that Inquisitor. They'll kill me!"

"We'll get you out of this," I tell her in songlight. I try to block Bel's terror out, knowing they will torture me as well.

"I want to die," she cries. "It's better to DIE!" And suddenly she bolts into the forest.

One of the men fires a volley of shots after her.

Bel's songlight sears through my brain. And then it goes silent.

I look at Kingfisher. He doesn't hear her either.

"Bel!" I scream in songlight. "Bel!"

All I sense is the forest, quelled into an eerie quiet by the gunfire.

"You're Mikane's Second Wife, aren't you," says the man holding me. "We've heard all about you on the radiobine. We know you've whored yourself to this Aylish bastard." My assailant holds me close, his blade touching my throat, and he presses his body into my back. His breath is raw onions. "There's a fine bounty on each of your heads," he goes on. "There's men gone right into the Tenmoth Zone looking for you."

"But we're the ones to have got you," says the man behind Kingfisher, whose voice rasps with glee. "Lighting a fire, that's your mistake. We could smell your smoke. Led us right here."

I notice that Ma has the sewing scissors gripped in her hand. She looks stricken at the loss of Bel and she's holding them fiercely, like a knife. I appreciate her courage but what can a pair of sewing scissors do? Heron is kneeling with his hands raised, a bounty hunter's pistol in the back of his neck.

"Look at this," cries his young captor. "The mighty Heron Mikane— caught snoring."

He laughs and Heron looks sick with rage. The men are delighted at the sight, praising each other on the big payout they will get.

"You've betrayed your country, Mikane," says Onion Breath. "You're the worst of them all."

"Why don't I brand the other side of his face on this fire?" asks the lad holding Heron. Quick as a flash, Ma sticks the scissors in his leg. He loses his balance, shocked at the sudden pain—and Heron flips him forward, using the lad's body as a shield. He grabs the pistol and puts it at the lad's cheek, aiming it up through his brain. It happens so fast I don't know how Heron's done it. The men fall silent.

"Let them go," says Mikane. "Or your friend is dead."

Onion Breath considers, torn between the lad and the thought of the reward.

"Pa," says the lad, looking at Onion Breath. "Come on . . ."

Suddenly the man holding Kingfisher falls. There is an arrow in his back. Another arrow hits the lad Heron is holding in the chest. Onion Breath lets me go, reeling backward, an arrow in the side of his neck. He tries to pull it out, staring at me in dazed shock. Another arrow hits him in the ribs. I spin around. We are surrounded. Our captors all fall at our feet, shot through with deadly accuracy. We breathe our shock, looking into the darkness. No one is visible.

Then I see shadowy presences coming through the trees. Heron aims the bounty hunter's gun. Ma stands, holding the bloody scissors. Kingfisher has the longbow primed and ready. I sense people, fierce as Hel, armed with guns and crossbows. But no one fires.

"Show yourselves," says Heron. "Let's make it a fair fight."

Slowly, from among the trees, people become visible, men and women in forest colors. A man slowly walks into the clearing. He's a stocky build, his hair threaded with feathers and beads.

"You're Heron Mikane," he says. "This girl is your unhuman wife and that's the Aylish fugitive you're shielding."

The air is taut with tension. And I sense something: songlight.

"Bel," I say.

Bel is brought into the clearing, held at knifepoint by a woman, a fighter dressed in black, her hair adorned with feathers. I sense this woman's songlight straightaway. She's a Torch.

"Your friend ran right into my arms," says the woman. "She's a little shaven-headed Siren. Tell me why I shouldn't run her through."

"We rescued her," I say. "She's one of us."

"Let her go," snarls Ma, "or you'll have me to answer to."

The warrior woman looks at Ma, taken aback by her bloody scissors and her deadly gaze. She makes her decision—and releases Bel. Bel runs into Ma's arms.

I feel a staggering relief that she's alive.

The stocky man lowers his crossbow. "Let's make this more friendly," he says. He eyes the woman—and at her signal, the shadowy people lay down their weapons on the forest floor.

"I'm Kam Fairley," he says. "This is Raven Pine. We're the Greensward militia. And if you're enemies of Kite, then you're friends of ours."

34 ✸ NIGHTINGALE

Troops are running like ants through the great hall and over the palace grounds. I see teams of Inquisitors and Emissaries, grabbing whips and guns and heading for the city. Swan ignores them all. She has me by the wrist and she's climbing to the council chamber at a speed that she knows is painfully hard for me.

She raided Alize's mind. She's discovered what I did.

I spoke to Carenza. I told her where Kingfisher is—I told her about Harrier.

I want to wrench myself free and run, but Swan's grip is like iron. She has shut herself off from me completely.

"Strange," she murmurs, "how Kite suddenly feels like my rock. No one else can be relied upon."

I pour out my songlight, trying to tell her that I didn't mean to go behind her back—I was going to tell her everything. Swan pauses on the stairs and tells me that if I hurt her with my songlight anymore, she will deliver me to Kite without a thought.

I fall silent.

The council chamber doors are opened in front of us and we enter to see Kite, on his feet, tearing a strip off his Ministers.

"Of course it's Harrier!" he cries. "Explain to me why he's still at large?"

Kite's Ministers come up with all sorts of excuses, but none of them has an answer. Swan quietly sits on her white seat, forcing me to stand beside her like a petrified dummy. Drake is listing all the measures they have taken to apprehend Harrier, but Kite won't be mollified.

"He's being hidden by a network of terrorists," he cries, admonishing his Ministers. "They're a foe just as dangerous as the Aylish—right here in Brightlinghelm. How have they been allowed to grow this powerful? How are they so hard for you to find?"

"We must round up every undesirable, strike fear into the city," says Ruppell. "I tried to tell Peregrine they should all be rooted out and brought to me in the Chrysalid House, but he was reluctant, and now they have grown into a plague."

I desperately want to warn Harrier.

"Why those particular buildings?" asks Greylag, puzzling over the bombs. "That's what we must fathom. A grain warehouse, the military museum, and a temple of Thal. What links them?"

"They're the city's largest murals of Lord Kite," points out Swan—and her laughter tinkles in the air. Kite's face is a mask of offense.

"Do you find this funny?" he accuses quietly.

"Harrier has always laughed at you," says Swan, with mock serenity. "He doesn't respect you, even as an enemy, and no one else here will tell you that." She pauses. "I know where Harrier is," she says—and her brazen stare gets Kite's full attention. My heart plummets. She is throwing in her lot with him.

"No, Sister, please," I beg her.

"Where?" demands Kite.

"For your ears only," says Swan.

"I insist that Lady Swan shares her information with us all," says Greylag, standing.

She's going to reveal me. Under my chrysalid's gauze, I pray to Gala. I ask for a quick death. And if it's to be slow, I ask her to help me with the pain.

"What I have to say is for Lord Kite alone."

Kite likes this. He rounds on his Ministers. "You have been sleeping on the watch. You have allowed this insult to happen. Now go."

"We will not go," says Greylag firmly, holding his ground. "We will all hear this, Kite."

The ground seems to move under Kite's feet. Greylag is defying him. The other Ministers look fervid with excitement at Greylag's show of strength. Kite has been undermined. He has shown his temper and made himself look weak.

I feel power shift toward his Ministers.

"Where's Harrier?" asks Kite, shaken.

"You will get him when we are alone," replies Swan, keeping her cool. She eyes Greylag defiantly and he leaves, fuming. The rest follow.

Kite reaches for the decanter that sits on the table and pours himself a big glass of amber liquor. He knocks it back. "Greylag is an ingrate," he says once the door is closed. "He was nothing under Peregrine. Peregrine despised him. I have raised him up and now he turns on me."

"Do you begin to recognize that I'm the only one who can truly keep you safe?" asks Swan, regarding him. "Your position is perilous and I can protect you."

"This is the wrong path," I plead with her in songlight. "Sister, I'm sorry for what I did. Please don't choose Kite. He will turn on you."

My songlight has no effect. Swan has blocked me out completely.

"Give me Harrier," pledges Kite, "and I will place you right by my side."

Swan stands, enjoying her height, taking her status.

"I've heard that before," she says, leaning over him. "If I am to help you, I will keep my freedom, you understand? You will not put that band on me again."

Kite sees that she is adamant. "I promise you," he says.

I feel a transfer of power in the air between them. And I have lost her.

"Break that promise at your peril," she says. And Kite feels her threat like a physical thrill.

Swan closes her eyes, heaving her breath, making a show of using her songlight. Kite gazes at her, envious of her power. I feel her songlight preparing to rise. The arch-Siren is going to hunt.

"Please," I say. "Don't do this."

Swan turns on me in songlight. I am expecting hot temper but her wrath is so cold and deep that only a ripple disturbs the black lake that sits at her core. She is beyond incandescent.

"Do you think I am so easy to seduce?"

Her question throws me, utterly. "Forgive what I did," I plead. "I was acting for our future."

"You're a rat from the gutter, Kaira. I picked you up and now I'll throw you back."

"This is your dark heart speaking, the dark heart that Kite made. It isn't your true self."

"On this day," she says, "when I strived to make you happy, when I gave you my love"—she falters—"you lied and you betrayed me."

"You think I don't love you, but I do," I cry in desperate songlight. "In your true heart you belong with Lark and Heron Mikane. You belong with Harrier and the Aylish. You don't belong with Kite. You have light in you and he does not."

"Where is Harrier?" demands Kite, becoming impatient. "Prove your strength."

"You are strong," I plead. "I've never admired you more than today. Don't do Kite's bidding."

Swan closes her mind to me. She raises her head, searching. And I realize that I have to act. I can find Harrier first. I can warn him.

I send up my songlight and listen. I open myself to the cacophony of the city. I sense the turmoil, the smoking fires, the forces of law and order being brutally deployed, the unsettled populace—and under it all, I hear a low whisper, a sense of achievement, a job well done. I home in on this whisper and follow its journey. Harrier's nature is becoming more familiar to me now and under the hubbub and the hurly-burly I sense it, a wisp of his laughter. Apple—I taste apple. And I am there. Harrier is on a river barge, hiding in its cargo hold—the cargo is apples. I creep into his consciousness, as Swan taught me, and for one breath, I feel the comfort of being with him. Perhaps Harrier senses me, for he allows my flame to brighten.

"Close your mind," I whisper, planting the thought as clearly as I can. "There's a Siren on your tail."

His mind instantly closes and his laughter grows quiet.

243

In the council chamber, I hear a tinkling laugh. Swan is smiling wickedly.

I realize what she has done, how skilled she is, how invisible. She has hooked herself into my songlight and traveled with me—a parasite.

"Thank you, dolly," she says in songlight. "Finally, you have served me well."

"No," I say, "no"—and my head spins in horror at what I have done. I can't react, I cannot move—I have no air in my lungs—

My legs go from under me. Swan watches me collapse.

"Poor dolly," she says, looking up at Kite. "It's a sickly thing and I'm bored of it." She speaks in her most velvet voice, as if she's swallowed oil from her black lake.

"You have him, don't you?" says Kite, seeing the triumph in her smile.

"Harrier is on the river, heading north," she tells him. "I picked up a wisp of his laughter. You can catch him at the floodgates in a cargo hold. Tell your men to look for apples."

Kite looks at Swan with a strange expression, a mix of admiration and something else I can't define. It's almost like a flash of fear. He goes to bark orders at his henchmen.

"Starling," says Swan. "My dolly isn't well."

I'm on the cold floor. I cannot move. My hope has gone. I see Starling's jackboots in front of my eyes.

"Take her to my rooms and lock her up."

Starling looks at me disdainfully. He hauls me over his shoulder, as if I am a sack.

Things come in and out of focus as he walks. I'm aware of being taken down the staircase and across the domed hall. I see a glimpse of Peregrine's statue upside down. I feel like I am drowning, drowning in midair.

When my eyes open, the dizziness has ebbed and I am lying on a narrow bed. I struggle to get the gauze off my face and I replace my dislodged spectacles. I see two of Swan's ladies sitting on straight-backed chairs, resting. This is their room, the little chamber behind Swan's bed. There's a sink in

244

the corner. I stagger toward it and I'm sick. One of the ladies stands and comes toward me.

"I don't need you," I say. "I'm fine." I straighten up and clean the sink. The lady hasn't moved. She's the one called Lady Scorpio. I wash myself, splashing water on my face, trying to revive myself. Lady Scorpio silently passes me a towel.

"Thank you," I say.

She isn't wearing her gauze and I am struck by her expression. Maybe it's just the way the light falls but I think I see something in her eyes, something human, far away.

"Who did you used to be?" I ask her. "What was your life, before? How long have you been like this?"

She doesn't reply, of course, but for a moment she seems to hold my gaze. She replaces the towel and returns to her seat, looking straight ahead.

I was sure that Swan was going to deliver me to Kite.

But she didn't.

Perhaps she didn't want to spoil her moment of triumph. Maybe, in the dead of night, she'll have Starling remove me to the Chrysalid House. I want Lark so badly but I daren't contact her. Swan's songlight is loose and she will know immediately. It will harden her resolve against me.

But I would rather be killed trying to escape than live like Lady Scorpio. I try the door. I pull the handle—locked. I try the heavily draped window. It looks out on a tiny enclosed courtyard—also locked. Even if I smashed it, I would still be stuck. I try to keep my desperation at bay. There must be a way out. I look around the stultifying room. There's a heavy curtain pulled across one of the walls and it's very slightly moving. There's a draft coming from under it. I pull it back.

A narrow spiral staircase runs down, disappearing into shadow. Ignoring my aching hip, I take a fluttering candle and walk down it as quickly as I can, praying that it leads into the labyrinth of cellars and storerooms that runs under the palace.

I find myself in a room full of hanging white dresses, all dripping wet.

The smell of laundry detergent hits me and it's strangely comforting. I never thought I'd miss my stepmother's kitchen but the smell transports me back to washing days in our tiny apartment. Ishbella and I would put aside our mutual dislike to tackle piles of linen and Inquisitor's shirts: soaking, scrubbing, drying, ironing. I walk on, grieving for my broken family. The room opens out into a turbine-lit laundry. A huge stove heats water and three of Swan's ladies are working, laundering her dresses.

Cassandra is there, cleaning dirt from a hem. I am so desperate for a friend I want to throw my arms around her.

It occurs to me that in this underground cellar, my songlight won't be detected. If I can't reach Lark, at least I can help Cassandra. If she were here, in her true spirt, she would know what to do; she would find a way to get us out alive. This is my sudden inspiration and it's desperate. I force myself into a state of tranquility. I calm my desperation and give every jot of songlight that I have to the task. I put my fingers on Cassandra's skull. I feel the scar lines hidden in her hair, where Ruppell made his cuts. And I let my full songlight go.

Cassandra, I need you. Please come back to me.

I hurl myself at the brick wall in Cassandra's mind. I concentrate my light on the scar tissue, trying to find a way through, to open up her memory, to give her access to herself. I put all my being into the task. I feel like something shifts—and then Cassandra jerks away from me.

She falls backward and I can't hold her. Her mind is a blinding shower of white. She utters a low cry—the first sound I have heard her make—then she's lying on the floor, her limbs jerking, her eyes rolling. I watch, terrified, as her whole body is seized by a fit. It rips through her as if she's in the grip of some monstrous turbine, forcing electric into her limbs.

When it's over, she lies collapsed. I cry her name over and over—but nothing I can do will get her to wake. Throwing caution to the wind, I hurry back up the spiral stairs. I don't care who hears me. I look for help in the only place I have left.

"Lark!" I cry. "Lark!"

35 ✶ LARK

Raven Pine draws her people together, using her songlight. They have been searching for us throughout the Greensward and each search party has its own Torch. Now they begin to congregate and together, they act as an escort for us.

"We have a camp at Sherlham," says Raven. "You'll be safe from bounty hunters there."

Kam Fairley says they will take us to Lake Lunen and help us on our way to Brightlinghelm. People keep joining us, coming through the darkness with small turbine lamps, rifles and crossbows slung over their backs. Some are Torches; most are just men and women of all ages who, for whatever reason, have fled the Brethren. One man, a veteran, comes and shakes Heron's hand, awed to meet the great commander. The militia is curious about Kingfisher—some of them outright suspicious of this Aylish stranger in their midst—and they want to hear the story of why Heron has risked so much to protect him.

I let the others tell it. No one pays me much attention and I'm glad of it. It twisted my heart to rags when I thought Bel Plover had been killed. Now I walk with her, glad she is still with us. Bel's trauma is receding but it's left her with an abiding fear of Raven.

"No wonder she wanted to kill me," she confides in a low voice.

"When I first saw you, I wanted to kill you too," I say. "Give her time."

"There's a price on Raven Pine's head," Bel tells me. "I know her name. My Inquisitor was after her. If I'd snared her, he'd have let me eat roast chicken for a week."

We look ahead at Raven, who is moving like a panther through the forest, as if it's been her home for years.

"She'll come to see your worth, just as I did," I assure her.

Bel shakes her head. "Some things can't be forgiven," she says. "Raven Pine lost someone to a Siren. I sensed it as she held me—someone she loved."

Bel falls silent, punishing herself, and I don't know how to comfort her.

The militia illuminates our way and we make fast progress. People climb ahead of us, high in the branches, making sure our path is safe. Some look like ex-soldiers, others like cadets and choirmaidens in borrowed fatigues. Kam Fairley tells us that at Sherlham, the river is deep and slow and full of easy fishing. It's well hidden but within reach of the Greensward's edge, where they can barter for food from farmers and villagers, friendly to their cause.

"I grew up in this forest," Ma tells him. "I remember Sherlham from when I was a child." I feel a great longing in her voice as she asks, "I wonder if any of you might have any news of my people?" She tells Kam about her family—our family.

"I've been moving through this forest a long time now," says Kam. "Most of the old Greenswardian tribes have gone."

"Gone where?" asks Ma, crestfallen.

"They didn't like the changes that the Brethren brought. So they took themselves north and sailed to the shores of Lador. Over the years, most of them have left."

"Lador?" I hear the disbelief in Ma's voice. Lador is an unpopulated wilderness.

"Many refugees have gone to join them too," says the man. "Not everyone stays with us and joins the fight."

I see Ma's disappointment and I sense her deep homesickness for her lost parents and her old way of life. I'm about to offer her what comfort I can when I see Heron Mikane quietly reaching for her hand.

I can't help but glance at Kingfisher. The distance between us holds, more taut than ever. I swallow my frustration, hoping that I live long enough to tell him what a fool he is.

"How many are in your militia?" Kingfisher asks Kam.

"Over three hundred," Kam tells him, "not including our children." He looks down, blushing. "I became a father myself, just last week," he says.

"He was a warrior till then," says Raven dryly. "Now all he talks about is babies."

Ma congratulates Kam warmly and wants to know all about his little son.

"He's been dying for another opportunity to talk about him," says Raven teasingly.

Kam laughs. "Listen," he says. "There are three hundred of us trained and ready to fight. More and more people are coming from all over Brightland every day—and we are all at your disposal, Mikane."

Heron takes this in. "What's your aim?" he asks.

"We're working toward revolt, preparing the ground, so we can light the fuse."

"Revolt?" Heron is skeptical. "Three hundred against Kite's armies?"

"Don't underestimate us," says Kam. "Kite is unstable. People don't like the way he grabbed power and there's a lot of damage we can do. We're stirring unrest in the city. Our Torches are in and out of Brightlinghelm all the time and we are linked with the network of resistance there. We think people will rise up for their freedom, if they believe they have a chance."

"The people of Northaven did," I say.

Kam's eyes flash in the dark as he hears this. "We know there's a lot of discontent in the towns. And we know that the army's got a fair share of men who'd lay down their arms if they could. But we've lacked a leader, until now." His voice is full of fervor. "Mikane, you've come to us from the north—and this very night, Brother Harrier is on his way here from the south. Harrier's for us, for the people—and Mikane, you're our greatest commander. Together, you could change everything. The time to strike is coming."

Heron is silent but I rejoice at everything Kam Fairley has said.

"How's that oath of yours, Heron?" I ask.

At that moment, I feel a blinding songlight.

"Lark!"

Nightingale's power almost sends me to the ground. I can see Kingfisher, Bel, Raven, and the other Torches all convulsed. I tell her she's hurting us and when her songlight has fallen back from its most painful, brilliant glare, I join her.

249

I find her in a stifling locked room.

"Swan's turned on me," she says. Fear for her leaps into my heart as Nightingale tells me what has just happened. I see it in jagged, jumbled images. She told Renza Perch who she was and Swan feels betrayed. But this isn't the main source of Nightingale's distress.

"Cassandra," she cries. "I have hurt Cassandra!"

"How?"

"I thought I could help her." I see Nightingale in an underground laundry room, forcing herself into a state of tranquility and putting her fingers on Cassandra's skull. "I put all my songlight, all my being, into the task. I tried to make a flow—but I hurt her." I see Cassandra fall into a fit. She's lying on the floor, her limbs jerking, her eyes rolling. "I tried everything. I can't get her to move or wake."

Without thinking, I pull Kingfisher into our harmony. He too sees the locked white room and we show him what has happened. He asks Nightingale questions: Is Cassandra breathing? Has her face gone slack? What position is she lying in? He gives her instructions: make sure Cassandra's warm, that her head is comfortable, that she's lying on her side, that her airway is not blocked.

Nightingale disappears down the spiral stairs to carry out Kingfisher's instructions. As she goes underground, we lose our connection with her. The sounds of the night forest come back into my consciousness. I realize that I'm on my knees and Kingfisher is holding me steady. He quickly lets me go—but damn, I want him to stay here forever with his mind in harmony with mine.

"What was that?" asks Kam Fairley. "What force is it, that can send Torches to their knees?"

"That was Nightingale," I say. I get my breath back, wondering how on earth I can explain.

"She's my friend," I tell him. Somehow, I have to convey how important Nightingale is and how vital it is that we rescue her—but I don't know where to begin. "Swan kidnapped her and she's trapped in the Brethren's Palace," I say. "She's been helping us in songlight, since we left Northaven."

"We owe Nightingale our freedom," adds Kingfisher in a low voice.

Then Raven Pine says, "I've sensed this girl before, in Brightlinghelm. She's a Flare, Kam."

"A Flare?" I question.

"A rarity. A Torch with uncommonly strong songlight. There's one or two in a generation. They are most precious."

A Flare. Nightingale is a Flare.

"I think she's the girl that Stork was trying to help when they took her to the Chrysalid House," Raven tells Kam.

"Cassandra Stork?" I say in disbelief.

"Yes," says Raven, her eyes fixed on me.

"Nightingale is with her now."

Raven comes toward me, helping me up to my feet. "Where?" she asks. There's a desperation in her voice. "Where's Cassandra?"

I see loss in Raven's eyes—and a surge of hope that there is news. How do I tell her?

"She . . . Cassandra is one of Swan's veiled ladies."

Raven lets me go. She turns away and Kam steadies her.

"I'm sorry," I say helplessly.

Raven is gutted to the core to hear what has become of her friend. "I knew they would make her a chrysalid," she says, keeping her emotions under tight control. "But I still hoped . . ."

I don't know how to comfort her. With every breath, I hear her anger growing, her determination to avenge her friend. Kam puts a hand on her shoulder and their warm regard for each other is visibly apparent. When Raven can speak again she asks, "May I talk to Nightingale?"

Kingfisher makes a quiet offer. "We could ask Nightingale to appear in such a way that everyone could see her."

"How?" I ask.

251

He's still unsettlingly close to me and I feel his presence with all six senses. My eyes take in his shoulders, the shape of his jaw, his eyes—I can smell his scent: forest and great-horse, fire smoke, the sweat of his labors, the river he almost died in. My lips are buzzing with the remembered onslaught of his kiss.

"We could use the power of three," Kingfisher says to me. "You already know how strong that is. You saved my life with it."

"Go on," I say.

"There are enough people with songlight here to make a circle of three, which sits within a circle of six. The rest of us form a third circle. We can hold Nightingale in the center, in our light." Kingfisher turns to the assembled company. "If she is willing and our concentration is sustained, she will appear so that you all may see her." I look at him, amazed. "Nightingale is uniquely positioned in the palace," he says. "She's right at the heart of power and I'm convinced that she can help us."

"Tell us what to do," says Raven.

Kingfisher instructs us. Bel and I sit with him, cross-legged on the ground. Raven and the militia's five other Torches form a circle around us, then Heron, Curl, Kam, and the rest of his people form a larger circle among the trees. Quietness falls. Turbine lamps light our faces and the branches hang over us, as if they're part of our circle too.

"Find her for us, Lark," instructs Kingfisher.

I close my eyes, concentrating on my task. I feel Nightingale pulling me and soon, I join her in the white room.

"How's Cassandra?" I ask.

"I've made her as comfortable as I can," she says. "She's unconscious, sleeping."

I tell Nightingale what we want to do.

"Let me come," she says. "I feel so alone. It would be wonderful to be with you."

I nod to Kingfisher and he looks up at the people in the outer circle.

252

"I need you to sing," he says. "It may sound strange, but what I need from you is a sustained harmonious chord of song."

There is silence. Then Ma's clear voice cuts through the night air, with a resonant note. Kam Fairley adds a low harmony and the rest of the crowd joins in, even Heron Mikane, who looks like he's never sung a note in his life. The chord they make builds around us, sustaining itself in the night air.

Kingfisher looks to the two circles of Torches. "Now we make a harmony of songlight," he says.

He takes my bandaged hand and I'm glad the pain of my wound is numbing the sensation. I take Bel's hand and she grasps Kingfisher's. Raven and the other Torches do the same. The song and the songlight swell. We concentrate, all of us together. I feel Nightingale's fatigue, her power stretched to the utmost, and I hope that she can last the course.

I sense the atmosphere vibrate and then the air takes on a light. Slowly, the shape of Nightingale appears in the center of our circle, her big eyes behind spectacles, her oversized white dress accentuating her youth.

She looks around. "So many people . . ."

I see wonder and pity on Ma's face as she takes in Nightingale's small frame.

"I can't be with you long," she says. "I can't leave Cassandra."

"We're all with you," I say. "We're coming for you. We're going to get you out."

"I don't think you can, Lark. But it gives me hope to see you all."

"Raven Pine would like to speak with you," I say. "She knows Cassandra. She is her friend."

I direct Nightingale's gaze toward Raven.

"Cassandra is more than my friend," says Raven, her songlight glistening. "She's everything to me. I don't know if you can understand it, Nightingale, but I love her with my heart and soul and I want you to tell her that. Whatever state she's in, please whisper in her ear that Raven is waiting."

"Yes, I understand it," says Nightingale, moved. "When I first met

Cassandra, I could sense love in her, like an anchor. She never told me about you, Raven, but somehow I always knew that you were there."

Nightingale looks down and I feel a beat of inexpressible emotion in her heart. I ache to be with her, to understand her, to hold her in the flesh.

"Tell us where you are," I urge her.

I want everyone in this circle to know exactly how Swan has treated her.

"I'm in Sister Swan's rooms, locked here, with her chrysalids," says Nightingale. "Swan thinks I have betrayed her. I revealed myself to the Aylish and it has provoked her."

"Don't make excuses for her," I say. "She's a monster."

We're all surprised at how Nightingale leaps to her captor's defense. "She's not a monster. Kite has bullied and corrupted Swan since she was young. She keeps fighting to be free of him but he's got a stranglehold on her. Kite is the monster, not Swan. Swan keeps trying to survive him." Nightingale sighs and I sense her deep nervous exhaustion. "I can't hate her, Lark. There is goodness in her. It has never been wanted, so it has withered—but she is capable of love. You should have seen her today with Commander Alize. She was open and honest in a way I've never seen. I began to think that if these two women had power, peace might really come."

"And then she turned on you like a fiend!" I cry.

"I hurt her," cries Nightingale. "I betrayed her trust."

"How?" asks Kingfisher.

"I told Carenza Perch who I was. I told her that you were alive in the Greensward. I told her that the Aylish should make contact with Harrier." Nightingale experiences a fresh wave of distress. "But Harrier has been found," she says. And emotion overwhelms her. "Kite has discovered him."

"They've caught Harrier?" asks Kam in dismay. "How?"

Nightingale's eyes dart over her shoulder, as if she's looking at the door. "I don't know," she says, and I feel immediately that there's something Nightingale isn't telling us.

The militia are devastated about Harrier and the harmony of song falters. The light that is holding Nightingale flickers, threatening to fade.

"Did Swan hunt him down?" I ask her directly.

"Whatever you think of Swan," says Nightingale, continuing her defense, "without her, there'd only be Kite's Ministers, and they're the real monsters. I have been trying to tell Swan that she could be the leader Brightland needs."

"She should be thrown in jail for what she's done to you," I say.

"I thought she'd send me straight to the Chrysalid House," says Nightingale. "But she didn't."

"Your predicament's my fault," interrupts Kingfisher. "I asked you to contact my people. I shouldn't have done it. Nightingale, if you agree, I'm going to speak with Swan."

I hold my place in the harmony of songlight, quelling every misgiving in my guts.

"If I can turn her attention on me," says Kingfisher, "it will take the heat off you. I'll tell her that we won't negotiate with Kite. I'll tell her that we see her as Brightland's leader."

"That's good," says Kam. "You can divide Swan and Kite."

"You can't trust that woman an inch," I say, unable to keep silent.

"But if we strengthen Swan," says Kam, "we will weaken Kite."

I feel agreement in the circle and I'm stunned that no one seems to share my objection to Kingfisher's plan. I bite back my misgivings. Perhaps they are colored by jealousy. Whatever I feel about Swan, I try to think about her rationally and I quash the voice inside me that's crying she's a snake.

It's not easy.

Heron speaks up. "Nightingale," he says, "I know how much you've helped us since we left Northaven, at great risk to yourself. We owe you our lives."

Nightingale flushes, shy at being spoken to by the great commander.

"Please don't feel you're on your own," says Ma. "Every person in this circle is standing with you."

"All strength to you, Nightingale," says Raven.

"You gave me hope," says Bel.

"One day soon, my friend," I say. "We'll meet."

Nightingale puts her songlight hand on my face. "Stay safe, Lark."

"You too."

We release each other. She descends the stairs to be with Cassandra and her songlight fades. The notes of song die away, leaving no sound but the rustling of leaves and the flowing of the river. I lie back, breathless with exertion, and Kingfisher sits, clutching his head. Using so much songlight has left us all drained. I see Raven and the other Torches similarly wearied.

"I suggest we rest here for a while," says Kam. "We're not far from Sherlham but I can see how exhausted the Torches are. We'll set off at first light."

"If Harrier has been arrested we must waste no time," says Heron. "Kite won't keep him alive for long. You said you had links with the resistance in the city. How soon can you make contact with them?"

I see a new side to Heron Mikane as he talks with Kam and Raven. He is a tactician, a strategist, a leader, no longer the haunted and embittered man I met back in Northaven, with a smoke in his hand and Death in his shadow. He's fully alert to every possibility, trying to turn the dreadful blow of Harrier's arrest into a galvanizing force.

"If Kite murders him," says Heron, "he must become our martyr, our figurehead."

"No," says Kam. "We can save him; we have to save him."

"We may not get there in time," says Heron. "We have to accept that Harrier might die—and we must think beyond it. That way we will not be disempowered. If he survives, we'll be in clover, but we can't rely on miracles."

"Mikane," asks Raven, who has now recovered enough to speak, "if we make it into Brightlinghelm, can you make contact with the military?"

Heron pauses.

"How's that oath of yours?" I ask him quietly.

He takes his time to reply. "Your friend Nightingale has moved me sorely. I have a battle still to fight." And Heron lets his oath rise into the night.

As we rest, I look across at Kingfisher. His eye are closed in an exhausted slumber; his lashes brush his cheeks. He wakes, as if he senses me—and I pretend to be asleep.

"I should never have asked Nightingale to speak to Renza," he says. "I have endangered her. It was selfish and I must put it right. You see that, Lark?"

"Yes," I say. "I see that." And then I realize what he's doing. "Are you asking my permission to reach out to Swan?"

"If you can think of a better way to reprieve your friend, then I am all ears," he tells me.

I can think of nothing. There is nothing in my mind at all.

I lie on my back and look at the stars, shining through the high forest canopy.

"I'll do everything I can for Nightingale," says Kingfisher.

"She's stronger than you think," I say. "Nightingale's a Flare."

I use Raven Pine's expression, thinking it will comfort me. But then I think of the flares the horsemen set off over the moors. They lit the whole landscape up, burning bright as comets—then they faded into darkness.

Flares burn bright and die.

Tormented with this thought, I know I will not sleep.

36 ✴ SWAN

Kite orders Harrier to be brought to the Chrysalid House. It's his favorite place to torture people. Rain starts coming down as he leads me there. We're surrounded by guards and in an uncharacteristically gallant gesture, Kite takes an umbrella from one of his aides and holds it over my head.

I will not think of my dolly. She lied to me and abused my trust. She never loved me, she's a fake. I thought her pure and artless but she's as cunning as a rat. I must cut her out. I hollow out my innards, as if I have a scalpel.

Starling Beech can dispose of her and I will never think of her again.

The rain comes down in torrents and the damp air, filled with smoke from the explosions, is making my lungs feel tight and pricking my eyes. There's a sore pain in my chest. I want some comfort and I put my arm through Kite's. He allows it. Things will be different between us now. I will not wear that Siren's band again.

As I think this, we enter the Chrysalid House and immediately, its lead walls extinguish my songlight.

Is this why he has brought me here?

Kite is told by the surgeon on duty that Harrier is being escorted from the river under guard and will arrive imminently. The surgeon offers Kite his favorite interrogation chamber.

Kite's in good spirits while we await our catch and when a ghoulish medic in a white coat brings us a decanter and some glasses, Kite pours me a whiskey and he toasts my success.

"To the radiant Flower of Brightland."

"Don't call me that."

"To Lady Swan." He clinks my glass. "I'm going to hang Harrier on the esplanade and make it a public event. I'll invite the Aylish to watch, just before the peace talks."

Alize. What was it she was trying to tell me?

I must put her from my mind and remember my hatred. My hatred of the Aylish has sustained me all my life.

"By the time the peace talks begin, I'll have everything in place," muses Kite as he drinks. "The Aylish will be signing their surrender."

"That will be a great day for Brightland," I say, "and a great day for you, my lord." I smile. But the whiskey burns my throat and drains into my hollow heart.

I should have found a way to contain Kaira's songlight. I should have made her a lead band, to ensure her loyalty. I'm sure that she's communing with that girl Lark even now, weeping and wailing, telling her how cruel and heartless I am. I should have known that behind those big, sensitive eyes was a mind full of guile. The pain of my foolishness pierces me.

But as the atmosphere of this place sinks into my bones, I remember her words.

"There is good in you. . . .You don't belong with Kite. . . .We both want this Chrysalid House to close."

What have I done?

Crush that voice.

Kite walks over to my seat. He raises my face to his. He plants his lips on mine. I don't move. "A taste of what's to come," he says with a grin.

This emptiness will leave me. I will soon start feeling safe. The thrill of power will be my solace.

At last, Harrier is brought before us. His presence brings a warmth into this cold place and his eyes smolder hot like coals. I had forgotten the effect that Harrier has on me. He's inches taller than Kite, with a head of dark curls, a dark beard. His hands are black with gunpowder.

"Kite," he says. And then his eyes fall on me. There's something in his expression. It isn't hatred or fury or contempt. What is it?

With him come two captured terrorists. One of them is a woman in her forties with blood running down the side of her face, the other a boy still in his teens, clearly a Torch, with eyes like a fear-struck deer. Kite addresses them, sipping his whiskey, telling them with understated malice that they'll both be chrysalids by dawn unless they tell him where they were escaping to.

"I know there's a nest of you hiding in the Greensward. Give me the location."

The terrorists stay silent and Kite has them removed. "You know what to do," he says to the medics.

Harrier remains, standing in a pool of light, knowing that his comrades are going to be tortured. I swallow more whiskey.

"My old friend," says Kite, offering Harrier a seat. "Won't you sit with us for a drink?"

"I'm not thirsty," he says. "And I'd rather stand." I swear there's something of a smile on Harrier's face, as if, even at this moment, he finds Kite absurd.

"It'll be your last comfort before I hang you with your wives and children," says Kite.

This hits Harrier hard. I see him try to collect himself.

"Do what you like to me," he says. "But my family's innocent."

Kite is savoring Harrier's helplessness, breathing it in.

What have I done?

The consequence of my spite now hits me. Once again, I have chosen Kite's side. My hand shakes as I empty the glass.

"You'd be a fool to hang my family," argues Harrier. "It would be obscene. There's little love for you in Brightland as it is. Killing my children would light a fire that will bring you down."

"Then keep them alive," says Kite. He sits back, crossing his legs in a pose of studied nonchalance, pretending he hasn't just heard Harrier calling him a fool. "Give up your insurgent friends and your children will go free. I want the location of their Greensward lair."

Harrier is ten times the man that Kite is, not just in looks but in character. To have lived with Harrier, to have borne his children, that's a rich life, and I feel a stirring jealousy for his wives. His must be a household that I can't imagine, a place I've never experienced—a household full of laughter. Harrier always flirted with me, he always made me believe I was special in his eyes. But now I see he played me too. Harrier's a family man. His heart is bursting with love for them.

"I'd like that whiskey," he says.

I pour him a glass and take it to him.

He drinks and I can't fathom his expression. He doesn't hate me, he isn't wishing me dead. He's looking at me as if there's some kind of understanding between us, *as if he respects me.*

The medic enters and clacks his way over to Kite, giving him a torture progress report.

What Harrier says to me next is intimate, as if Kite isn't even in the room.

"Thank you," he whispers.

Is he mocking me?

"I sensed you, the night Peregrine died. You warned me to leave the palace. Even today, you tried to help me. Your help came too late, but thank you, Swan."

He thinks I'm Kaira.

I feel a red heat burning through my body, a coruscating heat of shame.

"I don't deserve your thanks," I say. There's no power in my voice at all.

"You have great courage," Harrier says under his breath. "Use it."

My lip quivers and I drink my own whiskey to hide it.

Kite approaches us. "It seems that the boy broke down straightaway," he informs us. "The pathetic coward gave up all his comrades to save his songlight. I shall be destroying the insurgents' lair at first light tomorrow."

Harrier hangs his head, pitying the boy.

"So our meeting's over," says Kite. "I don't need your information after all."

"You will not destroy the insurgents," says Harrier. "Not with your planes, nor by hanging me and my family. You don't understand how much people hate you. They will keep on rising up—and if they don't topple you, your Ministers will. You've shown them how to grab power and they will take your lesson and serve it back."

These words make the hair stand up on the back of my neck.

But Kite saunters back to his seat. "Take the traitor away," he says to his white-coated torturers.

"I'll do what I can for your family," I whisper.

"Thank you. For all you have done," he says. "Keep the light, Swan."

Guards approach and Harrier is taken. The room is darker without him and the dreadful gloom seeps into my bones.

Kite pours us both another drink. A big one.

"I know you're soft on Harrier and I didn't think you'd give him up. But you tossed him to me like a piece of trash." Kite is walking toward me.

He wants to take me. Here. I knock back more whiskey.

I am the world's fool.

This is what I have brought up on myself. This is what I've chosen.

I can never refuse him. I'll never be free.

PART 4

37 ✸ PETRA

Garena interviews me for the airship's chronicle. I tell her in detail how we came to find Rye Tern, the first recorded natural eximian. She asks me how I feel about it and I say immensely privileged. I probably gush. But it is truly epic news. "Rye Tern says that he is one of many," I tell her. "So truevoice has developed in humanity without any scientific intervention."

Before I leave, I tell Garena my observations about Wren Apaluk. "Rye and Wren are sapien and eximian, yet they seem like brothers and treat each other with great affection, as if there is no difference between them." I notice that Garena doesn't write this last bit down. She apologizes, saying she has already filled the space allowance in her document.

I head back up to the medical wing, where I have been spending all my time. Rye Tern has been thoroughly checked for pathogens and he has been inoculated. Yesterday, once he was clean and showered, Mother injected him with a sedative. He didn't know this was going to happen and I don't think he would have agreed to it but Mother said it would give us the best opportunity to examine him.

Mother says he will awaken soon and I am to sit with him. She says it will be a good lesson in subject analysis. I am to monitor his vital signs and when he wakes I must encourage him to use his truevoice and I must then make notes about its quality. She warns me not to form any kind of attachment.

I lie, telling her there's no danger of that.

"No, I don't suppose there is—not when Charlus is around." She smiles knowingly and I feel utterly deflated. How can I tell her that Charlus asked to be my match and I turned him down?

I sit by Rye, noting his heart rate, thinking how peaceful he looks, trying not to be distracted by the shape of his shoulders, when something creeps into the edge of my consciousness—distant songlight. I like to use Rye's word for it. It's more eloquent than truevoice. I close my eyes and open my mind, listening.

I have learned lots of strategies for controlling my unwanted and intrusive excess of truevoice but apparently there is no cure. Father tried to tell me it was a rare gift. He said if I could master it, I would be a nonpareil, but it has always felt like a freakish burden. The first time it felt like a gift worth having was when I heard that voice—*Lark*.

Now, coming from the far northwest, I hear something else, little more than a cloud of whispers. This songlight grows as I tune into it, becoming more like the distant hum of bees. I strain further toward it, because what I hear doesn't seem possible to me. It sounds like many, many people all communing with each other, as we Sealanders do.

I wonder if any of our other airships have encountered such a thing? Now that we know wild eximians exist on the ground below, wild communal songlight becomes a possibility. It makes me wish I had listened for it farther south. I remember the nomads that we saw, traveling through the grasses with children on their backs. I swear there were Torches among them. Again, I use Rye's word. It's so much nicer than *eximian*. I listen to the distant hum, focusing my mind on it.

I think it may be a city. I will ask Rye Tern about it when he wakes.

I look down at him, taking in his clean-shaven face. His cuts and bruises have been healed with restorative gel and his skin is glowing. I study the shape of his nose and his brows. I look at the line of his jaw but words of description fail me. I just stare, liking everything I see. I wish I had my diary here. I badly want to write our story. How strange that it should start with cockroaches.

After a while, I hear a low moan. Rye's heartbeat is rising and I see that his eyes are moving behind his lids. He's dreaming—and his dream is not good. I wish there were a way that I could see it but no eximian, no Torch, no matter how strong their voice, can experience another's dreams. Rye moans again, louder. His breath starts to come jagged.

"Elsa," he cries, and he jolts himself awake.

"You're safe," I assure him.

He lies back, drawing himself into the waking world, remembering where he is.

Who's Elsa? I want to ask, but I hold back.

He takes me in with his eyes. "Petra," he says in mouth-words, as if he's reminding himself of my name. He looks around the tiny cabin and then looks down at himself.

"Your skin responded very well to the healing gel," I say, using my true-voice. "All the scans and tests have been done. You're in good health."

His eyes turn to me. "You're not behind that visor anymore."

"No," I say. "Your quarantine is over."

My hair is loose today and I can tell that Rye likes the way I look. I'm glad. I have made efforts.

Rye feels his face with his fingertips, where the medical team have tended to his salt-burned skin. He feels the line around his skull, where the cruel crown was placed. I speak to him in mouth-words, because that's clearly what he's used to.

"Our medics brought down the swelling and closed the flesh where your lead crown had cut into you," I tell him.

"My crown?"

"When I first saw you, I thought you were some kind of tribal prince."

He raises his eyebrows, as if the thought of it amuses him. "I'm just a soldier," he says.

"Are you thirsty?" I ask, and when he nods, I give him some water and he drinks.

"How long have I been asleep?" He's speaking with his truevoice now but it's raw and untrained. I don't think he understands how magical it is.

"Not much more than a day," I tell him. "You were in a deep sedation. Mother wanted to look at your genome."

"Where do I keep that?"

"It's in every cell in your body. It's what makes you Rye Tern."

"You mean like my spirit, my soul?"

Now it's my turn to look puzzled. I try to make myself clear using simple images, showing him the function of his chromosomes, making the molecular biology as plain as possible, explaining how his unique genetic data is in the nucleus of every cell. I see him trying to comprehend it.

"I'm not educated, Petra," he confesses. "What's your mother looking for?"

"Evidence," I explain. "You're an eximian, Rye, a natural eximian. It's indisputable. You're an incredible discovery."

Rye doesn't seem to share my excitement at this.

"News has gone around the ship like a comet," I assure him. "You've no idea the sensation that you've caused."

I can see he doesn't know how to react to this. He looks troubled and I kick myself.

"When can I see Wren?" he asks.

Mother comes in before I form an answer.

"Good, you're awake," she says, ignoring me. "I trust you're no longer in any pain?"

"None at all," Rye informs her politely.

"I have some questions for you."

"Of course."

Rye probably doesn't realize what he's let himself in for. My mother's questions can go on for days. She begins recording him without any preamble.

"Rye Tern, were either of your parents eximians? Or, in your parlance, did they have songlight?"

"No," he says. "At least I don't think so."

"Surely you'd know?"

"Not in Brightland. People go to all sorts of lengths to hide their songlight. There's only one other Torch in my town, as far as I know." His voice quiets. "Her name's Elsa Crane."

Elsa. The name he cried out in his sleep.

"So eximians are rare?"

He's regarding Mother curiously. "I've got some questions for you," he says.

I love the way he stands up to her.

"What's this flying battleship doing up above the badlands? Where are you going?" he asks. "And why separate me from Wren? Why isn't he here in this wing with me?"

"This wing is equipped to treat eximians," she explains, "and your fellow traveler is a sapien."

"What's the difference?" asks Rye. "We're all human."

This is such a shocking thing to say and Rye has said it with an easy certainty, as if it is a simple truth. Mother is thrown.

"It's the way we organize things here," she says, making it clear that there can be no argument. "As for your other questions, this is not a battleship, it's a reconnaissance vessel, on a mapping and research mission. We're one of six airships that the Sovereign Council has sent out from Sealand to discover our planet's state of health."

"Where's Sealand?" asks Rye.

"It's an island, two oceans away," I tell him. "We've been traveling for almost sixty days, mapping the entire eastern coast of this continent."

"We're heading north," says Mother, "to assess the ice cap. Then we'll return home through this continent's interior, so that our discoveries will cover as broad an area as possible. Does that answer you?"

"It's hard to take it in," says Rye.

Mother regains control of the conversation. "You say Torches in Brightland keep their songlight hidden. Why?"

"You saw that lead band they forced on me. Songlight is persecuted."

"Let me get this clear," says Mother. "You are persecuted by your sapiens?"

"If a sapien is a person without songlight, then yes."

269

"That is barbaric," says Mother. Her anger has risen. "What happened when they discovered you?"

Rye pauses. Then he sighs deeply. "I'm sorry," he tells her, "I can't talk about it like this. It's a hard story and I don't think I can bear to tell it more than once."

Mother looks irked.

"Of course," she concedes. "I'm sure my questions can wait a little longer. Admiral Xalvas is organizing a special communion of welcome for you. You may tell your story there." She looks to me. "Get him ready," she instructs.

"Will Wren be there?" asks Rye.

"No," says Mother, rising to leave. "Your sapien companion is still in quarantine."

"Is he all right?" asks Rye in concern. "When can I see him?"

"Quite all right," says Mother in a clipped tone. "We'll make arrangements for a visit in due course." And she goes.

"She's very direct," I say in apology.

"In Brightland," Rye tells me, "women are only able to be wives. It's good to see that you're treated the same way as the men. Wren noticed it straightaway. He liked it."

"Yes," I say, not wanting to go into the complexities of our differences.

Rye closes his eyes, gathering his energy. But there's one more question that I want to ask. I speak with mouth-words so it's easier for him.

"The girl who is the other torch in your town, Elsa Crane. Is she your match?"

"My match?"

"You said her name in your sleep."

I feel a wrench of emotion in him and he sighs out a deep breath. "Dreams can be bastards, can't they?"

"Bastards?"

"It's a swear. Don't go repeating it in front of your mother." He smiles again.

Those eyes of his, full of northern seas and skies. If I'm not careful, I will fall right into them.

"Elsa and I were very close," he says. "But now, she's someone else's match."

"She didn't stay loyal to you?"

"Girls have to marry. They've no choice," he explains. "We were going to run away. But I was caught."

"By the sapiens in your town?"

"By my friends and neighbors, yes," he says.

"And they put that lead band on you, because you have songlight?" I ask, using his word again.

"Yes."

Our faces are very close. I can see the flecks of color in his eyes.

"Petra," he says. "I think that your people might help my people. There are others like me who are suffering in Brightland, suffering terribly. You and your ship could change everything."

"Let me take you to communion," I say, seeing his endeavor. "I promise every one of us will listen to your story. The way you were treated is cruel and abhorrent. And if our questions are too much, you can tell us that we're bastards."

Rye laughs to hear me use his swear and I am glad. I think in his true nature, this boy would laugh a lot.

I show him the suit and shoes that I have readied for his use and I give him his privacy so he can dress. I sit outside his door, breathing my anticipation.

I feel as if life has altered its course in some profound way. Rye and Wren and Fenan, there's a connection between them that my mother cannot see. Rye is an eximian, yes, but he's a sapien too. In his mind, there's no difference between him and Wren. They understand each other—and they are the same. That's what I always felt with Fenan. Our difference meant nothing.

When Rye walks out, the suit fits him, the shoes are just right. His hair is long enough to hide the mark of his lead crown. He's as handsome as a prince. And for a moment, I can't speak.

We hold our silence.

"I'd like to hear your story too." He speaks in songlight. And our intimacy thrills me.

If Charlus were to walk in here right now, I'd tell him he could jump.

I have met the man I want to match with.

38 ✳ PIPER

I've woken in the dark with Finch lying next to me. I want to remember this. I want to relive and relish our whole day, because it was so perfect. Happiness is a strange thing. Lying with Finch, every single cell of me is rejoicing in being alive.

I don't think it's a lasting state. It cannot be in my case because of what I did to Rye, because of Ma and Elsa. But the feelings that I have here, now, I want them to stay with me forever.

I know I felt happiness when I was a boy. Pa would take us running on the sands and when we got home, Ma would be there and we would eat together and there would be stories told and I would fall into my bed, dreaming I could fly. They were sky-blue days when Pa was alive. As a cadet, after he died, I used to think that I was happy whenever I got praised. I felt a thrilling in my chest and my heart beat fast whenever I was first at something or the best. When they made me cadet captain I thought that I would burst. But this wasn't happiness. Looking back, I see there was a strange kind of desperation in it. I could keep running from the grief I felt and from the truth about myself, as long as I never stopped long enough to feel.

These last days, I have been happy.

"You're an odd bastard, Crane," said Finch yesterday, as we lay in each other's arms on the floor of a tool store. But he was smiling as he said it and he kissed me after. Finch seems to love me for my oddness. He thinks I'm strange because I am so silent. This boy could make conversation about anything. There are no boundaries in his mind. He thinks something and he says it without a moment's hesitation and I could listen to his bullshit all day long. His disposition is so warm, he makes everything amusing and he has such an easy way with words. I could hear him talk about a wrench and feel it was like poetry.

I love him. And even to think those words still shakes me to the core.

We keep everything hidden, of course. The tool store was our sanctuary yesterday but our meeting there was brief. So far we've been lucky and no one has disturbed us but we both live in a state of constant alert.

Yesterday, Axby sent our squadron out to the uninhabited islands off the coast. Before our visit they were full of nesting seabirds; now they are half-obliterated crags. We tested real bombs. They look like great orange-and-yellow flowers that bloom briefly beneath us, before they get consumed by billowing black smoke. As we returned to base we both felt bad about the seabirds.

"What will it be like when we drop these bombs on people?" I asked.

"The Aylish aren't people," said Finch. "They're fucking Aylish."

I wish he had not said this. Up there in the cockpit of our plane, I wanted to unpick Finch's loyalty to the Brethren. Rye started that process with me. When I realized that Peregrine was wrong about his definition of a man, the whole edifice began to crumble. I was about to open the subject up— but Finch started telling me about the crow he'd once kept as a pet and all the tricks he'd taught it to do. Soon, I was laughing and I felt actual joy.

I will speak to Finch today. Somehow I will find the right words to tell him about Northaven. He needs to know that Kite is not worthy of our devotion. Ma told me we must have peace. And I need to find the right words to unravel Finch's hate. We've both lost people we love in this war. Adding to the death count won't make things any better.

In his next long ramble, Finch told me how he'd like to own a café in a marketplace, where he could make people food and talk to them all day. Finch would be brilliant at this and my soul was smiling as I listened to him. In some other world, on some far shore, I might grow old with Finch.

"Perhaps I'd have the shop next door," I told him.

"What would you sell?"

I think for a while. "I'd have things on display," I tell him, "like my ma's carved animals and the birds and planes I used to make, like paintings and drawings and things that choirmaidens sew. They'd just be there to look at."

"That's not a shop, that's a gallery, you dummy. How would you make money? We have to make a living, Piper."

I feel a warm glow that he has said "we." He's imagining a future too.

When Axby gave us a few hours off base, Finch and I went down to the city and he took me into a grand old building, Brightlinghelm's gallery. We saw art from the Age of Woe, from the Traveling Time and things drawn and made by people now. I could spend a whole year in that place wondering at stuff and I was fully shaken by another happiness attack. I wanted to back Finch up against the wall among the landscapes and kiss him till it hurt. I settled for brushing the backs of my fingers against his. And even that touch was an electric risk.

The painting I liked best was of a field—but the field was tiny and the painting was really all about the sky. It's as if the painter was staring straight into the sun and he managed to capture the exact light of dawn. I stared for ages. The sun was yellow and white and thick with paint and I couldn't imagine how the painter had known what to do. He made me feel like I was right in the sunrise.

As it got dark, Finch and I wandered down to the riverside and got ink drawings done on our skin: a goldfinch for me on my chest above my heart, a sandpiper for Finch in the same place. We're on each other's bodies now.

Then came a moment of troubling reality, when the gods of catastrophe reminded us how close they are. As we were drinking our first beer, a great explosion came. People threw themselves down to the ground as debris landed all around us. There were men and women running and screaming. The whole side of a warehouse was blown to pieces.

We ran to see what had happened. A mural of Lord Kite had had its eyes blown out. As we watched, the whole wall destabilized and fell. By some miracle, no one was killed. Then two more bombs went off, causing a frenzy of panic. Dread began coursing through my veins.

"We should go back," I said. "Axby might need us."

"No," said Finch insistently, and he gripped my arm. "We must take the time we've got."

Finch drew me through the panicking crowd and into the Pink District. I knew exactly where we were going. When Finch paid the woman at the backstreet Pink House for our own darkened room, I didn't care that the place was dingy and the paint was peeling.

I have woken with him in my arms and I lie there, savoring the last hours of darkness. This is my chance to talk to him, to try and open his mind to the Brightland that I see. But how do I start when he's reaching up to kiss me? This happiness is irresistible.

Soon we'll have to leave. We'll go separately, back up to the airfield, boasting of the fun we've had with Brightlinghelm's Third Wives.

This happiness hurts.

But thank you, Gala, for giving it to me.

39 ✴ RYE

Petra walks me to a large chamber suspended in her world above the clouds, with floor-to-ceiling windows on every side.

"This is our viewing gallery," she says. "It runs almost the whole length of the airship."

This is some kind of room for gods, with burnished pillars and a view of the heavens. People are coming to meet me, introducing themselves in songlight. I soon give up trying to remember their names and their jobs, marveling at how friendly and richly dressed they are. They all have glossy, lustrous hair and skin like Petra's, totally unblemished. Their clothes are made of gorgeous fabrics and each individual is dressed how they please. I have never had so much attention paid to me in my life. I find myself badly wanting to be accepted by these brilliant people.

Petra introduces me to her father, Lukas, a mild-mannered man who tells me he's the airship's cartographer. I have no idea what that is. She senses my ignorance.

"Father's making a new map of the world, charting all the changes to our coastlines," she says.

"Sea levels have been rising for almost five thousand years," her father tells me in songlight, speaking as if I am a scientist. "They are only just beginning to stabilize."

I nod, struck by the fact that if Wren was here, he'd hear nothing but silence. There are what Petra calls sapiens in the room, standing with trays of drinks and snacks. They must be so bored.

I see the tall, angular lad who flew the scouting craft coming toward me and I greet him.

"Charlus," I say, pleased that I've recalled his name. I swear his suit has emeralds sewn into the cuffs and collar.

"They did a good job at cleaning you up," he says. I put out my hand to shake, but Charlus leaves a pause before he takes it. Perhaps it's not the custom here. Perhaps he thinks I'm dirty. We're sizing each other up and I'm not sure that I like him. There's something a bit superior in him that grates on me.

Petra brings forward a smiling young woman. "This is my friend Garena," she says. Garena is blushing like a choirmaiden. She's acting as if I were famous, someone like Heron Mikane.

"I'm the ship's archivist," she says. "It would be the honor of my life if at some point, you'd allow me to talk to you about some of your customs and your culture?"

"Happy to," I say.

"May I preserve your uniform for our records?"

"I'd like to keep my coat," I say. "It's a bit of a prize. I stole it."

Petra and Garena look at me like I'm some kind of pirate and they burst into laughter. It's amazing what a vivid impression you get of people communicating in songlight this way. These two young women are so open. I wish I were more at ease; they'd probably be great company. But I feel like a hundred pairs of eyes are watching me.

All the songlight suddenly falls silent and I realize that Air Admiral Xalvas has entered the room. He walks toward me. I don't want to offer him my hand only to have it refused, so I settle for a slight bow of my head.

"Rytern," he says, looking at me as if he's impressed with how much his team has done to improve me. "I'm pleased to welcome you properly to *Celestis*."

"I've been very well cared for," I say, making sure I'm as polite as possible. "My thanks to your crew."

"I see you're making new acquaintances?"

"Yes, sir. Wren and I are at your service." I try the slight bow again. It seems to go down well.

"Let's begin our communion," says Admiral Xalvas. He turns his back and I assume I'm supposed to follow him. I walk a few paces behind, noticing how no one fawns or looks away at his authority, as they did whenever Wheeler approached in Northaven. It strikes me as pathetic that Wheeler is the only example of authority I have ever met. I'm such a village boy. The admiral carries himself with ease, commanding respect rather than fear. I look for something to say.

"I can't help noticing the art everywhere. Petra was telling me the story of Terra Nova."

Xalvas pauses. "It's not something those of us who witnessed the end will ever find easy to speak about."

"I'm sorry." I kick myself. My first remark is a misstep. "We don't have a lot of art in Northaven, apart from murals of battles and portraits of our leaders, and they're not much to look at." I should shut up now. "Anyway, your airship is a credit to the artists and craftsmen who made it."

"Thank you. It's been designed to feel as if we're taking part of Sealand with us."

I feel a sense of history in Xalvas and a warm pride in his ancestry. He carries his family tree in his veins.

At the other end of the long viewing room, gilded seats covered in incredibly rich fabric are set out in a series of widening circles. Each crew member seems to know their place. The circles near the center hold those who have higher status, like Livia and, surprisingly, Charlus. The larger circles hold the rest. Xalvas waves me to a seat opposite his own.

His beard is fascinatingly well-kept. I find myself wondering how he keeps it so glistening and smooth.

"Rytern," he says. "We invite you to commune with us. The floor is yours. Please increase our store of knowledge by sharing your story."

I've lost sight of Petra. She's somewhere near the back and I look for her in songlight. She appears, her presence reassuring me.

"I don't know how to do this," I say to her.

"It's a matter of remembering things vividly," she says, "rather than 'telling' as you would in mouth-words. Open yourself, let us see what you saw and feel how you felt, and then we'll understand. You don't need to embellish or explain."

This is going to be soul-baring. There are things that I want no one to see. But it's important that these people know how bad things are. I take in a breath and open my mind to begin. I won't spare them any pain. Because they can help me. They can help Elsa. They can help us all to be free.

At first, I'm hesitant, but then it begins to come instinctively.

I show them Northaven, my life as a cadet, Emissary Wheeler with his rules. I show them my fear as a boy when I found out I had songlight. Elsa suddenly lights up my mind. I'm back on the deck of her boat, in songlight. She turns to me and smiles. Elsa . . .

I linger on her, feeling our love in the beating of my heart.

Then I go on, trying to build a picture of our lives. I show the Sealanders our murals as a way of explaining things. They see Great Brother Peregrine, holding a lead band over a lowly unhuman. Heron Mikane standing on a pile of Aylish dead. I come to the day of the shaming post.

This is so hard. I look around at the people watching me, sitting on their plush seats. I know they're sympathetic, I can see they're drawn in by my narrative, but none of them look as if they have ever known a single moment of violence or discomfort in their lives.

I'm not sure I can bear to relive what I went through on that day. I start on Bailey's Strand, pleading with Elsa to run away with me. I remember the surge of elation I felt when she said she'd come. But then I see Piper standing in front of me, telling me I am unhuman. I don't censor anything. I come to the beating that Wheeler gave me. I can still feel the pain in my ribs even now. I let them see through my eyes as I'm tied in that dungeon. Wheeler beats me so badly that I rise out of my body and watch him at work, battering me with his fists. When I am dragged up into the light, Elsa is my first thought. I find her on her boat, as dazzling as the sun. "Save yourself!" I cry.

When the lead band is welded onto my skull, I see some of the Sealanders react physically, as if this is the most horrific thing they can imagine.

But the shaming post is worse. Wheeler and Greening address the town, listing my crimes. I am unhuman, treacherous, a mind-twister. Wheeler makes sure everyone knows exactly what will be done to me in the Chrysalid House. His explanation will do for these Sealanders too. Petra's friend Garena looks too shocked to cry. My father disowns me and I feel the shame all over again. To be so utterly rejected by everyone I have ever known was and is unendurable. I see my mothers standing wretched. My father's handful of soil hits me in the face. I close my eyes then, feeling each thud against my body. Gala, the horror and humiliation is still so acute. I force myself to relive how every friend and neighbor, every cadet and choirmaiden threw dirt upon me, taking my name and my humanity. No one spared me. Then I see Elsa, her face a mask of pain, faltering in front of me. "Save yourself," I plead in my useless, smothered songlight. She throws the soil. She calls me an unhuman and the wave of pain carries me away.

I have to pause then. I ask for water, using my ordinary voice, and one of the non-eximians brings it. I thank them and drink it. The silence holds. My audience is rapt.

I tell the rest more quickly. I am chained in the hold of the transport ship. I make sure that the Sealanders see the chrysalids down there, toiling with gauze over their faces. I show them the holding camp in Meadeville and I let them see the other prisoners. I don't hold back my anger at the system that has ruined them. As Kite's planes take off and land behind me, I linger on the boy I met, whose crime was loving another boy. His name was Freed Atheson. Gala, that boy broke my fucking heart. He'll be a chrysalid now, like all the rest.

I show the Sealanders Piper Crane, standing in front of me in his pilot's uniform, a syringe held in his hand. We're in a kind of struggling embrace, loving and hating each other. Piper lets the contents of the syringe run into the ground.

I'm lying on the barge going up the Isis to the Chrysalid House, pretending to be unconscious, waiting for my chance. I dislocate my own thumb. I let the Sealanders feel how bad it hurts as, sweating with pain, I work one hand out of my manacles. Then I hesitate.

Do I let these Sealanders see what I did? I killed that guard. Will they judge me as a murderer? Will they decide I'm dangerous and reject me?

People are on the edges of their seats, wanting to know what happens next. It will be more powerful if it's honest. I show them my desperation to be free and I let them see how I struggle with the guard until he stops moving. It's him or me and I'm determined to survive. I take his keys, leave him for dead, and I dive into the river. An arrow hits me in the shoulder, another in my leg—but I don't die. I cling to the weeds and rocks on the riverbed like a lamprey. Then I float downstream and I live.

There's only one more thing I want to show them. The Sealanders haven't asked me for Wren's story and it isn't mine to tell, but I don't like the way they have separated us and I want to show them Wren's courage as best I can. I don't show them where Wren came from; that's his business, not mine. I don't show them the pink band around his neck or how important it felt when I cut his hair. I simply show them our closeness on that last night. It felt like we were both tiny parts of the same huge creation. I show them how we lay under the stars and fell asleep, face-to-face.

I end my story as we walk toward the city of cats.

In truth, telling it has exhausted me. I could lie my head back on this ridiculous plush chair and fall straight into a sleep. But I don't. I look up and see that some people are wiping tears from their eyes; others have looks of horror. One woman is being comforted by her friends. The admiral's handsome face is stern with outrage.

"You can see how things are now in my country," I tell them. "Girls are misused however the Brethren wills. Boys die on the battlefields of a senseless war. And you've seen what happens to people with songlight. I haven't even shown you the worst of it. I escaped before I saw the Chrysalid House, but I can tell you this. Its doors are open every day and it takes in people just like you."

Petra isn't crying. She's looking at me with her brow furrowed, like she's deciding something. I feel an urge to reach out to her but I hold it back. It seems important to keep talking to the group.

"I look at you all," I continue, "and I see a remarkable society." I look straight at Xalvas. "You could help Wren and me. Come to Brightlinghelm. The Chrysalid House needs to be destroyed. The Brethren must be brought down and the people of Brightland, freed."

Xalvas is listening very, very carefully.

"Your story is a revelation in so many ways," he says. "But I must tell you straightaway that *Celestis* is not equipped to do as you ask. We're a vessel for science and research, not bringing down governments."

"But even the sight of your ship, the threat of your great power would make all the difference."

"Return to Sealand City with us," offers Xalvas. "Put your case to our sovereign government. Ask for assistance and other vessels might be sent."

"How long will that take?" I ask.

"Too long," cries Petra, getting to her feet. "Xalvas, please, there must be something we can do. We've found natural eximians and they're being destroyed!" I hear a murmur of agreement from other voices. But I think Petra's broken some kind of rule by speaking out because her mother stands, angry, and her father just looks mortified. Perhaps if your seat is in an outer circle, you only speak by invitation here.

"I can't come with you to Sealand," I say. "If your government won't help me, I'd be stuck, two oceans away from home. I have to join the fight against the Brethren."

"What about the other city?" asks Petra suddenly.

"Daughter, you must take your seat!" says her father, Lukas, with his voice raised. He glances apologetically at Xalvas, as if his own central seat is suddenly under threat.

"Listen," Petra insists. "There's another city, northwest, a hum of songlight. There are more eximians there."

"It must be Reem," I say, inspiration hitting me. "It's Ayland's capital."

I can almost feel an aerial pull as the Sealanders turn their songlight. For a long while no one seems to hear anything and it occurs to me that Petra must be a very strong Torch to hear something so far away.

"I hear it," says one woman at last, standing.

"I hear it too," says Livia, sitting forward.

"Reem is the capital of our neighboring country, Ayland, where Torches are free," I tell them. "Wren and I were on our way there but our boat drifted south. If you can't take us to Brightland, please take us to Reem. Maybe the Aylish will help us. Or maybe together, you could stop the Brethren from destroying us."

Xalvas pauses, listening—and his expression slowly changes, as if he too is hearing something far away. He stands.

"Charlus, perhaps you'd allow Rytern to share your quarters?"

Charlus looks at him, surprised. "Of course, Father," he says, but I sense his reluctance. He seems almost affronted.

So Charlus is Xalvas's son? That's why he's sitting in the central circle; that's why he was flying that scouting craft with so little natural aptitude. My hackles rise at his privilege.

Xalvas walks toward me. "Petra will show you round the ship while we discuss all that you have told us. I assure you, we'll take it very seriously." He puts his hand on my shoulder and I feel the warm gravity of his power, as if he's pulling me toward him like a magnet. "Charlus will bring you our decision shortly."

"Thank you," I say. I take in the whole circle, meeting as many eyes as I can. "I thank you all for hearing me."

They get to their feet and I suddenly find myself held in a powerful chord of songlight. I think it's some kind of ovation. I find myself hot with emotion and I hang my head, my eyes pricking with tears. These people have listened.

Petra leads me across the long viewing gallery. Her back is to me the whole way and it gives me time to pull myself together. She doesn't turn around until we've climbed the staircase and we're on another long, burnished corridor with pictures etched into the walls. Then, to my astonishment, Petra draws me into an alcove and throws her arms around me.

"I can't believe what you went through," she cries. "I can't bear it."

I am completely taken by surprise. "It's all right," I tell her, returning her spontaneous embrace. "I escaped. I survived."

"Xalvas has to help you," she says passionately. "He has to." She starts to cry in earnest.

I just stand there, holding her. It's so strange that she's crying for my woes and I'm offering her comfort.

"It's abominable," she says. "It's unthinkable, what those people did to you."

"Don't cry."

"If Xalvas won't help you, I'll steal a scouting craft and take you to Reem myself."

"Petra," I say, touched.

And before I can say more, she kisses me. Gala in heaven, her lips are like honey and roses. Her lips are like the summer. I had no intention of kissing anyone today but this is so gorgeous, so ardent and unexpected, I can't stop. Her arms curl around me, pulling me close; my hands are on her back, one of them is in her hair. She smells so good. I feel her breasts pressing against me. This has to stop. It isn't wise. What if there are rules here that I don't understand? Maybe I'm breaking some invisible code. She's pressing her body against me and I'm hardening. Gala, oh Gala, this must stop.

"Petra," I say. But it feels like the height of discourtesy to push her away. I can't do it, I just can't. This is such unbelievable pleasure. I force my lips away from hers.

"What is this?" I whisper. "Is this your pity for me?"

"Does it look like pity?" she asks.

"No." We both want more.

"You say my people can bring change to your world," she says. "But you can do the same here. You and Wren, you change everything."

"How?" I ask with an urgency born of passion. "Why won't your people let me be with him?"

"They don't understand the bond you have with Wren—but I do," says Petra, fervent with emotion. "We'll find a way to see him."

"When?" I ask her.

"Now. Let's do it now," she says. But instead of moving off, her lips find mine again. I don't fight it. It's too wonderful.

Suddenly Petra springs away from me. I have sensed from the start that her songlight is powerful and her extraordinary perception has told her there is someone approaching. She starts explaining the artwork we are standing next to.

"This shows the beginning of the Great Extinction, when our sovereign founders took control of Sealand," she says. "See where our island is, in the middle of the ocean, far from any continent? Our sovereigns had the foresight to see that it would survive the worst of the war and the collapsing climate. They were the elite from all over the world and they brought their great wealth and scientific knowledge. They began to dream about how they could leave the planet Earth. . . ."

Charlus opens the door at the end of the corridor and approaches us at a saunter.

"Why did they want to abandon the earth?" I ask like a keen student, trying to calm the racing in my blood.

"Because mankind is a conquering species," says Petra, as if this is

286

something she has learned in school. "And our sovereigns could see that we'd run out of land to conquer. They sought a new dominion."

I don't have time to question her further as Charlus arrives.

"I expect you'd like to know what we've decided," he says.

He looks smug. I'm not going to beg him for news.

"We're setting course for the city of Reem," he drawls. "How about that?"

"That's very good," I say, wondering if I am flushing.

"The Senior Circle debated whether to make first contact with the eximian society there. Livia has made a strong argument in favor and my father's in accord."

"This is such an opportunity," says Petra. "My mother will be beside herself."

"You'd better run along to her, then," says Charlus.

Petra looks at him, her face falling. "Your father asked me to show Rye the ship."

"He's asked me to relieve you of that duty."

Petra doesn't believe him. But I can see that she daren't cross him.

She nods me a formal goodbye, leaving everything unsaid. I watch her as she walks away, wondering what will become of our plan to visit Wren.

"She's stunning, isn't she?" says Charlus.

I don't answer. I look at him, liking him less and less.

"That whole tale you spun back there was like a pirate story from a children's book," he says. "So it's hardly a surprise that you've turned her head. Word of warning, mate. She's mine."

This lad towers over me. But he's like a figure that someone's drawn upon the sand. There's power in him but no real strength. I stand my ground, unmoving.

"Petra didn't mention that she belonged to anyone."

"We're a match. It's been decided."

"Congratulations," I say. And then, unable to leave it alone, I ask, "What exactly is a match?"

"She'll be the mother of my children."

I'm a guest on his ship and I need his pa's goodwill. I mustn't say or do anything stupid. But I'm filled with a desire to rescue Petra from this prick.

"So, Charlus," I say. "Tell me about these sovereign founders. If they had so much wealth and knowledge, why did they abandon the rest of the world to die?"

40 ✳ PETRA

I can't take Rye, so I'll find Wren by myself. They deserve to have news of each other. I have no idea how to get onto the sapien floor but I'm pretty sure that Garena might know a way. As our archivist and chronicler, she knows a lot of secrets on this ship. I'm outside our cabin when I see my mother coming toward me, looking fierce.

"I hear that Charlus asked you to be his match," she says. "Why didn't you tell me immediately? And why haven't you given him a reply?"

I instantly feel like I'm five years old.

"I did reply," I assure her. "I told him that I didn't want a match."

Mother looks as if I've hit her with a thunderbolt. "Are you serious? He's an exceptional candidate."

"I don't want to be a parent yet."

"I don't think you fully understand," she says. "This is an ideal match. No one is suggesting that you have offspring immediately. It's a declaration of intent."

I'm as frank as possible. "I don't want to share children with Charlus."

"Whyever not?"

"I don't like him."

My mother looks at me in outraged disbelief. "Of course you do—you've been spending all your time with him."

"Because we keep getting forced together." I try to get past her to my room. "Mother, there are monumental things happening today and I can't believe you're even talking about this now."

She won't let me go.

"What is more monumental than your match? You don't have to like Charlus. It may come as a surprise, but when your father and I were matched I didn't like him either. However, I knew his genome was from excellent stock, and together, we've raised you. This match is a great advancement for you, Petra. The children you conceive will be part of a sovereign family."

"Mother, we're about to make first contact with another civilization—"

"You don't need to tell me that," she says, her truevoice rising with frustration. "Instead of preparing my department, I'm here, trying to get my daughter to see sense."

"I'm not promising myself to Charlus or anyone else," I say vehemently.

Mother pauses. "I see what this is about," she says. "This is about that sapien tutor back in Sealand."

"It's not about Fenan!"

Mother catches the color creeping into my cheeks. "Even worse," she says, realizing. "It's about that wild eximian."

"What are you talking about?"

"I told you not to get attached. He's to be kept at arm's length, like any foreign species."

"He's a human, not a foreign species. We're all human."

"Don't be facetious."

"I'm stating a fact."

"That sapien he came aboard with is a little savage and he's not much better. I'll be very glad when they're both off the ship." Mother takes a breath, reining in her emotions. "You cannot pass up the best chance of your life. If you turn Charlus down there'll be consequences for us all."

If I didn't know how indomitable she was, I'd say she looks almost desperate.

"So I must say yes to him, for your sake?"

Mother tucks a strand of hair behind my ear in a rare gesture of affection. "I trusted my mother and she was right. Your father and I have been a good match."

I decide to ask the question that's been troubling me.

"What happened to Caleb Ableson, Mother? Why was he executed?"

I see a flash of discomfiture on her face. "He broke a foundational law."

"It was Charlus's fault, wasn't it?"

"Charlus was the victim of sapien violence."

"But something incensed Caleb Ableson," I insist. "What did Charlus do to make him so angry?"

"What happened is none of our business and I urge you to—"

"It is my business if I'm to be his match. I don't like him and I don't trust him."

"Stop raising your voice!" Mother knows that sometimes my truevoice gets carried away and has occasionally burst beyond the boundaries of our privacy. Her own voice quiets to a whisper.

"We've fallen over backward to bring you into the fold, Petra. Don't be naive. One day you'll appreciate everything we've done."

Mother walks away. And I know this isn't over.

I tell Garena that Mother wants me to match with Charlus. I am hoping for her sympathy, but she congratulates me. She tells me she could see it coming. "When we get back to Sealand City, you'll be invited everywhere; no door will be closed to you. You've reached the top, Petra."

It's not really the reaction that I want.

"You refused your match, Garena. You said he was unfaithful and you didn't want him. What if I refuse mine?"

Garena just looks worried for me. "My match wasn't from a sovereign family."

I turn away, thinking of Rye's kisses, feeling a physical sensation running through me, an acute desire. He lit my body like a flame and I don't think I can go through my life and never taste his kiss again. I look down at the cloudscape as the airship slowly turns northwest.

"Do you ever wonder if we've got everything wrong?" I ask Garena.

"How do you mean?"

"Do you not think there's a different way to look at the world and we just can't see it?"

"Petra," she says with great kindness, "that kind of thinking won't make you happy."

I decide not to ask Garena for help with Wren. It will only get her into trouble. I must do this alone.

I have, however, taken her keys to the archive.

I open the door and the first thing I see is Rye's uniform and greatcoat, clean and mended, hanging on a rack. Immediately, I go to it. I want to pull it on, wrap it round me, breathe in his scent and imagine his touch.

In the ancient sapien texts that I used to read with Fenan, the word they use for this force is passion. Symptoms include lust, jealousy, wretchedness, and irrational behavior. Passion is to be avoided, say the ancient writers, as it invariably leads to tragedy. In their narratives, those who feel illicit passion end up broken in some way, or dead.

I'm a fool if I imagine that I'm free to love. I learned that with Fenan. My mother and father have me all sewn up.

Besides, I'm not sure if Rye feels the same. I know he likes me and he enjoyed the kiss but he's still in love with his girl Elsa and I can't compete with her. This passion is something I am carrying alone. The ancient writers call it an exquisite pain. They write poetry about it and this poetry is what I feel as I lay my head against an empty coat and put its empty arms around me. Rye . . .

I have things to do. I must pull myself together.

There's a rack of sapien uniforms and I take one, quickly dressing as a physical therapist. These sapien therapists come and go all the time, seeing to the needs of our crew. Our bodies suffer from inactivity and their task is to keep us in good muscular health. They wear pale orange, with a cap that comes low over the eyes. I won't attract much attention wearing it but I still don't know how I'm going to get up to the sapien floor.

I know there's no point asking the gatekeeper. He'll turn me straight back as he did before.

I go to the scouting craft hanger but as soon as I get there, I see one of Bradus's Division Enforcers coming down the staircase that separates the floors. He locks it closed behind him.

I decide to explore all the areas of the ship where I have never been and eventually, I come to the garbage area. Perhaps there is a chute that I can climb up. As I am holding my nose in the dismal place, a door in the wall slides open and two sapien cleaners come out of it. It's a service elevator. They politely hold the door open for me, thinking that I am one of their kind. It's my first stroke of luck. The elevator smells of rottenness, something an eximian never has to encounter.

I press the finger pad to ascend. The journey is only a few seconds long, but it will bring me out in a forbidden world. The metal doors grind open and at last I find myself on the sapien floor. I take my first steps. The corridor is narrow and the ceilings are lower up here. There is no art. It's not exactly unpleasant but the windows are smaller and everything is functional and plain. I realize that our floor is quite magnificent by comparison. The hum of the airship's great power source is all around me, its energy harnessed from the sun. I keep my head down and in my sapien uniform, with my cap over my eyes, none of these very busy people pays me much attention.

Their medical wing is directly above our own. When I ask to see Wren Apaluk I cause total consternation. The staff immediately know I shouldn't be there.

"You should go, miss," says the senior medic.

I decide that honesty is my best policy. I tell them I'm here on behalf of Rye Tern and that Wren Apaluk, as our guest, has every right to receive visitors. "Where is he?" I demand. "He's supposed to be here, in quarantine."

"Go back to your own deck, miss," says the senior medic. "We don't want any trouble."

"Any trouble is on my head, not yours."

"That's not the way it works." The senior medic says this as a statement of fact and I see a hint of resentment in his eyes.

"I'm very sorry," I tell him, "but I can't leave until I've seen Wren."

293

"If you don't go, I'll call the Division Enforcers."

I try a different tack. "Does it not strike you as marvelous that Rye Tern and Wren Apaluk are so close?" I argue. "Does it not give you hope for our people that such a relationship exists between an eximian and a sapien? They don't regard each other as different races. They're brothers; they're the same."

"You're Livia's daughter, aren't you?" says the junior medic.

"Yes," I say, "Petra."

The junior medic looks at her senior. "I'll walk her back to the gateway."

I realize it's a hopeless cause.

The junior medic leads me along the corridor toward the prow of the ship. I notice that she wears a silver hair clip with a dolphin on it and her identity pin tells me she's called Regan. The low throb of the ship's frontal power source gets louder and louder. She takes a circuitous route, and I realize we're not going to the gateway.

"The boy got upset," she says, turning to me confidentially. "He didn't like being in the small cabin and he hated that we locked the door. He didn't want to be separated from his friend. He wouldn't let us take his clothes away, not even to wash them, and he physically objected to our medical interventions. He wouldn't let us near him."

"I expect he was afraid," I say.

"Yes," agrees Regan. "He was—and none of the seniors took the time to speak to him. We were under orders to get the tests done as quickly as possible. When we failed, the chief biologist came up to oversee them herself."

"My mother?"

"I'm afraid she treated the boy like a sample of fauna."

"She treats everyone that way," I say, disappointed in her.

"The boy got very antagonistic," continues Regan. "He said that none of us had any right to touch him. He said he'd fought for his clothes and he was going to keep them. He had a knife secreted in his boot and when

Livia came at him with a syringe, he dived at her. We managed to restrain him but Livia was really shaken. Division Enforcers disarmed the boy and took him to the holding cells."

My hand goes up to my mouth. Wren has unwittingly broken a foundational law.

"Wren lunged at my mother with a knife?" I ask, appalled.

"Yes."

Now I know why she called him a savage. I feel a horrible foreboding. Regan has led me to a corridor right under the airship's frontal power source. There are small cells off to each side with glass doors. We're standing on a large glass panel in the floor. Looking down through it, I see that we are jutting out above the eximian viewing deck. I realize that the panel is a trapdoor. This is where they air-buried Caleb Ableson.

"Wren Apaluk is here," says Regan. "In the cells."

"Thank you for bringing me."

"I don't think it was his fault." I can feel the emotion in Regan's voice. "I don't want him to die like Caleb did. I don't think it's fair. He's just a boy and he doesn't know the rules here." I see a flame of anger that she's keeping buried under her politeness. Regan turns to go. "If you get apprehended . . ."

"I'll tell them that you took me to the main gateway—and I evaded you."

I give her my thanks and she walks away.

I look for Wren in each of the cells. They are all empty except for the last two. A young woman dressed exactly as I am in a pale orange uniform lies curled up on the bed in one of them. As I pass, she sits and looks at me and I notice that she's the heavily pregnant girl who was crying at the air-burial. I am desperately curious about her and I nod a greeting. A slim boy comes to the door of the cell opposite. It's Wren.

"Petra," he says.

"I'm here on Rye's behalf. He asked me to come and check on you."

"Is he a prisoner too?"

"No."

"You've no right to keep me here."

"I know. I agree."

"I want to go down to the ground. I was a prisoner in Brightland, trapped in a Pink House, and I won't be locked up again."

Wren's bravado is hiding his desperation. I cannot believe that my people have done this. Why, with all our scientific knowledge and technological advancement, could we not treat a frightened boy from a different culture with more respect?

"I'm going to help you," I say, making my decision then and there. "I don't know how yet but I will get you out."

"Where will I go? They say I've broken one of your founding laws by defending myself against that scientist. She was going to take my clothes off and there's no way—no way—" Wren cannot even articulate how violated he felt.

How do I make up for my mother's crass mishandling of a situation she didn't even try to understand?

"I will fly you to the ground," I say.

Wren puts his hands on the glass.

"You have to free Suki too," he says, and he nods to the cell behind me.

The girl is standing at her door, watching us. I look at her great pregnant belly in total fascination. She doesn't look much older than me. I wonder whose child she is carrying. Is it her own, or is she a surrogate for someone on the eximian floor? And why on earth is she locked up?

"Did no one teach you it was rude to stare?" she asks—which is uncommonly forthright for a sapien.

"Why are you here?" I ask her in bewilderment.

The girl sighs, as if the story is too exhausting to tell.

"She's here because the father of that baby is a shit-hound," says Wren.

I guess this is another Brightling swear.

296

"Suki didn't want the baby in the first place," he exclaims. "He forced himself on her. Then he abandoned her and now, once the baby's born, he's going to take it away."

"Wren," says Suki sharply. "I can tell her."

It takes a moment for me to untangle what Wren has said.

"Who?" I ask, already dreading Suki's answer. "Who's treated you this way?"

Suki hesitates as if she's scared to say his name and Wren jumps in, his anger burning like magnesium. "It's that useless stick insect who flew the plane."

"The admiral's son," says Suki quietly.

"Charlus." His name falls out of my mouth and leaves me without breath.

I suddenly see the spiderweb I'm standing on and I feel lightheaded. Whichever way I move, I'm going to get stuck and the more I struggle to find a way off, the worse the adhering threads will be.

Suki opens up. "He met me in Sealand City," she says. "I worked at his father's house and Charlus developed a fantasy that we were in love. But I was never in love. It's dangerous for a sapien to refuse a powerful man." Suki sits on the edge of her bed as she tells her tale. "My father tried to protect me. He wanted me to stay in Sealand City but Charlus insisted that I come on the airship. He wanted his child to be born on the voyage. But almost straightaway, he began to lose interest in me. I don't think he liked my pregnant shape. I was relieved—but my father pointed out that when my baby was born it would belong to Charlus. He wanted Charlus to sign a contract, giving me rights as the baby's mother. But Charlus wouldn't." Suki pauses. "My father went to speak on my behalf. I don't know what Charlus said but it must have been bad for my father to hit him."

"Your father was Caleb Ableson?"

Suki confirms it with a nod of her head. She won't allow herself to cry.

"I'm so sorry," I say. It feels ludicrous to say something so inadequate.

"I tried to stop the air-burial," says Suki. "I rallied others around me. My father was well-respected and I almost succeeded. There was a vote up here as to whether we should lay down our tools and withdraw our labor from the airship until my father was released—but someone betrayed what we were planning. I was accused by Admiral Xalvas of attempting to incite a mutiny."

"What will they do with you?"

"The admiral and his son are waiting for my child to be born and then I'll be redundant. I don't know what they'll do."

"Help her," says Wren, blazing. "You have to get us out of here. Let's go, now."

What do I do? Where can I take them? I look at the controls to the door.

"How well are you guarded?" I ask.

"A pregnant girl and a teenage boy?" questions Wren with a half laugh. "They feed us three times a day and we are allowed out once to wash. We're pretty much left alone apart from that."

A plan begins to form in my mind. I have no idea if I'll have the courage to see it through. My courage has never really been tested before.

"I'll help you," I say. "But you have to wait."

"What if Suki's baby doesn't wait?" asks Wren insistently. There's so much pent-up energy in him I worry that he'll throw himself against the door and break his shoulder bone.

"Xalvas has agreed to take *Celestis* to Ayland," I say. "We're on our way to make first contact. There's no point me rescuing you while we're over a poisoned desert. You must wait until we're near the city of Reem and there are people who can help us. I'll pack the scouting craft and I'll come back."

"Why would you help us?" asks Suki. "You, alone of all the eximians—why?"

Fenan Lee, Rye Tern, Wren Apaluk, Suki Ableson, me. We are all connected. I see Caleb Ableson falling through the air, his hands bound behind his back. I look at Suki.

298

"I saw your father die," I say, "and I thought it was wrong."

As I travel back down in the service elevator, I consider what to do.

I can't tell anyone. Especially not Rye. Rye dreams of my people helping him. And my actions in saving Wren and Suki might imperil that. If I'm caught, it must be my crime and mine alone. I walk along the wide, burnished corridors of the eximian quarters, with my pale orange cap pulled low.

It's dangerous to refuse a powerful man.

Suki is not the only one entrapped by Charlus. By freeing her, perhaps I'll also free myself.

I thank heavens for my status as a scouting craft trainee. It gives me access to the mainframe and I will be able to hack the codes that unlock the prison cells.

As I replace the orange uniform where I found it, I think how I'll spend the time till we arrive over Ayland's capital. I'll hone my flying skills on the flight simulator, preparing myself to steal a craft. I must think of every eventuality. Suki is a time bomb. I have no idea how babies are delivered and I must find out. I wish that I could ask the airship's chief biologist.

I lay my head on Rye's coat and breathe. In my heart, I know that my mother's trying to do her best for me but she is my adversary now.

As I slip back into our cabin to return Garena's key, I think of the spiderweb that I am standing on. I can't arouse anyone's suspicion. So I go to find the spider and do what must be done.

Charlus is in his father's stateroom with the Senior Circle. I think they must be discussing how they will proceed in Reem. I avoid Mother's eye altogether. I walk into the room exactly like a shy and silly girl of seventeen. Rye isn't there and in a way, I'm glad. It will make this easier.

"Hello," I say. "May I borrow Charlus for a moment? I'm trying to use the flight simulator and I can't get it to work." I smile a big wide smile and look coyly at Charlus.

He follows me down onto the flight deck.

"Why are we here, Petra?" he asks. "You know exactly how that simulator works. You're better at it than I am."

I turn to him. "Yes," I say.

"Yes what?"

"I hope you can forgive me for hesitating. It's such a big step. But if the offer still stands then yes, I would like to be your match."

He looks at me quizzically as I approach him.

"I thought you'd fallen for the lumpen refugee."

"It was seeing him next to you that made me realize. You're so much finer in every way."

I stand up on my tiptoes and I pull him down toward me.

His kiss tastes a bit like prawns.

"Wow," he says.

And I suppose that seals it.

41 ✶　　SWAN

Kite is in a whiskey sleep. I've hardly ever seen him drunk in all the years I've known him. Yearning for power has kept him stone-cold sober and as keen as a blade. But now that power is his, it's intriguing to see him stupefied with whiskey. When we got back from the Chrysalid House, he took me to his rooms and he drank until he flopped. I handled him as best I could until he slithered into bed. Now his snores are rattling the rafters.

Perhaps he's deadening his brain, in case Peregrine's ghost pays him a visit. This thought brings an absurd laugh up in me and I push it down, worried it will come out sounding like a shriek.

There's a pain in my chest, making it hard for me to breathe.

Kaira.

Shall I tell her that Harrier's family is doomed? Shall I lay their deaths at her door? If she hadn't gone behind my back, Harrier would still be free.

Treacherous rat. She betrayed me.

The pain grows tighter. My jaw is clenched, my fingernails are digging in my palms, I'm pacing, aggravated by Kite's snores.

I can't stay here. I'm going to suffocate.

I leave Kite's rooms and head toward my own. I feel dirty and I want to be clean. My whole body is aching with tension and I try to loosen my shoulders. I start to move them like a dancer, trying to lift the weight off my chest. I dance my way down the entire ladies' corridor, twisting, turning, until I reach my rooms. I'm sure I look mad. I close the door and step into the whiteness.

I decide that I hate the color white. I'm going to change everything in here. Tomorrow I will have it painted red or purple or shit brown, anything but this devastating, empty white. How have I endured it all these years?

I go into my bedchamber. I want to be cleansed and pampered and laid to rest. But none of my ladies are in sight. Starling Beech has locked them all in with the dolly.

He's left the key in their door.

I turn the key and enter the chrysalids' room. The smell of sleeping women fills my nose, the heavy perfume that I make them wear. There is no air.

"Kaira?" Two of the songless, soulless things stand, ready for my order. I ignore them. "Kaira?" I repeat.

Has Starling set her free? Did she mind-twist him into helping her? Gala, she's more cunning than I thought.

Then I remember the laundry room and I descend the little spiral staircase.

She's there, on the floor, under a quilt with one of the chrysalids. It's Lady Libra. Kaira is sleeping with her arm around this insensible creature.

Why?

For some reason, the sight cracks my heart. They're so close. There cannot possibly be any bond between them but Kaira's whole position speaks of tender care. How can Kaira care about this thing that has no feelings? They look so peaceful. I move away from them because my eyes are stinging, damn them both.

Why does she not give such care to me? Am I more repugnant to her than this senseless chrysalid?

I climb back up the stairs.

"Make me clean," I order the ladies. "I want to be bathed. Purify me. Get the stains off my soul."

They don't understand the instructions.

"Wash me!" I yell.

I am like a sterile statue while they wash me and dress me in white velvet. When they are finished, I walk into my wardrobe. White dresses hang on rails, one for every possible occasion. Tomorrow, I will need something fitting for a hanging. I take down a dress and give it to Lady Scorpio.

"Dye it black," I say.

When I get back to his rooms, Kite is stirring. His head is splitting and he's growling like a bear. I mix him some pain relief and sit him up on pillows while he sips. He runs his hands down the white velvet dress, which sits tightly around my hips.

"Nice," he says, pulling me toward him.

Fortunately, we have no time.

His manservants take him to his dressing room and I open a window to let out the whiskey fumes. It's still dark but the birds know that day is coming. I stand, listening, and their song is like a balm. I look down on the rose trees by a fountain and I breathe. The sound of the water feels like a trickle of relief, like a drink in the desert, and in the air, there is a faint scent of roses. My eyes close.

I want to be held, the way Kaira was holding that chrysalid. Why was she pouring all her kindness and compassion into that creature?

Because I frightened and condemned her, I rejected her and locked her up. She's seeking solace where she can. She's still a child and I abandoned her, she's—

I'm being watched.

My eyes flick open. A figure in songlight stands by the fountain, looking up at me.

The spy. Kingfisher.

He bows his head with something more than politeness. I hear my name in his clear songlight.

"Sister Swan."

I've played our duel over and over in my mind. Each time, it sears me with passionate fury. I feel it now, churning the hollowness inside.

"What do you want?" I make no effort to conceal my hate. I'm in that fight again, being locked to him, body and mind. I feel the same raw exposure now. I want to attack him, as he once attacked me. He senses it.

"We don't have to be adversaries," he says. He's not wearing his vivid azure. His plain blue uniform is ragged and worn. But his eyes are just the same.

"I think of you all the time," he says, and his songlight is as clear as the waters of the fountain.

I see what's happened here. Kaira has cried out to her precious Lark for help—and this Aylish Torch has been enlisted as her knight. Cunning. While I was in the Chrysalid House suffering mortification, Kaira was baring her soul to my foes.

"You must think I was born yesterday," I say.

"What if we were not enemies?" he asks. A finger of dawn creeps into the sky, casting light upon his face. "I'm coming to Brightlinghelm, so we may meet."

"You'll be dead before you get here," I tell him. "Kite will hunt you down."

"I have no interest in Kite," he says, stepping forward, gazing up. "I'd like to meet with you."

"Why?"

"I saw strength in you, and subjugated courage. I told my people you had the qualities of a leader. We want to negotiate peace with you."

I laugh. This is really funny.

"Do I look like a fool?" I ask this songlight trespasser.

Then I smell peppermint and whiskey. There's a rasping breath in my ear. "Why are you laughing?" asks Kite.

I spin round. He's there, dressed and ready.

"I'm just happy at the thought of the day. I am relishing my freedom."

His hair is slicked over his thin patch. "You were laughing yesterday too. What's funny?"

"Do you not believe that my present circumstances could be giving me pleasure?" I try to lay my head on his shoulder but it's slightly awkward because of my height. "I'm counting my blessings," I tell him. "I have everything I could ever want."

I want the Aylish Torch to see our tenderness. I want him to believe that I am cherished here. But Kite has got a headache and he hates affection.

304

He moves away and when I glance back at the fountain, the Aylishman has gone.

Kite picks up my Siren's band to put it on.

"No," I say, refusing it. "You promised. I am to be free."

"What were you doing just then?" he asks suspiciously. "A child could tell you were using songlight. Who were you with?"

I think fast. "Your position is vulnerable. You saw how Greylag undermined you. I'm trying to discover if he's plotting against you. I'm working for your safety, even while you sleep."

Kite considers. He puts the band in his jacket so I know I must behave.

If I use my songlight again, I had better make it subtle.

Ouzel is waiting outside Kite's rooms and they walk ahead of me, discussing their war games.

I process my encounter with the Torch. Was there any truth in it? Has he really been thinking of me ever since our fight? I know how often I've played it over in my mind. I recall the memory I stole from him: the boy, diving into a lake, coming up with a fish in his hand.

Kingfisher.

As we enter the great hall, we are met by Drake and Ruppell, who give Kite a full report of the arrests and roundups that have been made in the city. Ruppell tells Kite that the Chrysalid House is filling nicely with undesirables of every kind.

"Good," says Kite. "You know what to do."

"Indeed I do." Ruppell grins.

Instead of closing the Chrysalid House, Kite is packing it to the gills. Kaira begged me to help Harrier. I could have acted differently. I could have—

I see him, the Aylishman, at the foot of Peregrine's statue in audacious songlight.

"There's a different future," he says, "where we are allies."

"Get out, spy. You're not welcome here!"

I close him out and he disappears.

305

Greylag joins our retinue. He positions himself next to Kite. "Congratulations, my lord," he says. "I hear that Harrier awaits his trial."

Kite looks at him with narrow eyes and Greylag grovels, apologizing for his outburst, glancing at me resentfully. Kite accepts the apology but I can see that their relationship is shaken. Kite's trust in Greylag is melting. I can use this.

"Lady Swan," says Drake, looking at my breasts. "I see your sweet little dolly isn't with you today."

"No," I tell him. "The little thing gets tired. I have to let it sleep."

"I always enjoy the sight of your veiled ladies. Such fine beauties."

"Yes." I pull my face into a smile. "And they never answer back."

"Perfection," says Drake. "Sometimes I think my wives could do with a trip to the Chrysalid House." He is laughing. And I laugh too. This is shit-makingly funny.

I feel Kite grip my arm. My laughter is annoying him.

"When we get there," he instructs, "you'll speak to the airmen. I need you to be their inspiration. I want them filled with vigor for their task."

That's when I see the Aylishman again. He's by the doors, watching us approach. This spy does not give up.

"You don't belong with these people," he says in songlight.

And with a pang that rings right though me, I agree.

"You could be part of something new," he says.

"Tell Alize and her people to go back to Ayland," I whisper with a breath of songlight. "There's nothing for them here. Kite will not make peace."

"We know that. It's why I'm here, speaking with you."

I walk right past him without a glance. But his words resonate.

This youth is clever and he's bright. I felt his keen intelligence when we dueled. He knows exactly what to say and he will try to light a cruel flame of hope.

He keeps pace, striding at my side. And I have to admit that even as my

306

enemy, he's more companionable than this motley elite. The danger of this situation should make me shut him out. But it makes me feel alive.

"I know you've met with Eminence Alize," he says. "We cannot escalate this war. It would be catastrophic for both nations. Help us to secure the peace."

I should banish him. But I don't. We head into the grounds, where a funicular awaits to take us to the airfield. We climb aboard. Kite speaks into my ear. His mouthwash is wearing off.

"I intend to fly with the fleet today. It will boost their morale to have me at their helm. While I am gone, you are my eyes."

I nod my understanding and turn my head away. The whiskey fumes are bad.

Gala, the Aylishman is right in front of me in songlight. I look into his handsome, risk-taking face.

"You're a pearl," he says, "in a pigsty."

I bet he makes Kaira's girlish heart turn upside down.

"Where are you?" I ask him in songlight.

"Close enough," he says. And we take each other in. I sense forest around him but it really feels as if he's inches away.

"I saw your quality the day we fought at sea," he says. "You're a leader."

It's hard not to laugh at this. It's hard not to cry. I straighten out my song-light, enough so I can speak. "So Kaira Kasey has come to you about my wickedness and you are trying to flatter me?"

"Kaira will not hear a word said against you," says Kingfisher. "She's your greatest advocate."

"I commend your acting skills," I say.

"You're a good person, Zara, being used by evil men."

So subtle, the way he slips in my name, so charming, so thrilling.

"I'm not expecting you to trust me," he says. "But you should know who you are standing with. I want to show you something."

He's opening himself to me. This is the trick Drew Alize played yesterday. She convinced me that she had nothing to hide—but she did. I found it. What is this Kingfisher hiding? He's inviting me into his core.

I join him, feeling our harmony run through my body. He's showing me an image of his childhood: I see him as a boy, hungry, ragged, looking through a barbed wire fence.

His eyes are on Ruppell in the funicular. And in Kingfisher's memory, I see a younger Ruppell. He is in a doctor's coat, in some kind of prison camp, picking out people who all wear lead bands. They are taken into a low building. One woman turns round and gazes at Kingfisher, her eyes bidding him farewell—his mother. He watches her go, bereft. Then I see him staring down at her corpse. There's a clumsy incision in her scalp. She didn't survive the operation. I sense the full shock of his boyhood grief because he's feeling it afresh at the sight of Ruppell.

"You're standing among monsters," he says. "You know how it will go, Zara. Eventually, you'll end the same way as my mother."

For some seconds I just stare at him, Torch to Torch. The way he says my name sends a shiver down my spine.

"If we can't save Harrier," he says, "you are Brightland's hope."

This mention of Harrier throws me.

"I gave Harrier to Kite," I say. "You know that, don't you? Kaira will have told you." I let my songlight flow into him, opening myself, showing him exactly what I did. What difference does it make? This respect for me is all part of his playact, pretending I'm a pearl. He knows damn well how tarnished I am. "I destroyed Harrier and his family in a moment of blind spite. So look at me now and tell me I'm a leader."

I can see Kingfisher's shock. He knew nothing about it. Kaira kept my shameful act to herself. Even as she was seeking his help, she was protecting me, hiding what I'd done. This cuts me to the quick.

The Aylishman says nothing more. He vanishes. And tears fall down my face. I pretend I'm dazzled by the first beams of dawn and I wipe them hurriedly away.

When the doors open, Kite pulls me out onto the airstrip. We walk ahead of the others.

"What are you doing?" he asks. "You've been totally distracted, songlight pouring from you, tears in your eyes. Who are you with?"

I invent something. "Greylag plots against you," I say. "In his under-thoughts he is disloyal. He dreams of leading Brightland in the name of Thal."

Kite peers at me, envious. And I am steadfast in my lie.

The fleet salutes us as we walk into the hanger. I don't know where these airmen are going and I don't know why I do the things I do. What are these hot and cold moods I have, these acts of spite I commit? I have been Kite's creature since I was a girl. My need to please him is so ingrained that I betrayed a good man without thinking of the consequence. As we climb to the podium, I realize that Kite's been giving me instructions and I haven't listened.

I regard them, the rows of air force personnel standing to attention in front of me: pilots, gunners, ground crew. What am I supposed to say?

"I wish things could be different," I begin, my voice distorting in the microphone. "I feel you're all my brothers." Kite stiffens next to me. I try and focus—but what did he ask me to do?

"Looking at you now, I feel we're all one big family."

Kite hates this. It's cloying sentiment.

"Sometimes we are asked to do hard things, things that go against our better natures."

Kite clenches his jaw.

"But you are pioneers, flying at the cusp of a new dawn." I remember— yes—I must inspire them. "Sometimes, the greatest danger to a nation is not the foreign enemy. It is the enemy within, the enemy on our own streets. That enemy is the insurgent." I have it now, I'm back on track.

The Aylishman has gone for good, I expect. I saw the shock in his eyes and he won't come back. He'll be broadcasting my act of spite to all his comrades now. *Harrier will die because of Zara Swan.*

"Brave airmen . . ." Words fail me again. I am a shallow, treacherous Siren. "We must put our trust in Lord Kite. Lord Kite has our best interests at heart. May Thal fly with you. And may Lord Kite bring you safely home."

There is silence. I can't go on. The wind blows through me as I climb down from the podium. That's the worst speech I ever gave and Kite knows it. Drake leaps up to the microphone, lowering it so he can reach.

"There are rank traitors, hiding in our forests!" he cries enthusiastically. "Unhumans and villains, runaways, degenerates, whores and thieves who, like cowards, are planting bombs, killing our women and children, destroying our way of life! I say death to this scum, death to them!"

This is the kind of thing Kite wanted. He approaches me.

"I gave you a simple task," he says. "You can't be trusted, can you?" He puts one hand on the back of my neck, bringing me over to Ruppell.

Drake is whipping up the crowd. "Death to the traitors!"

"Death to the traitors, death to the traitors!" cry the airmen obediently.

"When you get back to the palace, would you assist Lady Swan?" Kite asks Ruppell. I see him draw the lead band out of his jacket and give it to the Minister of Purity. "Her head is troubling her."

"Dear lady," says Ruppell, grinning, "we know just the cure for that."

Not twelve hours have passed and Kite has gone back on his promise. I grab him as he walks away, hissing under my breath. "You gave your word you wouldn't put that band on me again."

"I won't," he says coldly. "Ruppell will."

As I recover from this contemptible duplicity, everything comes clear. Kingfisher.

"We know exactly where the insurgents have their base," continues Drake. "We're going to the Greensward to cleanse them with fire."

I send up my songlight, calling his name. I try to reach him but he doesn't respond. Perhaps he's blocking me out, telling the rest of his rabble of my ruthless act.

"Today, we destroy the enemy within," finishes Drake, "tomorrow, the Aylish. Victory will be ours!"

"Victory, victory!"

There is the usual cheering. Then the eight chosen pilots and their gunners go to their planes. Kite puts on an airman's jacket. He comes to me as if there's nothing wrong.

"In your radiobine address," he instructs me, "you must tell the people that Harrier's execution will be at dawn tomorrow. I want the whole city to be present."

His Ministers are listening.

"Yes, my lord," I say.

Kite turns his back and I see him go to greet his pilot. I stand unmoving, until Kite climbs into his chosen plane. The roar is deafening as the planes line up on the runway. We watch until they soar away. All the while I have been trying to reach Kingfisher.

I pull myself together. I must find out exactly where those planes are going. I ask Ouzel but he tells me it's top secret and moves away. I will get it out of Ruppell. But first, I see my opportunity.

I must do what I can for Harrier, as I promised.

"I'm thinking ahead to Harrier's execution," I tell the Ministers. "And I'm considering how we might best support Lord Kite. It was his plan last night to string Harrier's wives and children up with him. Much as I abhor the whole family," I say, "I can't help thinking that such an act might just backfire."

"Lord Kite knows best," says Drake.

"But I know the public," I tell the Ministers. "They will perceive such an act as wanton cruelty."

"I see what you mean, Sister," says Ouzel. "I believe Harrier's youngest is a boy of eight."

"How will it look to watch him hanging?" I ask.

Ouzel nods, pretending he has wisdom. "Perhaps Harrier's children are an unnecessary step."

"Quite so," I say. "We want Lord Kite to be cherished by the people, as our Great Brother was. They would appreciate an act of clemency for Harrier's family, I'm sure."

Greylag sniffs with his usual stony contempt but the other Ministers look convinced. I hope this is enough to save their lives.

Ruppell takes my arm to walk me to the funicular.

"Kite has given me a jolly little task, my dear," he says as we enter. "We'd better find a private place when we get back to the palace." He pats the lead band, which sits in his breast pocket.

As we ride down the hill, I think of what this man did to Kingfisher's mother. I think of what he did to the woman lying on the laundry room floor with Kaira's arms around her. I think of what he did to me. There's a lock that sits in my skull and I will never be rid of it.

"Remind me where's Kite's going, so I may think of him?" I ask.

"Sherlham," says Ruppell. "Exterminating this rats' nest of insurgents offers him the perfect opportunity to trial his firebombs, before launching them on Reem."

"Yes." I smile. "Sherlham."

Once more I send my songlight up. Once more, I hear nothing.

The funicular doors open and Ruppell leads me into the palace. He's far more subtle than Drake. He's fondling my inner arm with his thumb. Somehow, that's even worse than Drake's blatant stares and stupid lust. The Minister of Purity steers me into an empty office.

"Shall we secrete ourselves in here, while I remove your hair?"

I feel Ruppell's pleasure surging as he takes off my wig. One day, I will flush this man's remains down a city drain.

"I've always felt a strong bond between us, dear lady," he says. "I want you to know that if something untoward should ever happen to Lord Kite, I would be waiting to take care of you."

"What could possibly happen to Kite?" I say, blinking innocently.

"Well, for example, air travel is dangerous—so are Brightlinghelm's

312

insurgents. But you mustn't worry. I value your work for Brightland and I would want you to continue it."

I am astonished. Kite's greatest ally is plotting against him and I didn't even have to read the bastard's mind. He's told me to my face.

"Thank you," I say. "I appreciate your care."

It's while I'm standing with my bare skull on view that the Aylishman comes back. I make no attempt to hide what's being done to me. Kingfisher takes in the scene, visibly affected.

"I have met with my comrades," he tells me in his clear, unsullied songlight. "They are devastated by what you have done. But your confession goes a long way."

"I've been trying to reach you," I tell him.

"If you want to redeem yourself, the only way is to help us."

I sense people walking among trees. I hear a river flowing somewhere near.

"Kite's planes are in the sky," I say with the last of my songlight. "He's coming for the insurgent base. Make sure that no one you care about is anywhere near Sherlham."

I see a flash of horror in his eyes as Ruppell brings down the lead band. I feel the key turning in my skull. And the Aylishman is gone.

42 ✦ PIPER

Kite brings his Ministers and Sister Swan to see us off. We listen to some empty speeches and we cry the usual cries and Finch looks full of fervor. But all the while my eyes are on Kite, wondering how I ever believed that this man had all the answers.

As we prepare our plane, Axby approaches. He tells us that today, Finch will be flying as his gunner, as I have been tasked with piloting Lord Kite.

"Lord Kite would like to drop the first firebombs on our target," Axby tells me. "You must show him how it's done. Make sure the mission is a success for him."

"Yes, sir." I realize that I am expected to say, "That's a very great honor." So I say it. "But is it true that we're bombing people in the Greensward?"

"We cannot question these orders, Crane," says Axby firmly. And something in his tone makes me think he's tried.

I catch Finch's eyes as he prepares Axby's plane. How do I begin to tell him that I think Kite's a murderer and that this whole war is built upon a pack of lies? I should have spoken when we had our moment of time. But I didn't want to mar my happiness.

Before I know it, Kite is approaching in his flying jacket and I salute him, quickly hiding how I feel.

"This is a great day, Crane," he says, "and I'm pleased to be seeing it for myself."

What if I refuse to fly him?

I tell him it's the honor of my life to be his pilot.

"Let's have no crash-landings on the Isis today," Kite threatens, wagging his finger humorously, and I laugh like a good lad.

I show him the mechanism for releasing the bombs and I give him clear instructions on what he has to do. He fits well into Finch's seat.

"You'll have a good view from here, my lord," I say.

I remember the day I flew Wheeler to Northaven. He squashed himself in and found takeoff so frightening he was sick into a bag. I hope Lord Kite doesn't do the same but I stack some bags in the cockpit, just in case. As I buckle myself in, my discomfort at this situation grows. I've listened to every news report about the fugitives. I know that Ma is still alive.

What if she and Elsa are with the insurgents?

It's intimate, flying in a Firefly. It's just you and your gunner over the wide world. I am flying at the head of the formation, with Axby and Finch just behind. I see Kite looking down, taking in the view as the Isis winds through farmland and villages.

"Beautiful country, isn't it, Crane?" he remarks. "Best in the world. One of the few green and temperate places left, by all accounts. Ice to the north of us, toxins to the south. We're lucky to be Brightlings."

"Yes indeed," I say. And I get ahold of myself. I could give him two-word answers or I could be cleverer than that. "It's a gentle landscape down here in the south," I tell him. "Very different from Northaven. It's all moorland and mountains up there."

"Serious acts of treachery were committed in Northaven, wouldn't you agree?" asks Kite.

"Yes, sir," I say, recalling in a flash how Syker ran his bayonet through John Jenkins. "My sergeant was killed, Sergeant Redshank, the man who trained me. He was a good man, one of the best."

"I'm sure you'd like to see his killers brought to justice, wouldn't you?"

"Yes, sir, I would. Everyone responsible should face the highest justice."

Wheeler's already dead. What about you, Kite, when will you pay?

I remember the prisoners I saw manacled in the barracks as I left Northaven: Heron's men, Gailee Roberts, Mr. Malting and his family, Hoopoe Guinea.

"What will happen to the Northaven rebels?" I ask.

"I'm pleased you asked," says Kite. "I'm having them brought to Brightlinghelm. I want the whole nation to know how insurrectionists are dealt with. I'm building a gallows along the esplanade and once Harrier and his

315

family have been executed, I will deal with those who ended your brave sergeant's life."

I sit back, stunned. Thal's teeth, this man can't be hanging Gailee Roberts?

"You've gone quiet, Crane."

"It's hard for me, sir, to comprehend such deep corruption and iniquity. My own town has been riven in two."

"All the more reason why it must never happen again. Insurgency cannot be given any oxygen. Hence, our mission today."

We're above rolling meadows now. I see sheep looking like tiny maggots on the land. Ahead lies Lake Lunen, glittering blue in the sun.

"One day, Crane, when this war is over, we'll develop planes that can cross the wide ocean. We shall lay claim to new lands and people them with Brightlings."

"A noble ambition, sir."

Kite tells me his vision of a great Brightling empire. A few days ago, it would have inspired me, but as we fly over the wilderness of cut-down stumps that marks the beginning of the Greensward, I'm only half listening. I think of those bombs waiting to fall.

How can I stop this?

"Sir," I say. "My mother's family is from the Greensward."

Kite turns round to stare at me. "I know all about your mother. She's on the run with the fugitive Mikane. I'm prepared to show her leniency for your sake but the rest of them will hang."

"I understand that, sir, and I thank you from my heart for such great clemency. Do you have any news of where the fugitives are?"

"Three different groups of bounty hunters all claim to have found them. You'd better hope they're not in Sherlham, Crane."

Be clever.

"In war," I say, "the way to victory is to avoid what is strong, and strike at what is weak."

Kite looks pleased at this. "Those are my own words," he says.

"Yes, my lord. If there are casualties today, it's in pursuit of a greater good.

You also said that the supreme art of war is to subdue the enemy without fighting. That's what we're doing, isn't it, subduing people, without fighting?"

"You have it, Crane. You have it. Eight pilots and their gunners can subdue a whole treacherous rebellion." Kite sits back, satisfied.

"What if we hit innocent people, forest people, families with children?"

This question is a mistake and I know it straightaway.

"If they're with the terrorists, they're not innocent." Kite takes time to explain. "Those people are part of an equation one must make. The Light People called them collateral damage."

Axby's voice comes into my radiobine headset.

"Target approaching. Prepare to fire."

I look down into the green. I see Kite's hands curl around the release rod. Far below, in clearings beneath the trees, I see people running like ants. I see crafts being pushed onto a river. Do they know what's coming?

If they knew, they would be screaming.

Do something.

A feeling of paralysis takes hold of me as Axby talks us down to the firing point through our headsets. I have never felt more useless in my life.

"Three, two, one. Fire."

Kite releases our bomb. It falls and explodes into a huge billowing orange flower.

I am a coward. Somehow I could have prevented this. And I did not.

"Show me, show me!" Kite is squealing in excitement like a schoolboy. I veer round and he watches in awe as Finch drops his bomb and another fireball engulfs the trees.

I keep circling, making sure that Lord Kite sees what we do to the people of the Greensward.

"Incredible," he says, as the orange-and-yellow flowers suck all the oxygen out of the air and black smoke billows up. "Magnificent."

I see it too.

And I will never forget.

317

43 ✳ LARK

We waste no time. As soon as Kingfisher leaves Swan, we Torches begin to cry warnings to Sherlham. Now we're running toward it, praying we arrive in time to get people out. Raven tells us that the encampment is in the next valley and we're climbing a steep hill as fast as we can. Kam Fairley is sprinting through the trees. His partner is there with their baby son and he disappears over the brow of the hill. Bel is to one side of me; Ma and Heron follow behind. Kingfisher is ahead, running with Raven Pine.

I hated him communing with Swan. I felt my exclusion like a hot sore. Kingfisher's still affected, I know he is. Swan's talons pierced right through his skin. I don't have time to dwell on this but the thoughts keep intruding even as I run. Swan has *moved* him.

I force them both from my mind, pouring out my songlight.

"Run! Kite's planes are coming! Run!"

We hear an alarm sounding down in the valley. People will be waking, leaving everything they own, fleeing. We Torches make sure our warnings are crystal clear, telling the camp at Sherlham what is about to descend. We sense people scattering, running for their lives.

Not fast enough.

Gala, we can hear them coming. The planes.

We reach the brow of the hill but the forest is still too dense to see the encampment. We know it's down below us but it's hidden perfectly in the trees.

"Run!" we Torches cry. "Save yourselves. Go to the river!"

The planes are visible in the distance, glinting in the golden dawn like droning wasps. I come to a halt and see Ma nearby. We're both thinking the same thing. I'm the one who says it.

"Piper."

"They're using him," says Ma. "He's a boy who loved planes and they're using him."

When the first explosion comes, Kingfisher holds Bel. I hold Ma. The fireball is terrifying. When the bomb hits the ground it explodes in white and orange flames right up to the top of the canopy. I hear piercing screams. Someone is on fire down there. I can't look. I close my eyes, hugging Ma.

If Piper is up there, the rift between us cannot be healed.

Another bomb drops—closer. Heron stands watching powerlessly, as all the air is pulled from around us to be consumed in the fire. We see whole trees crack and shatter in the explosion. Splinters become missiles and Heron puts his hand up to his face. There's something in his scarred eye socket—a piece of wood like a dagger. He turns to me and to my horror I can see his face is pouring blood. Another bomb falls, uprooting trees, sucking all our oxygen to feed its flames. We can't breathe. There's not enough air.

"Turn back," says Kingfisher. "Turn back now. Run!"

We grab Heron, who seems puzzled by his injury, and we retreat as fast as we can. No one dares touch the wooden dagger in his eye. I thank Gala it's the scarred one and not the one he sees with. The fourth bomb hits and I hear more dreadful screaming coming from the camp. The inferno roars behind us, coming closer. The bombs keep coming. Each one splits our ears and causes tremors in the ground.

I pray that people have made it to the river. I pray the smoke doesn't kill them.

I look up and see the final plane in the formation releasing its load. A tiny black dot falls from the sky. It's going to land right on top of us.

"Faster," I scream. "Faster!"

We run like the wind, helter-skelter down the hill toward the river. We're part of a crowd of terrified, fleeing people now. We're pulling Heron. Ma runs with Bel. The bomb lands to one side of us and we're thrown to the ground. I see a man impaled as he runs toward us. The trees are death traps of sharp wooden missiles and his body is shattered before our eyes. There is no oxygen, the fire is taking everything. The roar and boom of the impact has deafened me. I am disoriented, terrified, and next thing I know, my lungs are full of chemical smoke.

I make it onto my hands and knees. The chemical is in my eyes now. Through the pouring tears I see Bel helping Ma away. I see Heron, picking himself up off the ground, the hideous missile still in his eye. He lets out a roar of rage and pain.

Where's Kingfisher? I can't see him in the blinding smoke and I start to panic. Where has he gone? Why isn't he with me?

Then I perceive her.

She's there, grinning at me in delight amid all the destruction, that bony figure, Death. She's staring right at me, as if I am hers. I seem to lose all ability to move. I hear the air cracking all around me but everything sounds as if it's far away. I hear my own name being yelled but my ears are ringing and the sound is distorted.

"Elsa!"

Suddenly a figure lands on me, pushing me.

With a howl, Kingfisher propels us both forward. I hadn't seen the falling tree. He throws me to the ground and it crashes, burning, behind us, exactly where I was standing, landing inches from Kingfisher's heels. The sound reverberates through the earth, through our bodies. I hit the ground on my back, all the air forced out of my lungs. I feel Kingfisher gripping me in shock and I don't let go of him for the longest time.

"Elsa," he says. And he lays his head on me. My arms wrap around his back.

I cannot speak. Not even my songlight can be mustered. I hold him tight. Time stops.

"Don't die," he says.

I press my cheek against his and when I can finally breathe, I whisper: "So you do care."

His lips brush my neck. And I know it then. This wordless thing between us—it is love.

Gradually, my heart starts to beat. I become aware of blood, pouring down Kingfisher's arm, of flames licking at our feet. He loves me. It is clear.

We help each other to stand, pulling each other away from the mighty,

320

burning tree. The ringing sound in my ears recedes and I can hear Ma, screaming my name.

"Here!" I manage to call. "I'm here!"

When I look back to where it was standing, the bony figure is gone.

Kingfisher and I move as one, gripping on to each other, and somehow, we get to the river's edge. Ma and Bel have Heron between them. I see Ma's relief as we approach and she turns her attention on the wooden spike embedded in Heron's eye socket.

"Gala in heaven," I hear her say.

Heron smiles grimly, blood all over his teeth. "I already lost that bastard eye," he says. "It makes no difference to me."

I dread to think of the pain he must be in.

Fire is coming at us, eating its way through the trees. Roaring flames, screaming people, falling branches.

I see Raven Pine, coming out of the smoke, holding a tiny new baby in one arm. In the other, she's supporting a young woman.

"Kam," screams the baby's mother. "Kam!"

"There's nothing we can do," cries Raven, over the sound of the fire. "If we go back for him, we'll die."

Raven puts the baby in Bel's arms and goes to lift the stricken young mother onto a raft.

I see Bel looking down at the tiny human scrap. She's staring at him, stupefied.

"He isn't breathing," she says. "We need to help him."

"Ma!" I cry. "Ma helps women with their labors," I tell Bel. "She sees babies into the world. She'll know what to do."

Ma and Bel climb onto the raft and lay the baby on his side. Bel talks to him, while Ma massages his tiny heart, breathing her breath into his mouth.

"We've got you," says Bel in gentle tones. "You're coming on the river now, and everybody loves you. . . ."

321

I can sense her pouring calming, loving songlight into this tiny, struggling boy. His mother looks on, distraught, as Bel and Ma work. Ma holds the baby upside down by the feet and strongly taps his back.

"Breathe!" she orders.

I can't describe what I feel when the tiny baby fills his lungs and starts to scream. Ma looks drenched with relief.

"He'll be all right," she says. "If we get him away from this chemical smoke."

I'm standing waist-deep in the river, pushing the raft away from the bank, when I see Heron pulling the wooden missile out of his eye. It's a mistake. Blood pours and the pain must be very bad because Heron's legs go from under him and he sinks into the river. I cry out:

"Heron, Heron!"

Kingfisher helps me grab him.

"Get him on the raft," I say. Ten pairs of hands help get him on Ma's raft.

Kingfisher and I heave it away from the edge. We watch them drift downstream, Bel seeing to the needs of the tiny baby, and Ma trying to relieve Heron's agony.

I keep up a silent prayer to Gala as we work with Raven, roping together more logs to make another raft for the remaining survivors. We work till we're exhausted. The river saves us from the worst of the blazing heat but my lungs are sore with smoke and we are all coughing badly now. Raven hauls us onto the last crowded raft and we push away, leaving a furnace behind us.

"No one else is surviving that," says Raven, looking at the sheet of fire. "If there are any stragglers left, they must work their way around it. They know where to come."

I take charge of the raft, feeling it's the natural thing to do. I stand, instantly feeling stronger, more at ease on the water, using a staff to steer us to the far bank away from the treacherous fire. The river is wide and deep, full of mountain rain, and the current lifts us, carrying us downstream. I am ignoring the pain in my hand. It's insignificant compared to the roaring outrage in my heart. Raven is kneeling, holding a young soldier as he cries. Kingfisher is pouring his songlight into a woman's painful burns. Children are sobbing, terrified. My eyes are watering so much I can hardly see the rocks ahead.

"Where are we headed?" I ask Raven.

"Lake Lunen," she replies. "There's a place we can shelter, on the far shore."

Kingfisher tends to the wounded, holding their burns under the cold water. Our eyes meet. And we flow together.

Leaving the fires of Hel behind, we head down into the rapids and away.

44 ✦ PIPER

"That was incredible," says Kite. He is laughing, thrilled with excitement, like a boy.

The plumes of thick smoke behind us grow higher.

I got a strong image of Elsa running through the trees. Why did I see that? Is she down there? Is Ma there? Was it my imagination, my guilt?

I feel nauseous and lightheaded. It's all I can do to keep staring at the controls.

Gala, fire is the worst death. The worst I can imagine.

"You must be proud of yourself, Crane."

I make myself speak. "Yes, my lord. Now I truly know what we're capable of."

Kite turns round in his seat, grinning at me.

"Your next mission will be Reem, you understand? I'm telling you first. Not even Axby has the details yet."

Reem. He wants us to do this to a city. A city.

"Tomorrow, you'll attack the Aylish capital."

My nausea rises. I grip the controls, so Kite can't see my shaking hands. "So soon?"

"The Aylish won't know what's hit them. That circular parliament of theirs; it will be a crematorium. You'll fly back to Fort Peregrine to refuel and by the time you get to Brightlinghelm, the war will be over and you will be heroes."

Words fail me. There's a very real danger that I will be sick.

Elsa. Ma. Where are you?

"What of that Aylish ship on the Isis?" I ask. "I thought they'd come to make peace, my lord."

"The Aylish aboard that ship will never see their homeland again unless they agree to an unconditional surrender. That's the only kind of peace I want."

"Yes, my lord. You have it all sewn up."

"This is victory. It's what we promised since the war began and I will deliver it."

Don't vomit. Keep it down. Say something.

"Warfare is the only thing I've ever known," I tell him. "What will Brightland do when it's at peace?"

"When it's victorious, I think you mean."

"Yes, my lord."

"Ayland will become a tributary state. They will pay for this war in every way." He goes quiet for a while, empire-building over the clouds.

If this is what victory feels like, you can keep it.

"You must feel very close to Thal up here," says Kite.

"Yes, my lord. We have done his work today."

Kite looks at the plumes of black and gray, eating the blue sky above the forest canopy.

"The bombs are ingenious," he tells me with pride. "Not just firefuel—it's mixed with a paste of white phosphorus, a Light People recipe. The phosphorus eats all the oxygen so people can't breathe and it burns three times hotter than gunpowder. I had to develop it in secret. Peregrine would never have allowed it."

Is that why you murdered him?

Kite is expecting a response but with every breath, I am swallowing my nausea. I must say one of his quotes. He likes that.

"If ignorant of both your enemy and yourself, you are certain to be in peril," I say.

"What?" says Kite.

I realize I have made a mistake. Kite never said this. Peregrine did.

"Oh—Sergeant Redshank used to say it. He'd make us repeat it every day. He said it was a saying of yours, my lord."

"Are you trying to flatter and please me, Crane?"

It won't do to be weak.

"Would you rather that I chide you, my lord?"

Kite laughs, as if nothing in the world could bring down his mood. "I'd like to see you try." Then he says, "That sergeant of yours will be avenged. When the transport from Northaven comes in, I'll send for you. I'd like you to bear witness."

"Thank you, my lord."

I think of that fire burning people alive and the vomit creeps up. I looked down through the trees and I saw the camp: tents balling with flames, people blazing, writhing, trying to outrun the fire that was eating their flesh. I can't do this again. I can't.

"I want you to come to the palace tonight, to join my celebration. I will be having victory drinks. The insurgent rebellion is dead."

I say thank you and what a great honor but if this puke comes up, everything is over. My hands are clammy on the controls. My forehead is prickling with sweat.

My mother. My sister. What if they were there?

The self-disgust is like a tide that comes up in a retch. I manage to make it sound like a cough and I force the rest of it down. I hardly hear what Kite says.

As we prepare to land, I look at the back of his head, his balding pate.

How vulnerable he is. That soft patch above his nape—if I was armed, I could slide a knife right into it.

No, there is a better way and more simple. I curse myself for thinking it too late.

My plane is an instrument of murder.

High above Lake Lunen, I could have let go of the controls and smashed this bastard to an early death. My nausea has blinded me. But the thought hits me like a revelation.

I am going to kill Kite.

As I touch down on the runway, I prepare myself.

Your next time in my plane will be your last.

"Will you be flying to Reem with us, my lord?" I ask as I taxi into the hangar. "I'd be honored to be your pilot."

"I'd like that very much, Crane. Nothing would please me more. But my duty lies here in Brightlinghelm. I must leave the fate of Reem in your capable hands."

"My life belongs to Brightland."

He grips my hand as I help him out of the cockpit. "I am Brightland, Crane. Your life belongs to me."

"Thal keep you, my lord," I say, and I salute him. Standing on my wing, I watch him depart.

Next time, Bastard, I will kill you.

I manage to hold on until I get to the latrines. Then I vomit to high heaven. I stay in my cubicle until the worst of the shaking stops.

When I get to the sinks, Axby is there, bathing his face in cold water. He must have heard me. I am consumed with mortification that my commanding officer knows my weakness and my shame.

Axby dries his face with a towel. His expression is inscrutable.

"Kite was most satisfied," he says. "Well done, Crane."

"Thank you, sir." My voice has no volume.

"Are you pleased with how it went?" asks Axby searchingly.

I notice myself in the mirror and see my clammy complexion. This is not the heroic airman that I dreamed of being. This figure staring back at me is a frightened boy.

"Lord Kite told me that we are to attack Reem with firebombs tomorrow, sir."

"Reem?" questions Axby.

"Yes, sir. He wants to see it burn, like the Greensward."

Axby exhales, leaning forward, staring at the mirror. He is gripping the sink with both hands and he stays motionless, his fingers turning white with effort. "Tomorrow?" he asks.

"That's what he said."

"I'm grateful for this information, Crane."

Axby slowly turns to me. He takes me in and there's a strange look in his eyes full of an emotion that I can't fathom. I wonder if perhaps he's thinking of his son again, the boy who died of wasting fever.

"When I'm on missions over the Tenmoth Zone," says Axby, "I often wonder how it got destroyed. There were more than half a million people living there in the time of the Light People. We have evidence that a single bomb shattered the place and left it uninhabitable." Axby's eyes are full of intensity as he stares at me. "What if the man in charge of dropping that bomb had questioned his orders and said no?"

45 ✳ NIGHTINGALE

The floor is hard under my bones and my hip aches. The pain of it has woken me. I realize immediately that Cassandra is gone.

Where is she?

I sit up on the floor of the laundry room. A blurred figure passes in front of me. The veiled ladies are already at work. I reach for my spectacles and put them on, getting to my feet.

I see Cassandra at a great laundry tub, working with Lady Scorpio. A wave of relief comes over me that I haven't further damaged her. She looks just as she did yesterday before she had that terrifying seizure. The tub is full of black water and I watch Cassandra and Scorpio pulling something out of it. They hang it and winch it to the ceiling. It's a dress with a wide hooped skirt. They have dyed it jet black. They seem unaware that their sleeves are covered in black stains. The dye drips on them from the dress above, falling down their veiled faces and onto their white dresses. The effect is macabre.

"Cassandra?" I say.

She doesn't react. There is more black fabric in the tub and she tends to it.

"It's me, Kaira, can you understand me?" I approach, my hip aching with every step. "I spoke with Raven Pine last night." I look through the gauze into Cassandra's eyes. "I met her. Raven says she loves you. She's in the Greensward and she's waiting. Raven loves you." The focus moves in Cassandra's eyes, almost as if she is looking at me. Does she comprehend what I am saying? For a moment I think I see something in her dark pupils, a beam of puzzlement. But her eyes slide away. It's only the reflection of the turbine lights.

Cassandra plunges her arms in the black water and blankly performs her task, pulling out a black hooped petticoat. Lady Scorpio takes it from her and puts it on a hanger, winching it up to the ceiling. Black drips of water fall upon us all.

This is too cruel. Curse everything. This is too fucking cruel and I mean that swear.

I pick the blankets up off the floor and I climb upstairs. I throw them back on Cassandra's narrow chrysalid's bed. I can't bear this stifling room. My songlight feels as if it will explode and I must send it somewhere before it consumes me.

Lark. It comforts me just to think about her. I want Lark.

I go toward the window and I release my songlight. No one is going to keep me from Lark, not Swan, not anyone. Lark is my freedom.

I find her on water, on a makeshift raft. She's standing on great logs tied with ropes. Kingfisher is there, and Raven Pine. They sit amid a crowd of other people and their emotion hits me like a wave. Something terrible has happened. Lark can't form words. She turns around and through her eyes, I see the inferno.

The shock runs through my whole body. Black smoke towers up above the trees like a mountain range. Frenzied flames leap from the canopy. I notice that many of the other people on the raft are coughing, crying, injured, bleeding.

"Where's Curl?" I ask, distressed.

Lark can hardly articulate herself. "Heron's been wounded. She's ahead, with him and Bel."

Kingfisher senses me and he wakens his songlight, asking to join our harmony. Between them, they tell me all they can. I see their flight through the forest, their fear and confusion as the firebombs fell. Lark owes Kingfisher her life. I sense the emotion in them both and I swallow my own loneliness.

"Kam Fairley is dead," Lark tells me. "We don't know how many more have perished in the flames."

"Swan's warning saved a lot of lives," says Kingfisher.

"Swan's warning?" I ask, puzzled.

"I spoke with her," he tells me. "She discovered where Kite was flying and she told me."

"I'm glad," I say. "I'm glad of it."

"Don't heroize Swan," says Lark darkly. "She betrayed Harrier. She confessed it."

"Swan admitted what she'd done of her own free will," says Kingfisher, tempering Lark's anger. "She accepted the blame. And she regretted her action, the minute it was done."

Lark doesn't reply. I can tell that Swan is a source of painful contention.

Kingfisher shows me the line of rafts far ahead, each one crammed with survivors. "Kite thinks he's destroyed the Greensward militia," he says. "But see how many have escaped."

Swan warned them. I am deeply heartened by this.

Then I hear something in my own reality. I part from Lark and Kingfisher and find myself back in the quiet, low-ceilinged room. I go to the door and listen. There's a strange sound coming from Swan's bedchamber. Uselessly, I try the handle, expecting it to be locked. To my surprise, I find it open.

Swan is there, standing in the middle of her room, staring at nothing, her wig in her hand, the lead band round her head. The sound is a high-pitched cry she is making, despairing and disjointed.

"Zara," I say, and she falls silent.

Swan turns to face me, looking as hopeless and as desolate as I have ever seen her. Her eyes slowly rise to mine, and I see her terrible remorse.

"Kite will hang Harrier," she tells me. "I did what I could to spare his wives and children. He's gone to destroy the insurgents' camp."

"I've been with Lark," I tell her. "The forest is in flames. No one yet knows how many have died. But it would have been worse, without your warning."

Swan takes no comfort. She crawls onto her bed and lies in a heap. "Kite will attack Reem with his firebombs next. Then he will force Drew Alize into a surrender. It will seal his power and he will be our lord forever. It's nonsense to believe that Kite can be resisted. Men like Kite will always win. And even if he dies, there are others waiting in the wings. Others who are even worse."

I won't get sucked into this maudlin self-pity.

"Last night you locked me up and threatened me. What will you do with me, Zara?"

331

Swan is lying like a crumpled corpse.

"I can't ask you for your love or loyalty," she says. "You're free to do as you please."

"As I please?"

"Starling will take you into the city. You can go."

Is she *serious?*

"You mean just leave the palace?"

Swan closes her eyes and nods. She's letting the waters of her black lake engulf her.

"Go home, Kaira."

I wasn't expecting her to be like this. I'm surprised by how painful the thought of leaving her feels.

"Do you really expect me just to walk away?" I ask.

"I'll pull whatever strings I have to get your papa out of jail," says Swan, numbly. "I don't want you anymore."

I want Papa to be free; I want him to be a better man. When I first came here, I would have leaped at this. But I'm a different person now.

"I can't go home," I tell her. "I'm needed here."

"Not by me," says Swan.

"Especially by you. I'm part of this fight now and so are you."

I climb up on the bed and lie facing her. "I'm sorry that I spoke to the Aylish behind your back. I'm sorry for everything I did. But Kite must be stopped. Lark showed me what his bombs have done to the Greensward. He's annihilated people and destroyed Gala's forest. He cannot be allowed to win."

Swan's fingers touch mine. "Brave dolly," she says.

I grip her hand tightly. "Zara," I say, "you have to understand something. I'm not your dolly and I never was. My songlight name is Nightingale."

Her tears fall as she looks at me. "Nightingale," she says. "What must we do?"

332

46 ✳ LARK

The current takes us downstream and our roughly made raft moves at its own pace. It has no comfort but it keeps us afloat and carries us toward Lake Lunen. My one consolation is being back on the water. It's not the sea but even so, I relish its flow, and I realize how much I have missed my element. We bathe our eyes in the river and the dreadful, blinding chemical is washed away. My vision is clearing, my body stops shaking, and as the river takes us farther from the flames, my emotions begin to calm.

There is little conversation. Ahead of us we see the other rafts. We are too far behind to make out individual figures but knowing that Ma is there makes me feel a little more safe. People share what comfort they have and Raven and I steer the crowded raft on, avoiding rocks and banks of shingle, finding the safest route. After an hour or so, the forest gives way to a landscape of stumps and huge bullrushes. We see distant farms, dragonflies, and a family of otters but little else.

Raven takes control of the staff for a while, steering the raft through the current, while I pull some of the wooden shrapnel out of my arms and legs. Kingfisher is pouring his songlight into a woman's burns, trying to help her with the pain. I see that blood is congealing all the way down his left arm. A jagged piece of wood must have ripped his skin. There are bloodstains all over his torn Aylish shirt.

"Someone needs to tend to you," I say.

He looks over at me and in a heartbeat I am reliving what has just happened. Kingfisher pushes me out of the way of that falling tree. I see the same memory in his eyes—and then he turns his face from me.

"The laceration isn't deep," he says, glancing down at his arm. "The wood hit at a good angle. It'll heal by itself."

"I thought the same thing with my hand. It needs cleaning and stitching," I insist.

Kingfisher doesn't reply, concentrating on the woman's burns. He'd better not be trying to distance himself from me again. After what I sensed when he saved me from those flames, it just won't wash.

At last, the river drops us into Lake Lunen. For a while, all I can do is take in the beauty. Light dances on the blue-black lake, insects fly in glittering clouds, and water birds take off at the sight of us, hundreds of them in a wheeling spectacle, looping high in the sky and then landing again when they realize we are not a threat. Far ahead of us, we see the rest of the rafts, spreading out in the middle of the lake. The water becomes too deep to steer the raft so we let the current carry us and we drift. We are closer to Brightlinghelm than ever—but our plans of making inroads on the city have been smashed.

Raven lies on the raft, allowing herself a moment to acknowledge what has happened. I lie with her, staring at the sky, and I let my songlight float. I reach out to Bel and ask her about the tiny baby and about Mikane.

"Heron is unconscious," she says. "But your ma says his pulse is strong. The baby's name is Kamlyn, after his father. He's stopped crying now, he's feeding. But his mother's grieving, sore."

I let Bel go, noting how much it means to her to be useful.

I sense Raven, quietly communing with her fellow Torches, those who have survived on the other rafts. They are trying to work out who is dead and who has made it. They count up men, women, children, trying to keep each other strong. Some of their friends and comrades have been witnessed as dead; others are lost, their fates unknown. I want to find out what Raven will do.

"I'm so sorry about Kam Fairley," I say, when she comes back to herself.

"He was a good friend," she tells me, as if her heart is beating under a great weight. "We all know the risks—although that doesn't make it any easier. It's why we have many leaders, so our struggle can survive every loss."

"Will you survive this one?" I ask.

Raven pauses. "We must," she says simply. "We must survive the loss of Harrier too. These things seem crushing but they will bring us closer to the tipping point."

"The tipping point?"

"A moment when enough people just won't take it anymore. If they believe that things can change, our ranks will swell, new leaders will arise—and Kite and his men will be brought down."

I am humbled by Raven's refusal to be beaten.

"Those firebombs are an evil I never thought I'd see," she goes on, "not even from the mind of Kite. I've already contacted our agents in the city. They know what we have just endured," she says. "They'll find a way to show Kite that he is never going to win."

There's something in her that reminds me of Heron. I would fight for Raven Pine.

We lie for a moment, letting the sun warm us. The serenity of this place is seeping into me. Crossing the tranquil waters, I feel that we're being held by some benign force and that for these brief moments, nothing can harm us. I sense rainbow fishes swimming beneath us, and here in the sunlight, all is at peace. A trout leaps out to catch a fly, disturbing the glassy surface, and I watch the rings of water grow wider and wider. I'm aware of Kingfisher next to me and Raven, staring at the clouds.

I am connected to everything.

As we approach the southern bank, I see that the rafts ahead of us are aiming for a large cluster of low brick buildings. There are turbines above them but it doesn't look like a village. The buildings are all identical and too austere. It doesn't look like a barracks either; there's no barbed wire or parade ground, no military flags. As we get closer, I see that there is agriculture all around. In the distance, there are grazing meadows and farmed fields. The low brick buildings are surrounded by gardens with vegetable beds and displays of climbing flowers soften their austerity.

"What is this place?" I ask Raven.

335

"It's called Lunenbourn," she says. "It's a hospital for incurables. We have friends here."

Raven tells us that the hospital is a regular stopping place on the militia's forays in and out of Brightlinghelm. "It was built as a recuperating hospital for injured soldiers," she says. "Some are sent back to the front lines; others desert and join our ranks. But for the veterans who can't be used anymore, whose injuries or nervous disorders are too severe for them to go home, this is a lifelong dumping ground. The Brethren don't want such broken men affecting Brightland's national morale, so they hide them away."

Men in a worse state than Heron and John Jenkins?

"It's also a dumping ground for Third Wives," says Raven. "Peregrine decided that after ten years of service, Third Wives were not fit to return to their towns and villages, so they become nurses, to care for the veterans."

It takes a while for anger to hit me. I had a feeling that Chaffinch Greening's stories about Third Wives getting rich enough to retire was some kind of Brethren bullshit. Their service never ends.

"Lunenbourn has made itself a strong community," continues Raven. "Over time, they've become good friends to our militia."

I'm still digesting this when Nightingale's songlight crashes into my consciousness.

"Listen," she says, pulling me with her. "Lark, come."

I sit up, energized by her urgency, and I join with her.

I see that she's with Swan and they are in the council chamber.

"Swan's on our side," she says. "She's resolved against Kite."

"How can you trust that?" I ask. "Swan is on no one's side but her own."

She's sitting on her white seat, dressed in a luminous gown, her hair— her wig—in an elegant bun at her nape. This woman is the architect of so much pain and carnage. I know she gave Kingfisher a warning. But she betrayed Harrier—that's how Kite discovered Sherlham in the first place. As far as I'm concerned, Kamlyn Fairley will grow up fatherless because of Zara Swan.

336

But Nightingale hasn't summoned me to talk about Swan. There's a senior airman standing in front of Kite. "That's Wing Commander Axby," Nightingale tells me. "Kite is planning an attack on Reem. He's sending his air fleet with firebombs. You have to warn Kingfisher."

I immediately take Kingfisher's hand, alerting him. I let him in to our harmony and wordlessly, he witnesses the scene.

"I want the fleet over Reem at noon tomorrow," Kite is saying. "The sun will be at its height, blinding the Aylish on the ground."

"May we give the civilians any kind of warning, my lord?" asks Wing Commander Axby.

"A warning? So that they can prepare their defenses?" asks Kite in disbelief. "No," he says, "categorically, no. And I can't believe as my chief airman that you would even suggest such a thing."

On the raft, Kingfisher sits forward, appalled.

"There were women and children in the Greensward when we attacked this morning," Axby tells Kite. "There will be even more in Reem tomorrow."

"And your point is . . . ?" Kite dares Axby to object.

Axby takes in his breath. "My lord," he begins, "I have always found it impossible to comprehend how the Light People destroyed each other's cities. I am increasingly of the belief that the craft of war should never be practiced on civilians." Axby's gaze is fixed on Kite. "Bombing Reem would be an atrocity."

Silence falls. There is shock on every face, tension, even in Swan's hairstyle. I am applauding that man, Axby.

"Reem is populated with unhumans," says Kite, as if he is rationally debating. "This is an act of purification, of cleansing," he explains. "And before we sit down for dinner tomorrow, the war will be won. We will have our triumph."

I feel Kingfisher's outrage.

"Do you understand your orders?" Kite asks Axby.

337

Axby pauses, as if he's preparing himself. "I can have no part of it," he says. "I refuse to deliver your orders to my men."

Kite's lips have spread into a thin grimace. "I'm sorry to hear that you're unhappy," he says with mock sympathy. He leaves his seat and strolls toward Axby. Nightingale is stricken with dread.

"It's terribly disappointing," Kite says to his Ministers, "to discover that a man in such a high-ranking position, a man I have trusted and allowed to rise, is actually a self-righteous and disloyal coward."

"I will not be an instrument of mass murder," says Axby.

The Ministers glance at one another, unsettled by Axby's unshakable integrity. Axby seems to know what's coming. I see him grip his hands behind his back as if they are already cuffed. He's a lot taller than Kite and he looks down on him, his expression one of resigned dignity.

Kite takes his time. "When I hang Raoul Harrier tomorrow, he will have the full honors: crowds, guards, a marching band," he says. "A man couldn't have a better death. It's more than he deserves. Harrier really deserves a death like this."

Kite sticks a blade up into Axby's ribs. So fast I didn't even see the knife in his hand.

On the raft, Kingfisher yells out as if he has felt the pain himself. Nightingale utters a cry of horror and Swan covers her—pretending that the cry is hers. She tries to turn it into a cry of surprise: "Kite!"

Axby barely moves. He uses every last effort to hold himself, looking Kite straight in the eye. Kite twists the knife. It must cause Axby intolerable pain.

"Thal's teeth, Kite," says Ruppell in distaste.

Swan is on her feet, her eyes darting between Axby, Kite, and the Ministers. Kite twists the knife further, holding on to Axby in a deathly embrace.

"I lay down my life to stop this madness," says Axby, and his strength falters. "When my men discover what you've done to me they will refuse this mission too." Kite pulls out his knife. Axby drops to his knees, his hands pressing on the wound in a futile attempt to stop the surge of blood.

I feel Nightingale's extreme distress and I don't know how to calm her, as I am so horrified myself. "Don't give yourself away," I beg her.

All the Ministers are on their feet. I realize that Kite has done this to show them what happens when someone crosses him.

Axby curls on the floor, dying. Blood is pooling under him. He cries out a woman's name.

"Please," says Swan, looking genuinely stricken, "may I leave?"

"Dear lady, let me escort you," says Ruppell.

Kite raises his voice. "No one will leave this room until our plans for tomorrow are secured!"

I can't bear Nightingale witnessing this horror with these monsters.

"Ouzel," says Kite, "as Minister of War, you're taking command of the air force."

Ouzel accepts this sudden command but he can't tear his eyes from the dying man. "I'll tell the pilots that Axby's been called home on compassionate leave," he says. "I'll tell them he has a sick child."

"My son," utters Axby, his lungs now gurgling with blood. "My son . . ."

"I don't care what you tell them," says Kite, "as long as my airmen are ready at first light."

Kite and his Ministers continue to make plans for the attack on Reem. But Axby disrupts them by writhing in agony.

"Shut the fuck up!" yells Kite at last, his mask of authority slipping. He has to stab Axby again, this time in the throat, to make sure that he dies. It's bestial.

Kite looks at the bloody mess on the floor. He looks at his hands, covered in blood.

"Get it cleaned," he says to Drake.

His plans laid, he takes Swan by the arm and leaves the room. Swan pulls Nightingale with her—and our link is broken.

339

I am back on the raft, gripping Kingfisher. Neither of us moves as what we have witnessed sinks in.

"What is it?" asks Raven. "What have you seen?"

When we her, Raven stares at us in disbelief, as if such an obscenity cannot be true.

"We can use our songlight, all of us, to try to reach Reem," suggests Kingfisher. "We can warn them. We can share our light, as we did in the Greensward. It's possible," says Kingfisher, looking quite desperate, "that with the greatest effort, we could reach the coast of Ayland."

"And every Siren in between." Raven has to let him down. "If we send a great, forceful beam of songlight now, we'll give away our position and they might attack again. I'm sorry, Yan, but I must protect people," Raven tells him. "We have suffered enough."

Kingfisher reluctantly accepts this. "I have to get to Alize," he says, his mind whirring. "We have to stop Kite before those planes leave the ground."

"I'm with you," I tell him, sharing his urgency. "I'm not leaving Nightingale in that madman's palace for another day."

We are arriving at a long and sturdy jetty, which reaches right out into the lake. People from the other rafts are already being helped ashore. Nurses and veterans in shirtsleeves are aiding the wounded. There's a sense of urgency, as the whole of Lunenbourn aids with the rescue. Everyone is trying to keep their emotions under control, working together for the worst of the wounded. I see Bel supporting Kam's young widow and her son. Heron Mikane is on a stretcher being carried toward the largest building by veteran soldiers, the residents of Lunenbourn. Ma is bent over him in concern. His hand falls limply to the side.

Has his condition deteriorated? Brightland needs him—but more than that, I need him; Ma needs him. My heart is thumping through my chest.

Not Heron. Not Heron. That bony poacher Death can't have him.

Nurses and veterans pull in our raft and help us off, treating us with kindness and concern. I want to thank them but I leave Kingfisher and Raven and I run.

Not Heron.

I run after him as fast as I can toward the largest building, where the veterans take his stretcher. I fly through the doors and find myself in a hall with long tables and murals of gardens and the lake. It's some kind of refectory and it has become a field hospital. There are medical staff assessing burns and injuries. Some of the survivors are being treated on the spot but the more seriously injured are being helped away. Veterans are acting as hospital orderlies, doing what they can to help the nurses. Some of the men are amputees; others bear burn scars worse than Heron's. A blind man is serving water to the new arrivals. Other men have the troubled, nervy look of John Jenkins. I digest all this in a moment, but my focus is on one of the long tables. Heron's stretcher is being laid upon it. Ma is at his side.

"Heron!" I cry. "Heron!"

To my great and enduring relief, I see that he's coming round.

"What's all this fuss?" he mutters.

One of the nurses is washing the blood from his face and he pushes her hand away.

"I'm fine," says Heron. "Leave me be. I just need to . . ." As he tries to lift his head he runs out of words. His mind is fogged with pain.

I see Ma looking at me and I know immediately that Heron won't be coming with us. He needs doctors, surgery—and he needs it now. Somehow, Kingfisher and I must manage without him.

"We have to get to Brightlinghelm," I tell Ma in a low voice. "Kite is going to firebomb Reem. Kingfisher has to get to Alize."

Ma grips my hand at the sheer danger of it all.

"No," she says. "Not you. The militia will help Kingfisher. Let Raven or one of the others go with him. They're trained soldiers—you can't even fire a gun."

"Nightingale needs me."

341

"What will you do for Nightingale if you rush in and get killed? You've been through Hel and high water, Elsa. Stay here with me."

I realize that Ma won't be coming with us either. Somehow I understand that her place is with Heron, strengthening the people, regrouping. She is wracked with concern for me, and right now I don't want to add to her burden of worries.

"Elsa," says Heron, "just give me a day."

When the doctors hear they have Commander Mikane in their midst, they give him their full and immediate attention. His hand is gripping Ma's, as if she is the steadfast beam, holding him to his purpose.

"I'll be right here," I say, backing away. "You let the doctors do their work."

My eyes find Kingfisher and I see him, shirtless, wiping the blood off his arm, trying to bandage it himself. I feel a pang at the sight of him—and I help him fix the laceration up as best I can, dressing it with mesh.

"We can slip into the city, unnoticed, if there's only two of us," I say.

He lets out a long, slow sigh. "It's best if I go alone," he says.

I give him a long, hard stare. "Let's just forget you said that."

I see the hint of a smile dawning on his face as he looks at me. "Elsa Crane," he says, and he lays his head on my shoulder.

The fate of Reem, and the fate of Nightingale, might hang in the balance, but it's every bit as urgent to show this Aylishman, just for a moment, how I feel. I put my arms around him and I hold him.

"We cannot rest here, even for an hour," he says in songlight. "Alize is in great danger."

"I'm ready," I reply.

But I don't want to let him go and I think he feels the same.

At last we separate. A veteran in a wheeled chair approaches, offering us food. I take what he has, thanking him. As we leave, I see a doctor shining a light into Heron's eye socket. Heron is trying not to yell. I take in Ma's beloved face and I go, following Kingfisher. Outside, we find a pump and we wash some of the fire smoke from our hair and skin.

342

"We'll need a boat," I say.

As we're heading back to the lakeside, we see a nurse walking toward us. She stops and greets us and to my surprise, I realize that it's Bel. She has rid herself of her Siren's yellow dress.

"I tied it to a brick and threw it in the lake," she says.

"Where did you get the uniform?" I ask.

Bel takes us to a storeroom. "In there," she says, and she waits outside, keeping watch as we take what we need.

I look at Kingfisher in his ragged, bloodstained Aylish clothes. He looks at me in my torn and ruined Northaven dress. Without another word we find clean, fresh uniforms that fit us and put them on. I try not to look at Kingfisher as we change—but I cannot help taking in his beauty. I see his eyes on me in the same way as I stand in my petticoat. Two breaths, maybe three go by and our stare holds. Then I turn away, transforming myself into an auxiliary nurse. When I next look at Kingfisher, he is a medic. I grab a pair of white shoes but I don't put them on. It feels like my boots have taken me the whole length of Brightland and I can't yet bear to be parted from them. Besides, Heron's knife is tucked down one of them and I am going to need it.

"With any luck, we'll be in Brightlinghelm by dawn," I tell Bel. "Please don't tell my ma we've gone until Heron's out of danger."

Bel wants to object but she sees our determination. "I'll take care of them," she says. "And when you need to speak with them, I'll be your voice."

I thank her with a hug. There's so much that I want to say to her. I want to say that I know she's a good person, I have seen it—and that I hope she finds her little girl. But it feels too much like a final parting, too much like I'll never see her or Heron or my ma again. So I say nothing.

Bel walks with us down toward the jetty. Kingfisher is already looking at the ambulance boats, long and narrow, sleekly shaped.

"One of these might give us speed," he says.

I jump aboard the closest one and see the strong battery, stretchers for

343

the wounded and a stock of medical supplies. I can see how useful these boats must be to the Greensward militia, providing them with cover to come and go from Brightlinghelm. I feel bad stealing one but I think of Nightingale and everything we have to do.

No one pays us much attention as Bel loosens the ropes and pushes us off.

"Gala keep you safe," she says.

Kingfisher thanks her as I power the boat out onto the lake. I face southeast, away from the distant towers of black smoke. Soon I feel a current picking up beneath us. It's the pull of the River Isis, taking the crystal waters of Lake Lunen down to the ocean's edge. The riverbanks close in, hiding our boat from the passing farms. Kingfisher looks at the view ahead, his mind on all he has to do. I set the tiller.

"Yan," I say, and he turns to me. "We have to win this fight."

Before I know it, he is in my arms, his lips on mine. I want him so much that I find myself in tears.

"If this is our last night on earth," he says, "let us spend it living."

"Never let it end," I whisper.

As darkness falls, we lose ourselves in each other's arms. I tear at his new shirt, so recently put on. His skin feels beautiful. I feel no barriers between us, nothing keeping us apart. There is a desperation in me as I pull him closer, gripping his back, wrapping my legs around him. The sensation of pleasure hurts my heart and I cry out in an exquisite pain.

Tonight we will have love, for tomorrow we might die.

The current takes the boat downstream, toward our destination and our fate, in Brightlinghelm.

PART 5

47 ✴ SWAN

Kite takes me to his bedchamber after he's killed Axby. He tries to pretend that it's normal, walking through the palace with his hands covered in a dead man's blood. I send Kaira to my rooms with an insistent nod. I know what Kite is after and I don't want her to witness it. Kite will want to be told that he did the right thing, that Axby was an ingrate, a traitor, that he, Kite, is like Thal himself. And he will want me to use my body to prove it all to him.

As we walk, Kite gives me instructions for the reception that he wants me to host, to celebrate his destruction of the insurgents. He's behaving as if nothing has happened, as if his businesslike tone can make up for the grotesque slaughter I have just witnessed. I can see the lust in his eyes, even as he talks about this evening's table plan.

Someone has to get Brightland out of this quagmire. Fate points at me.

Kaira, Alize, Kingfisher: all three have told me I could lead.

Are they right?

I have to get this cursed Siren's band off my head. Then I must speak with Kingfisher again.

I have spent years in the company of selfish, aging men. Every one of them has been a politician, a player. Kingfisher is different. He makes me remember that I am still young. There's time for me to start again. I think of his audacity as he walked in songlight among Kite's Ministers.

Zara, he said. And I heard my name afresh. I heard it in my heart's core.

I look at Kite in comparison as he scrubs his hands at a washbasin. He's disgusting.

I fix him a whiskey, wondering how I can evade his embraces, while he tells me how much he's going to relish watching Harrier hang. He dries his hands and, throwing his towel on the floor, comes toward me, unbuttoning his blood-streaked uniform.

No. Get away from me.

I cannot show my repugnance or I'll end like Axby. But when I feel Kite's damp hands pawing at my dress, I pull away, saying:

"Unlock my Siren's band."

"Why?" he asks, slugging his whiskey. "I have no task for your songlight. My enemies are dead or waiting to be hanged."

"That isn't true," I tell him with a steady gaze.

There's a wound of mistrust in Kite and I will pour salt in it. That's my only plan.

"What do you mean?" he asks.

"Axby has just proven that your enemies are everywhere," I press. "I should have been free in the council chamber, free to pick up on how your Ministers reacted, on the true depth of their loyalty. I saw Drake look away when you killed that traitor, Axby. He caught Greylag's eye and they were both disapproving. There's something afoot between them."

"Busy little spider," says Kite, pulling me closer, "always trying to spin discord."

"It would be disloyal of me not to tell you what I saw. Your Ministers are all ambitious. They covet everything that you've got—including me." I top up his whiskey. I need him to be drunk. "I hardly like to tell you, but Ruppell made a play for me."

"He wouldn't dare."

"Watch him tonight. He never takes his eyes off me. When he locked the Siren's band on me this morning, his hands roamed where they should not. He took the opportunity to offer me a future, should anything ever happen to you."

Kite eyes me, drinking, running his tongue across his teeth. Paranoia is cooling his desire.

"I can't trust any of you," he says.

"My poor lord," I say. "You must trust someone. And the person who has never let you down is me." I draw him to the bed and take his boots off. Hopefully, he'll fall asleep.

Kingfisher.

I thought I hated him. It's strange how that passion has become something else. I suppose the seeds of strong feeling were always there. I feel him like a kindred spirit, a survivor of war, a fellow orphan. His songlight is clear and pure. He wouldn't lie to me and abuse my trust. He wouldn't fill me with hatred and bitterness, like Kite. I have felt lonely for so long.

"What are you musing upon with that faraway look?" asks Kite. "Are you plotting my downfall with Greylag and Ruppell?"

"I'm daydreaming," I say, turning to him, "about the day when you finally trust me."

Kite meets my smile with narrow eyes. "I don't appreciate your efforts to put rancor between my Ministers and me. Ruppell has been my lifelong ally."

"Take off my band," I insist. "Throw the thing away. You promised to make me your equal."

Kite pats my bottom. "But without your lead band," he says, "you have the advantage. How can we be equal then?"

I realize there is only one way out of this. The thought comforts me and I let it grow.

Murder.

48 ✳ RYE

Charlus, my reluctant guide, is showing me the airship's library. I see rows of flat black screens—nothing in the way of books. Charlus says these black screens are the gateway to all the knowledge in the world. I ask him how they are used and he laughs. He tells me it would take me years of study to learn. In Sealand, he says, children start learning how to manipulate these screens before they can even walk, then he starts talking a lot of jargon that I don't understand. He seems to take pleasure from my incomprehension. Next, he takes me to an empty gymnasium where everything is made of a dramatic black alloy. He picks up the thinnest sword I've ever seen and asks me if I can fence. I say I can box. He asks me if I'd like to try and he spends a while adopting weird positions and pointing his sword at my neck and my ribs. Truthfully, I'm running the risk of punching him hard in the face. So I ask if I could have a bite to eat.

He shows me the cramped and busy kitchens next to a luxurious dining hall and I'm relieved to talk with my mouth instead of with my songlight for a while. I ask some of the chefs how they keep the ship supplied. Again, I delight to see men and women working together. They show me what they're making and I tell them it looks like art, not food.

"It's a whole lot better than our Brightling ship's biscuits." I can see they find this amusing but the staff here are full of reserve. I ask one of the chefs if she's seen any sight of my friend Wren Apaluk. She shakes her head apologetically, glancing at Charlus with mistrust and dislike. I'm clearly not the only person on the ship who thinks this lad is a woeful prick.

"I'd like to see Wren," I say to Charlus. "I'm sure as the admiral's son, you can arrange that."

"Sure," he says. "No problem, Rytern. Let's have a drink."

Charlus takes me to a wide corridor and opens a door into a suite of rooms. I see an opulent sitting area, leading into a finely furnished bedroom.

"For some unknown reason, Father wants you to share my quarters," says Charlus, pouring me a drink.

"So, I'm on the bed, right, Charlus?" I ask. "And you get the sofa?"

"Very funny," he says. "You're a funny guy. I like that."

But he doesn't. The dislike between us is as taut as a bowstring.

As we drink, he tells me the value of some of his fancy objects and he's so dull I find my eyes are closing.

I soon find myself on the cliffs in Northaven. Elsa is standing by her father's grave. She asks me how I've been. I tell her that it's good to see her. We sit together, looking at the sky and the sea. She stands and I ask her not to go. She cracks a smile and tells me that she's with me all the time.

I wake weirdly comforted. It's the first dream I've had about Elsa that didn't jolt me awake with a rush of pain. I think of her as she must be now in Northaven, a young wife, sharing a home with Heron Mikane. I have been riven with a jealous grief. Now I try to think rationally.

What will happen if I reach Northaven, at the head of a Sealand force? Will Elsa run into my arms, or tap her pregnant belly and tell me sorry, she's in love with someone else? How can I compete with the hero of fucking Montsan Beach? I have to protect myself from the worst.

Is that why I kissed Petra?

Petra, with her strange, uncompleted name and her open heart. Her songlight is always at a low pitch, as if the full force of it would spin me right into the blue.

What's going on with me?

Fuck.

I sit up, my head thumping. It seems like about ten minutes have gone by since I dozed off, but when I look out of the window, I see that night has fallen and we're hovering under stars.

Gala—did that fuckwit Charlus drug me?

Why?

I send out my songlight, trying to reach Petra, thinking once more of that unexpected and delicious kiss. She's my only friend among the Sea-landers and I'm longing for her company.

Is that disloyal to Elsa? Or will Petra help preserve me, if Elsa's heart has fallen to Mikane?

I find Petra sitting at one of the black screens in the scouting craft hangar. I get a starburst of her emotion—her acknowledgment of me—and then a veil comes down. When I ask her for news of Wren, I get nothing. She closes herself off, as if she's blocking all contact.

When I told Charlus I wanted to see Wren, he drugged me. What's going on?

I step into Charlus's fancy little bathroom and run cold water on my head, trying to clear my mind. The fog in my brain begins to lift. I leave the bathroom on a mission—and I almost run into Charlus.

"I've come to get you for dinner," he says with a bland smile. "You were pretty tired back there. How did you sleep?"

Do I accuse him of drugging me? Or pretend it hasn't happened?

"I want to see Wren Apaluk," I say.

"Yes, I asked about your sapien friend," says Charlus, "and unfortunately they discovered a virus is in his system. He's still in quarantine."

"There must be some way I can speak to him?"

"Ask Livia at dinner. She's the boss."

We walk along the burnished corridors toward the dining room. "Petra and I have made it official," Charlus tells me. "She's pledged herself to me. She's my match."

I can't begin to comprehend it. Is this why Petra has closed herself off?

I organize my features and congratulate Charlus but truthfully, I feel gutted that Petra could be contemplating any kind of congress with this fop. I know it's her choice and this is not my culture. But why did she kiss me like that? She kissed me like she meant it, that's for sure. Some force must have acted on her, making her accept him.

I will do everything I can to help this girl.

In the dining hall, Charlus leads me up to the top table and I nod a greeting to my fellow diners, Petra's parents and Commodore Bradus. My eyes scan the room for Petra and I see her sitting with her friend Garena. Her head is bowed and she doesn't meet my eye. Strange.

Everyone stands when Xalvas comes in and the first thing he does is to congratulate his son on making his match. He slaps Charlus on the back and I look at the contrast between them. The father, so handsome, so enlightened, so charismatic—and Charlus. Every feature seems to have come out wrong and his character, in my view, is a cocktail of defects.

"The young lady in question took a while to accept him," says Xalvas. "She kept him waiting for an answer, but I'm delighted to say that Petra will be the mother of my grandchildren, and that another generation of this sovereign family is secured. Petra, my dear, come and join us."

Petra looks hot with confusion as the assembled company gives her a songlight ovation. She sits between me and Charlus, her mouth locked in an awkward smile, her eyes firmly on the tablecloth. She won't look at me and I don't know how to communicate with her. I don't know the rules of their truevoice here, and my own songlight is so inexperienced. Will we be overheard? Will I endanger Petra with my clumsy thoughts?

I decide to bide my time until I've figured out what's going on.

I'm about to turn to Xalvas and ask him about Wren. But his eyes are on his crew and in confident songlight, he illuminates his plans.

"*Celestis* will approach Reem at dawn," he says. "First contact must be carefully handled and it must be done by me, alone. There's an interdiction on all other communication with the natural eximians of Reem. Anyone caught breaking this will face consequences and Bradus and his Division Enforcers will be listening to all. If the Aylish should invite us to meet in person, the ground team will consist of myself, Livia, and our new friend Rytern. My son, Charlus, will pilot the scouting craft."

"What about Wren Apaluk?" I ask immediately.

"I beg your pardon," says Xalvas, who is clearly unused to being interrupted. "I hadn't yet mentioned our sapien colleagues. We will be joined in the craft by Jem Kahinu as engineer and our Brightling guest, Wren Apaluk."

I'm reassured.

Xalvas signals for the meal to be served and the non-Torches bring in an array of dishes. Xalvas asks what I know about Ayland and I tell him everything I remember from Sergeant Redshank's lessons. Ayland has a Head Torch with a name that was etched into us with fear, Sorze Separelli, their mind-twister in chief, a warrior with a reputation for brutality. And the leader of their parliament is a woman. I wrack my memory for her name, Odo something. I tell Xalvas what I can, trying to shake off Brightland's bigotry. Bradus wants to know if Reem has airpower and what kind of ground-based heavy artillery they might have. I wish I could be more helpful to him.

As an array of picturesque desserts are served, Petra's father, Lukas, asks me about the climate and topography of Brightland. I have to reveal my ignorance.

"What's topography?"

"It's the study of land features," says Petra quietly. "My father's asking you what Brightland looks like." She doesn't lift her eyes but for a brief second, I get the full beam of her truevoice. It feels like a lightning bolt in miniature.

There's something wrong.

I begin to tell Lukas what I know, but really, I'm speaking to Petra. I tell her about Northaven and the hills and moorland that surround it. I tell all I know about the Greensward, the mountainous forest that covers the center of our island. I tell her about the mysterious Tenmoth Zone that we are all taught to fear, a place worse than the cockroach city—and I tell her about the south, the scene of my recent adventures, salt marshes and rolling hills, populated with towns and rich farmland.

"How much of the year are you icebound?" asks Lukas.

"It's cold and wet but it's not like the ice lands of the north and our summers are warm and beautiful." I show Petra what it's like lying on Bailey's Strand, the sun on your face, the waves lapping at your feet.

The whole table has fallen silent, listening with interest.

"Is Ayland temperate too?" asks Xalvas.

"Our climates are very similar. We have a lot in common with the Aylish and I wish we were at peace. I hope this mission can be part of that."

Xalvas seems impressed by what I have said. I feel his warm interest.

"We want to help you, Rytern, but more than that, it occurs to me that we might find friends and allies in the north, like-minded people who could help us with our mission."

"What is your mission?" I ask.

"You could be part of it," he says. "We want to populate and regenerate the Earth. We eximians are seeking new lands."

"You mean to regenerate places like the cockroach city that you found me in?"

"Over time, we'll make our mark, even in places like that," says Xalvas thoughtfully. "Over time, we'll bring our science and our culture to every corner of the globe."

I sit back, reassured. Whatever my problems are with Charlus, I feel I can trust his father. These people really could bring peace and enlightenment. They really could help the Torches of Brightland. Perhaps they could even help our chrysalids.

I'm sure that these Sealanders have their flaws. They're only human, after all. But how can I doubt them, when behind every one of their black screens lies all the knowledge in the world?

49 ✳ NIGHTINGALE

Night is falling. Swan is in her bedchamber, being bathed by Lady Orion, getting ready for Kite's banquet. Her cropped hair is on view and she is wearing her lead band. She's hardly spoken since she came back from Kite's rooms, as if she has to get clean before she can think.

Axby's death has frightened her. It's a lesson in Kite's authority. No matter what she does, Kite will never free her.

I am desperately trying to reach Reem. I have been trying this all afternoon. Someone has to warn them. I send my songlight up as high as it can go.

Reem, I cry. *Reem.*

It always felt so easy, making the leap to Northaven. I remember the first time that I heard Lark, crying her soul out on the beach, grieving for her Rye. Whenever I went back, Lark was my compass point. But what is my fixed point in Ayland? Who am I trying to reach? I listen for any distant whisper of songlight, pouring my energy into the task.

REEM! I cry. *REEM!*

But the horrible murder of Wing Commander Axby keeps invading my mind. My concentration flies apart and I see his suffering again. All I hear is my own heartbeat, the blood pumping through my ears.

Exhausted, I pause.

I watch Cassandra as she styles one of Swan's wigs. Her arms are bare and I look at the ink drawing of the stork that she has on her wrist. Above it, high on her arm, is a black raven in flight. I never noticed it before. I touch the image. "That's for Raven Pine, isn't it?" I say.

Cassandra looks down at it.

"Raven loves you very much," I say. "You have someone who cares for you and accepts you and understands you. It's a precious thing. Not everybody has that."

Cassandra pauses, then she goes back to the wig, insensible. I shall go mad in these white rooms.

"Stop it," I say, gripping her wrists. "You're Cassandra Stork. Stop being like this and help me." Her empty eyes are pulling out my heart. "Help Raven. Raven loves you. We need you. Help us!"

Cassandra falls still, staring at me, blank.

I turn away from her.

Lark. I want Lark. Lark will give me strength.

I send up my songlight to find her—she is on water—a long, narrow boat—and my heart rejoices; Lark is on her way to Brightlinghelm.

But she's in Kingfisher's arms. They are lovers. It's a fatalistic passion that I sense, as if they both believe some unknown doom is going to befall them and their time is running out. I remove myself, mortified to have invaded their privacy.

Gala, I feel so alone. I want love. Proper, enriching, beautiful love. Love like Lark has.

"Kaira," says Swan, startling me.

She's approaching, dripping wet, a towel wrapped around her, the light dully glinting off her lead band. "I want you to reach Kingfisher. I have to speak with him."

What can I tell her? I pretend to use my songlight. I am certainly not disturbing him now.

"He must be sleeping," I say, after a while. "I can't reach him."

"I want to know as soon as he wakes." There's a desperation in her eyes. Kingfisher has gotten under her skin.

I exhale slowly. He's playing with hearts—playing with fire—and I don't think there is a more dangerous game. If Swan discovers where Kingfisher's heart truly lies, if she were to sense him, lost in love with Lark, his duplicity would ignite a furnace of destruction. If my minor betrayal led to the arrest of Harrier, what would Kingfisher's betrayal do? Swan's loneliness is even more acute than mine. It isn't fair to pretend with her and I will tell him so.

If Swan's feelings are truly entangled, she is vulnerable—and it will make her dangerous.

Swan walks back into her bedchamber to dress. Cassandra follows with the wig, which she has coiled into braids that look like fighting snakes.

I am left with Harrier in my thoughts. His execution is tomorrow. I know that there is nothing material I can do for him. I cannot offer any hope of a reprieve. But I want him to know that he is not alone. I'd like to tell him what he's meant to me.

I have to concentrate a long time before I find him. He's here, in the dungeons of the palace, and that deep laugh of his is silent. He has been tortured and his body is in pain. Harrier is preparing to die. I surround him in songlight.

"You're here," Harrier says. "My angel in white."

I try to tell him how I feel but I'm not sure he understands.

"Zara," he says, "this time, you can't help me to escape," and his spirit seems to smile.

He thinks I'm Swan. What do I do? Do I tell him he's mistaken or do I simply beam him my admiration, my compassion, my solidarity, my thanks?

"I'd lie if told you I wasn't afraid," he says. "But I have lived well." Then he says, "I hope you can do something for my children."

I tell him that I won't stop trying to get them all released. Harrier seems to take this in. And it comforts him.

"Things may look insurmountable," he says, as if he senses how I feel. "But people have always struggled against tyrants. Kite's time will pass. Keep the flame, Zara."

It doesn't matter if he thinks I'm Swan. I will keep the flame for him. I pour out my songlight, wanting him to believe that his legacy will live.

Then I feel a talon on my cheek.

"Who are you with?" asks my mistress suspiciously. "Is it Lark?" She spits out the name. In her wig, she looks like a snake goddess.

358

"I'm with Harrier," I say. "He's preparing to die."

Swan turns away, guilt curdling her.

"He thinks that I am you," I tell her. "He says Kite's time will pass. He says keep the flame, Zara."

Swan hangs her head and seconds tick by.

"Does he know what I did?" she asks.

"No. And I won't tell him. He believes in you. If you want to atone for what you did—"

Swan cuts me off. "We've just seen what happens when you cross Kite," she cries. "Death is a knifepoint away."

She is gravely upset and I don't press her.

"It's done," she says under her breath. "I can't undo it. I can't help him."

I come closer, trying to comfort her. "He asks you to help his children."

I watch Swan pull herself together, forcing the guilt down into her black pool.

"I will find my own way to atone," she says. And a veil of ruthlessness comes over her. "Get dressed," she instructs me. "Kite wants us to shine."

Swan goes to the mirror, where Lady Scorpio is waiting to adorn her with jewels.

Cassandra approaches, with a petite white evening gown draped over her arms. She helps me dress in it. It's not as little-girlish as my usual clothes and I am glad of it.

"Thank you," I say, when she has finished.

Cassandra pauses.

Suddenly, she grips my arm. A shock shoots through me. She holds my gaze. There's something there that isn't dead. A question.

She makes the sound of a single syllable, a hard C. I don't know if she's trying to say my name or her own.

But it's beautiful to me.

I put my finger over my lips, warning her that everywhere's unsafe.

And we take our place, behind the goddess of the snakes.

50 ✴ PIPER

I'm alone in the tool room, sitting in the corner.

I should be in the canteen with the other lads but my insides have turned into ash. Something in me got burned over the Greensward.

As it's growing dark, Tombean Finch finds me. I want him to say, "What's the matter, my boy?" and put his arms around me. But he says, "What the fuck's wrong with you, Piper?"

I tell him I'm upset by what we did. Finch looks puzzled. "That mission was a success. You had Kite slapping you on the back. You're made."

Where do I begin?

"We're tainted with it," I say. "It was an act of evil."

Finch looks worried. "Look, no one likes to see stuff like that. But it wasn't our evil. We just followed orders. If a crime's on anyone, it's Kite." I feel his sympathy for me—but not his understanding.

"What if my mother and sister were down there?" I ask, sharing my distress.

Finch holds out a hand to help me up. "Piper," he says, "this is brainsick. Your mother and sister could be anywhere. You need to stop."

He is firm. I grip his hand.

He tells me to get my arse in gear. Commander Ouzel's in the hangar and he wants us all. I follow him. Truthfully, I would follow this boy anywhere.

Ouzel is in the hangar with a senior airman I have never met. He tells us that at dawn, our mission is to firebomb Reem. He introduces Air Marshal Judd.

"Judd has come up from Meadeville to lead you," he says, "as Axby has been called home."

This instantly gives me a very bad feeling. "May I ask what's happened to him, sir?"

"Axby's son is gravely ill," explains Ouzel.

"Axby's only son died of wasting fever, years ago," I inform him.

"I didn't mean his son," responds Ouzel, harassed. "I meant his wife. It's been a very busy day and I've had to do a lot of rearranging. Any more questions?" His tone is so aggravated that no one wants to ask one.

Ouzel leaves us with Air Marshal Judd, who says that history is in our hands. He says a lot of other stuff that I don't really listen to. We go to prepare our kit bags for our flight.

"Axby would never leave us in the lurch like that without telling us why," says Finch as we walk back to our dorms. "What's going on?"

"I don't know," I reply.

I think back to how somber Axby looked when I met him at the washbasins. He stared in that mirror like he was looking into the corners of his soul.

"We don't know this Air Marshal Judd," says Finch. "What if he's a wanker? I don't want to be up in the air above enemy land without a leader that I trust."

That's when I remember Kite's invitation to his drinks reception at the palace. I tell Finch that I'll go and find out what I can.

"A drinks reception?" says Finch in frustration. "Could you crawl any further up Kite's arse?"

It's time to tell Finch everything. Tonight. I'll talk to him tonight.

I put on my dress uniform and set off across the palace grounds.

Under floodlights down on the esplanade, I see a line of prisoners disembarking from a transport ship, cuffed to each other in pairs. Some of the figures look familiar. The men are being separated from the women and I walk closer, recognizing Mr. Malting, our baker from Northaven, and some of our seaworkers and their wives. The men are being escorted up to the prison on the hill, but Brightlinghelm has no women's prison, so the women are being detained in the Chrysalid House.

My eyes pick out Gailee Roberts and I feel a dreadful pang.

It was so easy to tease Gailee when we were kids. She was one of those girls who was scared of everything: spiders, mice, eldermen, wasps. I think back to how we treated her when we were junior cadets. Everyone knew that Galilee's dad had been taken as unhuman, and we used to do impersonations of him as a chrysalid. I remember Chaffinch Greening standing with us, laughing. I close my eyes in shame. What a bunch of heartless little shits we were.

Gailee's whole body shows her dread as she looks at the Chrysalid House. But instead of collapsing in fear, she is comforting Hoopoe Guinea, the choirmother. Mrs. Guinea has surely never broken a rule in her life and I find it unbelievable that she is here, a prisoner. Some kind of fatal fascination draws me toward them.

"Gailee," I say.

I see her eyes shining at the sight of me.

"Piper," she says, "help us." She wastes no time, telling me that Mrs. Guinea has done no wrong. "I took up arms with my husband—but our choirmother did nothing. You saw her, Piper, you were there. She stood with Sergeant Redshank as a voice of reason."

I nod but no words come.

"I was trying to serve Great Brother Peregrine," says Hoopoe. "He wanted peace. I was trying to keep the peace."

"I'll do what I can for you," I say.

"Where's Elsa?" cries Gailee as the guards start to pull her away. "Is she alive? Is your mother still alive?"

"No one knows," I tell her.

I see grief and hope on Gailee's face. "They've not been caught?"

"No," I say. I don't tell her that their bodies might be cinders, cremated in Kite's forest fire. But this is the thought I take into the palace.

The reception is in a banqueting chamber that has murals on every wall, of soldiers feasting and cavorting with Third Wives. Sister Swan is acting as hostess. She's greeting people at the door in a dress like ice, with snaky hair.

"Airman Crane," she says, her voice like sweet honey. "Lord Kite will be so pleased you're here. "He has talked of nothing but his flight to the Greensward."

"Thank you for inviting me," I manage to utter.

"Thank our Lord Kite," says Swan.

Gailee will be in the Chrysalid House by now.

"Sister," I tell her, my words spilling out, "there's a line of gallows being built on the esplanade, for the townspeople of Northaven."

"For the insurrectionists, yes?" Swan's smile is beginning to look fixed.

"I was in Northaven on the night of the riots. Forces of hatred came to the town and stirred up division between us. My neighbors are good people. Is there anything you can do to intercede on their behalf?"

Swan's smile fades away. "We must talk another time," she says, and she turns to greet the next guest.

"When?" I ask.

But Swan doesn't answer. One of her ladies, a petite chrysalid, offers me champagne. I take a glass. The tray looks almost too heavy for her. Other women are serving us with little snacks of food, each wearing a gauze over her face. I don't like getting too close to these chrysalids. The air feels empty around them. I stand in my uniform, champagne in my hand, not a word in my head.

If I can't help Gailee, how can I help Axby, or the citizens of Reem? I am afraid of my own weakness. I am such a worthless wretch. Do I really think I can find the courage to—

"Hallo, Piper."

I look up. The last person I'm expecting to be greeted by is Chaffinch Greening. She's wearing an extraordinary dress in the very latest fashion, so low-cut it embarrasses me.

"Chaffinch," I say.

"I've been hearing things about you," she says. "Are you really Lord Kite's personal pilot?"

"He was my passenger today," I tell her.

"That's incredible," says Chaffinch, giving me an approving smile. "Who'd have thought Piper Crane would turn out to be so dashing? You were always such a spud."

She giggles. I think her insult is meant to be flirtatious.

"Are you here to speak for Gailee?" I ask, hoping for an ally.

Chaffinch lowers her voice. "I'm sorry for Gailee but I can't. Papa's brought me here to testify against the traitor Heron Mikane. Through no fault of my own, I'm trapped in wedlock to the biggest villain in Brightland. I'm here to get my marriage annulled."

"Gailee and Mrs. Guinea are being held for execution," I tell her. "They're not criminals. Will you help me speak for them?"

Chaffinch's eyes hit the floor. And suddenly, she's tongue-tied. I know immediately that she won't do anything—and that she feels bad about it. Her face flushes with guilt as Gyles Syker comes to her side. He has overheard us.

"No one's going to speak up for those traitors, Crane," he says. "They chose their side and they must take the consequence."

Syker takes Chaffinch away proprietorially, looking for someone more important to talk to. I have failed. I remind myself of my main purpose: to find out what's happened to Wing Commander Axby.

As Lord Kite enters, the whole assembled company applauds him. Kite looks supremely confident as Swan congratulates him on his mission. She tells us that Lord Kite personally dropped incendiary bombs into the Greensward, incinerating a whole village of tents. She sounds as if she is full of praise but there's something odd in her tone, something shrill, as if what Kite did was faintly ridiculous. "The rebellious inhabitants will have certainly learned their lesson." She finishes to applause.

I can't tell if Swan is being respectful or impertinent. Kite rests his hand on the back of her neck and I notice that his finger presses one of the bones of her spine as he speaks.

"Friends, old and new," he says, welcoming his Ministers and the people of Northaven. "It's good to see you on this momentous day. We have smashed the insurgents who have been blighting our lives in this finest of all cities," he tells the crowd, and there's spontaneous applause. "Tomorrow, justice will

364

be done," he continues. "We will hang the man who murdered our Great Brother. Then talks with Ayland will begin. Before sundown, there will be a new chapter in our relations with our enemy. I'm not at liberty to tell you much, but I assure you that the outcome for Brightland will be good." There is more enthusiastic clapping. To my utmost surprise, Kite picks me out. "I'd like to take a moment to celebrate the achievements of our air force and in particular the skill of one young man, our star pilot, Piper Crane."

I feel all eyes upon me.

"This young man first came to my attention when he landed his plane on the River Isis. I was struck by his mettle then and he's gone on to prove himself one of our finest."

Mortification creeps up my cheeks.

"Flight is a new science and it needs the young," continues Kite. "A new generation must rise to the task. And in this spirit, I reward your diligence and enterprise." Kite is pinning something on my chest. "You are now Flight Lieutenant Piper Crane."

There is loud applause.

"Thank you, sir," I say stiffly. "I live to serve."

Kite indicates that the music should start up and the hubbub of chatter resumes.

"When you fly your mission tomorrow," he instructs, taking me aside, "you will be second in command, after Air Marshal Judd. Afterward, I'd like a full report, preferably over a glass of something strong."

"Yes, sir."

"You'll drop the first bomb on Reem's precious Circle House. It's a hilltop citadel—you cannot miss it."

"Where's Wing Commander Axby?" I blurt.

Kite's smile shifts. As the chatter swells, he says, "He's sick."

This is a lie.

"I'm sorry to hear that," I say. "Is there some way my comrades and I can pass on our best wishes?"

365

"I shall do that for you," says Kite. He pins me with his gaze. "Destroy Reem's Circle House and you will have Axby's place. I will make you wing commander."

He ends the conversation, turning to greet the power-dazzled delegation from Northaven.

I put my unwanted champagne back on the petite chrysalid's tray. Under her gauze, she's wearing spectacles and she's staring at me in a way that doesn't seem . . . quite dead. It's disturbing. She has flecks of green in her eyes and her expression is intense.

I feel something move in my mind. I see a sudden image. Axby and Kite are in an embrace. At first, I do not comprehend it. Then I see the flashing blade. Kite stabs Axby, twisting the knife up into his guts. Axby falls, writhing with pain. I see his lifeblood pooling beneath him.

I am so shocked that I take a step backward.

The chrysalid holds my gaze. I understand that she witnessed it.

"Save Reem," she says.

Her words implant themselves in my core. Tearing my eyes away from her, I find the exit door and leave.

She is not a chrysalid. She has mind-twisted me. She has put images in my head.

Unhuman.

I wait until my ingrained fear and visceral horror of her subsides.

She's just a girl. A girl like Elsa.

As I climb up to the airfield, I concentrate on what she showed me.

Axby refused Kite's order to bomb Reem. And Kite has murdered him.

I halt on the airstrip, breathing the cold night air, looking down on Brightlinghelm, letting it sink in.

What do I do?

I put my hand to the badge of rank that Kite pinned to my jacket.

Axby.

I will not let you down.

51 ✴ NIGHTINGALE

After the reception, there's a banquet. I serve the food with my songless sisters, my arms bare, my face veiled. I hold trays, plates, and bottles until my muscles ache.

I sensed a longing for the truth in Piper Crane and I took a desperate chance with him. I pray there's something he can do for Reem.

It was a mad risk. But mad risks are all I have left.

As the meal is served, my eyes keep going to Cassandra. She works with her usual blank grace but once or twice, I notice her pausing mid-action, as if puzzled by the scene that she finds herself in. I don't know what it means, but it mesmerizes me.

Kite and his Ministers are buoyant with drink. The girl from Northaven, Chaffinch Greening, is a big hit. She is full of bigoted wisdom about the uprising in her town and her angry contempt for Heron Mikane simmers under her sparkly chat. Ouzel is particularly taken with her and she flirts with him outrageously. I don't think this girl has any idea what she's playing with and I wish she could see what these men really are. She's singing her pink-and-golden song to a table full of predators.

Suddenly, there's a cry and Minister Drake leaps to his feet, revealing a puddle of hot custard in his lap. Cassandra is standing over him with a dripping jug.

"Clumsy fool," he cries, the custard running down his breeches. "She did it on purpose, I swear!" My heart leaps to hear it.

"How can she have?" asks Ruppell. "She's an utterly enchanting dummy like the rest. In fact, I remember this girl. She was an insurgent and I consider her among my finest works."

"I gave the creature a friendly stroke," says Drake in a hurt tone, "and I'm telling you it willfully poured hot custard in my lap."

Cassandra stands like a statue, holding the jug. But behind her gauze, her eyes are shining. Some beautiful life force in her resisted Drake's repugnant touch.

"Bravo, Cassandra," I whisper in songlight.

"I can assure you, brother," says Swan, "my ladies are exactly what they appear to be. I couldn't tolerate any spark of personality or will." She barks to Cassandra. "Go back to my rooms."

Cassandra puts down the jug and leaves. I don't know if she can hear my songlight but I tell her that she's wonderful and I'll be with her soon.

Drake is huffing and puffing as he wipes up the custard. "She meant it, I tell you."

Ruppell is piqued by this. "I feel you're calling my work into question, Drake, and I don't like it. Through years of experiment I have perfected the art of severing free will. If that chrysalid covered you in custard, it's because you were feeling her up and you nudged her hand."

There is laughter at this and Drake smarts.

"Can they ever recover?" asks Kite. "Because we need to know their servitude is permanent. We cannot offer unhumans a single chink of hope."

I lean in, listening to Ruppell's response. "Sometimes, a flicker of self-will reappears," he says, enjoying his expertise. "Occasionally, we've been sent a chrysalid who's exhibiting resistance. On one or two occasions, the personality has returned. The brain is an organ of magnificent complexity and it finds myriad ways to navigate an injury. But it's simple enough to ensure continued obedience."

Chrysalids can come back to themselves. This is news.

"If you bring me your troublesome handmaiden," says Ruppell, treating Swan to his most charming smile, "I'll examine her most thoroughly."

"Thank you," says Swan graciously.

"Anything for you, dear lady."

I notice that Kite is staring at Ruppell in mistrust.

After the coffee is served, Kite sends his guests away. Chaffinch Greening leaves on Ouzel's arm, floating like a bubble, full of champagne.

368

"Won't you stay a minute, old friend?" Kite asks Ruppell. And his Minister of Purity remains smiling smugly. Greylag looks furious at not being invited into this inner circle. He leaves in a fog of bitterness, with Drake. Kite turns to Swan.

"Go and wait for me in my rooms," he orders.

Swan makes no move to leave. "Shall I serve the sugared almonds, my lord?" she asks tartly.

Kite doesn't appreciate this reference to Peregrine's murder. Swan, for all her fear of him, is walking recklessly close to the line.

"Thank you for your magnificent efforts this evening," Kite says to her coolly. "As a reward for your sterling service, I'd like you to read out the public condemnation tomorrow, at Harrier's execution. You delivered him to justice and I think it's only fitting." His eyes are steely.

Swan's face falls. "For your own good," she says in earnest, "spare his family."

Kite throws a look to Starling Beech, standing in the shadows. "Take Lady Swan to my rooms. She isn't wanted here."

Swan rises to her feet, knowing that some kind of punishment awaits. "Good night, Minister," she says to Ruppell, holding out her hand for him. He stands as she leaves and his eyes linger on her with an amorous gaze.

Swan flicks me a look as Starling Beech escorts her out. I understand that I must be her eyes and ears.

Kite and Ruppell remain as we dummies clear the table.

"Swan wants clemency for Harrier's wives and brats. Where do you stand?" Kite's question is curt and his gaze is direct.

Ruppell clasps his hands under his chin. His head is shiny in the turbine light. "I suggest she should be listened to. Lady Swan best knows the people's mood."

"Interesting," says Kite, filling his own glass. "Interesting that you should take Swan's side."

369

"These are volatile times," says Ruppell. "And I happen to think she has a point."

Kite's jaw twitches as he looks at Ruppell, trying to fathom his loyalty.

"Is something ailing you, my friend?" asks Ruppell, looking concerned.

"She spins mistrust," says Kite. "She makes a web of it, all around me." He looks as if he might unburden himself—but at that moment, the Northaven captain, Gyles Syker, returns.

"Sorry to disturb you gentlemen," he says confidently, as if he's interrupting a picnic. "I forgot my smokes." He has left them on the table—on purpose, I swear.

"While I'm here," he says, eyeing Kite, "there's something I ought to tell you. I thought I'd wait until you were alone."

"Well?" asks Kite. "My Minister and I have no secrets. We're lifelong allies."

Ruppell smiles his shiny smile. Syker takes a seat and gestures for me to pour him a drink. Kite enjoys his impertinence.

"As you know," Syker begins, "I was among the horsemen that were hunting down the fugitives. We had a Siren with us, a nasty thing, but she had strong unhuman powers." Syker offers out his smokes and Lord Kite takes one, intrigued by this real soldier. Syker lights it for him.

"This Siren led us to a boathouse where we almost caught the lot of them. But as we were about to strike, the Siren fell to her knees and she was crying out, as if there was a force in her head so strong that she could neither function nor resist. She was literally blinded."

"By what?" asks Kite.

"Powerful songlight."

"Go on," he says, with interest.

I find myself stock-still, listening. I remember that I must keep moving, doing my stupid tasks, or I will give myself away.

"Whatever this force was, it wrecked the Siren—and the fugitives escaped. The Inquisitor was furious. Under duress, his Siren said that the

370

songlight had come from the Brethren's Palace. There was a Torch, she said, a woman in white, who was helping the fugitives."

Silence falls. Kite's eyes land on Swan's empty chair. I don't think I can stand this dread; I should just open my mouth and cry out that it was me.

Syker carries on. "The Siren was different after that. Less compliant. I don't think it's any surprise that a day later, she attacked her Inquisitor and ran off with the fugitives."

"That's a very interesting story," says Kite, exhaling smoke. "Thank you for sharing it."

"One final thing," says Syker, "and I'll leave you gents to your affairs of state." He knocks back his port. "It surprised me greatly to see Piper Crane in here," he says. "I'm sure he's a good airman and all that, but blood's thicker than water. The mother's an adulteress, the sister's unhuman. The Cranes are all the same under the skin—deviant. If I was you, my lord, I'd treat that boy with caution."

Kite exhales his smoke, inscrutable. "Remind me of your name," he says.

"Gyles Syker, Captain. At your service." I swear he almost calls Kite "pal."

"Dismissed."

Syker nods a bow and saunters out.

Both Kite and Ruppell are shaken.

"You don't seriously think it could be Swan?" asks Ruppell.

Kite stubs his smoke out on a plate, saying nothing.

I want to rush to warn her—we must escape the palace now, tonight.

"What could her motivation be?" Ruppell is completely puzzled. "She's our most effective propagandist and loyal to her core. How could she be aiding an Aylish fugitive, when every speech of hers reminds us to revile them?"

Kite silently considers. His trust is like mercury, settling nowhere, running away from him, impossible to grasp.

"Surely Swan is innocent," reasons Ruppell. "You keep her on a tight leash. That band is hardly ever off. What if it's one of these chrysalids?" he questions. "That one who spilled custard on Drake—she was once a rebel, a real firebrand. What if her songlight has crept back?"

Kite eyes us all as if we are dangerous.

"Why don't we bring in the Sirens?" suggests Ruppell. "If there's an unknown Torch in the palace, it will be found."

"Yes," says Kite, "I will have evidence."

He calls his guards. "Take these creatures to Swan's rooms," he says. "Keep them under lock and key."

We are lined up and marched to the door. There is no escape.

"But what of Swan herself?" presses Ruppell. "I simply can't believe it, Kite."

Kite's eyes are glinting with suspicion. "You're very quick to rush to her defense."

"That Northaven captain is no witness," continues Ruppell. "He's repeating something a Siren said under duress. That's hearsay." Ruppell reaches across the table to reassure Kite. "We'll get to the bottom of this, old friend. I will have five Sirens in this palace by tomorrow. And you need Swan at that execution. A brilliant piece of statecraft, getting her to read the condemnation."

Lord Kite fixes his trust on Ruppell—for the time being.

"When I have evidence," he says, "then I will strike."

I hear no more. The guards escort us out, leaving Kite and Ruppell to decide our fate.

52 ✳ SWAN

I'm in Kite's closet, rummaging through every pocket. His scent is strong in here: mint, cloves, and violence.

He will have a spare key somewhere, I know it, a tiny key that will slip into the lock on this lead band. I will free my songlight. I should have done this years ago. But there was never anyone I wanted to commune with.

Now there is him—Kingfisher.

I open every box on Kite's dresser: unguents, hair gel, powder, an old watch, some rings. This man is so austere. I go into his bathroom and rifle through his cabinets. Razors, shaving gel, a kit for manicures, more overpowering scent, a shelf of bottles filled with different colored pills.

I go back into his closet and hunt through all the drawers containing underwear. I find some letters from his mother and, disturbingly, some locks of women's hair, each one tied with black ribbon. I know immediately that these are Kite's conquests, all now chrysalids. There's a lock of hair my own color, tied with a ribbon of pink. I pick it up, remembering how he cut it off me when I was just sixteen. He pretended he was going to cut my throat and sliced through my hair instead. He found my terror amusing—it was Kite's idea of a joke. For a while I stand holding it, confounded.

My eyes are on the row of Kite's gleaming boots. I've missed something. Behind them, tucked away, is a dark wooden box. I draw it out and open it.

Phials of poison. Like the one he gave me to kill Peregrine. Nestling between them, a velvet pouch. I open it. And drop a tiny key onto my palm.

The anticipation draws a moan of pleasure out of me. I cannot go elsewhere. Kite's men are guarding the door. So I must lose no time. Kneeling, I pull off my wig. Fingering the lead band, I find the tiny lock. Using the mirror to assist me, I insert the tiny key.

I am free. I let my songlight surround me, strengthening me.

I don't rush straight to Kingfisher; I hold myself back. I must be ready.

I tousle my cropped hair and step out of the dress, standing in my petticoat. I get rid of my lipstick and my jewels. I stand, gazing at myself: ardent, captivating, strong but vulnerable.

I am Zara Swan. I desperately need a friend, a champion.

I run my tongue over my bare lips. The Aylishman will not resist.

53 ✴ LARK

We've been entwined in each other's arms, letting the boat drift on the widening river. But we have not made love. I sense the fight in Kingfisher every time we get close. I can feel his self-control battling his desire. Now I sit up.

"Kingfisher," I say, "Your plan with Swan won't work. She'll find out how you feel about me."

"She won't. I'm too well trained."

"She'll damage you. You'll damage her."

"Tell me, Elsa, what else have we got?" he asks. "She's the only one capable of stopping Kite."

"It's wrong," I say emphatically.

He's silent. I watch him grab his shirt and dress. "I'm sorry," he says, at last. "I shouldn't have done this." And he turns to leave.

"You can't pretend it hasn't happened," I say, as gently as I can.

But his response is vehement. "There are forces here bigger than you and me. If Sorze Separelli knew what I'd just done with you, he would consider me a spineless libertine, a traitor to the Aylish cause."

"We didn't do anything except admit a truth," I tell him. "There is love between us and it changes everything."

Kingfisher doesn't deny it. He lets out all his breath, then he raises his eyes to mine. "It's too late," he says. "I've already placed myself as Swan's ally and protector. You have to let me go."

I stare at him, silent. I hold back the urge to scream FOOL. He moves out of the cabin. I hear him drawing water, washing. *FOOL* . . .

I'm about to go to him and force him to see reason when Nightingale comes. Her urgency lights up the night.

"Kite is bringing Sirens into the palace," she says in songlight. "I don't know how I'll speak with you again." Her anxiety comes pouring out. "Kite knows there is a Torch working against him. I have to find Swan and warn her but I'm locked here, under guard. And Cassandra . . ." Nightingale's songlight is almost painful. "She's gone."

It takes me a moment to unpack this density of information. I start with the last thing first.

"Cassandra has gone?"

"She's not in Swan's rooms, I've searched everywhere. She isn't here." Nightingale describes the events of the night, ending with Syker's revelations about the woman in white who helped us to escape.

My panic matches hers. Nightingale is in terrible danger.

"We're almost in Brightlinghelm," I tell her, unhesitating. "I'm going to get you out."

"Don't risk yourself. Go to the Aylish ship with Kingfisher. Stay with him," she insists. "Keep yourself safe."

"I love you, Nightingale," I tell her. "I'm coming for you and I'm going to get you free."

I sense Nightingale shimmering with tears. "I love you too," she says. "It's meant everything to me to have you as a friend."

This girl. She cuts me up so bad that I can hardly speak. Her songlight resonates right through me as I sit in the dark, floating downstream.

"Stop talking like it's over," I insist. "Kite will be stopped and you're going to survive."

"Brave Lark," she says, and her light glows warmer. We hold each other tight, as if we're standing on a precipice and either one could fall.

"Swan is in even worse danger than me," Nightingale whispers. "And she's the key to everything. Lark, you must do what you can to help her."

I feel my throat tightening with the effort of keeping down my deep antipathy. But Nightingale is right; if Swan acts against Kite, she'll be a powerful force.

I manage to tell her that I'll do what I can. "Don't you dare give up. You will survive this and be free."

Nightingale goes, searching the palace with her songlight from the confines of Swan's rooms, trying to find Cassandra while she still can.

376

I become aware of the boat again, the sound of the river, the waterbirds, the breeze. It's the charcoal hour, where shades of gray creep into the sky, just before night becomes the day. I can't tell Nightingale what I am planning in the secret parts of my head because it is too desperate and too unlikely. But waves of hatred and anger keep crashing over me when I think of what Kite's done. He has to die. Someone has to get near him with a knife.

And that someone's going to be me.

It's nonsense. It's wishful thinking. It's actually depraved. I couldn't even kill that poxy Inquisitor, never mind a man like Kite. But there we are. I will die trying.

It's a heavy thought.

I think back to what passed between Kingfisher and me. Now that the intensity of hurt has subsided, I try to think rationally about what he has been tasked with. His people are asking him to love Swan, as some kind of national duty.

The wrongness of it scrambles me.

Zara Swan is no fool. She will find out his duplicity. He has to go to Alize and tell her that this ruse is now unworkable. I resolve to tell him so.

I find him at the other end of the boat, sitting cross-legged, just as he was when I first met him. Except that he is shirtless. His eyes are open, facing the water, and he doesn't notice me approach. He's communing with someone. I see his expression—this is something intense.

Swan.

That woman—

Swan.

The jealousy I feel wrings me, twists me like a rag-worm.

He *wants* this.

He's letting her see his strength, his vulnerability, the wound on his arm, heroically sustained. Yan Zeru, what a player.

I turn away, keeping silent, retreating to the back of the boat, sitting at the tiller. I try and stamp my feelings down. They aren't rational. Or even dignified. There's every good reason he should speak with her—for his people, for our cause. Nightingale is right; if Swan was on our side it could make all the difference.

I long to break into their precious harmony and declare myself. I want her to know that I am here, a force to be contended with.

But I wrap myself in silence. I won't endanger him.

I turn my eyes to the riverbank, trying to think of something else. We are going through a town. A boy and his mothers are herding cows along the towpath. I see river traders pack their boats and I look at the turbines high above, like protective gods, turning in the still night air.

When Kingfisher finds me, I'm staring at the dawn.

"Zara's in a dreadful situation. Her life is in danger."

I nod, staring at the warehouses on the bank, thinking this might actually be the outskirts of Brightlinghelm.

"You know what I must do. Please don't make it any harder."

I still can't look at him.

"Kite's fleet is leaving for Reem. Zara can tell us everything, how many planes, their route, their plan of attack. It's vital, essential information and if she can help me to save my city I'll take everything she has."

My head keeps nodding, but I can't find any words.

Suddenly, I'm consumed with grief for Rye. I think about the last time I saw him, tied to that post, muddy and bleeding. Rye had no one but me and I abandoned him. The pain of it still kills me.

Rye.

Kingfisher approaches me. Perhaps he sees how much I'm hurt. I have to move away because if I open my mouth I might croak with tears and I have too much dignity. He will play this game with Swan until it becomes real. He's already falling. I stand alone at the tiller, steering us toward the looming city.

And this is how we enter Brightlinghelm.

Estranged.

54 ✳ PIPER

My mind is racing. I keep seeing what the chrysalid showed me: Kite sticking Axby with a knife, Axby dying in a pool of blood. Toward dawn, I'm wracked with doubts. What if she's trying to confound me, as mind-twisters do? I want to know the truth. So I go to the morgue, looking for proof.

It's dark and deserted but I hammer on the door until a caretaker answers. I give him my name and my rank and I tell him that I've come from the airfield to collect Wing Commander Axby's things.

The caretaker swears under his breath. He shuffles off, and when he comes back, he says that Axby's personal effects have already been sent to his wife with a letter of condolence.

"I'd like to pay my last respects."

"Too late. He's been sent for cremation," says the caretaker, and he shuts the door.

This tells me all I need to know.

Once I explain things, Finch will be my ally. Kite's mission to Reem must not succeed—but I can't yet see how to make it fail. Finch will help me. I will talk it through with Finch and together we will find a way.

As first light comes, I prepare myself. Somehow, word of my promotion has got round and lads congratulate me right and left. When I finally see Finch, he's smiling with delight.

"Flight lieutenant," he says. "You surely are the golden boy of Brightlinghelm." He wants to kiss me, I can tell, and a sweet longing seizes me. I follow him to the airstrip, just glad to be in his slipstream as he laughs and jokes with our comrades. When we get to our plane, I pull Finch up on the wing, where no one will hear us.

"Axby's dead," I say. "I went to the morgue during the night because I could not believe it. But it's true."

"How?" asks Finch, stricken.

"Kite killed him."

Perhaps I've been too blunt because Finch immediately rejects it, shaking his head. "No." He keeps repeating, "No."

I can't explain to Finch about the chrysalid—who is clearly not a chrysalid at all—so I tell him I overheard talk at the reception. "Axby refused an order. He didn't want us to fly to Reem. And Kite stabbed him in cold fury."

Finch cannot comprehend it. "That's not true. For a start—why would Axby refuse Kite's order? We're one mission away from winning the war."

It guts me that Finch has said this. I thought he would immediately see Kite's evil. I try to explain.

"Axby knew this mission was a crime."

"That can't be it," says Finch. "How could Axby object? It's not like bombing our own people in the Greensward. They're the fucking Aylish. I don't believe Kite killed him—why would he do that?"

I go quiet after that. Finch's hatred for the Aylish is in every artery. And Kite is his hero—as he was mine. I felt the same way that Finch does, just a few days ago. The scales have fallen from my eyes but it has taken time. I wish I had confessed my change of heart to Finch when I had the chance. I put off the hard conversation fearing he'd object—and now it is too late. Hatred of the Aylish is the lifeblood of our nation.

I expect the Aylish feel the same hate for us.

Before I can say more, Air Marshal Judd calls us over. He gives us relief maps of Ayland and issues our coordinates. We will stop in Fort Peregrine to refuel and then proceed west, to Reem. Judd tells me that Finch and I will be flying in Axby's plane.

"I know I'm a stranger among you, Flight Lieutenant," says Judd. "The airmen know you. They'll respond to your voice better than mine. So I will be using you to instruct the fleet."

"Yes, sir."

We take our things to Axby's plane. It's a brand-new model, the Firefly II. It's more sophisticated than the others, flying farther on its fuel, with improved communications. In my previous Firefly, I could only hear Axby's instructions. Now I'll be able to issue them.

380

A rash plan comes to me. This plane will help.

"Finch," I say, "I'm sorry for what I told you, but please believe me when I say that it's true."

Finch works on, without replying. I hope that he's digesting what I said. He fits two incendiary devices below the fuselage. Both will deliver devastating damage. Judd inspects his work, admiring the bombs. He says our success is assured, as most of the buildings in Reem are made of wood.

"The city's on a high plateau," he tells us. "The mountain winds will blow the flames sky high."

"I'll hit my targets, have no doubt," says Finch. "Those Aylish won't know what's coming."

This is meant for me, and my heart sinks. He's weighed what I've said and rejected it. How can I stop this attack when even my dearest friend, Tombean Finch, wants it to succeed?

When Kite, Swan, and his Ministers arrive to witness us take off, I still haven't found an answer. We get more speeches.

"No one undertakes such a task unless the outcome warrants it," says Kite. "And today, the outcome is clear: victory!"

We chant until we're hoarse and then Sister Swan comes onto the podium. Her smile looks strained, like it's held in place with wire. She tells us we will make our grandchildren proud. "You are the stuff that myths are made of." I mishear her and for a while, I think she has said moths. Kite stands with her to watch our takeoff, tightly gripping the back of her neck.

Finch and I climb into the cabin of Axby's plane. We familiarize ourselves with the controls and taxi toward the runway.

"You heard them," says Finch. "This is the right thing."

We are the first aircraft to take off into the pink beauty of the dawn.

Somehow, I must stop this.

But all I can think is that Finch and I are the stuff that moths are made of.

Dust. We are dust.

55 ✳ RYE

As first light breaks over the horizon, I see the shape of the whole planet. The sky turns from a black, starlit dome, through every shade of blue, into a low blush of gold in the east. I am transfixed. As we slowly move north of the badlands, forests begin to spring up beneath us. This is a region of lakes and rivers and I stand at the viewing window, tracing their meanders, awed by the massive scale of creation.

I send up my songlight. "Petra, let me know that you're all right. Let me know if you need help."

No response. There has been no response all night and I have tried and tried. I don't accept that Petra regrets the kiss we had. She was so full of emotion at the table last night. I twist my head, looking up at the rest of the airship, wondering where she is. The sapien quarters tower above, where Wren Apaluk is on his own. Today, I will get to him. I will find out what's going on under the polite friendly behavior of the Sealanders.

My movements are constantly being watched and guarded. When I crept out of Charlus's rooms an hour ago to search for Wren, one of Bradus's men was sitting outside the door, springing awake in his chair. He followed me when I came down here to the viewing deck, under the guise of being a friendly guide. It's pretty clear that I'm not allowed to go anywhere alone.

I must keep faith in these people. They're still my only hope. Today, we will reach Reem.

"It takes some getting used to, doesn't it?" says Xalvas in his songlight.

I turn to see him approaching me.

"It gives one a feeling of majestic grace, moving slowly over the globe," he continues.

"Yes, sir," I say, politely agreeing.

"Sovereignty," says Xalvas. "It's only natural. Here we are, above nature, in our high dominion. As eximians, we are above everything. You understand that, Rytern? You are one of an elite."

What I'm feeling is the same insignificance that I felt with Wren in our tiny acorn boat, but I don't correct him.

"Yes, sir," I say.

"It's time for us to make first contact," says Xalvas. "I'd like you to be with me."

I tell him that I'm grateful, thrilled, honored, and he takes me to his own suite of rooms, front and center of the ship. The opulence makes me gasp. Livia is there, waiting at a round table, and there's another figure at the window, staring at the growing beam of dawn on the horizon. My heart leaps—Petra.

"I have asked my first science officer and Petra to join us. Petra—soon to be my daughter—has a good knowledge of ancient sapien languages. And you may have felt the potency of her truevoice already, Rytern."

"I have, sir, yes." I feel more than her truevoice as Petra's eyes flicker briefly to meet mine.

Xalvas invites us to sit. "Your country is at war with these Aylish?" he asks.

"Yes, sir."

"Then we must establish that you are not a threat to them."

"Absolutely." My only job is not to fuck this up.

The Sealanders sit straight-backed with their hands upturned in their laps. I do the same. I can see they are already making a harmony of truevoice and before I join them, I take a deep breath.

This is for Brightland, for our Torches and Third Wives.

My songlight leaps. I feel the electricity of Petra's presence and I let go into her incandescent beam. She steadies me, keeping her distance. She was an open book yesterday but now she will not let me see a single underthought. I respect this, realizing that any show of feeling might somehow endanger her. I concentrate on what she's asking me to do. My coarse songlight must find its place in this sophisticated harmony.

383

I feel as if I am in my body and outside it; I am in *Celestis*, yet I am hurtling through the blue-gold dawn.

"*Reem*," whispers Petra. Her songlight reverberates right through my soul.

Xalvas and Livia are letting her lead. Our four hearts seem to beat as one as we hold the chord of this powerful communion. We are apart and yet together in a way I do not fully understand.

Petra's beam of songlight intensifies, moving our minds in her direction. I feel as if I'm falling through gravity as she homes in on a presence. I get a rushing sense of buildings—no time to take in anything—I see a small study—a young woman getting to her feet, paperwork spilling around her, a writing pen in her hand. She looks up, connecting with Petra, and there is wonder on her face. I see an impression of her dark hair, her azure shirt, an amber jewel at her neck. She has a headful of figures that shimmer and dissipate as she tries to hold us. An exam; she has been up since before the dawn, studying for an exam.

"Who are you?" she asks, and her songlight ripples like water.

Xalvas, takes the leading note in the harmony, introducing us as the eximians of Sealand. "My name is Air Admiral Xalvas." He gives her a whole bewildering string of his titles and his genealogy and finishes by saying, "I would commune with your leader."

"I'm Janella Andric," says the young woman, who has no titles at all. We sense her trying to contact someone in songlight. "Our leader is Sorze Separelli," she says. "He's asleep."

"Our airship has come from afar," says Xalvas. "We're pleased to make contact with a race that has truevoice. Waken him."

I see Janella thinking fast, trying to hold our harmony. Her heartbeat is pounding in my ears. She leaves her study and runs down a corridor past a vast library and out into a square. I see that this is a mountaintop citadel. Pines sway in the breeze and valleys fall away steeply on every side. I get a shimmering sense of a whole city nestling below, with its tall turbines rising around us. Janella runs past a building bigger than any I have ever seen, circular, like one of the fabled temples of Brightlinghelm, unimaginable to a small-town lad like me. She picks up her pace, belting across the square, and opens a door into a tall white tower. I notice with surprise that it isn't locked or guarded. By the time Janella climbs halfway up, she is completely out of breath. She can hardly hold us anymore. Petra takes the lead again, encouraging Janella, telling her not to be afraid.

"I am Petra," she says, and Janella pauses, as if she's really seeing Petra.

"Petra," she repeats. And she stands in wonder. "Have you crossed the badlands?"

"Yes, high above, unscathed by the irradiants. If you look to the south you will see our airship, *Celestis*," says Petra. "We've been voyaging for over sixty days from our home, two oceans away."

Janella peers out a narrow window and through her eyes I see a tiny pin of light on the horizon. The first rays of the sun are reflecting off *Celestis*. Janella is struck silent, as if she is witnessing a miracle. I see the strain on Petra as she tries to hold the harmony.

"Your leader," insists Xalvas impatiently.

Janella hurries on, up flight after flight. At the top, she raps on a door. Her songlight is exhausting itself as she waits for a response. The connection flickers in my mind like a flame in the wind. She raps again.

"Separelli!" she cries, using her mouth-words. "Torch Sorze, wake up!"

At last, a man pulls open the door, aggravated to be woken, naked from the waist up. A warrior, whose long hair falls almost to his waist. He's the size of an ox and I can see that all three Sealanders are taken aback by his big hairy chest. Janella pulls him into our communion and immediately we are conscious of his songlight, as deep as a river, as strong as the mountain upon which he stands. In a whirlwind of images, Janella fills him in.

"Tell Odo to come," he says to her, and Janella turns away with a last look at Petra, fading from our communion.

Sorze Separelli breathes our harmony. He goes to his windows, glancing

385

first at the tousle-haired woman who is waking in his bed. He throws open wooden shutters, gazing to the south. I feel his unshaven potency, pulling us toward him. He separates the strands of our chord and I feel his light entwining us, exploring us. At first, I lay myself open. This is a man with no airs and graces, a soldier, like myself. Then I feel it: *Brightling*, he says. And the hairs stand up on the back of my neck. He's turning my spirit over in his hands and I shudder to I think how many Brightlings this man might have killed. My feelings boil up in me. He is my enemy. And yet— compared to Xalvas—I feel our sameness. We're caught in the same war. He can see the scars around my skull from the Brethren's lead band and I know that he has scars too, not visible on his skin.

"I'm a Brightling Torch, as you can see," I tell him. "I've come to seek your help."

Sorze Separelli turns his beam on Petra.

"A powerful Flare," he says, impressed. "You carry three Torches."

Petra introduces Air Admiral Xalvas but Sorze Separelli interrupts her, halfway through the list of his titles.

"Xalvas," he says, "I sensed your people coming days ago. I heard you, like a distant choir."

Xalvas is wrong-footed. I think he's taken aback by Separelli's potent songlight and his lack of awe. The woman in Separelli's bed comes to his side and she takes his hand. She is not a Torch.

"What is it?" she asks. "What do you see?"

"A new dawn," says Separelli. I feel his songlight smile. "Sealand," he says. "You are welcome here."

56 ✴ NIGHTINGALE

I am woken by the noise of Firefly planes, taking off from the airstrip, one after another. I count forty, and watch as they rise over the Isis and veer round to the west. I pull myself together, gathering my songlight. I will try again to reach Reem.

I stare out the window, hoping that the new day will give me adequate strength. And the first thing I see is a group of Inquisitors crossing the courtyard. There are Sirens with them, two men and two women. They are already hunting.

Any thought of using songlight now comes with a death sentence.

I crouch, hardly daring to breathe.

This is a day I don't want to live through. And it will start with Harrier's execution.

Cassandra has not returned. No one has found her. No one even knows she's gone. In spite of my worries about her, this gives me heart. Somewhere, Cassandra Stork is finding her liberty.

The door unlocks and two guards come in, holding Sister Swan. I stand with the other ladies, trying as hard as I can to keep the consternation off my face. Something's badly wrong. As soon as the guards exit, Swan collapses. There are lurid red marks all over her neck.

I shout for the ladies, asking them for blankets, an ice pack, anything I can think of. Lady Orion and I lift Swan onto her white chaise and I prop pillows around her. She pulls off her serpentine wig, revealing the lead band locked tight round her skull. I cover her with a quilt and put my arms around her.

"I found the spare key," she says. Her voice is low as if it hurts her to speak.

She tells me what's happened. "I freed myself. It felt like the sweetest liberty I've ever known. I went to Kingfisher. He's coming, Kaira, he's on his way. He'll join the Aylish and they will help me." She pauses to sip the water I give her. "I parted from him when I heard Kite returning. I just had time to lock my lead band and replace the key before he found me in his closet. He could see that I'd been searching—but I made him believe that I hadn't found it."

Kite.

"He thought I was searching for poison. He tried to strangle the truth out of me."

I feel a rage so deep that I worry it will twist my songlight into some howling and misshapen force.

"He accused me of helping the fugitives to escape."

"Sister," I say, "that was me."

I expect her fury, but Swan is not angry.

"I was able to swear, hand on heart, with complete integrity, that I was innocent," she says. "He began to believe me. But his trust in me is hanging by a thread. I think there's only one reason I'm not in the Chrysalid House already," says Swan. "He's got to hang Harrier. It's a public event. He needs me."

I wrap some ice in a towel and put it on her neck, hoping it will bring the bruising down.

"You could have given me up," I say, "but you took the blame for what I did."

"If I gave you up, it would reveal my even greater treachery," Swan points out. "Kaira, if Kite ever finds out about you, I am utterly finished."

Lady Scorpio approaches us. She stands with a pitch-black dress billowing in her arms like an organza thundercloud.

Swan stares at it. "What's this?" she asks.

"You asked her to dye it," I remind her. Swan gets to her feet. She looks at the dress—huge hooped skirts and a long train. There's even a black veil to go with it. The sight of it imbues Swan with a new energy. Clothes have always been her inspiration.

388

"We're going to watch a good man die," she says. "Let's put on our best."

Wasting no time, the ladies and I dress her. Swan makes no attempt to hide the bruising on her neck and her tear-smudged eyes. We put the black veil over her cropped hair, letting it cascade down the dress. Her reflection strengthens her.

"I'm not inclined to go down without a fight," she says. "Kite should not have made an enemy of me."

Everything about Swan is brave and magnificent this morning. As we leave the room in our funereal procession, I wish that Lark could see her. Even she would be impressed.

57 ✶   LARK

The guards at the city's river gate wave us on, two medics on our way to pick up the wounded—a sight they must see all the time. In spite of everything, I feel like an excited child to see Brightlinghelm for the first time. I have only seen it through Nightingale's songlight, where it had the shifting, glimmerous quality of a dream. Now I see how vast it is. Shops and houses are dwarfed by great turbines, climbing up the city's hills as far as the eye can see. We drift by warehouses, a hospital, a fish market. Even this early, the river is busy with boats and no one pays us a second glance.

On one side, the palace complex comes into view, stretching up a hill. I see the domed great hall and sweeping lawns leading down to high walls and an esplanade. I slow the boat. My heart turns cold when we pass the low-level building that fronts the river. A barge is outside and I see two men unloading unconscious figures. The reality of the Chrysalid House is stark and Kingfisher comes to me, perceiving my dread.

"That won't be your fate," he says. And he puts his arms round me. He's trying to mend things between us.

"You can't know that," I say.

Yan Zeru doesn't realize that he and I are about to part. I can't go with him onto the Aylish ship. That has become clear to me. I have to go my own way, solitary, invisible.

As we emerge from under an ancient bridge, we see the masts and turbines of *Aileron Blue* ahead of us, docked near the palace gates. Only when we're very close can Kingfisher make his presence known to Renza Perch. Her sensitivity to songlight isn't strong enough for anything else. I cut the battery and we slowly drift. Kingfisher pours out his songlight and before long, two faces appear over the ship's rail ahead of us—Renza and Cazimir Cree, fraught with relief at seeing us. Two rope ladders are thrown down.

"We have to leap from one vessel to the other," says Kingfisher. "This boat can drift on downstream."

I wait until the last moment because I know Kingfisher will object to what I am about to say.

"I realize it's your task to get Swan on our side," I tell him. "I respect that. But I can't watch it. If I'm there, I'll only hinder you."

"What is this?" he asks.

"I'm not coming," I tell him. "This is your path. You have to be with your people. I have to save Nightingale."

"But our ship's the safest place," he says. "We can both help Nightingale."

Renza and Cazimir await, their arms outstretched to help us aboard. Our boat drifts alongside. I step back.

"Go," I say.

"Lark." His voice falters. He sees I am in earnest. "What are you thinking? What are you planning?"

"Go, or you'll miss your chance!" He pulls me tighter into the embrace. I see that he is going cling to me and keep me with him. I force myself out of his arms.

"Go!" I say. At the very last second he leaps from boat to ship, grabbing the ladder, pulling himself up.

"Lark!" he cries in frustration. "Lark!"

I look back at him, not daring to use my songlight. I put my fist high in the air, wishing Yan Zeru strength and honor, success in his endeavors.

"Lark!" His voice fades under the blanket of mist and I sail on, downstream, alone.

He's been my constant companion since we left Northaven. And we have not parted well. My heart is instantly telling me I've made a terrible mistake. But I have only one idea of how to rescue Nightingale, and Kingfisher can't help me.

I take the ambulance boat over to the other side of the Isis, the city side, where people live. A host of boats are moored outside warehouses and market stalls. I see brown canals leading into a close-packed district where taverns front the river, many of them painted dirty pink. I look for an empty mooring and I bring in the boat. No one pays me much attention.

I have a sewing job to do and I execute it with the utmost speed. Sewing is a skill that I always resented learning in Northaven but now I thank Ma and Hoopoe Guinea for every chiding they gave me. Using my white auxiliary nurse's dress as a base, I cut and shape a sheet into a passable long skirt. I leave a gap where I can reach into my pocket and I secrete Heron's knife. I don't know if I'll have the guts to use it but I am getting Nightingale out, come what may. I use medical gauze to make a veil and I fashion it like Cassandra Stork's. I watch people walking past the boat as I work. They look grim-faced and bitter and I wonder if they're on their way to witness Harrier's execution. I don't have much time. I must be in this crowd, as close to the front as I can get.

As I put on the white nurse's shoes, Bel Plover comes to me in songlight. I instantly warn her there are Sirens here.

"I know their tricks," she says, as if no Siren in Brightlinghelm could outsmart her.

She tells me Heron has woken. "The surgeons say he'll be all right."

I feel a flood of relief. "How is he?" I ask.

"He hates the fuss that people have made and he's mad with frustration that you and Kingfisher went ahead. He wants to be in Brightlinghelm right now," says Bel. "He's trying to get up and he says he's fine."

"He isn't fine," I tell her. "Heron Mikane is careless of his life. He needs to be watched or he'll throw it away."

Bel takes this in.

"How's my ma?" I ask.

"Worried. But proud of you, Lark. What you and Kingfisher did, it's fired people up—to go off like that into danger, alone. The militia are shaking off their grief, turning it to purpose." Bel's eyes are alight. "We're coming. Raven has been communing with the insurgents in Brightlinghelm."

"You must tell her that there is hope for Cassandra Stork," I say. "Tell Raven that Cassandra's mind is injured but not broken. She's recalling herself and she has left Swan's rooms."

"Heron says don't do anything until he arrives. You understand? He says I'm to order you most forcefully—don't do anything."

I know they will be hours and hours behind me but my relief starts to flow. They're coming.

"What are the Brightlinghelm insurgents planning?" I ask.

"Fireworks," says Bel. As we part, she gives me a piece of good advice. "If you want to use your songlight, make sure you're in a crowd. The Sirens lose their accuracy. They won't be able to pick you out."

I thank her.

"Be safe," says Bel, fading.

I think how much Bel Plover has changed in the days since I met her, how much more herself she is. As for Heron's exhortation not to do anything? I forget it instantly.

When my makeshift dress is ready, I put on a blue nurse's coat. I roll my gauze veil up and put it in readiness round my neck. I will be able to transform when I must. I will become a chrysalid. I step off the boat on to the flat street and immediately I miss the feeling of my element, the water.

I lose myself in the crowd heading toward the palace. I flow with the mourners, each of us dreading what we're about to see. The silence is heavy.

This is an execution we're attending after all.

58 ✶   RYE

We're in the scouting craft hangar, preparing to make the trip to Reem.

"It's right and fitting that you come with us," Xalvas says to me in his rich songlight. "You're the reason we are here."

"You have my thanks," I say. "All the more for bringing Wren Apaluk."

Something changes in Xalvas's smile and he excuses himself to make arrangements with Commodore Bradus, who'll take command of *Celestis* while we're on the ground.

Livia comes to my side. "Before you ask," she says in songlight, "I'm afraid I have some troubling news about your young companion. He hasn't allowed us to treat him medically. He won't suffer anyone to touch him and I'm afraid he's contracted a fever. He's too unwell to travel this morning."

Somehow, I knew this was coming. "I'd like to see him," I say immediately.

Livia apologizes. "Wren Apaluk must remain in quarantine." She assures me that he's in good spirits and has been apprised of our meeting with the Aylish.

"I don't have to break quarantine," I tell her. "Just let me talk to him through his door."

"I'd be happy to arrange that but the scouting craft is leaving directly. I'm afraid you'd have to remain on board *Celestis*."

"So if I see Wren I will miss Reem?"

"I'm afraid so."

"You can't delay by five minutes?" There is anger in my songlight.

"Diplomacy is a delicate business," she explains. "The Aylish are expecting us and any delay may be misconstrued."

This is bullshit and my anxiety for Wren is now acute. But Gala, what can I do? I must meet the Aylish. Yet how can I leave him here alone? And why is my only ally, Petra, continuing to ignore me?

"I have no choice," I tell Livia in defeat. "I must meet the Aylish."

I walk away angrily, and see Charlus in his uniform, languidly watching the non-Torches prepare the scouting craft for him. He doesn't lift a finger. I am disappointed to see Xalvas putting a fond hand on Charlus's shoulder and talking to him under his breath. Parental love must be blind.

I'm waiting to board when Petra approaches. She has my sergeant's coat in her arms.

"I brought you this," she says. "You should wear it." She's keeping her songlight studiously calm—not a hint of what might lie beneath.

"Are you sure?" I ask her with a half smile. "Brightling sergeants aren't so popular in Reem."

"Wear it." She puts it in my arms and it seems important to her.

"Petra," I tell her sincerely, "I'll do anything you ask of me."

She flushes. "I hope this trip brings you everything you need," she says, turning away.

"Aren't you coming with us?" I ask in dismay. "I was hoping we would get a chance to speak."

"Garena is taking my place," she says, without meeting my eyes. "I asked to be excused."

"Why?" My songlight is insistent.

"My truevoice is weary after the exertions of this morning."

I have to accept this but I don't believe it. I ask her about Wren. What does she know about him being ill? Petra is evasive and it feels like she's throwing cold water on my question. She walks over to Charlus. He bends down and gives her a proprietorial kiss, right in front of his approving father. It's sickening to watch and I climb aboard the craft so I don't have to see. Jem Kahinu shows me to a seat and I thank him. I ask him if he's heard anything about Wren.

"No," he says, his eyes hitting the ground. "I'm very sorry."

I put on my coat and I sit, brooding. I smile a greeting at Garena, who looks genuinely thrilled to be part of the excursion. Xalvas and Livia join us, strapping themselves into their seats. Xalvas is in good spirits. He tells me he's not been on the ground since *Celestis* left Sealand, so this is a big day for him. He watches as his son turns the craft around, taking us up and out through the wide hangar doors, into the open blue. Charlus manages to keep us steady. We fly northwest at speed and soon we are descending in a great circle, giving our ears a chance to adjust to the rapidly changing altitude.

Out of the window, I see a sprawling city, wrapped around a high-topped plateau. Close-packed houses, turbine towers, and precipitous streets lead the eye up to an ancient citadel, on which there is a large tree-lined square and the extraordinary circular building that I noticed in Janella Andric's songlight. I get the full view of it now. Only the foundation walls are built in stone. The roof, which reaches a dramatic high point, is intricately carved in wood. I see the white tower where Sorze Separelli sleeps. This time it's not shimmering in songlight. Everything is starkly real.

A crowd has congregated in the square. They are cheering with delight and their expressions are full of wonder. As the scouting craft descends, they make way for us to land. They must have a clear view of *Celestis*, approaching in the sky. What on earth do they make of it? I remember my awe when I first saw it. Xalvas leans into me and says, "Let me do the talking, Rytern. Sorze Separelli knows about you and your plight. Let me negotiate a future for you."

"Of course," I say. But my trust is shifting and I decide then and there that I'll speak for myself. Charlus wobbles the scouting craft down to the ground. The eyes of two nations are upon him—and he lands us with a jolt. I bash my head on the seat in front and Livia bites down on her lip and makes it bleed. I sense Xalvas's bland vexation with his son, as if this embarrassment is a minor mishap.

As we prepare to leave the craft, Jem Kahinu picks up the object with the round lens that Livia was using in the cockroach city. He tells me it's a recording device for images. He will capture our meeting with the Aylish and send it, by some process I cannot understand, up to the airship so that the crew can watch it, eximian and sapien alike. I am amazed.

"So Wren will see what we're doing?" I ask.

"I hope so, yes," says Jem.

"Will he be able to hear what we say?"

Jem tells me that the device also records and transmits sound. I will speak for Wren and I won't let him down.

I stand with Garena, behind Xalvas and Livia, as the scouting craft doors open. A hush falls over the Aylish crowd as we walk out. I see people holding Aylish flags. Banners are waving, covered in long lines of Aylish script. Musicians start to play—a searing melody of drums and violkas. I step onto enemy soil. Human voices join the melody. The people of Reem are singing an anthem—joyful, welcoming music. Brightly dressed children come forward bearing wreaths of flowers that they reach up and place over our necks. I am impressed with how quickly the Aylish have organized all this, crowding into the square to greet the strangers from the sky.

Janella Andric is in the crowd, looking at me curiously, perhaps wondering what this shabby Brightling sergeant is doing with these Sealanders.

Jem keeps filming as we're met by Sorze Separelli.

He is even more imposing in the flesh. His long hair is tied in a knot and he's wearing an azure greatcoat, open over a plain Aylish suit. Next to him is his wife—I assume it's his wife—the woman who was in his bed. She's dressed in a long, dark green dress, her hair in a high ponytail. She has a ruby jewel around her neck. With them is a tiny woman in a simple cotton suit, so old her back is bent. Her smile beams with a deep radiance.

When the anthem ends, I am expecting Separelli to greet us in songlight, but this tiny woman steps forward and it's she who speaks, using mouthwords as she's not a Torch. The crowd hushes in expectation.

"My name is Odo Swift," she says. "I am Prime Minister of Ayland. News of your arrival has spread through all our Circle Houses. The people of Reem warmly welcome you."

There is cheering from the crowd at this. Xalvas is puzzled. He addresses Sorze Separelli in songlight, saying that this is a great day for Sealand and, he hopes, for Ayland too.

"Forgive me, friend," says Separelli, using mouth-words, "we never use our songlight when there are those present who don't have the skill. I must ask you to speak so that everyone may hear."

Xalvas exchanges a look with Livia.

"That's not our custom," Livia tells Separelli. "Admiral Xalvas always speaks with truevoice."

"Then we will translate for him, but we must insist," says Separelli. "It's our first rule. No one shall be excluded from our full communication."

Xalvas must hate using mouth-words because he nods to Garena to translate for him and he stands, smiling tersely in silence. This seems wrong to me, deeply undiplomatic. Why doesn't he just say hello?

"We're from the island of Sealand in the Santific Ocean," begins Garena, once she has introduced us. It takes her a long time to get through all Xalvas's titles. Her speech is halting and it makes me realize how skilled Petra is at mouth-words. Xalvas is looking increasingly unsettled.

"Our airship *Celestis* is on a reconnaissance mission, making an inventory of Earth," says Garena, gesturing up at the mighty airship, hanging in the sky like a burnished copper moon.

Odo Swift thanks her for her courteous translation. She introduces Sorze Separelli and the Aylish poet Zia Benn (the woman in Separelli's bed). She doesn't mention whether Zia Benn is Separelli's wife. Odo beams goodwill at Xalvas.

"Come into our Circle House," she offers with her disarming smile. "I'm so curious to know about you. And you must have many questions for us. We'd like to honor you with a feast and a display of our culture. And then you might like to tell us of your country and your way of life. With your consent, our Torches will relay your answers throughout Ayland."

Jem Kahinu keeps recording his images. He seems galvanized by what is unfolding, as if Odo and Separelli have said something revelatory and profound, instead of their simple welcome.

Odo Swift is walking toward him. "I see your comrade forgot to introduce you."

Jem gives her his name, embarrassed to be noticed. He says he's just the engineer.

"You are very welcome too."

I sense Xalvas sending a lightning-quick instruction to Charlus. Charlus immediately goes to Jem Kahinu and as we follow Odo Swift and Sorze Separelli into the Circle House, I see him take away Jem's recording device. Jem objects—and Charlus escorts him back to the scouting craft. Whatever's going on here, Xalvas doesn't want Jem to record it or take part in it. Why not? What has spooked Xalvas?

"Won't you come in, sergeant?" I turn to see Janella Andric at my side, gesturing for me to follow the others into the Circle House.

"Thank you," I say, "but I'm not really a sergeant. I stole this coat, escaping."

Livia sees us and instantly, she calls me away. "Rytern, Xalvas wants you by his side."

I look at Janella.

"There's another Brightling on their ship. We need your help" is all that I have time to say.

59 ✴ PETRA

I have lost no time since the scouting craft left. I am in my borrowed sapien clothes, standing in the service lift, feeling terrified at what I have to do. I close my eyes as I rise up, as if somehow this might block out the smell of garbage. My hands are clammy with a cold sweat of fear. I am breaking foundational rules now and I dread the consequence. I almost capitulate to my misgivings and run back to my cabin—but I think of Suki Ableson, having Charlus's baby in that prison cell, and I harden my resolve. I think of Rye and it all becomes easier.

Petra, he said, *I'll do anything you ask of me.*

I find that I'm pressing my hand into my heart, not just because I'm afraid but because I am rejoicing. I could see in his eyes that he cares about me. He is concerned for me and more than that. More than that.

The lift opens. No one is around. I pass a refectory and see a crowd of sapiens, their attention glued to screens. The scouting craft's cameras are showing the descent and there's a loud derisive laugh as Charlus touches down with a clumsy jolt. I would love to see our first contact but I hurry on.

Avoiding all the main corridors, I make my way toward the prow of the ship and the two prison cells. I have the codes memorized in my head. There's a man guarding them today and my heart sinks when I see him—but he too is watching the meeting between the nations. I hear the foreign sound of Aylish drums and a choir—some kind of anthem is being sung. I sneak past the guard and turn into the row of cells. I bash the codes into the keypads on the doors, releasing Wren first. I have brought clothes to disguise him as a scouting craft engineer. He refuses when I tell him to undress. He backs away.

"I killed to get this uniform," he says. "No one's taking my clothes from me."

"I'm risking my life for you," I say. "If you want to get out of here, put the bastard suit on."

Wren appreciates the urgency inherent in my Brightling swear. He takes the outfit. His sleeves are rolled up and I see there's bruising on his arms.

"What happened?" I ask.

"The scientist woman came in the night with that man Bradus. They held me down and injected me with something."

My heart fills with apprehension. What has my mother done? "Did they tell you what it was?" I ask.

"No. I resisted. But I don't feel good," he says. "As they left, the science woman said that nature will take its course."

My blood runs cold. My mother is a villain.

"Are you well enough to run?" I ask him.

"Fuck yes," says Wren. "Now get out while I change."

I unlock Suki. She's kneeling on the floor, gripping the bed. There's a pool of water beneath her and a wave of pain renders her silent. When it passes, she says, "My waters have broken."

"I don't know what that means," I confess.

"It means this baby's coming."

This is my worst fear.

"Take Wren," she says, heaving in her breath. "I'll slow you down."

I can't leave her here. Charlus and Xalvas will own her baby and they'll have no further use for her.

"This is your only chance," I say. "Your baby could be born on Aylish soil. You could claim sanctuary."

"We'll help you," says Wren, entering Suki's cell. "And we're not fucking leaving you." He's dressed as an engineer and he's not taking no for an answer. "Come on," he insists.

Together, we help Suki to her feet. We pass the guard, who is crunching nuts in his mouth as he watches his screen. Sorze Separelli, looking stunning in blue robes, is speaking to Xalvas in mouth-words.

Wren halts, seeing Rye. "He went without me." Wren is most upset.

"My mother told him you were ill. She gave him no choice."

Wren's face falls. "They've injected me with fever, haven't they. It's going to make me sick. That's what they've done, isn't it? They're trying to get rid of me."

I feel a confusion of acute pain and deep shame to admit what my people have done.

"You're a problem to them, Wren," I tell him. "You're a sapien who doesn't know his place."

"Gala," says Wren, fear rising in him. "Gala."

I pull him on. We could be discovered any second. "There'll be medicines on the scouting craft to heal you," I assure him.

I hope I'm right.

We're almost at the service lift when Suki Abelson doubles over again. She kneels on the floor as a great wave of agony engulfs her. Nearby, in a laundry room, I see a crowd of sapien workers gathered round a screen. The image shows one of the Aylish leaders, an elderly lady, coming toward the camera. She has such a compelling face that I find it hard to look away. She's speaking to the camera, gesturing to the man behind it to accompany her. This must be Jem Kahinu. The old lady walks into the big imposing building and I see Charlus pass in front of the lens, his expression hostile. Shortly after, the screen goes black. Our moment of time is running out.

The crowd of sapien workers wait to see if the filming will resume. Then they start to complain. I kneel down with Suki.

"We have to go," I whisper.

At that moment, an alarm goes off. The guard must have noticed that the cells are empty. With excruciating slowness, the elevator opens. Wren and I help Suki in. She's on her knees, pallid with the pain, but to her credit, she makes no sound. The doors close, far too slowly. I hear a shout.

"Hey, what are you—"

It cuts off as the doors seal and we are moving down. Suki throws up in the corner of the lift. The smell is really very bad. Wren has his arms around her.

"You're doing great," he says. "You're doing brilliantly. I was there when my sister was born. My ma screamed blue murder. You're fucking brave, Suki Ableson, and you can do this."

"Hold on, little baby," says Suki, rubbing her hand over her huge belly. "Please hold on."

When we get to the eximian floor, I run ahead to make sure the coast is clear.

The eximians don't need screens to show them what's happening on the planet's surface. I feel them all communing, their focus intent on the historic meeting. In the hangar, the scouting craft I have prepared is tantalizingly close. If we sprinted, we could make it—but Suki is at the mercy of her baby. I don't know how she's managing to move at all. My brain is screaming that we're going to get caught and I have to force myself to a state of concentration, wiping my clammy hands on my suit.

I have to open the hangar doors. I have it all planned in my head. I quickly go to the door mechanism and put in the codes. Then I hurry back to Wren and we both support Suki. She's walking as fast as a woman in labor can possibly walk across the hangar floor. Then I hear a deep male truevoice.

"What are you doing?" It's Bradus.

My mind starts swimming with dread. We're almost there. Another few feet.

"Stop or I'll fire. Those sapiens will die."

I turn to face him, supporting Suki. "Wren, go," I say.

Wren sprints into the craft and Bradus fires his blaster.

"You have no right!" I scream, and I think my truevoice must sear him, as he winces in pain and his aim goes wide.

Suki is furious. "Are you going to murder us?" she yells. "I'm having a baby. This is Charlus's baby, you shithead."

Bradus looks at her, bewildered, as if childbirth is something dreadful that he's never had to contemplate. His moment of confusion gives me time to pull Suki into the craft. I grab the blaster by the door and keep Bradus back, firing on stun mode at his feet.

403

"The red button on the control panel," I yell at Wren, "Press it."

Wren slams his hand down on the panic lock. This is designed to protect the craft from any wild sapien attack. It's bombproof, bulletproof, and the doors instantly lock shut, hard-sealed. Bradus is trying to close the hangar doors but I have foreseen this and overridden the mainframe. I fire up the engines and we hover off the ground. It's just like the simulator, I tell myself. Flying the real thing can't be very hard.

What I don't foresee is what Bradus does next. He points his blaster into the hangar door controls and melts them. The doors halt, halfway open. And my resolve crumbles. A flood of terror overwhelms me.

Our way is blocked. We can't get out.

60 ✳ PIPER

I can feel Axby's presence here. Pinned to the instrument panel in the cockpit, there's a pencil sketch of a woman and a boy—Axby's son and his wife. If I survive, I will go to this woman and tell her everything: how Axby died, what he lived for, and how much he meant to me.

I look at Finch, bent over the relief map, carefully navigating our route. We don't speak much. Our disagreement at the airfield has upset us both. I look down at the view as we reach the coast of Ayland. Fort Peregrine is our main foothold here. We will land there to refuel, before proceeding on to Reem. There's a weight in my heart as I begin the conversation that I know we must have.

"Finch," I say. "I'm not going to be part of this."

"What are you talking about?" he asks.

"I know you don't believe me, but I can tell you for a fact that Kite killed Axby."

"Fuck, Piper," exclaims Finch in exasperation. "Why would he do that, unless Axby was a traitor?"

"Think beyond your love of Kite," I beg him. "I know Kite is a brilliant man. I know the air force is his brainchild. But think what he is asking us to do. Kite is power-sick. He killed Axby for refusing an order, but the order is obscene."

I've chosen these words carefully. Finch goes silent and I begin to hope. Down below, we're following the coastline. Coming closer is a brand-new airstrip and a military town. I ask Finch if he's with me. "We can persuade the others. We can halt the mission."

There's a pause, as what I've said hits him. Then he turns round and stares at me.

"That's mutiny," he says. "Halt the mission? For a start, they'll shoot us as deserters. And Piper, the Aylish killed my brother. They killed your own pa. Reem is their power base, full of unhuman scum. Why would you halt the mission?"

"Didn't you hear what I said?" I ask, tasting bitter disappointment.

"I'll pretend I never heard any of it. It's fucking treason."

I'm completely wrong-footed. Finch turns round to face me and I see his eyes are not without sympathy. "I know things have been hard for you. I know how fond you were of Axby, but this is bigger than all of that. We might end this war today. It might be over." His eyes are shining. "We can get our lives back. If we do this, we can find a way to be with one another. We can grow old together."

"Look at us," I implore him. "I'm in love with you. But Kite himself tells us that's an aberration. We know we can be hanged, just for being who we are. How is that different from being unhuman?"

"Piper," I can feel the emotion in Tombean's voice as he tries to explain. "Those unhumans will take over the world if we don't keep them down," he says. "If we don't cull them, they will wipe us out."

I am silent then.

I switch on the comms and tell the fleet to prepare for landing. I circle around, making sure I come in last, behind Air Marshal Judd.

One conversation is never going to unpick years of hatred. I've left it far too late.

"You're feeling a lot of grief," says Finch as I make my final descent. "But I'm the one who'll drop the bombs, not you. You don't even have to look. Just think about ending this war."

"Yes," I say.

"It will be over and we will have won." Finch believes it.

"Yes," I say.

I touch down and bring the plane to a standstill. It's Finch's job to liaise with the ground crew preparing to refuel us. He opens the cockpit and jumps off the wing. His expression looks troubled and he doesn't meet my eye as he walks toward the other gunners. I close the cockpit and look at my fuel gauge. In Axby's superior plane, I still have half a tank. That's enough for what I intend. Immediately, I turn and taxi back to the runway. As I take off, I switch on my comms and the words begin to come.

"Brothers, those of us who saw the destruction of the Greensward know what will happen when we get to Reem. Thousands of people will burn in an all-consuming fire, men, women, children. We are bringing Hel." Every word I say strengthens my resolve. "Our beloved wing commander died to prevent this. Axby thought Kite's order was obscene and he refused it. Kite murdered him for insubordination. Axby died to protect us and to protect his enemy because he was more than a soldier. He was heroic." Something tight in my chest releases. "With the fuel I have left," I tell my comrades as I ascend up to the heavens, "I will warn the people of Reem, so they can defend themselves against the coming slaughter. Tombean Finch is innocent of my intentions. He believes, like many, that he's flying to end the war. But I say if we carry out Kite's orders, the name of Brightland will be blackened in the fire. The Aylish will retaliate and peace will never come."

I turn off the comms device and veer inland to face the mountains. I take off the pin that says I'm flight lieutenant.

I am in no one's air force now.

I leave Fort Peregrine behind, knowing that by the time Air Marshal Judd refuels and comes after me, I'll be far ahead of him. I don't have enough firefuel to get me back home. This is my final flight.

I fly to honor Axby. And I fly to honor Rye.

61 ✶ LARK

The rain comes down in sheets, the wind driving it in from the east. I have to admire Swan for the stunt that she pulls with that black dress. She and her ladies process across the lawns, with guards surrounding them. Swan holds a bouquet of black tulips and her dramatic veil flies around her in the wind as she glides up to the podium. She looks like Death herself. I pick out Nightingale behind her, in Swan's retinue of ladies, smaller than the rest, holding a single black tulip, the horrible gauze covering her face.

The crowd on the esplanade is tightly packed, spilling over the bridges and back into the city. My progress has been slow but I am determined to work my way to the front. For my plan to have a chance of working, I must get close to Nightingale.

People are hushed, waiting in somber respect or macabre eagerness, depending on whether they support Harrier or Kite. As I pass the *Aileron Blue*, I look up, and it heartens me to see Alize and her crew solemnly standing to attention on the deck.

Kingfisher is there, back in his Torch's azure uniform, and I wish that he would look at me. But when I follow his gaze, I realize that it's fixed intently on Sister Swan. Emotion impales me—disappointment, jealousy. I swallow it and tell myself that Kingfisher's doing what he must. But Gala, the way he's staring at her—nobody can act that well.

I force my eyes away from the pair of them. They're nothing but a sore distraction from my task.

I edge my way through the crowd in my nurse's coat, so I can better see the small girl in white, standing on the podium. Behind her white gauze, Nightingale is scanning the crew members on Alize's ship. She thinks I am with Kingfisher and she's disturbed that she can't see me. I wish I could tell her how close I am; then I remember Bel's advice: *If you want to use your songlight, make sure you're in a crowd.* I stand in stillness as people push and shove, and I fix my gaze on Nightingale. With a wisp of songlight, I will her to meet my eyes. She moves her gaze into the crowd.

And finds me.

So much passes between us, even without our songlight. We're here, within sight of one another. We have got this close. We drink each other in as the rain pelts down.

Harrier is brought to stand beneath his noose, his hands tied behind his back, looking as dignified as a man can be. His wives and children are brought up and placed in position at the row of gallows next to him. Harrier is devastated by the sight of them. His wives look stoical but Gala, the children are terrified.

Kite keeps the whole crowd waiting in the rain. At last he and his Ministers appear, exiting the tram that has brought them from the palace. I wonder if he knows how weak this makes him look. An aide trots beside him, holding a large black umbrella over Kite's head. The Ministers hold black umbrellas too, and I'm reminded of a line of wet dung beetles pushing shit toward a hole.

As he climbs the podium, Kite looks at Swan's black dress and his eyes narrow. The whole city is watching and he can't send her back to change without looking petulant. So he steps up to her and takes her hand, as if her outfit was all his idea. He whispers something—probably a threat—and he plants a kiss of ownership on her. It's strange to see him in the flesh, this tyrant, who has so much power. He looks like a commonplace nonentity. I feel Heron's blade in my pocket, near at hand.

Kite hands Swan a speech to read and she steps up to a microphone. She makes a point of spreading out the scroll, letting the rain soak it, as if to tell us in the crowd that these are Kite's words, not her own. She glances at Harrier—I see a flash of guilt—and she begins. A stiff little aide holds an umbrella over her while she reads out a list of his crimes in a monotone. Her voice is lifeless. She informs us that the whole family has been a magnet for treachery and insubordination.

"Raoul Harrier," she says, raising her eyes to the man she betrayed, "for the murder of Great Brother Peregrine . . ." She leaves a pause. "The sentence is death."

Harrier doesn't know Swan's guilt and I can see that he too is struck by her bruised and broken beauty. He looks up at the sky, as if it should be riven with thunder and lightning.

"What about my children?" he cries.

Swan abandons the soggy script. In a great sweep of her dress she turns and kneels before Kite, supplicating to him.

"Free his family," she pleads. "They are innocent." I hate to admire her for this, but I do. The veiled ladies follow Nightingale's lead, kneeling with Swan. Kite is put on the spot.

"My first act today is an act of mercy," he declares. "I have decided to release the traitor's wives and his children. Take them down." He pulls Swan to her feet—his cheek twitching with anger. She will pay for that gesture later on.

But it pleases the crowd. We all watch in relief as Harrier's family is spared. The mothers hug their children and they are led away.

Kite moves to the microphone.

"This will be a historic day for Brightlinghelm," he says, staring down at us. I think he's trying to adopt a friendly tone. "We begin with justice and we'll end with peace. Peregrine's murderer will die this morning—and by this evening, the war with Ayland will be over. We will have victory."

I think Kite is expecting the usual victory chant but the crowd is silent in the rain.

Harrier speaks, his cry of truth coming from the gallows: "The Aylish came here seeking peace. Peregrine welcomed them. We want peace. Peace. Peace."

His words instantly become a chant that ripples through the crowd. Feeling the safety in our numbers, we dare to utter our heart's desire: peace. My eyes go to the Aylish ship and I see Alize coming to the ship's rail, where all the citizens of Brightlinghelm can see her. She has a microphone and her voice booms powerfully. The crowd quiets.

"Kite," she says. "Show your clemency. Spare this man. Then call off your planes. We know you have sent them to destroy our capital. My family is in Reem, one of thousands of ordinary families. To attack us in a ceasefire is obscene. Call off your planes."

Kite looks livid at her interruption. He ignores her. "Prepare the prisoner," he says.

Alize does not give up. "If your planes attack, we will retaliate with firepower that will leave this city burning too. There is no victory in carnage, Kite."

Kite hurls his response at her. "Your presence here incited the insurgents. You're working with them, to damage Brightland from within."

Alize ignores this lie. "The only way to end this war is through a peaceful settlement. It is within our grasp. All we have to do is talk."

Harrier cries out again. "Peregrine wanted peace—and he was killed for it. Citizens, his murderer is standing before you on the podium—"

For a second, Kite is thrown. Then he acts. "Hang the traitor!" he barks.

The executioner releases the trapdoor and Harrier swings.

I feel Nightingale's high whine of pain. She closes her eyes, her face is screwed up—and suddenly, several things happen at once:

BOOM

A bomb goes off in the grounds of the Brethren's Palace.

BOOM

A warehouse explodes across the river.

A rifle fires—Harrier drops.

A rifle fires again—and a bullet lands in the lectern just in front of Kite.

These are fireworks indeed. The crowd goes wild with alarm.

Kite panics. He grabs one of the veiled ladies and pulls her in front of him. The third bullet, meant for Kite, hits this lady in the forehead and blood trickles down her gauzed face. Kite drops her and he hits the ground himself, cowering.

Nightingale's high whine of distress turns into a blinding cry of woe.

"Get down," I cry to her in songlight.

"LARK!" she screams. "LARK!"

I hear more rifle fire. This time, it's returned by guards. They come barreling into the crowd, looking for the sniper. People are screaming, trying to get away. The crowd quickly becomes a writhing mass as a frenzy of panic takes hold. The crush is lethal as people try to get back to the bridge.

"LARK!"

When I look at the gallows, my heart skips a beat.

The rope has been shot through. And there is no sign of Harrier.

I try to fight my way back to Nightingale, feeling a surge of hope. But the crowd is becoming a stampede for the bridges as people flee in terror from the gunfire. People are crushed, falling into the river. People are going to drown and die.

Kite gets to his knees, using the podium to hide behind. He grabs the microphone.

"This is the Aylish!" he screams. "The Aylish are attacking us—board their ship!"

Alize and her crew take defensive positions on the deck as Kite and his Ministers are being bundled by guards and Emissaries into a tram. The tram takes Brightland's leaders up the hill, back to the palace.

Cowards. They are cowards.

I can't get breath into my lungs. I am crushed.

The Aylish ship is being overrun by troops. I cannot turn my head—I crane my neck, trying to breathe—I see Alize and Kingfisher held at gunpoint. A girl next to me disappears. She's being trampled underfoot and I grab for her, trying to hold her up. Gala, we will die here. My ribs will break. And Nightingale is flooring me with her searing panic.

"LARK!"

She can't find me. I can't answer. I can't breathe. The girl next to me—her face is going blue. Gala save us, give us breath. I'm carried farther, my feet no longer on the ground.

Next thing I'm aware of is Swan's voice, appealing for calm.

"LAY DOWN YOUR ARMS!" I admire her guts. The sniper could easily finish her but she stands at the podium, raising her voice.

"People of Brightland, BE STILL!"

Her voice is so familiar and has such authority that the pressure in the crowd slightly abates.

"THE VIOLENCE IS OVER," cries Swan. She goes on, calling for order, for stillness, managing the crowd. "MOVE AWAY FROM THE BRIDGES. THERE IS NO DANGER. THE VIOLENCE IS OVER. MOVE AWAY!" she orders.

Something eases. I pull the girl next to me back up. I fill my aching lungs.

"REMAIN CALM," says Swan. "GUARDS, PUT DOWN YOUR ARMS. WE WILL HAVE PEACE. PEACE. PEACE."

The pressure continues to ease, as she echoes Harrier's words. The girl next to me finds her breath. I hold her up until her mother takes her, then I begin to work my way back toward the podium. Somewhere in the crush, I have left my coat behind. I check in my pocket for my knife. Still there. I could feel it pressing hard into my thigh. I am breathing.

"LARK!" Nightingale's songlight must be confounding every Siren with a hot pain.

"I'm here," I whisper in return. "I'm all right."

I see her now. She is kneeling, stricken, by the dead veiled lady. Nightingale sends out a wail of deep distress. This is dangerous.

"Nightingale," I beg her. "Don't give yourself away!"

Swan must be wearing her lead band because she's unaffected, but I feel as if a shower of sparks is burning in my head. I implore Nightingale to quiet her songlight, hoping the crowd protects her. I tell her I am safe.

413

Swan continues to appeal for calm and I know that later, when people go over these events, it will not go unnoticed that Swan was the only Minister with the guts to stay. Her actions have certainly saved many, many lives.

I hate that I have to respect her for this.

I sense Kingfisher, searching for me. I tell him I am fine. I see Alize through his eyes. The ship is being boarded by guards and she is ordering her crew to put down their arms. They will not use violence.

I am almost at the podium, almost out of this sea of people when I see the empty tram returning from the palace. Swan continues to orchestrate the crowd, telling people to go calmly to their homes. I look for Harrier. The rope dangles, no corpse upon it. He has vanished like a specter. Either the guards have already taken him, or his comrades have spirited him away.

I have the faintest hope that he is living.

Is that what the bombs and fireworks were about? A distraction to cover his rescue?

I take my hat off to the Brightlinghelm resistance.

Swan turns her attention to the Aylish ship, where Kite's guards are roughing up the crew.

"GUARDS," she says firmly. "THE AYLISH ARE OUR GUESTS. NO HARM WILL COME TO THEM. THAT IS AN ORDER." Her voice carries absolute authority. "The Aylish are not responsible for anything that's happened here," she says. "I am determined that Brightland and Ayland must have peace."

Swan is speaking like a leader. And I see what she is doing. She is staking her claim on Brightlinghelm. The crowd chants again: Peace. Peace. Peace.

Her eyes search the deck of the *Aileron Blue*. She finds Kingfisher, held at gunpoint. He gazes at her and the bastard, the bastard, he makes his hand into a fist and presses it to his heart. Swan is *moved*.

Yan Zeru, the king of hearts, pledges himself to the queen of the hour. I can't watch it.

They can keep each other.

Guards begin to bundle the veiled ladies into the tram. Nightingale is picked up and pulled away from the dead woman. I put the veil I have made over my face and I work my way toward her. She sees me and another wave of songlight crashes in my consciousness as she realizes my plan.

"Lark, no!"

Swan makes one more exhortation for peace, then Emissaries and aides remove her from the microphone and forcibly take her to the tram.

I am glad of the rain, glad of the chaos, the crowd, and the mud, because in this instant, I look as bedraggled as the other chrysalids and my dress doesn't look like the amateur costume that it is. Nightingale is taken into the tram. She has to be silent, unresisting. But her eyes remain on mine. As the tram leaves, I climb onto the stage, where the guards have left the dead woman's body. I stand impassively in white, my face covered with my gauze. I will wait for them to find me. They will think I'm one more of Swan's women and they'll take me into the palace. That was always my flimsy plan. In my heart, I believed it was doomed to failure, but this chaos has strangely assisted me. The guards will take me to Nightingale.

"What are you doing?" asks Kingfisher in songlight. Through his eyes, I see guards swarming over the *Aileron Blue*. He is on his knees, a gun trained on his chest, but his focus remains locked on me. I don't reply. I must play the veiled lady for all I am worth and I hide my songlight deep inside my core.

"Lark," he says. "Don't throw yourself at death." I feel his deep emotion. "Don't ignore me, Lark, I know you hear me."

I have to block him out in case he weakens me. I kneel down next to the dead woman and I take her hand.

My ma once told me that death doesn't happen instantly. She said it takes time for a person's spirit to leave, as if there's part of our soul in every cell and some part of us is still alive, until every cell has released its hold on life. I don't want this woman to be here alone. I sit with her and under my gauze veil, I pray to Gala to take her soul.

I pray that she'll be whole again.

62 ✸ NIGHTINGALE

Harrier is dead. Lady Scorpio is dead. I sit on the floor of the tram where the guard has put me. I don't move. I don't speak. I am a blank nothing.

Shock waves are pounding through me, like storm breakers on a beach.

Lark, what are you doing? Don't risk your precious life.

I'm aware of Swan and I should be supporting her. I sense that she is facing shock waves of her own. She's been heroic and I want to tell her so but I must be a dummy, a dolly for the guards. We travel in silence.

And that's when I hear her. A voice coming from far away. A girl.

"I hear you," she cries, *"who is Lark?"*

Too far away to be a Siren. Her songlight is a gossamer thread. High, high above, I pull it toward me.

"Lark is my friend," I tell her.

"I hear your pain," she cries. "I've heard you before. Where are you?"

I try to clear my mind so I can reach her better. I think she is in Ayland, farther than Northaven, farther than the sea. Yet I don't sense any ground beneath her. She's on the edge of a distant cloud.

"I am in Brightlinghelm," I tell her. "Who are you?"

It comes, her reply, the thread stronger now. "Petra."

She's a girl, a girl like me, a girl with Torchfire.

The tram arrives outside the palace. I should stand at Swan's side but I can't get to my feet. I feel like my legs are made of air.

"Let us out," Swan orders the men.

"Lord Kite's orders are to keep you here," says one of the guards.

I see Swan's frustration and her growing fear. Her songlight is confined under that lead band and she's stuck, trapped, at Kite's mercy.

I close my eyes. "Petra," I cry. "Where are you?"

It takes all my songlight straining to hear her reply. "Reem."

I can sense her now. A pure song, as clear as a spring. She's my age, in a small, enclosed place. It shimmers. There are others with her. I sense great emotion. Fear and courage are surrounding her. It's clear what I must ask this girl to do. I force my songlight into its brightest beam.

"Warn your people," I tell her. "Tell Sorze Separelli there are firebombs coming."

"Firebombs?"

"Lord Kite is sending his planes. They are on their way to destroy Reem."

"Who are you?" cries Petra.

"I am Nightingale. Tell Separelli that Drew Alize needs help."

"Drew Alize needs help," she repeats.

"Save Reem," I cry.

"Nightingale," she says in her golden voice, "I hear you."

The thread between us breaks. A tidal wave of weariness hits me. This exchange has taken everything I have. With the last of my energy, I tell Kingfisher what I have done.

"Reem knows," I say to him. "There was a girl, her songlight strong as mine. I've done what I can. I've warned them what's coming. Reem knows."

I feel a weight lift from him.

At that moment a shaven-headed figure comes running to the tram. His fists bash on the windows, a man with desperate eyes, wearing a shabby Siren's suit.

"There!" he cries, pointing at me. His Inquisitor follows, coming to his side.

"Her songlight is scorching me. That girl is a Flare!"

I see Swan turn to me, her eyes full of dread. I have given myself away. But I have nothing left. Reaching Petra has taken everything I have. Black dots crowd into my field of vision. I feel like my body is turning into air. I lie depleted on the floor of the tram and I let exhaustion carry me away.

63 ✶ PETRA

As soon as I am safely in the craft, I roll up Wren's sleeve and inject him with an antiviral serum from the craft's emergency medical kit. Mother's abhorrent plan to let illness carry him away will not succeed.

Bradus is furious. He is hammering on my mind, demanding entry. I tell him our demands. Wren Apaluk, Suki Ableson, and I want sanctuary in Ayland. I tell Bradus I have not used my songlight yet, but if he doesn't let us go, I will tell every Torch in Ayland how Sealand treats its people.

Suki's had a few minutes of respite, but now another contraction takes her down onto her hands and knees. Wren and I do what we can for her. It is deeply moving watching her labor and I find myself thinking about my surrogate, the sapien woman who birthed me. She is the one who must have suffered in pain when I was born, not Livia. She is the one who held me, all new and bloody, who fed me and nursed me and cared for me until the age of three.

I think I have missed her all my life long.

When I get back to Sealand, I will find out who she is. I will go to her and tell her that she is my real mother.

"You're all right, baby," Suki tells her child as the contraction passes. "Everything will be all right. We're going to be fine."

Then my father's truevoice breaks into my mind. "Petra, what have you done?"

I see him standing in the hangar outside the scouting craft. I tell I him what Mother did to Wren. And I repeat our demands. "Let us go."

It's harder to be firm with Father. His hurt and disappointment consume me with guilt. First, he tries entreatment, telling me how much he loves me; then he coaxes me with lies—telling me there will be no repercussions if we come out now—then plain anger: "This rebellion is inconceivable. How could you shame us like this? Your behavior is verging on deranged."

I tell Father it is shameful to lock up pregnant women and deranged to inject a boy with pathogens that might kill him. He becomes desperate. He puts his hands on the glass, peering at me. "We are all finished," he tells me. "Your mother, me, the whole family. You have ruined us. If you embarrass Xalvas in font of these primitives, I swear, Petra, he will stop at nothing. He could have you air-buried for mutiny." My father wipes his tears.

This is hard to hear and it saps my resolve because I fear that it is true. I am nothing but a troublesome girl and I can be silenced as easily as Caleb Ableson.

"Please," begs Father, "please come out. I'll help you all I can. I'll make sure no harm comes to you or your companions. I promise I'll protect you."

I'm afraid his assurances are empty. Father has little power and I have even less. But his distress is unbearable and it's making me feel hopeless. We will never get away. I'm on the point of giving up when I hear the faraway songlight.

Lark . . .

It's her. The girl I heard.

Lark . . .

I reach her. I speak with her.

I somehow know that Nightingale is a prisoner too, that her situation is as perilous as mine. She asks me to help her save the people of Reem. My mind is exhausted with the effort of reaching her. I sit back, closing my eyes, and I realize that I am not powerless. There is so much I can do.

Suki is having another respite from her pain. Wren is holding her, comforting her. He is remarkably unruffled by her labor pains and he seems to know exactly what to say. Suki relaxes in Wren's arms. She feels safe. I tell Wren and Suki that I'm going to commune with the Aylish. And I let my spirit go.

I feel my own power, tumbling through the blue. I can use this situation to my advantage. I can try to save us all.

I find Rye, Xalvas, and my mother at the center of the round building.

419

But it is the Aylish that I seek. Janella Andric senses me. She holds me firm, drawing Sorze Separelli into our communion.

"I bring you news from Brightlinghelm," I say—and I give them Nightingale's message.

Janella is about to translate what I say into mouth-words but Sorze Separelli asks if he can make me visible to everyone in the room. He would like everyone to hear me. I consent and he makes concentric circles around me with Rye and more of his Torches. The whole building makes and holds a chord of song, sapiens and natural eximians alike. Xalvas, Garena, and my mother look on, astonished. My eyes meet Rye's and I feel my songlight grow brighter. The chord of song holds me, giving me courage. I appear in my truevoice in front of the whole assembled company. Mother looks at me, too shocked to speak.

"What brings you to us, child?" says a small old lady with wise eyes. She speaks in mouth-words and I answer her the same way.

I pass on Nightingale's message, word for word. I tell the assembled company that planes are coming to firebomb the city. I tell them Drew Alize needs help.

I say nothing about asking for sanctuary. For this is the embarrassment my father fears. Xalvas would never forgive me and he would punish us all.

I will have to help Wren and Suki a different way.

Some of the Aylish rush to prepare their defenses. Others discuss whether they should send their missiles upon Brightlinghelm. There is a strong feeling that they should. The years of warfare have taken their toll and the Aylish say they have suffered enough.

"The Brightling girl I spoke to, Nightingale, risked her life to help you because she hopes for peace," I say, held in the chord of song. "With the help of our scouting crafts," I offer, "we can divert this catastrophe. Peace can be achieved."

I look at Xalvas, putting him on the spot. He agrees with a nod and I sense him communicating with *Celestis*, giving Bradus instructions.

420

"Thank you for coming to us, Petra," says Sorze Separelli. "You're a friend to our city. Your news will save many lives."

The chord of song dies down and my songlight is released. Before I leave, I join with my mother, making my songlight no more than a whisper.

"I know what you tried to do to Wren Apaluk," I accuse.

This throws her. "That sapien attacked me," she begins.

"There is no excuse for what you did," I say. "It's attempted murder."

"Petra," she cries, "you have to understand—"

I vanish from the circle. I don't want to hear it.

The core of my songlight seeks out Rye. He marvels at what I have done.

"You reached Brightlinghelm?"

I hold him. In the middle of this crowd, we commune alone. The warmth of his regard lifts my feet up off the ground.

"Wren is with me," I say. "I have rescued him but none of us are safe."

"Bring him here," says Rye. "The Aylish will protect him."

"I can't. Xalvas would be mortified and I'd embroil the Aylish in his wrath."

"Petra, I will come with you—"

"You have to go to your people in Brightland," I assure him. "You must try to free them. Free Nightingale, the girl I met. She is in grave danger. If I accuse Xalvas of any misdemeanor, he will never help you."

I show Rye my reality. He sees Wren, holding Suki as she labors. I show him what is happening, outside in the hangar. The other scouting crafts are being manned and told to stand by. If an air fleet from Brightland comes, Bradus will use the scouting crafts to protect *Celestis*. He will have to override the melted controls and open the hangar doors. We'll be able to leave then.

"Where will you go?" he asks me. "Where will I find you?"

I have no answer.

"Beware of Charlus," I warn him. "Beware of Xalvas and my mother. There's a system of injustice on my ship and Wren Apaluk fell foul of it.

My people cannot comprehend your kinship. To them, sapiens are a different breed, a dying breed. But Wren is your brother and that's the way I want to live, Rye—with everyone, equal, as we are."

"I'll find you," he says.

I let him see my feelings and my feelings are in flame. Rye steps into this flame and kisses me in songlight. It feels like the purest essence of who Rye is, and of what he intends.

"I've left you a gift," I say. "Look in your coat."

I leave him.

Back on the scouting craft, I feel as if my heart is torn out and left behind in Reem.

I can only hope the ancient poets are mistaken about passion.

I hope it leads to freedom, not inexorable tragedy.

64 ✳ RYE

She's gone.

I try to take in what she's said. She has saved Wren, this exceptional, courageous girl. Petra.

I am reeling. My desire to be with her in that craft is so strong I can hardly see where I am or hear what's being said. One of my hands closes around something in my coat pocket. A small book. I work my way through the letters on the cover. My reading is not good.

Petra's Diary, it says. Precious gift. I will decipher every word. Then I will know her. Then I will know.

We leave the Circle House and I join the efforts to defend the city, moving like a sleepwalker, processing everything she said.

Beware of Charlus. Beware of Xalvas.

I watch Air Admiral Xalvas as he puts his scouting crafts at Ayland's disposal. In songlight, he tells Separelli that he will help to protect the city. I can see he's worried for *Celestis*. It has few defenses, as the Sealanders were not expecting to encounter civilizations with air technology. He comes toward me and I calm my mind.

"These Brightling planes of yours," he asks me, "what powers them?"

I tell him what I know about Kite's firefuel. Xalvas sends his songlight up to the ship, ordering Bradus to bring the scouting crafts down to Reem.

Almost immediately, I see a white craft leave *Celestis*. It soars like a bird and then shoots at full speed toward the north.

She's gone.

I look at Xalvas again. What on earth have I done, tying the fate of two nations to this man? I thought him so enlightened. Now I see him through different eyes. The system of injustice that Petra spoke of suddenly comes clear. All he thinks of is sovereignty and dominion.

He sees sapiens as a dying breed.

I watch him exchange a glance with Charlus and I know they are communing.

What must they think of Ayland, where everything is organized for fairness and balance? If the sapiens on his own ship knew that such a society was possible, Xalvas would have a mutiny on his hands. No wonder he stopped Jem Kahinu from filming and sent him to wait in the craft.

I see Xalvas now for what he is. The Brethren; he's the Brethren in a different form. And I have exhorted him to come to Brightlinghelm. I am bringing this man, with his ideas of supremacy, toward my own conflicted people.

At that moment, Jem Kahinu comes out of the scouting craft. He tells Charlus something and Charlus relays it to us in songlight. Jem has noticed on the craft's instruments that there is a small airborne craft approaching the city limits. The Aylish immediately spring into action, assuming that this is a harbinger of the attack. I turn and look, seeing a black dot coming toward us over the mountains. As it nears the turbine towers of Reem, I see that it is a solitary Firefly.

I release my songlight into the air, greeting my countryman, whoever he may be. It's unlikely that he'll be a Torch but all the same I am willing him, pleading with him not to drop his bombs.

The Aylish are readying their guns when I sense a presence that turns me upside down.

"Hold your fire!" I cry. "Hold your fire!"

65 ✴ LARK

As the guards escort me up to the palace, they are arguing. "Who left this bitch behind?" They swear at each other and they swear at me: I'm a fucking chrysalid, a freak, a fucked-up, unhuman whore. I'm fine with that. It means that my improbable disguise is holding well. I must have no reaction to them, even if they touch me. My skin is bristling and my fists are clenched, ready to punch. But I must be empty and rise above it all.

I sat in the rain for a long time, holding the dead woman's hand as it went cold. I looked at the city from inside this gauze and everything became strangely clear.

It isn't enough to rescue Nightingale. I'm being taken to the very center of power. I have a knife in my pocket, a warrior's knife with a good, sharp blade. I will find the man who is responsible for the pool of blood around that dead woman's head, responsible for hanging Harrier, for the attack on Reem, for the fear that Nightingale endures, for Cassandra Stork and for the system of horror called the Chrysalid House.

All my thinking about justice resolves into this blade. The knife I'm grasping in my hand will be my instrument. Without justice, there is only violence. And violence will be met with violence. I am going to force change.

But Gala, I'm afraid.

I think about Bel's Inquisitor outside our cave. In the heat of the moment, I was going to stick my knife into his belly. Kingfisher killed him in my stead but I had no qualms; I would have been killing him to save Bel. I have even more reason to kill Kite. What's hard is the thought of doing it in cold blood. I'm a choirmaiden, not an assassin.

We're inside the palace. I've seen this great hall before through Nightingale's eyes. I know there is a vast statue of Peregrine, presiding over all, but I cannot look at the splendor of the place. If my eyes roam, I will give myself away. The guards take me down a corridor.

I can do this. I'm more than a choirmaiden, I'm a seaworker, and I kill every day. I see big, expressive eyes, desperate flapping gills, and I turn away ruthlessly and let them die. I'm skilled with a knife. I can gut a tunny fish and they're almost the size of seals. I go in at the bottom and I slice up to the top. Removing the gore is part of my job. I can do this. I have had the perfect training and it's in my blood. I remember my pa, teaching me, when I was just a little girl, how to cut the tender flesh and take out the digestive tract. I can fillet a tunny and turn it into steaks. Kite should hold no fear for me.

With Kite, I must aim higher, straight for the heart. I must get the knife in just beneath the ribs and twist, as he did with Wing Commander Axby. I will learn from this ruthless killer, and deliver his murder lesson back to him.

66 ✳ NIGHTINGALE

Someone is shaking me awake, shaking me hard. I want to stay drifting up here in the clouds but someone is gripping my shoulders. The shaking gets vicious and I hear Swan, crying out, "You'll hurt her, please leave her alone!" I force my eyes to open.

It's Kite.

He's staring into my face. His hands are on me. Gala.

"There it is," he says with a grimace. "The dolly." His expression is full of hate.

I remember too late that I'm supposed to be a chrysalid.

"So, little dolly," says Kite. "You've been a spy in my chambers?"

"Let her go," pleads Swan. "She's just a dummy, she's nothing." I see her cropped hair, her lead band. Her black dress lies torn in a heap by the door and a petticoat is all she wears. I see that she is bound and Ruppell is holding her arms behind her back.

Kite rounds on her. "This creature is your songlight, your own unhuman. I knew it was strange, the way you lavished it with love—brazen, barefaced treachery."

Swan has nowhere to hide. She has played such a bold hand. But in reaching Petra and saving Reem, I have fatally exposed her. Her eyes dart like a cornered rat's.

Kite turns back to me. "You've been working against me, helping my enemies. What do we do with traitors, dolly?" he asks.

I can't think why I would reply.

"We hang them by the neck until they're dead," says the tyrant. "But that fate is too good for you."

This is what Kite said to Axby, just before he stabbed him. I close my eyes and prepare to die. I have such a yearning for more life. There is so much I want to do. But Kite drags me to my feet. "It's cunning isn't it, Minister, the way these mind-twisters exploit each other?"

"It is indeed," says Ruppell. "But Lady Swan will soon be safe with me in the Chrysalid House and when I return her to you, she'll be the pinnacle of obedience."

Swan half collapses, a mess of horror and panic. She can't believe that her long game of survival will actually end here. She looks at me, pained, and I wish I could reach her with my songlight, to tell her what I did.

"You care for these creatures, don't you?" asks Kite. "It will make you sad to see them die."

"They're just chrysalids, I swear," says Swan.

I can't bear him tormenting her like this.

"They're easy to kill," says Kite. "Watch me."

And before anyone can stop him, he runs his knife into Lady Orion, straight into her heart. She utters a cry—the first sound I have ever heard her make.

"Is that really necessary?" asks Ruppell in distaste.

Kite lays her down as she expires. He pulls his knife from her and turns to me. He has a taste for blood and I am next.

"Don't," begs Swan, "please don't."

I feel a flame of outrage flickering. If I'm going to die, this man is going to know what I have done.

"I warned Reem," I say. There's pride in my voice.

Kite looks at me. "What did you say?"

"I used my songlight to tell Reem that your planes are coming. Sorze Separelli knows of your attack."

Bastard. Now your face is falling.

Kite stares at me, uncomprehending. And Ruppell isn't grinning anymore.

At that moment, two guards bring in Lark.

67 ✳ LARK

A suffocating white chamber, an atmosphere thick with violence, a dead woman on the floor—this is my welcome.

"This chrysalid was left behind, my lord," says one of the guards.

Their presence distracts Kite. "Get out," he barks, and guards depart, leaving me behind.

I see Swan, crop-haired, her lead band on, staring at me, realizing who I am.

Yes, Sister, I am here.

Kite doesn't give me a second glance and neither does the Minister who's holding Swan. Their eyes are on Nightingale.

"Lark," she says in songlight. "They killed Lady Orion. They're going to kill me." I look at the dead woman lying on the floor and all my fears fall away. This is easy. It's going to be easy.

My hand curls around my knife. I tell Nightingale, "Be ready to run."

Kite squeezes her arm. "What do you mean, you warned Reem?"

She's standing up to him, so strong, so fragile. "I reached their strongest Torch," she says. "They will be well prepared."

This incenses him. "You're lying!"

"No," says Swan. "Her songlight is exceptional. She's a true Flare. She could reach Ayland in a breath."

"Their Torch took my news straight to their Circle House. The whole of Ayland will know by now."

"What if she isn't lying?" asks Ruppell. "What if our planes are flying into a trap?"

"Go to Drake in the war rooms," says Kite, livid. "Call the air fleet back to Fort Peregrine."

Ruppell exits, running down the corridor.

"I will break your unhuman neck," cries Kite. He is lifting Nightingale off her feet, swinging her round.

And I am running at him, my hand gripping the knife, releasing the blade.

Kite realizes I am armed. He tries to use Nightingale to shield him. I pull her away—and my blade makes contact with Kite's chest. I force it in with a cry. I force it with all my might. Kite stumbles backward. He falls onto a white chaise.

I see his shock.

"I am Elsa Crane," I say. "And I will see you die."

But he's not dying. He's not weakening. Why is he not dying? Something is blocking my knife. I feel Kite's hand on my wrist, his iron strength, shock replaced by fury in his eyes. I try twisting the knife but it's no good. He is wearing some kind of armor under his suit. Of course he is. Bastard coward pig. Kite wouldn't go in front of the whole city unless he was protected. I scream in frustration as he pries the knife out of my grasp.

Gala, I have failed. Gala, I should have stabbed him in the neck. Kite will kill me now and I have failed. He gets me on my back.

"Elsa Crane"—I hear his contempt—"you think you're good enough to kill me?"

I fight him off but he is all sinew, made of steel. The knife comes up—

And Nightingale throws herself on Kite's arm. "No, no, no," she yells.

Her whole body weight can't prevent him from stabbing me. He lifts the knife. This is it. He'll kill me now.

Suddenly Kite's body jerks. He looks like a man in agony. His knife hand loses power and he collapses. Nightingale's eyes are locked on him. I feel her songlight, an incendiary force. She's in Kite's mind, searing everything she sees. She's burning him, destroying him as he destroyed the forest. I force myself into her purifying fire and I see her in a furnace of Kite's memories. Nightingale sets alight his triumphs, his ambition, his intellect; she incinerates his lust. She is a bright blade, a scimitar of light. Her fire scorches through his landscape, eating his machines of war, his game of chess with Peregrine, consuming his desire for control and

430

domination. Nightingale blazes—and I worry that the flames will burn her up.

"DIE," screams her songlight, "DIE."

I give Swan the knife. She takes it in her bound hands. "He's yours," I say.

And I lift Nightingale away.

"Leave him now," I whisper, cooling her. "You're not a murderer."

I put my arms round her as the conflagration fades, leaving Kite to Sister Swan.

68 ✴ SWAN

I have the knife in my hands, poised to strike. But Kite's eyes are dull, expressionless. He's lying limp beneath me and he breathes, staring blankly, as if his body has lost none of its function but all of its will.

"Blink," I whisper. And his eyes blink. They are as empty as interstellar space.

"Sit up," I order. Slowly, my tormentor sits.

Kaira Kasey has done her work. Kite is alive in death. Slowly, he slumps to one side, his eyes without expression. It's as if the girl has made a chrysalid of him.

I am humbled by her power. And in truth, I am afraid of it.

I stare into the void of his eyes. His lips hang open. Gala, he's finished. This man who has abused and tormented me is finished.

What will I be without him?

Kite lies like a sack, breathing. I take hold of his arm, pull up his sleeve, and I use the knife to cut the tiny key off the chain around his wrist. Instead of killing him, I stand and push him backward with my foot. I lean over him.

"Who's the dolly now?" I ask.

Elsa Crane laughs. Holding Kaira in her arms, she laughs. For long, slow seconds we all breathe. How that girl got in here, I will never know. Reluctantly I toast her courage. But when her laugh dies down, she is clinging on to Kaira and her look says *keep away*.

How hostile she is, this peasant girl.

I can hear distant shouts. I find the lock in my skull and turn the key, taking off the lead band, determined I will never wear the hated thing again.

"Kaira," I say. "You are one in a million." I want this girl by my side, always. Her sweetness hides a formidable power.

Elsa Crane helps her to stand—but Kaira's expression worries me. She doesn't look proud of what did; she looks afraid.

I rush to my dresser and put on the wig that sits there, ready for the day. Elsa Crane watches me as if I am a vain, conceited creature, but I know from years of experience that appearance matters; it is everything. I bend down over Kite and I pull the ring of state off his finger, the ring he stole from Great Brother Peregrine.

"What are you doing?" asks Elsa Crane suspiciously. "What are you planning, Swan?"

She uses my name as if it's an insult.

"Survival," I tell her.

As the door bursts open, she has to bite back her reply and stand as a chrysalid with Kaira and my two remaining ladies. Ouzel strides into the room with officers and guards. Starling Beech is among them. Good.

"Thank heavens you're here," I cry, thinking fast. "I thought you'd never come." I caress Kite, as if trying to rouse him. "He needs help!"

My hands are tight bound, my hair tumbles loosely and I make sure I look helpless in my bare feet and petticoat. The men see Kite lying prone, next to Lady Orion's corpse. Ouzel rushes to Kite's side. He cries Kite's name but Kite's eyes are glazed and he's drooling.

"What's happened to him?" asks Ouzel, staring at me in shock.

"I think it's a stroke," I say. "He had a seizure."

Ouzel sends his men running for medics. He takes Kite's pulse.

"It was a dreadful scene," I continue. "He killed my lady. He believed she was a spy. He was quite apoplectic. Ruppell went for help—and Kite, at the very height of his rage, collapsed into a fit." I cry a useful tear.

But Ouzel glares at me, unconvinced. "Take them to the Chrysalid House."

"Even Lady Swan?" asks Starling.

"Especially Lady Swan," he replies.

"Ouzel," I say, stopping him. "You cannot think that I did this?"

"Kite is strong and healthy," he cries. "How has he fallen . . . ?"

I leap on his confusion. "I don't know—but you can bet Ruppell and Greylag are already staking their claim on Brightland. Ruppell's in the war room now, calling off the attack on Reem. Whatever comes next is up to you. You could rise and forge the future."

Ouzel says nothing, staring at me. I hope the idea of his own greatness drips like poison into his soul. "Whatever you think of me, I always thought you were Peregrine's finest man. I was never free to say so, until now."

I beam my songlight on Ouzel, fertilizing seeds of ambition in his mind.

"I'll find out the truth of this," he says.

My eyes are brimful of sincerity. The ring of state is in my fist.

"Take them away," he tells Starling. But the contempt has left his voice. And the seed might germinate. Greylag, Ruppell, Ouzel; they will be set against each other now.

Starling takes me by the arm and marches me out with Elsa Crane and Kaira. As we walk, my vision expands until I see the whole of Brightlinghelm. My survival isn't enough. I grip the ring so hard it hurts my palm. One day soon, I will wear it on my hand.

I consider how I might save Kaira. I want her with me. I can't do this alone. But no plan presents itself. Starling will risk himself for me—but not for Kaira Kasey. I'm not blind to his antipathy for her. My mind whirls and every step takes me closer to the Chrysalid House. I can't set foot in there again, I can't. I have to save myself first.

When we approach the radiobine recording room, I plant an idea in Starling Beech's head. It's a bold idea and at first he is afraid. But I make him realize that such an act would be heroic.

"Kaira," I say, in my new, free songlight. "I won't abandon you for long."

But Kaira's mind is still in pain from her attack on Kite and I'm not sure if she hears me. I know how she dreads the Chrysalid House and I would do anything to keep her from the place. But it's her relationship with Elsa Crane that has led us to this crisis. Elsa Crane has endangered and abused her. She manipulated Kaira into helping the fugitives and warning Reem—and I was almost killed for it. If my plan succeeds, Kaira will be reprieved.

But Elsa Crane? Not my responsibility.

We approach the radiobine room and I continue to pour ardent songlight into Starling Beech. Suddenly he turns to the guard captain and says: "Take these two to the Chrysalid House. Lady Swan has business here."

Before the captain can object, Starling pulls me into the radiobine room and he bolts the door behind us. He thinks that this is all his own idea.

"I had to save you, Zara," he says. "I love you. I would lay down my life for you." Pathetically, he offers me his lips and I give him one long grateful kiss. It's a tedious necessity, but it must be done. Only when I'm free can I save Kaira. I gauged the feeling of the crowd at Harrier's hanging. The crowd wants an end to the war and that is what I'll give them. I'll earn my power by bringing peace to Brightland.

I'm glad that I have cultivated my engineers. They set me up for an emergency address and listen loyally to my words, making no attempt to stop me. I tell the people that Kite hanged Harrier, an innocent man, for his own crime of murder. "Kite poisoned our Great Brother because Peregrine wanted peace with Ayland." I tell the people that I share this vision, that I stand with Peregrine and Harrier. I tell them that I am under arrest and that this may be my farewell address. I build my speech to a climax, telling the people that I love them. Then I say "Kite's health is in the balance and his Ministers are scrambling for power. But if you see a better way, then rise up and fight for—"

The power cuts off. The microphone goes dead and the room is plunged into darkness. There is rapping on the heavy doors. But I have said enough. Starling lights a small turbine lamp.

"How else may I assist you?" he emotes. "What else can I do?"

I look fondly at this servile rabbit.

"Dear Starling," I say. "You must lend me your clothes."

Starling sits, wearing my wig and petticoat, watching me put on his uniform. He has his back to the door, and in my imagination, I relish the Ministers' faces when they see what I have done.

The engineers, moved by my address, offer me their help. There's a

435

trapdoor in their office that leads down to their power room. By the light of Starling's turbine lamp I follow them down into the cavernous cellars. The engineers lead me through a labyrinth that snakes under the palace. It's an escape route they have worked out over many years, they say, and they are glad to put it at my service.

The fresh air strengthens my resolve. All I have to do is cross the lawns and get to the *Aileron Blue*. I tighten Starling's belt and I slick back my cropped hair. I am wearing the insignia of Kite's personal aide and I hope that no one will stand in my way.

As I set off, I think about the power that men have. And I dare myself to believe that Kite no longer has a hold on me.

For now, my path lies with the Aylish. I have chosen the ascendant side and I will be a peacemaker. I will do more than survive. I will prosper. And Kaira Kasey will be my secret weapon.

I dare myself to begin again, to start afresh with a new heart.

I am going to Kingfisher.

69 ✦ PIPER

The clouds clear as I fly over Ayland. Below me are the battlefields where most of this war has been fought. I see the catastrophic stalemate on the land: the remains of trees and farms, blackened and broken, filthy craters, a muddy no-man's-land of barbed wire and dugouts. This Helscape has been fought upon for years, mile after mile of bleak ruination.

Time and again, doubts assail me. I imagine Finch, how betrayed he must feel. I think of my pa, who died somewhere on the blasted land below. What would Pa think of my actions now? I can only hope he understands. I think of Elsa and my ma and I pray to Gala that they live.

I fly on toward the snow-covered peaks. Away from the battle lands I see towns in green valleys and wide, glittering rivers. The weather is beautiful in Ayland, blue skies and cotton clouds. I rise over foothills into the mountains, following Finch's navigation to the letter, and I'm on my fuel reserve when I see an urban sprawl. The city clings to a mountainside, climbing up toward a citadel on a high plateau. Reem.

There is something in the sky hanging above it, a burnished metal cloud. What is that?

Gala in heaven, *what is that?*

Fear strikes me. What are these Aylish? How have they made such a thing? Is Finch right about them? *Those unhumans will take over the world if we don't keep them down.*

Whatever I think, it is too late. Either I must fly on until my fuel is gone and crash into these hills, or I must land. But I realize with alarm that the plateau is too short to be an airstrip. My plane will not have time to come to a halt and I will crash into that round building. I descend steeply and my wheels touch down right at the plateau's edge. I see people running, clearing out of my way, and I hit the brakes with everything I've got. I stop inches away from the circular wall. I become aware of people screaming in fright and of Aylish soldiers taking positions, pointing guns at me. Slowly and carefully, I open my cockpit and raise my hands.

I'm expecting to be blown to pieces as I hold up a white handkerchief. "I come in peace," I cry. "For the sake of peace, hear me!"

I am underneath the huge weapon, the airship that the Aylish have hanging in the sky. It casts a shadow over everything. We believed that Ayland had no airpower. How ignorant we are. How we have been lied to. My comrades are flying like innocents toward this monstrous machine.

What do I do?

People are coming toward me as I climb onto the wing of my plane. I see it is not the only aircraft on the square. There are winged *things* here. Three crafts crouched like white eagles, ready to strike. They make my Firefly look like a toy. People in strange white suits stand outside them, with some kind of weapons aimed at me. They don't look Aylish.

A group of dignitaries outside the circular building slowly moves toward me. These people look like princes and kings. But I notice that one of them is wearing a Brightling coat, an army coat like Sergeant Redshank's. It's draped over his foreign suit. I can't take my eyes off this Aylish lad because he looks for all the world like Rye Tern.

"Don't shoot," he yells at the others. "Hold fire."

Rye's voice. He comes toward me. I blink my eyes. He's a mirage brought on by wishful thinking. Rye is a chrysalid; he's dead. My sanity is shaken and I tear my eyes away from him.

"Brightland is sending its air fleet against you," I shout to the crowd. "This is all the warning I can give. I do this for the sake of peace between our nations. Defend yourselves."

The lad who looks like Rye is standing underneath my wing. He's looking up at me with Rye-like eyes.

"Piper fucking Crane," he says.

I don't know anything else. I scramble off the wing. He's here. He is in front of me. Suddenly, I'm in his arms and Rye is holding me.

438

70 ✶ LARK

As the guards take us to the Chrysalid House, we hear Swan's radiobine address in the halls and palace corridors. When they lead us out into the grounds, it's being relayed by metal speakers over the lawns. It is everywhere in Brightlinghelm and by the time it gets cut off, Swan has said all that she needs. She has positioned herself as Peregrine's heir, as Harrier's ally, as a heroic fighter for truth, peace, and freedom. So clever. Had she not just thrown us to the lions, I would applaud her.

Swan's songlight is at liberty. She doesn't need Nightingale anymore, so she has tossed her aside. My anger at this grows and becomes all-consuming. How could Swan abandon Nightingale after everything that Nightingale has done for her? Her ruthlessness is shocking and her cunning scares me. This woman is a danger.

As Swan's address is cut off, the speakers blare static. I look at the low building ahead of us. I've known since the day my songlight came that this might be where my journey would end. Rye was brought here. Now I will be joining him.

I hear Kingfisher calling me, his songlight frantic, like the beating of wings. I join with him, smiling with as much wryness as I can muster, feeling infinitely sad. When I show him where I am, I feel his cry of woe.

"We destroyed Kite," I tell him. "Nightingale finished him; she attacked his mind with her songlight, filled him full of white heat. She saved me."

I feel Kingfisher's disbelief. Then his admiration.

"That's strong Torchfire," he says.

My fingers touch Nightingale's and I decide that I don't give a damn if these guards see that I'm not a proper chrysalid. I put my arm through hers and pull her to my side. I feel our togetherness, our camaraderie, our love.

"She must be saved," I say.

Kingfisher shows me his constrained reality. Brightling guards have him at gunpoint on the ship's bridge. He's on his knees, his hands behind his head. I see Alize, furious, at his side.

"Kite is as good as dead," I tell him. "The scramble for power's already begun. And Zara Swan wants her piece of it."

"She's better than the rest of them," he says. "I heard her address—"

"She's sent us to the Chrysalid House," I tell him. "She saved herself without a thought for Nightingale. Beware of her."

Kingfisher acknowledges my warning.

"I should have stayed with you," he says. "We should never have parted, not for a moment, no matter what was at stake." He's wracked with pain at losing me and without words, I share the loss of everything we could have had.

The building has a yawning entrance. No windows. It goes down underground for floor after floor. Like Hel, they say. Nightingale grips me tighter.

"Lark," says Kingfisher, "Mikane is on his way. When the moment is right, we'll come for you. Stay strong." This gives me hope but Kingfisher and I both know that next time he sees me, my face may be expressionless. I want to tell him how I feel. But love is so hard and painful to convey. In songlight, I let go. I feel him do the same. Our hearts are open. We're as one.

—And then I sense her.

She's trying to reach him with her songlight. She has escaped. She's coming to his ship to be with him.

Zara.

I feel how he is torn. He wants me—but he needs her.

We all need Zara Swan.

Her songlight will sense mine. She'll see Kingfisher's heart—and she will withdraw from him, slighted, vengeful, stung. She will be dangerous then. She'll ally herself with Ouzel or Ruppell—ever the survivor.

"Goodbye," I whisper, and I slip out of his harmony.

We're underneath the yawning entrance when I halt, stricken.

Hope leaves me. Fear grips me. But Nightingale is there.

"We won't give up," she says, and I feel her hand gripping mine.

The captain nudges me on.

"Petra is coming," says Nightingale. "I spoke with her. She will bring a different world."

I look at the hope in her eyes, remembering how she first appeared to me, when I was grieving for Rye in Northaven. She sat on a roof with me one night, her song as loud and piercing as a nightingale's. We have been through so much and yet this is the first time I have seen her in person, the first time I have ever held her hand.

My friend.

She will keep me strong through whatever we have left.

"We did well, Nightingale," I tell her.

"Brave Lark," she says. "We did everything we could."

There are guns pointing at our backs. And facing the darkness, we proceed.

ACKNOWLEDGMENTS

My thanks to Matt Charman and Josh Fasulo at Binocular for their continued time and support in helping me to realize the world of *Songlight* and enrich this narrative. You always know the right questions to ask.

My thanks to Anwen Hooson at Bird for always being in my corner. You have been the trilogy's advocate and angel.

Thanks once more to my early readers, Martin Biltcliffe, Bridie Biltcliffe, Nuala Buffini, Fiona Buffini, Nigel Burrows, Andrée Molyneux, and Hugh Williams. My thirst for feedback was intense and you were there.

My thanks in particular to Maya Gannon for coming with me through the Greensward and into Brightlinghelm. I greatly enjoyed our weekly meetings. Thanks for putting me right in no uncertain terms.

Massive thanks to Alice Swan at Faber for guiding me and trusting me. You have taught me so much. And to Tara Weikum at HarperCollins. It is a gift to have two editors. The book couldn't have a better first audience and your notes always encourage me to dive deeper and write better. Alice and Tara, you have worked together seamlessly and that is much appreciated.

Huge thanks to Allison Hellegers and Rosemary Stimola for all their sterling efforts in helping this book to connect with its audience.

My thanks to the whole team at HarperCollins for diligence, for excellence, and for believing in this book and putting the weight of the entire company behind it. You continue to go beyond the call of duty and that is much appreciated.

Thanks to David Wyatt for his awesome cover design.

And finally my loving thanks to my family: Bridie, Joe, and especially Martin, who bore with my absent presence while I was in the forest, writing. Please keep reminding me to look up.